# Coalescence

I Found My Heart in
San Francisco
Book Three

Susan X Meagher

Susan X Meagher

# COALESCENCE

## I FOUND MY HEART IN SAN FRANCISCO: BOOK THREE



ISBN 0-977088-53-7

THIS TRADE PAPERBACK ORIGINAL IS PUBLISHED BY BRISK PRESS, NEW YORK, NY 10011

FIRST PRINTING: FEBRUARY 2006



---

# Acknowledgements

Thanks to the following people who helped proof this edition. It took a lot of time and effort on everyone's part: Stefanie, Edye, Judy, Karen, Laura, Lori, and Elaine.

To Carrie for knowing that a relationship is an always-changing work in progress. Thanks for taking the journey with me.

# By Susan X Meagher

## *Novels*

Cherry Grove

All That Matters

Arbor Vitae

## *Serial Novels*

*I Found My Heart in San Francisco:*

Awakenings

Beginnings

Coalescence

Disclosures

Entwined

Fidelity

Getaway

## *Anthologies*

Girl Meets Girl

Tales of Travelrotica for Lesbians: Vol 2

Undercover Tales

Telltale Kisses

The Milk of Human Kindness

Infinite Pleasures

# Chapter One

The massive six-lane thoroughfare was jammed with people. Some sat upon sleek, brightly colored racing bikes, unwilling to dismount even after so much saddle time. Small packs of people clad in bright, primary-colored T-shirts said their good-byes with emotion-filled hugs. Coworkers, family members, friends, and lovers shouted greetings and ran to meet their loved ones, welcoming them home from their long journey. So many people—so much emotion; the scene was close to chaotic, save for one small oasis of tranquility.

Two young women sat alone on the edge of a large, balloon-bedecked stage. They were holding hands and the smaller of the two leaned heavily against her companion. Her fair head rested against the broad shoulder of her friend, who supported her with a strong arm tucked around her waist. A banner over their heads proclaimed, "California AIDS Ride 6 – Welcome Home, Riders", but neither woman seemed particularly cognizant of her surroundings.

They gazed blankly at the throng of people below them, their unfocused eyes only partially taking in the joyous celebration that showed no signs of abating. As a group of stagehands jumped onto the platform and began to break down the stage, the smaller woman spoke. "I know we should go, but if we do, I feel like the spell will be broken."

"Spell?" Her lover's voice rumbled huskily, its normally smooth tones rough from singing and shouting farewells.

"Yeah. This week has been so magical for me that I'm afraid to have it end."

"Jamie," the deep voice crooned, "the magic has only just begun, baby."

Sighing heavily, Jamie cuddled up tighter against her partner. "Really, Ryan? Are you sure we'll be able to hold on to this?" Her voice held a wistful note, and it was clear that she hoped that her friend would reassure her.

Ryan sat up tall, separating a bit from her companion. She allowed her considerable confidence to show as she sought to convince her partner. "Guaranteed, babe. This feeling is all about love and passion and commitment. We've got tons of that!" A gentle laugh floated up to Ryan, and both women smiled as they considered that thought. "I could sit here all day, but I guess we'd better go find Mia or she'll ditch us," Ryan said, a small chuckle showing that she was partially kidding.

"More likely she'll hook up with someone, and *then* ditch us," Jamie laughed, acknowledging her roommate and long-time friend's tendencies.

She got to her feet and stretched for a minute to get some of the kinks out of her back. She was bent over at the waist loosening up her hamstrings when Ryan chortled, "You know her too well. She's hooked up alright—ooh—an older man."

"Probably the head of the studio," Jamie said absently, alluding both to her friend's propensity to attract attention from a wide variety of males, and her summer job working for a movie studio in L.A.

Ryan jumped to her feet and gave a hearty wave as Mia jogged over while holding the hand of a middle-aged, sandy-haired man. Ryan turned to comment on Mia's date but caught sight of her partner's stark white, terror-stricken face. "Jamie, what's wrong?"

"M … m … my f … f … father!" she squeaked out, looking like she was going to faint.

Ryan's hands dropped as she whirled to stare at the approaching pair. Her eyes focused on the tall, athletic-looking man and immediately saw the resemblance to her partner. Not bothering to process the information her brain was receiving, she leapt from the platform and intercepted Mia, grabbing her in an enthusiastic hug, while Jamie's father, his attention centered on his daughter, continued towards the stage.

"Miss me?" Mia giggled, her feet dangling a foot off the ground.

"What did you see?" Ryan hissed into her ear.

Mia leaned back in the embrace, staring at Ryan for a moment. "What do you mean? We saw a bunch of people on bikes."

Ryan's heart was pounding in her chest. "You didn't see us on the stage?"

"Well, yeah, we saw you on stage. It was like thirty seconds ago, Ryan. Do you have heat stroke or something?" the curly-haired woman asked with concern as she looked into Ryan's eyes.

Exhaling heavily, Ryan placed Mia back on the ground and leaned over, resting her head on the small woman's shoulder. "Thank you, Jesus," she breathed.

Mia placed her hands on Ryan's shoulders and moved back a few inches, staring at the normally implacable woman. "What in the hell is going on? You look like you had the scare of your life!"

Turning her head to catch sight of her partner, Ryan murmured, "We almost did. We almost did."

"Daddy," Jamie whispered, her voice far too soft for her father to hear. The beaming man extended both of his strong arms, and without a second thought, she clasped his forearms and let him grab her waist and lower her to the ground. "Daddy," she whispered again, the weak voice now filled with tears. Her panic had morphed into shock, but when she saw how happy her father looked her mood changed once again—now she was filled with appreciation that her father had gone out of his way to be here for her. "How … when … God, I'm glad to see you," she finally got out.

"Nothing could stop me from being here for you, cupcake," he murmured, his voice cracking with emotion. "I'm so proud of you, Jamie. So very proud." The hug in which he had enveloped his child had grown progressively tighter as he spoke, and he had to force himself to loosen his hold. "I don't think I've ever been prouder in my whole life," he finally whispered. "I'm so happy that you're my daughter."

Hot tears began to course down Jamie's cheeks, her body weak with emotion. "Thank you … thank you for coming, Daddy." She wiped the tears away with the back of her hand, the gesture ineffectual since the flow hadn't stopped. Jim Evans retrieved his clean linen handkerchief and gently dabbed at her eyes, the tender gesture causing the emotional woman to cry even harder. "It … it means so much to me. I'll never forget this."

"There, there, baby," he murmured, hugging her tightly. "It's all right. It's all right."

It took another minute or so for Jamie to control herself, but she finally took a deep, ragged breath and stood tall. "Wow, that knocked me out," she said, a little embarrassed at her uncharacteristically emotional display.

"This was a very big day, honey. It's perfectly understandable that you'd be emotional about it. While we were waiting, Mia and I heard some of the families talking about their loved ones who were participating. There are a lot of very courageous people on this ride."

"Oh, I know," she said, smiling. "And here's one I want you to meet." She extended her hand and grasped Ryan's arm, pulling her close. "Daddy, this is Ryan O'Flaherty." She didn't know quite what adjectives to use to express the deep bond she had with her partner, so she chose to say nothing else.

Ryan stepped forward and extended her hand. Her eyes grew wide as the grinning man enveloped her in a hug, whispering, "Thank you for helping Jamie accomplish this, Ryan. I know how instrumental you were."

Ryan was stunned, at both the display of emotion and the warm appreciation that the man offered. "I … I'm … pleased to meet you, Mr. Evans," she got out.

"Forget the Mr. Evans stuff, Ryan," he said, releasing her. "Please call me Jim."

"Me too?" Mia piped up, poking her head around Ryan's shoulder.

"You too, Mia," he laughed. "You girls are adults now, and it's time we treated each other that way."

"Cool," the cherub-faced brunette beamed.

"I've gotta get my bearings here," Jamie muttered. "I still don't know how you got here, or why you're not still in Italy."

"It's simple," he said as he slung his arm around his daughter. "Let's go get your things and I'll tell you all about it." As they started for the "Meet and Greet" area, he explained, "I needed to be at work on Monday for a meeting, so I decided that if I had to be in California on Sunday, I might as well come on Saturday. I called Mia's dad, got her number, and she and I met up this morning."

"So, you're staying over?" Jamie asked, hoping that was not the case. As grateful as she was for her father's generous act, she had a deep need to spend the evening in her partner's arms, and she doubted that would happen if her father were to stay the night.

"No, baby, that's why we came to look for you. I've got very little time. My flight is at seven o'clock, so I need to be at LAX by six."

"It's nearly five now," Jamie said, looking quickly at her watch. "You have to leave now to be sure you make it."

"My point exactly," he smiled. "We thought you'd never get over here, so we had to come find you."

They were now at the gear pick-up area, and since they were so late, their things were easy to find. "It's amazing you found us in this crowd," Jamie said.

"Not really," Mia piped up. "I saw a big group of women with matching T-shirts that said … uhm … that said … that they were from San Francisco." Mia discreetly failed to mention that the complete slogan was, *The Lavender Menace—San Francisco.* "On a whim, I asked if they knew you or Ryan, and they did! One of them said you guys were still over at the stage, so we high-tailed it over there."

Mia's huge, rather impish smile indicated that she had more to add, but Jamie, wary of Mia's propensity to reveal all, didn't want to ask for too many details. Therefore, she tailored her query to obtain the minimum of information. "Did you see the whole ceremony?"

"Yeah, but we didn't hear it," Mia said, laughing. "We watched from your dad's office." She turned and pointed to one of the gleaming stainless steel office buildings that flanked the wide street. "Up there, on the fifteenth floor."

Jamie offered up a silent prayer of thanks that her father had an office in the neighborhood, since he surely would have seen the impromptu serenade if he'd been in the crowd. "That's fantastic," she said, the relief evident on her face. "I'm so glad you saw it all."

"Yeah, it was pretty cool from that perspective," Mia said. "It was a sea of people and bikes."

Jim nodded enthusiastically, smiling broadly at his daughter. "It was very impressive, Jamie." He took a quick glance at his watch, pursing his lips as a worried frown settled on his forehead. "I hate to leave so abruptly, but I really have to run."

Mia and Ryan busied themselves with grabbing all of the gear so that Jamie could have a moment alone with her father. Once the gear was secured, Ryan paused to take in her future father-in-law. Her previous glimpses of the man only allowed her to identify him from an angle that she hoped she was never unlucky enough to see again. Viewing him fully clothed allowed her to concentrate on the overall package, and she was pleased with what she saw.

He was tall, much taller than Ryan would have guessed—actually about Ryan's height—and his build was amazingly similar to Jack's. His hair was mostly blonde with a good smattering of gray that, with his vibrant demeanor, actually looked premature. After another minute of reflection, however, Ryan amended her opinion.

Jim Evans did not really look that young when judged solely by his features or his hair, but there was something absolutely boyish about his sparkling eyes and energetic enthusiasm. Ryan had always prided herself on being able to judge people based on their physical appearance and energy level. After spending a moment looking at Jim, she decided that things would probably go just fine between them. He looked friendly, and open, and very at ease with his emotions. He reminded her a bit of Jamie's grandfather and she prayed that Jim took after his father in personality and open-mindedness as well as in appearance.

*No matter what happens when Jamie comes out to him, he's shown that Jamie means a lot to him*, Ryan thought, watching father and daughter talk quietly. *He really went out of his way to be here to support her and for that, I'll always be grateful.*

Jamie stared at her father for a few minutes, enormously pleased that he had realized how important this event was to her. He seemed to understand her unspoken words as he placed his hands on her shoulders and smiled broadly. "Your mother and I worried about you all week. We must have mentioned you at least twenty times on Sunday alone." His smile broadened as he revealed, "I called my secretary as soon as the office opened on Monday to see if she had watched the news about the start of the ride. She went on and on about how many people were riding, and how much money had been raised, and I decided that if I could rearrange my plans a little in order to be here with you, it was well worth the effort."

As she wrapped her arms around his waist for another hug, he continued, "You know, Jamie, it's one thing to give money to a charity, but quite another to make this kind of physical and emotional sacrifice. You've really shown me what you're made of."

She snuggled into his embrace and let the sobs take over. He patted her back and rocked her slightly, just as he had when she was young. When she was in control, he held her out at arm's length to inspect her. He was both surprised and pleased by how muscular and fit his little girl looked. Her skin had tanned during the ride, even with Ryan's obsessive sun block application, and she looked healthy and vigorous and very mature. Tears formed in his eyes once again as he held her tightly and allowed himself to share in her accomplishment.

"Ryan seems like a lovely young woman," he said after a minute, sniffing slightly.

Jamie shook her head and wiped at her eyes, her enthusiasm immediately bubbling out. "Oh, she is! She's absolutely remarkable, Daddy. She's been losing weight all week, and she was so sick this morning that I don't know how she continued, but she got back on that bike and forced herself to finish. I'm just so proud of her," she choked out.

"There, there, sweetie, it's okay." He soothed her tenderly, rocking her in his arms. Looking up, he motioned to Mia and Ryan. They both looked a little embarrassed at witnessing such a private moment, but he put them at ease. "I've got to leave, girls. Will you make sure my baby's taken care of tonight?"

"We'll take very good care of her," Ryan said, as she cast a fond glance at her partner.

Jamie kissed her father goodbye, then with a sob, she turned and fell into Ryan. Jim gave the tall woman a small nod as he passed his only child over to her. He clasped her shoulder, giving it a good squeeze, hugged Mia goodbye, and disappeared into the crowd.

Mia looked at Ryan and made a hand signal to ask if she should make herself scarce. Ryan shook her head, knowing that Jamie just needed a moment to collect herself. "Time to go," she said, stroking her partner's back. "Can you make it?"

Jamie took a deep breath and straightened up. "Yeah, I'm okay." She tilted her head back and paused for a moment, trying to calm herself. "This is an awful lot to take in at once."

"What happened before we saw you guys?" Mia asked, aware that she had missed something momentous.

Ryan wasn't in the mood to explain and, since Jamie didn't look able to, she suggested, "Let's get out of the crowd. I'm getting a little claustrophobic. I'll fill you in on the whole thing when we get to your apartment."

Ryan hoisted her own bag in one arm and shared the burden of Jamie's with Mia. Jamie stayed right by her partner's side even though the bag prevented them from touching. They located the car in the subterranean parking structure of Jim's office building. Mia got in to drive, and after stowing the bags in the small trunk, Ryan climbed into the back, right next to her partner.

They struggled through the traffic-clogged streets, finally making their way to Santa Monica Boulevard. Mia peppered them with questions and Ryan answered most of them. Jamie was largely uncommunicative, curled up on the seat and leaning against her partner, who had an arm wrapped around her protectively.

Ryan kept the conversation going by asking Mia all about her job as a script reader for a major film studio. The work sounded fairly interesting and Mia was meeting a lot of people. She'd found a fantastic sublet for the summer, and she raved about the apartment all the way to Santa Monica.

When they reached Mia's place, both guests were suitably impressed with the rather opulent apartment. It was a spacious two-bedroom unit, furnished in a rich tapestry of greens and golds and yellows. The style was vaguely Italian—modern, sleek and elegant. The most stunning element, however, was the beautiful, unobstructed view of the ocean. They could see the Palisades and the sharp drop from the street to the shore. Hundreds of people were on the beach and the bike path was also full on this cool but sunny day.

The unit had come completely furnished and sported a very well appointed kitchen. Since Mia had yet to make anything more adventurous than microwave popcorn, they decided they would order dinner in.

Ryan stowed their bags in the spacious, understated guest room, then asked Jamie if she'd like to shower first. Receiving only a vacant nod, she gave Mia a shrug, pulled Jamie into the bedroom and pushed her gently onto the bed. Kneeling at her feet, Ryan looked up at her with concern. "Are you okay? You look pretty out of it." While waiting for her answer, she brushed the hair off Jamie's forehead and felt her cool skin.

"I'm okay," she said. "It was all so overwhelming."

"Do you want to take a shower? Or would you rather lie down for a while?"

"I can't decide whether tired or dirty wins," she muttered, wiping at her eyes with an annoyed swipe. "I guess dirty takes it," she groused. "I've got a nasty combo of sun block, sweat, sand and tears going on here."

"Need help?" Ryan asked ingenuously, batting her big blue eyes.

"Yeah," Jamie smirked, her normal attitude reasserting itself. "Take my shoes off."

Ryan returned the smirk, grumbling, "I get all the crummy jobs."

"You wait, Buff," Jamie promised. "Tomorrow, you'll have full access."

"Tomorrow?" Ryan gaped.

"Oh, shit," Jamie cried. "I mean Monday." She dropped back onto the bed and let out a frustrated moan. "Damn, maybe we should just go home tonight."

"Nah … we can't do that. I think Mia's looking forward to spending some time with you. We can't blow her off now."

A heavy sigh greeted this thought. "Of course, you're right. I can't let my baser instincts rule my world."

"Base? You think I'm base?" Ryan pounced on her partner, pinning her to the bed and tickling her furiously. Jamie squirmed and cried, seeming more like herself every minute.

"Okay, love-bug," the breathless blonde managed. "You go play with Mia … and get a snack."

"Snack? Did somebody say snack?" The always-hungry woman rose immediately and left the bedroom, nose twitching—every sense attuned to the presence of food.

Ryan went out to chat with Mia for a few minutes and look for that snack. The good news was that Mia was familiar enough with Jamie's emotional responses to not be bothered by her withdrawn behavior in the car. The bad news was that there was nary a bite to eat in the house. Her desires frustrated, Ryan went back into the bedroom to organize her things.

Jamie wasn't in the shower very long and when she emerged, wrapped in a big towel, Ryan expressed surprise. "That didn't take long. Weren't you tempted to stay in there all day?"

"As a matter of fact, I was, but I decided to make it quick, since I knew I had to leave some water for you." She tilted her head and grinned at her partner, and Ryan was reassured to see the playful glint in her eyes once again.

"Well, I'm not going to be so moderate. I'm gonna stay in here until my fingers prune."

"You go right ahead, pigpen," Jamie teased, lightly flicking her thumb at the dirt-smudged face. "You're my little dirt raccoon."

"Dirt raccoon?"

"Yeah. The dirt sticks to your face, but it doesn't get behind your sunglasses. So you get this raccoon effect. It's pretty cute."

"Dirt raccoon, indeed," Ryan grumbled, going into the bath to dispute the moniker. After looking into the huge, well-lit mirror over the double sinks, Ryan had to agree that she looked more raccoonish than human. "I'm going to scrub every particle of dirt from myself, babe. Would you see what you could get for us to eat?"

"Sure, anything in particular you'd like?"

"I'd eat the back door buttered," Ryan assured her in her best Irish accent.

Jamie shot her a fond smile, always amused by her partner's endless Irish aphorisms. "I think I can do better than that, my little colleen. You take it easy and take a nap when you're finished with your shower, okay? You've had a tough day, baby."

"Okey dokey," Ryan agreed, shutting the bathroom door.

Ryan stayed in the shower for a good fifteen minutes, even though she knew that water conservation was important in Southern California. She needed to pamper herself a little bit today, so she indulged in the extravagance without guilt—washing her hair three times before she finally felt that all of the grit was washed away, then shaving her legs carefully, luxuriating in the feeling of actually being able to move freely in the pounding water after a week of showers in facilities the size of a phone booth.

When she'd finished, she was pleased to note that she was feeling much like her old self. Her energy level was better, and she felt so clean that her mood was much improved. Pulling on her cleanest sweats, she climbed onto the neatly made bed and was asleep within seconds.

While Ryan was in the shower, Jamie put on a tank top and a pair of running shorts and went out to join her friend on the balcony.

Mia was sitting in the cool ocean breeze, the wind blowing her jumbled curls all around her head. "Hey," she said in greeting when Jamie poked her head out.

"Hi," Jamie smiled. "Do I look like a human again?"

"Yep. I knew it was you under that layer of grime, but you look perfectly normal now. Feeling better?"

"I feel pretty good. The ravenous beast is going to need to be satisfied soon, though. Where can we get plenty of food really fast?"

"Mmm, we can order in or walk some place close. The nearest place is a little Chinese …"

"Sold!" Jamie decided. "That's Ryan's favorite."

"It's not fancy. It's cheap and quick, though."

"Even better," Jamie laughed. "Those are Ryan's primary requirements in a restaurant."

After they both got shoes on, they started off on their short quest. As soon as they hit the street, Jamie stretched her arms out and took in a deep breath, tilting her head back to gaze at the milky blue sky. "God, it feels good to be off that bike!" she cried to the heavens.

Mia draped an arm around her shoulders and gave her old friend a squeeze. "Was it really hard, James?"

Pursing her lips together, Jamie considered the question. "Yes and no. In a way, it was absolutely ridiculous, it was so hard," she laughed. "If I never see another hill it'll be too soon. My legs feel like I ran three marathons, and I have no feeling left in my ass." She paused and considered the conflicting feelings that flooded her brain. "It's hard to explain, Mia. I never thought I'd say this, but in a way, it was easy. The energy of the group was so infectious that you found yourself doing things that you didn't think possible. And mealtimes were so nice! I met tons of people—and some of them hadn't even slept with Ryan!"

"Yikes!" Mia cried. "Did you run into old lovers?"

"Yep. All ages, all sizes, all shapes. The only thing I'm sure of is that she never slept with a man. Other than that, all bets are off!"

"You seem awfully cool with it," Mia said with a suspicious glance. "Why doesn't that bother you?"

Jamie thought about that for a minute. "Oh, probably because it wasn't a surprise. I knew that she'd slept with tons of women, and it stands to reason that lots of them would be on the ride. It was a little weird, but in a way, it helps me to know her better."

"Yeah, that sounds like you," the mischievous woman teased.

The no-nonsense look on Jamie's face gave Mia a clear signal that she was completely serious. "Well, it is like the new me. I don't wanna change her. I love her just like she is. And if I really love her, I have to accept that she is who she is because of everything that's happened in her life—even the stuff I don't like. What matters is that she loves me now, and I believe that she's committed to me."

"Are you really sure about that?" A niggling doubt about Ryan's ability to be faithful troubled Mia. As much as she liked Ryan, her loyalty was first and foremost to Jamie, and she wanted to protect her friend as much as possible.

"Yes. I am." The confident look had not changed, and Mia found herself smiling at her friend's assuredness. A gentle smile slid onto Jamie's face, and her voice turned wistful. "She's soooo cute about telling people about our relationship. She introduces me as her partner, and when I asked her why, she went into this explanation about all of the terms she'd thought about using, and why each of the others wasn't quite right."

"She told everybody about you?"

"Uhm, we both did," Jamie said, taking a noticeable gulp. "And I do mean everybody."

"Huh?"

"Right before you found us, a group of her friends got the band to play a song for us. We were up on that stage with thousands of people singing to us!"

"Holy crap! What were they singing?"

"Going to the Chapel," Jamie informed her with rolling eyes. "It's an old song that I think I've heard. My beloved knew every word, of course, and we ended up with me sitting on her knee while she serenaded me! We were making out in front of that huge crowd!" As these words left her mouth, all of the color drained from Jamie's face, and she reached out blindly to steady herself against a building. "We were making out in front of that huge crowd," she repeated in a whisper, clutching at her suddenly pain-wracked stomach, eyes wide with alarm.

A short time later, Ryan woke with a start as her partner hurled herself onto the bed. "Shit!" the dark woman cried as she jerked up into a sitting position. Turning wide eyes to her partner, she asked, "What's wrong?"

"We were making out in front of that huge crowd," Jamie moaned, still clutching her stomach.

"What?" Ryan demanded, sleep-fogged and confused.

"We had thousands of people singing to us. We were making out in front of all of them. There were probably television cameras there. My parents' friends might see us on the news. Cassie might see us on the news. What part of that don't you get?" The words came out in a monotone, all of Jamie's emotion lodged in her cramping stomach.

"Ahh, shit," Ryan slammed her fists down onto the bed. "God damn it!" She was off the bed in a flash, pacing up and down the large room in a tight oval. "Damn it, damn it, damn it!"

Seeing how upset Ryan was made Jamie immediately try to collect herself. "Honey, honey," she said at higher volume. "Why are you so upset?"

"Because *you* are," Ryan cried. "I was so involved in the joy of the moment, that I didn't even consider the repercussions! That was so stupid! I can't believe I let that happen ..."

Ryan started to pace again, muttering under her breath, but in that instant a perfectly clear thought came over the smaller woman, and she looked up at her partner calmly. "It's okay, Ryan. It's really okay."

The pacing stopped and Ryan crossed back to the bed, climbing on and scooting across the surface on her knees. "What?" she asked in a subdued voice. "How can it be?"

"It can be because I've decided that it is," Jamie said, her voice full of her growing conviction. "I'm not ready to tell my parents yet, but if they find out … they find out." She looked completely normal now, and her lips had even curled into a sunny smile. "I'm not ashamed of you … I'm not ashamed of myself … I'm not ashamed of our love. I refuse to be ashamed, Ryan," she added softly. "This is too precious a gift to ever be ashamed of."

Ryan lifted her hand and began to stroke Jamie's face, fingers gliding over the smooth planes of her face. She stared at the earnest woman for a few minutes before tilting her head and bending for a kiss. Their lips merged in a tender touch as Ryan's fingers threaded through her partner's fair hair. Both women rose to their knees and continued the embrace, which was now rapidly escalating in intensity. The kisses grew more heated, more passionate, as each claimed their right to love who they chose, as they chose. Shaking with emotion, they slowly broke apart, finishing with a small flurry of tender kisses.

Ryan's heart was filled to bursting with emotion for the gentle woman in her arms. Jamie's heartfelt words seemed to break the shackles Ryan had used to control her desire. Her hands shook as she trailed them over Jamie's face, lovingly touching each feature. Her eyes were dark with yearning, and her breathing had become more rapid until she was panting softly. "I want to make love to you, Jamie. I need to love you." Her grip tightened, and they tumbled onto the mattress, with Ryan's powerful body poised over her beloved.

Summoning all of her resolve, Jamie placed her hands on the sides of Ryan's clenched jaw, sliding her fingers across her ears and down the tightly corded tendons in her neck. "I want that, too," Jamie said, reaching up to place gentle kisses all over Ryan's flushed face. Jamie blinked slowly, realizing that Ryan was allowing her to make the final decision. The sensations were overwhelming as she tried to calm her racing pulse, feeling the heat radiating from her partner. To her own amazement, she slowly shook her head and tried to kiss away the disappointment revealed in the dark blue eyes "This isn't the place, honey. Mia will be back soon, and the last thing I want is to have to rush, or be interrupted."

"But …" Ryan began to beg, her arousal clouding her judgment, "we could just not answer when she comes home …"

Jamie was firm in her resolve. "No. This isn't what we've waited for. This isn't special, or private. We deserve that," she insisted.

Ryan slowly lowered herself onto her partner, then rolled onto her side and tossed her arm over her eyes. Just then, Mia called out, "Dinner's ready!"

When neither woman responded, Mia opened their door a few inches and said, "Let's go, you two. I've got enough food for the whole building."

"Thank God you were in your right mind today," Ryan muttered, "'cause if I were in charge, Mia would have been eating alone, and we would have missed our plane tomorrow!"

At eight, Ryan's eyes blinked open, the bright sunlight streaming into the bedroom making it hard to stay asleep. She was lying on her back and Jamie was spooned against her right side with both an arm and a leg thrown over her.

She gently pried Jamie's sleep-heavy appendages from her body, marveling at how her partner could be manipulated in her sleep. As she stretched and flexed all of her muscles, she gratefully acknowledged how a little affection, a lot of loving attention, ten hours of sleep, and a fabulous dinner could restore her good humor.

She found her sweats and padded into the living room, looking for Mia and a little snack. Their hostess, dressed in running shorts and a tank top, sat on the balcony sipping from a large Starbucks cup while she flipped through the L.A. Times.

"Hey, Ryan, I brought back coffee for you guys." Ryan had poked her head around the doorframe when she spotted Mia, but pulled it right back in when she realized that a cup of coffee was waiting for her somewhere in the kitchen.

A delighted moan reached Mia's ears when Ryan found the huge cup sitting in the microwave. "God, I've missed this," Ryan groaned. She spent a minute figuring out the mechanics of the machine and then turned it on for two minutes, watching the cup twirl around, her anticipation building. She pulled it out when the timer rang and closed her eyes, taking a big sip, then holding the cup up in adoration, "Aah, I've missed you so." She walked back out to the balcony and kissed Mia on the top of her head. "You have my undying gratitude for this." She hoisted the cup again, gazing at it like a long-lost friend. "I think I missed caffeine more than anything else."

"I'm really surprised they don't give you guys coffee."

"Oh, they do, but it's a diuretic. It's hard enough to keep fluid in me without peeing it out unnecessarily."

Mia giggled when Ryan's statement reminded her of something. "I've gotta tell you, I was the most surprised person in the world when Jamie decided to do this, but when I heard that she was gonna have to use a porta-pottie for a week, I knew she'd lost her mind!"

Ryan gave her a smirk as she was forced to agree. "I don't think either of us will have fond memories of those little beauties. You'd be surprised at Jamie, though. She can rally when she needs to."

"You don't have to defend her to me, Ryan. I love her like a sister."

"She feels the same about you. I'm glad she has you."

A massive smile lit up Mia's already sunny demeanor. "So, what are your plans for today? Do you want to go to the beach?"

"I'd love to spend some time playing in the surf. I want to go to church first, though."

"Church? Really?"

"Yeah, I'm going to St. Monica's, just down California. Would you like to go with me?" She was teasing Mia, already knowing the answer.

"Gosh, I'd love to Ryan," she said with innocent, wide eyes, "but I wouldn't want to break my record of never having been inside of a church except for funerals and weddings."

"Far be it from me to try to convince you to give up your beliefs. Hey, isn't your mom Italian?"

"Yeah, her parents were both born in Italy. Why?"

"How did you escape being Catholic?"

"Oh." Her laughter acknowledged that it was an anomaly. "My mother was raised Catholic, but she had a big fight with her parents and the Church over something and she quit on the spot. She's not the woman you want to piss off," she said with a chuckle.

"What were they fighting about?"

"Not sure. Maybe my dad, he's a heretic Lutheran, you know."

"So you didn't go to his church either?"

"He belongs to the church of the holy dollar sign," she scoffed. "He believes God lives in Ft. Knox."

"Must be funny to have no organized religion growing up. How do you know what to rebel against?"

"Yeah," Mia laughed. "That's about it, isn't it? Jamie's the only one of my friends who goes to church, and I think most of them were raised in some religion. I guess you don't miss it if you don't know it." She gazed at Ryan thoughtfully for a moment. "So, you and Jamie are both regular churchgoers? I hate to admit it, but I wouldn't peg you as religious."

"Jamie goes more often than I do, but I get a lot out of a service if I'm in a receptive mood. I guess you could call me religious, if being religious means looking for ways to make life make some kinda sense. But I break more than my share of commandments."

There was a brief moment of silence, and it gave Mia an opportunity to decide to take a plunge. "Do you mind me asking you a really personal question?"

"No, not at all."

"What are your … uhm … intentions … towards Jamie," she finally got out.

"My intentions?" she asked, surprised at the form of the question. "Oh, my reputation …" she said, as realization dawned on her. "You want to know if I'm going to use her up and toss her out when I'm through with her."

"Well, I wouldn't put it like that, but I've heard that you really get around. I'm worried about Jamie, 'cause this is all so new to her."

Ryan put her cup down and raised her face to the sky, composing her thoughts so that Mia would understand her completely. She turned so that she faced her squarely. "I'm deeply in love with Jamie. I'm going to spend the rest of my life with her, if she'll have me. I have been with a lot of women, but none of them has ever affected me like she has. She's one of the nicest, sweetest, most generous people I've ever met, and I'm honored that she's chosen me."

Mia sat in stunned silence for a moment. "God, Ryan, I had no idea you were that serious." She reached out to grasp Ryan's hand, giving it a friendly squeeze. "I knew Jamie was wild about you, but I was afraid it might be a little one-sided. Damn, I'm really sorry that I thought that about you."

"I've got no one to blame but myself," Ryan grumbled. "I've never intentionally hurt anyone, but a lot of women were hurt by my inability to form an attachment. I can't change what I've done in the past, but it'll never happen again. I'm gonna put every ounce of my energies into making this relationship work."

Mia leaned over and kissed her lightly on the cheek. "I'm really glad that you found each other. She doesn't know this, but I was really worried about her when she decided to marry Jack. I mean, he was a really great guy and all, but it was obvious that she wasn't hot for him. With you, she really acts like a woman in love. It's great to see her so happy."

Ryan paused at that statement, and uttered a small, wry chuckle. "You know, sometimes I feel so sorry for Jack that it makes me want to cry. If he loves her anything like I do, I can't imagine losing something that precious." She shook her head at the thought, allowing herself to feel how devastated she would be if Jamie no longer loved her.

"I know he said he loved her, but how much can you love someone who doesn't love you back in the same way? I think he may have been in love with who he wanted her to be, rather than who she was." She added, "I think you love the real Jamie."

"The real Jamie is so much better than anything I could fantasize."

"Could you *be* any more wonderful?" came a soft voice over her shoulder.

Ryan's face lit up in a luminous smile as she turned and caught Jamie's loving gaze. "C'mere, sweet stuff," she commanded, as her partner came out onto the balcony and curled up into her lap. Ryan placed several small kisses on her lips, smiling through the tender touches. "Hey, guess what Mia brought?" She provided a fairly large clue by holding up her cup.

"I changed my mind," Jamie declared, getting off Ryan's lap and climbing onto Mia's. "I love you the best," she said as she snuggled against Mia's chest.

"Looks like you were worried about the wrong person's fidelity," Ryan joked to Mia as she left to prepare her partner's coffee.

"What did she mean by that?" Jamie asked.

"I uhm ... kinda made the mistake of assuming that she wasn't as serious about you as you were about her."

"And she set you straight."

"Completely," Mia agreed, rolling her eyes. "She said the sweetest things about you, James. It was really darling. I had no idea that she was so open about her feelings."

"I've never known anyone who was so connected to how she feels," Jamie said. "It's really easy for her to express her feelings if she trusts someone."

Ryan came back onto the balcony just as Jamie finished speaking. "I'm going to Mass just down the street at nine-thirty, Jamie. Do you want to go with me?"

Jamie checked her watch and saw that it was just quarter to nine. "Yeah, I'd like to. Do I have time to take a shower?"

"Sure," Ryan replied. "We don't need to leave until about 9:10."

"Oh, but I don't have any decent clothes," she said as she did a mental inventory. "I didn't know we were going to church."

"This is a Catholic church in Santa Monica. I'm guessing the dress code is 'no swimsuits'."

"Really? I usually wear a dress to church. Are you sure?"

"I'm wearing my purple T-shirt that we got yesterday, and some khaki shorts. If you want to look like you're with me, dress accordingly," she ordered. "Could I use your shower so we can get ready at the same time, Mia?"

"Sure, no problem."

When Ryan was out of earshot, Mia turned and asked, "So what's up with that? Don't you two lovebirds shower together?"

Jamie blushed to the roots of her hair as she confessed, "We haven't really done … uhm … everything together."

"What kind of everything haven't you done?" Mia asked, narrowing her eyes suspiciously.

"We haven't really had sex together yet."

"What?" Mia shrieked. "Why the hell not?"

"It was only a few weeks ago that I decided that this was right for me and that I was ready to take the plunge. We couldn't find anywhere to be together that was private. We can't do it at her father's house, and Cassie was still in Berkeley."

"So why didn't you go to a hotel?"

"I wanted it to be special, you know, a time we'd always remember."

"How could you not remember the first time you make love to a hottie like that?" Mia cried. "You could do it on a bus and have it be memorable!"

"I know, I know," she muttered, her embarrassment growing. "I'm really struggling with this. Cut me some slack, okay?"

"Oh, shit, I'm sorry, James. I don't wanna give you a hard time. I'm surprised, that's all. I never would've asked her if she was serious about you if I'd known this! She must love you an awful lot to wait all these weeks."

"Uhm … months," Jamie corrected shyly, flinching in anticipation of Mia's reaction.

"What do you mean, months?" Mia was dumbfounded, and her expression reflected her surprise.

"She didn't sleep with the woman she saw before me either, mainly because I talked her into trying to build a relationship based on something other than sex."

"So how long has it been for her?"

"She's only had sex once in seven months," Jamie figured with a gulp as she realized how long that really was.

"Seven months! Seven months! Are you crazy? When you finally unleash her, she's gonna devour you in one bite! That's not natural, Jamie. You could hurt yourself waiting that long!"

"Well, if you hear screaming coming from Pebble Beach tomorrow, you'll know that you were right." Jamie got up to take her shower, hoping that her insistence on celibacy would not prove to be her demise.

# Chapter Two

During the walk to the church, Jamie quizzed Ryan about the service. She'd never been to a Catholic Mass and found herself intensely curious. They arrived at about 9:25, and the pews were nearly full. They wound up sitting three rows from the front, right in front of an open door. Ryan was quite pleased with their placement, since she was usually warm, but Jamie knew she'd be cold with the rather stiff ocean breeze blowing in on her. To her great pleasure, they closed one side of the double door just as the service began, and she was much more comfortable.

The service began with an upbeat song, which Ryan sang from memory. Next came readings from the New and Old Testaments, followed by the gospel reading and a relatively brief sermon. The priest looked around as he wound up his remarks, then asked how many people had participated in the AIDS Ride. Jamie was surprised and pleased to see about fifteen people stand up, all wearing their T-shirts. She and Ryan hopped up as well, and the large crowd gave them a heartfelt standing ovation. The priest praised their efforts and congratulated them for their caring and dedication.

Jamie was quite touched when they took their seats again. "You knew that was going to happen, didn't you?" she asked in a whisper.

"I had a feeling it might. They have a really big gay and lesbian outreach group in this parish, and I know the pastor is very supportive. He rides a bike, too, so he knows what a big deal it is."

"Well, it was very sweet. Thanks for bringing me."

As they walked back down California after the service, Jamie asked Ryan about her current relationship with her church. "It's funny, but I've been thinking about going more regularly. I have so much to be thankful for that it makes me want to give thanks in a more formal way."

"Do you like your parish?"

"It's okay. But if I had a church like St. Monica's, I'd really love to go. How do you feel about yours?"

"I love it, but maybe that's because my grandfather's there. Would you consider going with me?"

"Yeah, let's try your grandfather's church and see if we can both be comfortable there. I'd really prefer to go with you, if possible."

"I would too. If you don't like the Episcopal Church, I'd be very willing to search for a Catholic church that we both liked. I think that going to church together would be a very good thing for us."

"It's a deal."

It was 11:00 a.m. when they arrived home, and Mia was ready for the beach. Her father belonged to a prestigious city club in San Francisco that offered reciprocal privileges for her to use a local beach club in Santa Monica under his name. Since none of them had eaten, they decided to have breakfast when they got there.

They walked the short distance and were shown to a nice white, wrought iron table with a forest green umbrella that shielded them from the intense sun. An eager young man came to take their order, and Ryan ordered for all of them, choosing eggs benedict, banana pancakes, pecan waffles, a green chili omelet, and steel-cut oatmeal with cream and brown sugar. They each ordered another coffee and a glass of juice as well. Given the size of the order, Jamie thought she could see the waiter trying to figure out where the other members of their party were, and when he brought out the dishes, he was completely unsure of where to put everything. Ryan noticed his confusion and told him to put it anywhere that it fit. He did, looking over his shoulder as he walked away.

Jamie and Mia laughed at his confusion, but Ryan couldn't spare the time. She dug into the oatmeal, performing her usual pleasure dance. Jamie knew that she had to get cracking if she was going to get food, so she grabbed the plate of pancakes before Ryan could. "You'd better grab something, Mia. Time is of the essence with Ryan around."

Mia reached for the waffles just as Ryan did. Those big blue eyes narrowed dangerously, and a firmly held fork pointed right for her hand as Mia meekly relinquished her tenuous hold. Ryan threw back her head, laughing uproariously. "You'd starve to death in the O'Flaherty household," she chided. "You can never give up on a plate you've claimed. It's a sign of weakness that the others will surely exploit!" She politely placed the dish in front of Mia, snagging only one quarter of the waffle as her prize.

"Is she like this at every meal?" Mia asked incredulously, starting to eat more quickly than normal to make sure she didn't wind up hungry.

"Yep. It's a constant struggle," Jamie said. "We almost always have to order three entrees if I'm gonna get anything at all."

"What do you do with all of those calories?" Mia asked, turning to Ryan. "You're as lean as a greyhound."

"I don't know," she replied through a mouthful of waffle. "I've always eaten this much. I must be used to it."

"Don't let her kid you, Mia," Jamie smirked. "She runs around like a hyperactive two-year-old all day long."

Ryan was preparing her defense when three women beginning to limber up to play volleyball on a sand court caught her attention. Her eyes began to sparkle as she said, "I gotta check something out." She jumped up and ran over to the women, engaging them in conversation for a moment before she was back again, grinning like the Cheshire cat.

"What was that all about?" Jamie inquired.

"Jamie, sweetie, honeybunch," Ryan said, as she got down on her knees in front of her partner. "Would you mind terribly if I spent just a few minutes with my new friends over there?" she asked coyly, pointing at the women who were now watching her for an indication of her readiness.

"What are you going to do with your new best friends?" Jamie asked, as she affectionately fluffed the bangs out of Ryan's innocent blue eyes.

"We're just gonna play for a little while, if you don't mind, that is," she said solemnly.

"Do you know how to play volleyball?" she asked, in her best maternal voice.

"I think so," Ryan said as she nodded her head, her face brimming with childlike innocence.

"Okay, you can play for a little while, but don't get hurt." She leaned over and whispered into her ear, "You need to be in tip top shape for tomorrow."

"I won't!" Ryan said as she stripped out of her clothes. Jamie noticed, with surprise, that Ryan's swimsuit matched the outfits that the other volleyball players wore: high cut briefs and racerback sports bras. The other women sported logos on their outfits, but Jamie knew that Ryan hated to use her body as a billboard. When they were shopping for gear they had actually spent the better part of an hour finding bike shorts that didn't have the manufacturer's name on the thigh.

"Just wait one more minute," Jamie said, rooting around in her pack as Ryan fidgeted, anxious to start playing. "I have to put some sun block on your shoulders before you take off."

"The sand will stick to me," she whined.

"You won't get sand all the way up here," Jamie reasoned, as she slathered gel on her shoulders and back.

"Hmrff," was all that Ryan could summon up as a rejoinder. She used the time wisely, though, grabbing the omelet and finishing it off while Jamie worked away.

When Jamie finished, she slapped her on the butt, saying, "Go get 'em, Tiger."

Since breakfast was finished, she and Mia found a pair of comfortable Adirondack chairs and turned them so they were facing the court. She noted that although Ryan's new playmates were in fantastic shape, they were all less muscular than her generously sculpted partner, with long, lean bodies, rather like whippets. While Ryan was also very trim, she had a solid, muscular build that made her look somewhat formidable next to the other players. They warmed up for a few minutes, casually tossing the ball back and forth.

"I didn't know she played volleyball," Mia said, as they watched them prepare.

"I didn't either," Jamie admitted. "I just found out on Friday that she played basketball in college. She seems to really like having little secrets that she only reveals when I ask her a direct question."

*I just bet she does*, Mia mused, not thoroughly convinced that Ryan was completely reformed, even though she believed that she was sincere in her attempt. "She doesn't look like the other women," Mia observed, echoing Jamie's earlier thought. "I wonder if she'll be any good."

"I don't know," Jamie said. "I've only seen her play rugby, and I had no idea what was going on in that madness. I do know one thing for sure. Whether or not she's any good, she'll play hard."

Their questions about Ryan's abilities were answered about four minutes into the game. The score was tied, two to two, and Ryan's partner had just served. The ball flew back and forth a few times, finally coming to Ryan who was standing right next to the net. The ball was high—actually so high that Jamie assumed it would sail over Ryan's head and land between her and her partner. The green eyes grew wide as Ryan coiled, gathering her muscled legs beneath her, and then began to rise. She kept going, up, up, up, until her head was above the net. She pulled her right arm back as she rose and chopped at the ball, hitting it right at its apex with unbelievable force. At that instant, the opposing player dove to the spot that she anticipated the spike to hit. She misjudged and over-committed, falling to the sand as the ball hit her right on the butt with stunning velocity. The ball ricocheted as it hit her, changing direction and flying nearly to where Jamie and Mia sat watching, openmouthed.

Ryan trotted over to retrieve the ball, a huge grin on her face. She cast a glance at her friends, wiggling one eyebrow at Jamie, saying, "That had to sting!" She grabbed the ball and headed back, both spectators watching her firm butt twitch as she ran.

"Did you see . . .?" Mia stuttered.

"Yeah, I think I did . . ."

"That wasn't human!"

"Can you imagine the bruise that poor woman is gonna have on her ass?" Jamie finally gasped, as both she and Mia collapsed with laughter.

The game continued at a rather frenetic pace, and Ryan's partner looked mighty pleased that she had been paired with the dark stranger. Jamie felt her ire begin to rise as Ryan's partner beamed over at her. With some difficulty, she forced the jealous feelings down, knowing that Ryan was more interested in the match than in her teammate.

As the game wore on, the intensity of the match increased dramatically, and Jamie noticed that the women on the other team now seemed more interested in stuffing the ball down Ryan's throat than in actually winning the game. "You know, she was telling me about how a player on another team beaned her with a basketball during a game. She didn't seem to have any idea why that would happen, but after watching this, I think I have a clue," Jamie said reflectively. "It looks so effortless for her. That could really start to piss you off if you were busting your ass playing against her."

Focusing on the game and the interaction of the players for a moment, Mia had to agree. "Yeah, she just looks like she's having fun. The others look like they're working." After a pause, Mia added in a quiet voice, "God, will you look at that body."

"Hey, I've got dibs on that body, you know," Jamie said as she poked her in the ribs.

"I don't know, Jamie," Mia mused, surveying the lanky woman with studied interest. "You've only got a lesbian learner's permit. Taking her on would be like driving a Ferrari," she observed. "I mean, look at the power in those legs. You could bounce quarters off her ass! Whew, the thought of those legs wrapped around me makes me want to swoon!" she said dramatically.

Casting a puzzled glance at her friend, Jamie tried to step back and look at her partner from a purely physical perspective. "Well, if we're gonna analyze her, I've got to vote for her back and shoulders. I love the way her back tapers down to that lean, narrow waist. And her shoulders are so broad and strong. You know, she tossed me over her shoulder the other night like I didn't weigh a thing. She carried me all the way back to our tent, and it must have been three hundred yards. She wasn't even breathing heavily!"

"Oh," Mia sighed deeply. "I love it when they pick you up and carry you. I love to feel that power."

"You know, I hated it when Jack would pick me up, unless he was carrying me to bed after I fell asleep. With a guy, it feels like they want to show you how strong they are, and how weak you are. With Ryan, it's like … play. I know she would never use her strength to overpower me."

"How can you be so sure, Jamie? She might show you a whole different side when she gets you between the sheets."

"Nope. You don't know how she is. I've never been around anyone who's so considerate of my feelings. When we first started playing around, it all kind of freaked me out. She told me that I could do anything I wanted to do to her, and she wouldn't go further than I did. And I have tortured her, Mia. I mean, I've really tortured her."

Jamie saw the mischievous glint in her friend's eyes and knew that she'd set herself up. The curly head tilted, and Mia said thoughtfully, "I never figured you for a dom. You're just coming out all over the place, aren't ya?"

"I'm hardly a dom!" Jamie cried, slapping Mia sharply on her bare leg. *I think I know what that is*, she thought to herself, but there was no way she was going to ask for verification of her guess.

"I don't know, babe," Mia muttered, rubbing the red handprint on her thigh, "you pack a wallop, and I think you enjoy it!"

"Only with you," Jamie said, with an overly sweet smile affixed to her face.

"So how does Ryan react to your little torture sessions?"

Jamie paused for a moment, recalling all of the times she had pushed the obviously turned-on woman further than she should have. "She's been the soul of restraint. She never—not once—tried to go further than I wanted to. Well …" she amended, "She almost lost it once, but she let me decide."

"And you said no?"

"Yeah. It just wasn't the right time or place. But other than that, she's spent most of this spring trying to talk me out of doing stuff."

"God, if I don't want to do it two minutes after getting to L.A., Jason has a fit! Come to think of it," she mused reflectively, "I don't think a guy has ever tried to talk me out of doing anything!"

Jamie shook her head briskly, reflecting on how proud she was that Ryan was so gentle with her. "She never gets mad about it. As a matter of fact, she's downright adorable about it. There's this hungry look she gets that just about breaks my heart. I know it's hard for her, but she controls herself because she knows that I want her to."

"Jeez, maybe we're both wrong about her," Mia mumbled. "Maybe she's not really hot in bed. It could just be an act."

"No. Trust me," Jamie said slowly. "Just the way she kisses is enough to melt you into a puddle. Plus, I've … seen her in action."

"I don't doubt it!" Mia cried. "I'm surprised she doesn't run down the street grabbing the first woman she sees, after what you do to her!"

"It was before we started dating," Jamie said with another smack to her thigh. "I saw her practically making love to a woman in a lesbian coffeehouse. She didn't know I was there, and I assume she didn't think anyone was watching her, but I got so turned on … whew! She's not all talk, Mia. Trust me."

"God, that sounds hot!" Mia squealed. "What else ya got?"

Mia was getting so much pleasure out of this interchange that Jamie didn't have the heart to tell her these topics were too private. Besides, if she was really honest with herself, she got a good deal of enjoyment from talking about Ryan in this frank manner. "Well, she took me to a women's sex toy store, and they made a big deal about her not breaking any more of the toys in the try-on room."

"Yikes! How do you break a sex toy? Was she alone when she did that?"

"Nope. She apparently used to take dates there to have a quickie."

"Dates—sex toys, dates—sex toys," Mia mused, deep in thought. "That's a match made in heaven! She's a genius! What else?"

"Well," Jamie began, blushing mightily, "even though we haven't made love … we've uhm … you know …"

"Touched each other," Mia supplied helpfully, batting her big brown eyes at Jamie.

"Yes, of course we touch each other," Jamie scoffed. "I'm not *that* hung up!"

"So … if you're already touching each other, why do you keep insisting that you haven't had sex? That's all there is with a girl, Jamie."

"Oh … well … we haven't touched each other … that way," the blushing blonde said. "I meant that we touched each other when we kissed."

"Oooh, you mean you don't stand two feet apart, put your hands behind your backs and lean over to kiss," Mia drawled, obviously enjoying her friend's embarrassment.

"God! Must you harass me like this?"

"Well, yeah," Mia laughed. "It's what I'm best at, James."

"I guess you have me there," Jamie agreed. "What I was getting at is that even though we haven't gone very far, I can tell how passionate she'll be by the way she responds to my kisses. She's just so … I don't even know the word for it. She's …" a heavy sigh followed her comment, and she looked towards her partner with a wistful smile, "wonderful."

"Do you have any idea how many women she's been 'wonderful' with?" Mia asked, shattering Jamie's romantic reverie.

Jamie tilted her head back, dramatically rolling her eyes at her friend. "Does everything have to be about sex?"

"Come on, do the numbers," Mia begged.

Jamie gave her a look, but she complied. "Well, she's been sexually active since she was seventeen—that's six years. She's basically never had a girlfriend, and until this year her able-bodied record for going without sex is two weeks—and that didn't happen very often from what I can gather." As Jamie did the math, her eyes grew wider. She gulped noticeably when she considered the tally.

"Are you sure you don't want me to break her in for you, Jamie?" Mia inquired solicitously. "I don't want you to get hurt, you know."

Smirk firmly in place, Jamie patted her friend on the leg. "You're a real pal. As much as I appreciate the offer, I think I can handle her. Besides, what makes you such an expert?"

"I'm not as naïve as I seem," Mia scoffed, assuming a haughty look.

"You haven't been naïve since you were in diapers. Now what are you hinting at?"

"I've had a few bites of the lesbian apple."

"You have not!" Jamie shrieked as she slapped her friend's arm.

"Have too," she insisted, rubbing at the reddening skin and scooting back in her chair to avoid a repeat.

"When? With whom?"

"It's a long story, babe. I'm sure you don't want me to bore you with it now."

"*Bore me?*" Jamie cried, causing every one of their neighbors to turn in her direction. "Bore me?" she repeated at a more moderate level. "You've got to be on drugs! Now tell me the whole story—and don't you dare leave anything out!"

The curly-haired woman sighed dramatically, but couldn't keep the smile off her face. "Oh, all right," she said. "I should've told you before now, but I promised I wouldn't."

"Promised? Who did you …?"

"That's part of the story," Mia said. "I shouldn't tell, but I know you won't spill it."

"No, but if you promised …"

"Statute of limitations has expired," Mia said. "She's either married or she's joined your club by now."

"Huh?"

"Okay, here's the whole deal. Remember when I started hanging out with Melissa Johnston during senior year?"

"Yeah," Jamie agreed, a small frown settling on her brow. "What's Miss Homecoming Queen got to do with it?"

"Well …" Mia drawled. "We started to hang out because our boyfriends were buddies. Remember?"

"Oh yeah, I forgot how close Mark and Trey were. You know, I was pretty jealous when you started spending all of your time with her. I felt like she was taking you away from me."

"You had nothing to worry about, honey, but Mark should have been shaking in his boots!"

"What does your old boyfriend have to do with the story? This is confusing the heck out of me."

"Patience, girlfriend. All will be revealed." Mia took another deep breath and continued her tale. "Melissa and I got to be really good friends. We were together a lot because of Mark and Trey, and over time we started to hang out when the guys weren't with us."

"I remember," Jamie pouted. "I could hardly get a minute of your time."

"I know, and I'm sorry you felt shut out. Things were … complicated for me then. I really liked Melissa, and before I knew it we were inseparable."

"I've never understood why you stopped hanging out with her so abruptly," Jamie said.

Mia chuckled. "Can I finish?"

"Sorry." Jamie shook her head. "It's your story—run with it."

"Okay, we were getting to be really close. One night we'd been out with the guys, and I decided to stay overnight at her house. We were hanging out in her room, talking and smoking a little weed. My leg was bothering me—I forget what I'd done to it, but it was stiff. Melissa offered to massage it for me. I thought that was nice, if a little odd, so I took her up on it. She gave me a short robe, and we got onto her bed … hey, don't pass out on me here." Mia laughed when she caught sight of Jamie's shocked expression.

"I … I … did you …?"

"Patience is a virtue, sweetie. Just hold on a sec," she urged, patting her friend's leg reassuringly. "Okay, I was on the bed, and she started rubbing my legs. She kept going higher and higher, well past the painful area, and as she kept going, something else started to throb."

Jamie's mouth was open so wide that Mia was afraid her jaw was going to pop out of joint. "You … you slept with Melissa Johnston?"

"No … we didn't sleep," Mia corrected. "She slid her hand up between my legs, and within seconds we were rolling around on that bed like a couple of rabid chipmunks!"

"Mia! How can that be? You're both straight!"

The curly-haired woman tossed her head back and laughed heartily. "That's so cute! You sound like my grandmother!"

"What?"

"That's so old school! Nobody's into those silly labels anymore! She was into me, and I was into her. We were both in the mood, and had the opportunity—so why not?" She shrugged as if it were an every day occurrence.

"But … but …" Jamie sputtered. "She's a girl!"

"I know," Mia agreed. "A very hot girl, who knew how to make me come better than any guy I've been with, before or since. She was a cheerleader you know. She was practically double jointed!"

"Jesus, Mia! You can't sleep with every person who asks you to!"

"And that would be because …?" the chestnut haired woman asked, holding up her hands in a questioning gesture.

"Because … because … I don't know why. I just know that you can't!" Jamie finally decreed.

"Well, I beg to differ, sweetie, I can, and I do! No harm has befallen me, I might add."

Deciding to table her discomfort for the moment, Jamie let her curiosity take over. "So, what happened with Melissa? Did you stop seeing each other because it was uncomfortable?"

"No," Mia laughed. "We stopped seeing each other because she wanted me to be exclusive with her! Jeez! I certainly wasn't exclusive with Mark, why would she think I would be with her?"

"She fell in love with you?" Jamie was stunned at this revelation.

"She said she was," Mia mused, the smile vanishing. "It was really kinda tough for me, to tell you the truth. I liked her a lot, and I loved having sex with her. I still don't see why we couldn't have kept on doing what we were doing."

"She wasn't able to, huh?" Jamie knew that she wouldn't be able to share someone she loved with another.

"No, she wasn't," Mia said. "It got to be too hard, so we finally had to stop seeing each other completely. The guys were kinda pissed off, because we'd all gotten along so well. I honestly think that's one of the reasons Mark broke up with me. I think he liked hanging out with Trey as much as he did with me."

"Maybe Mark and Trey …" Jamie began to suggest.

Mia tossed her head back and laughed. "Now that, I would pay to see!"

"I bet you would," Jamie muttered as the server came by to ask if they wanted anything to drink. Mia was flirting outrageously with the twenty-something man and Jamie sat back to watch a master at work. She decided that her friend possessed the perfect blend of openness and playfulness needed to flirt successfully. Mia didn't seem overly aggressive, and her cherubic face made her appear more innocent than she was. She gave the accurate impression that she was funny, witty, open-minded and very interested.

By the time the server, Chad, left, Mia had received an invitation to attend a jazz concert on the Santa Monica pier on Thursday night. "You are really good at that," Jamie mused, as she watched her friend put Chad's phone number into her bag.

"It's a gift," Mia agreed, tossing her curls in the breeze.

"I take it you and Jason aren't exclusive any longer?"

"Mmm, we're taking it a lot more casually now," Mia said. "I've seen him about three times since I got here. I think he's trying to make me miss him by playing hard to get."

"Oh yeah, that'll work!"

"He obviously doesn't know who he's dealing with," Mia agreed with a sympathetic smile. "I invented hard to get."

Getting back to their earlier discussion, Jamie said, "Did you promise Melissa you wouldn't tell?"

"Yeah, but I figure it's safe to tell you now since you're a member of the same club. I mean, I always knew I could trust you, James, but now I think you have a better sense of why she wouldn't want this to get out."

"Yeah," she laughed wryly. "I'm certainly not ready to shout it from the rooftops. Just a stage in front of thousands of people," she added, shivering with the memory. "So … back to your story. Once you got it out of your system, you've stayed with men exclusively, right?"

"Not exactly."

"Give!"

"Okay, okay, jeez, you're so pushy!" Mia laughed. "I had sex with a woman at Cal."

"When … with whom?" Jamie persisted, unwilling to forego any of the details.

"Freshman year. Remember Dave, that guy from Oregon that I dated for a while?"

"Yeah, vaguely. You didn't see him for very long did you?"

"No, thanks to him, I didn't. He wanted to do a three way with another girl. I didn't really object, so he set it up with this woman he knew. We all get together and have a pretty hot time. Problem is, he thought I liked it too much, which I did, as a matter of fact. The woman and I really went at it, and he got all pissed. He thought we would both do him and be happy, but we spent most of our time on each other. He actually had the nerve to call me a lesbian, and say he didn't want to see me anymore because he didn't want to date a dyke! The nerve!"

"God, Mia!" Jamie said, wide-eyed. "What haven't you done?"

"Besides barnyard animals and children, not much," she admitted. "I figure you're only young once, but if you do it right, once is enough."

"Is that it? Just that one girl?"

"No … I had one more little dip in the pool … last week. A bunch of us from work went out to this club, and it turns out it's mostly lesbian. We were all drinking and dancing and having a good time, and this fine-looking redhead asked me to dance. We had a really good time together, and she asked if I'd go home with her. I didn't have any good reason to say no, so I went."

"Did you enjoy it?"

"Oh, yeah!" Mia readily agreed. "This girl had been around the block a few hundred times. She really knew her way around a woman! I'm certain I've never had that many orgasms in one day. I could hardly walk the next day at work."

"What does all of that mean to you? Doesn't it make you question your sexuality?"

"Question my sexuality," Mia repeated slowly, tilting her head up, and staring pensively into the blue sky. "I think I've given pretty good evidence than my sexuality is quite robust."

"I mean your sexual orientation," Jamie insisted. "Doesn't it ever make you think that you might be gay?"

"No. Why should it?" Mia asked blankly, clearly not understanding why that would even be a question.

"Well, when I saw that I wanted to be with Ryan … that way … I started asking myself if I was gay."

"I'm not *gay*, Jamie!" She laughed heartily, looking at her friend with a big smile. "I love to have sex. I'm primarily attracted to men, but if I meet a hot woman, I can have just as good a time. Actually, in some ways being with women is a lot easier."

"How?" Jamie asked, longing for support for her own choice.

"Number one—no birth control. That's a very big deal for me. Number two—lots of orgasms. Also a big deal," she laughed. Number three—the women I've been with have been all about pleasing me. A very, very big deal, as you might have guessed."

"So why not go lesbian?"

"I find men really hot. I like 'em big, and strong, and powerful. And there's nothing I like better than to have a guy show me how much I'm getting to him—they're like compliant little pets. I gotta tell you, though—I might switch for a woman like Ryan. She is definitely a hottie. And boy, can she kiss!"

"Thanks for reminding me," Jamie scowled. "Now I'm mad that you kissed her after finals. I thought you were just drunk!"

"Oh, I was drunk," Mia laughed. "Just not too drunk to enjoy that sexy little mouth!"

"You have no idea," Jamie sighed, her pique replaced by the delicious thought of Ryan's lips. "God, Mia, when I wrap my arms around her to kiss her, my knees get so weak I'm afraid I'll fall. She's so strong, but she holds me so tenderly, like she's afraid I'll break."

"Sounds heavenly," Mia sighed.

"It is, it really is. I know we're gonna have fantastic sex together. I've never, ever been this turned on by anyone. She gets aroused so easily, it's amazing, but she's been so tender and patient with me—it's been wonderful."

"Well, all I'm gonna say is, you'd better keep her busy, or I'm coming after her ... and her brother!" she added with a defiant slap of her hand on the wide arm of her chair.

They'd lost track of the game even though Jamie had kept her eyes on her partner throughout her talk with Mia. She was surprised to see Ryan come trotting over, covered in sweat and sand, looking for a bottle of water. "Did you win?" Jamie asked a little hesitantly.

"Jeez, weren't you keeping score?"

"Uhm, we got kinda involved talking, and I lost track."

"Uh-huh," she replied, as she narrowed her eyes at the duo. "Let me guess what you were talking about." She put her hand up to her eyes as she closed them for a moment, pseudo-seeking psychic vibrations. "I'm gonna say ... sex," she declared. As the blush on Jamie's cheeks rose past her ears, Ryan leaned over to kiss her gently. "Don't give away all my secrets," she said, as she tweaked her nose and jogged back to her position.

"Okay, this time we pay attention," Jamie said as the second game began. They kept their focus for less than two minutes before they were analyzing Ryan again, comparing her to the other women in the game, and to the hundreds of women who passed by on the bike path—walking, skating and jogging. "You know, the only thing she doesn't have is a really ripped stomach. It's rock hard when you push on it, but there's a thin layer of fat that's kind of cushioning. Still, I think I prefer it that way," Jamie mused. "If she was all hard, I don't think I'd like sitting on her as much as I do."

"Oh, I bet it feels great to climb on top of her," Mia moaned.

"I'm drawn to do that like a moth to a flame," Jamie admitted. "I start to kiss her, and within minutes I'm straddling her hips. It's like you're sitting on a panther. She's all coiled energy and power, but she's purring like a little kitten."

"Jamie, we've gotta stop this. I want your girlfriend as much as you do! Let's talk about something else—anything else!"

"Okay, you're right. Let's talk about your job."

They tried to concentrate on Mia's job, but the sweating, laboring bodies of the volleyball players drew them back into a discussion of what constituted the perfect body, and before long Jamie was waxing poetic over the gorgeous body of her partner.

A grinning Ryan, towering over them and blocking the sun, interrupted them. "You weren't watching, were you?" she demanded, her hands on her hips.

"I had my eyes on your butt the whole time," Jamie replied honestly.

"Me too!" Mia smiled, proud of her powers of concentration, until Jamie knocked the smile off of her face with a punch in the arm.

Ryan shook her head as she grabbed a bottle of water and ran back to play another game.

They did a little better this time but they got sidetracked when Ryan kept turning around to point at Jamie, then at her own eyes, reminding her to pay attention.

Jamie then started to regale Mia with the numerous ways that Ryan teased and played with her. They talked a lot about the ride and the little tricks that Ryan had used to get her up the hills. She talked about how thoughtful Ryan was, setting up camp every night, and went on and on about how wonderful it had been to hold her at night and wake up in her arms in the morning. She was about to go into how cute she looked in her little bike outfits when Ryan towered over them again. "What's the score, Jamie?" she demanded, eyes twinkling.

"Uhm … a whole lot for you and very little for the other side?"

Ryan tilted her head back and drank a bottle of water in one long gulp. Both women ogled the line of her throat and the play of her neck muscles. Oblivious to their admiration, discarding the empty, Ryan smacked her lips together, gazed at her partner and shrugged her shoulders. "That's about right," she agreed with a wink, running back across the sand to finish the game.

"Hey, speaking of scoring, tell me about all of the ex-lovers you met," Mia asked with a mischievous grin.

"Got an hour?" Jamie replied dryly.

"So what … she showed up at the ride every year, grabbed a woman and threw her in the tent?"

"No, I think she was a little more moderate than that … at least I hope she was," Jamie laughed. "Actually, it turns out that she trained for each ride with a different group of people. She usually hooked up with someone from the training group, and then slept with her during the ride."

"So … what did they look like? Were they all gorgeous?"

"Thanks." Jamie beamed a smile at her friend.

"You know I think you're gorgeous," Mia laughed. "Are you her usual type?"

"I think her usual type is the double X chromosome. I've seen her with women from twenty to fifty plus, thin, chunky, tall, short, brown, black, and white. She claims that she's more attracted to energy than looks, and I'd have to concur with that. But I'd also have to say that she didn't always choose nice women."

"Oh, somebody gave you a hard time?"

"Just a little," Jamie conceded. "One woman was kinda pissy at first, but she apologized later. Another one was a real bitch, though! She sought me out to give me a hard time because Ryan dumped her after the ride was over."

"Did ya deck her?" Mia asked, always loving a good fight.

"Yeah … that's my style," Jamie agreed. "I loosened a couple of teeth and ripped out a handful of her hair." The smirk now firmly attached to her face belied her statement and, after a second, Jamie continued, "I told her not to dis my lover, and that was that."

"Mmm, I liked the story better the first way."

The imposing shadow of a sweaty, sand-covered woman interrupted the discussion. "Score?" Ryan asked.

"Uhm … you won?" Jamie guessed.

"That's not a score, that's an outcome," she said sternly.

"I … I … I guess I wasn't paying attention," Jamie admitted with a little downward glance.

"Just for that, you have to go rent me a boogie board so I can cool off and get this sand out of my pants," Ryan said with a grimace, as she tried to shake some of the sand out of her tight suit.

"I'll rent two, we can go out beyond the breakers, and I'll help you get that sand out," Jamie teased, as she got up to run over to the rental stand.

Five minutes later they were frolicking in the cool water. Jamie had spent a decent amount of time in the ocean and she was fairly fearless. She was a good swimmer, and she really loved to hop on her boogie board and catch a good wave. Ryan was also perfectly at ease on the ocean. They ranged farther and farther out until they were just beyond the waves, where they sat astride their boards and stared at each other lovingly for a long time. Jamie was perfectly content to smile at Ryan and watch her sweet face, but they finally maneuvered their boards so they could kiss a bit without falling off. It was a struggle to remain upright, so they turned and rode the waves for a while. After a good hour of play they ran back up to Mia, who was lying on the sand on a large towel. Jamie went to the bar and got them all drinks, along with a club sandwich for Ryan. Her partner had not asked for any food, but she knew that it would be devoured in moments. Ryan's eyes grew wide as Jamie put the plate in front of her. "I love club sandwiches," she said with delight, as she dove in happily. "Thanks."

"I can't ignore the most important person in my life all day," she said, as she gave her a little kiss. "You really kicked ass today, didn't you, Tiger."

"Yeah, we did pretty well," she admitted. "My partner was really good."

"Uh-huh," Jamie nodded. "I'm sure that was the reason."

"She really was good," Ryan insisted.

"I'm sure she was, sweetheart." After a beat Jamie asked, "Are there any more sports that you excel at?"

"There might be a couple more that I've played a little bit."

"Do you want to tell me about them?"

"Nope," Ryan said as she happily munched away on her sandwich. "I like to keep an air of mystery about myself. I don't want you to get bored too fast."

"I don't think I could get bored with you in a million years," Jamie said as she gazed into her eyes.

"I need to run down to the Venice boardwalk to pick up a couple of things," Ryan said when she finished her snack.

"Yeah," Mia drawled lazily, clasping her unhooked top to her chest as she rolled over to tan the front of her body. "Two dollar sunglasses are pretty hard to come by."

"No, wise-ass," Ryan scoffed, leaning forward to tie her friend's string bikini. "I need to buy a T-shirt for a friend."

"A T-shirt?" Jamie asked, in a cadence slightly slower than Mia had used. "Honey, who do you know that can't get a T-shirt in San Francisco?"

"It's just a ... thing ... that I do when I travel," Ryan explained. "I'll run down the bike path and be back before you know it."

"Okay," Jamie said laconically. "We won't move a muscle."

Jumping to her feet, Ryan surveyed the listless roommates. "I think you can both easily accomplish that goal."

Since they were now both lying on their backs, they jointly watched Ryan's departing form. Jamie turned to catch Mia holding her head up to get a better look. "Off limits, babe. She's all mine."

"I wouldn't dream of it. Well, I might dream of it," she amended, "but I wouldn't actually do it."

"Thanks, Buddy," Jamie smirked, lying down and wriggling around to get comfortable in the sand. "I gotta admit, I'm starting to feel less nervous about tomorrow after talking to you."

"Why are you nervous?"

"I don't know," Jamie mused. "I trust her, I love her, and she's gentle and patient. It doesn't make logical sense, but I'm ... I guess that I'm afraid I'll disappoint her. I mean, we've waited so long—I really feel like there's a lot of pressure to make tomorrow perfect."

"I can see that," Mia agreed. "But you've got to remember that you're in this for the long haul, babe. Tomorrow isn't a one shot deal."

"You're right. I know I shouldn't build it up bigger than it already is, but I want so badly to please her. She's been with so many women—I worry that I'll be a dud."

"It's not that hard, Jamie," Mia soothed. "Really. You start at the top and work your way down. Stop when you get to something that interests you, hang out there for a while, and move on when something else grabs your attention. It's no big deal!"

"It's that moving down part I'm worried about," Jamie admitted, getting to her biggest concern.

"What? Oral sex?"

Draping an arm over her eyes, Jamie muttered, "Yes, Mia, oral sex. It freaks me out to think that she'll expect that."

"Well, hell yes, she'll expect that!" Mia laughed, her outburst falling well short of the reassurance that Jamie sought.

"Now I feel better," Jamie muttered.

Mia sat up, crossing her legs and resting her elbows on her knees. "Jamie, it's no big deal because I guarantee you'll want to do that to her. Trust me on this, babe. You'll get involved, and it'll happen. You'll be munching away before you know it, and I guarantee that you'll wonder why you ever had any doubts."

"God, I hope so," Jamie groaned. "Sex is so important to her … and it's becoming important to me, too."

"It'll be fine, babe. You'll call me when you get back, and I guarantee that you'll laugh about your nervousness."

"Either that, or I'll call you tomorrow night and beg you to come to Pebble Beach to be my stand-in."

"Either way, babe," Mia laughed. "You know I'm a giver."

Forty-five minutes later, the sweaty shopper returned, amused to find her companions out cold. She tucked her purchases into her gym bag, kicked off her shoes and socks, and scampered across the hot sand for a refreshing dip in the water.

When she returned, she couldn't resist the impulse to straddle Jamie's somnolent body, allowing the cold droplets of water to rain down on the shocked woman.

"Yeow!" the blonde cried as she shot up into a sitting position. Only Ryan's quick reflexes allowed her to jump back a foot to avoid having Jamie's head do a number on her pubic bone. Shaking her head, Jamie asked, "Did you leave?"

"Ahh, I've been gone for over an hour, sleepy."

"Oh, yeah," Jamie said, lazily scratching her head. "Did you shop?"

"Yep. All done."

"Lemme see." The tousled blond head looked around for a package but found none.

"Ahh, okay," Ryan stalled. "I … uhm … Ally and I have this … thing," she stumbled. "We … ahh …"

"This I gotta hear," Mia said, sitting up alertly.

Now two sets of eyes focused on the uncharacteristically bashful brunette. "Oh, all right," Ryan said, grabbing the bag and handing it to Jamie.

As the T-shirt fell out and was unfurled, brown and green eyes trailed from the fabric to Ryan and back again. "This is for … Ally?" Jamie finally said, as Mia got ready for the fireworks to begin.

"Now, Jamie," Ryan soothed. "It's a … joke between us. I told you that I was going to keep her as a friend, and …"

"Sleeps well with others?" Jamie finally uttered, her eyes focused on the writing on the shirt. "You're giving your ex-lover a T-shirt, that you buy on our honeymoon, that says, *Sleeps well with others?*"

"Well, when you put it that way, it sounds kinda bad," Ryan admitted, shifting her weight nervously from foot to foot.

Mia was utterly fascinated by this exchange. Her dancing brown eyes darted from one woman to the other, waiting for the next volley. Jamie spoiled her fun by taking a deep breath and neatly folding the shirt. "Whatever," she muttered, before placing it back in the bag.

"No, no, no," Ryan said, sitting down on a portion of Jamie's towel. "Not so fast there, sport. Here's how it is," she explained, ignoring Mia's presence. "Ever since we've known each other, we always, and I do mean always, buy each other a T-shirt on every trip we take. The game is to make sure you get the one with the most sexual innuendo, or the most politically incorrect one that you can find. I like Ally as a friend, Jamie, and I want to keep the friendship part of our relationship like it used to be. Do you understand?" She lifted Jamie's chin with her fingers and leaned over to place a gentle kiss on her lips. "Please try to understand. I don't want to hurt your feelings."

"Couldn't you have gotten another one?" the smaller woman asked. "There had to be less … provocative ones."

"Well, I could have bought the one that said, 'FBI' in big yellow letters."

"That sounds better," Jamie said.

"Yeah, but underneath it said, *Female Breast Inspector*." Ryan chuckled. "Most of the rest of the suggestive ones had something to do with penises, and that just wouldn't do."

"Let's go back to the boardwalk," Jamie offered, as she stood and extended a hand to her partner.

"Really? Why?"

"Because I want that 'FBI' shirt," she laughed. "And I'm starting with yours … tomorrow!"

After the second shopping trip, they relaxed on the sand for a while. All too soon they had to pack up and head back to the apartment. A thorough shower for Ryan was first on the agenda, and Jamie was next on the list. By rushing a little, they were cleaned and dressed in time to head out to LAX. Traffic was pretty slow and, since none of them knew the shortcuts, they had to stay on the freeway. They wanted to be there an hour early, but Mia dropped them off at the departure gate barely forty-five minutes before their flight. She quickly kissed Ryan on the cheek, and gave Jamie a heartfelt hug, whispering, "I know you'll be fine tomorrow. Have a great time, James, and call me when you get back."

"I promise, Mia, and thanks for everything," she said as she kissed her. "You're the best."

"I hope, for your sake, that I lose that title tomorrow!" she laughed as she pinched her friend's blushing cheek.

An hour and fifteen minutes later, they were in the air for the fifty-minute flight to SFO. Martin had agreed to pick them up after Ryan had called earlier in the day. They were both excited about seeing the family again and Ryan jabbered throughout the trip about Caitlin, and Duffy, and how she'd missed them. "You are such a little love bug," Jamie said, giving her a kiss. "I adore how much you love your family."

"I do love my family," Ryan agreed. "And now that you're part of it, my whole world is complete."

"That definitely deserves a kiss." Jamie leaned in for a big, wet one.

Martin picked them up at eight. They headed home in his truck with Ryan talking nonstop about the ride, and how proud she was of Jamie, and how pleased she was that Jamie's father had made a special trip to L.A. to see her. Martin hardly got a word in edgewise, but he happily let his daughter speak her mind.

When they entered the house, Duffy leapt on Ryan and licked her from head to toe. She quickly got down on the floor with the squirming dog, as he joyfully began to lick her eyes and ears. She giggled like a child as the big dog lapped at her energetically. Both Martin and Jamie had to laugh at the spectacle the pair made. Ryan finally caught her breath and demanded that Jamie join her. The smaller woman rolled her eyes at Martin, but dutifully joined her partner for the tongue bath. Conor was out for the evening, but Martin had saved some dinner for the travelers. The three of them sat down at the dining room table as Ryan focused on her dinner, with Jamie taking up the slack in the conversation as she filled Martin in on the things Ryan hadn't covered.

He asked a few questions about the ride and how Jamie had experienced it. She related a few small stories about her experiences and told him of how loving and thoughtful Ryan had been. She decided not to bring up Ryan's near collapse on the last day, figuring that was for Ryan to tell, if she so chose.

Martin tried to draw Jamie out about their plans for Pebble Beach, but she ducked that question as gracefully as possible after sharing a surreptitious glance with her partner. She knew that their main plan was to have sex and plenty of it, but she guessed that Martin didn't want to know those details. Since they really had no plans that called for them to be in a vertical position, she adroitly steered the conversation back to the ride.

By the time they cleaned up the kitchen, it was nine-thirty and they were both beat. They hadn't discussed how they would handle sleeping arrangements and, rather than bring it up at this point, Ryan decided that one last night alone wasn't such a terrible thing. She took Jamie's bag down to her room and snagged some sweats for herself. After Jamie had finished in the bath, she tucked her into the big bed, kissing her tenderly for several minutes. Ryan rose to leave, but Jamie tilted her head up and gave her such a winsome look that she couldn't help but dash back for another round of tender kisses. They started to move against one another slowly, but Ryan called a halt to the escalating passion and wrapped her arms tightly around her partner. "Guess what we'll be doing this time tomorrow?"

"Sleeping," Jamie said dreamily.

Ryan pulled her head up and stared at her with a quizzical look. "Sleeping?"

"Yep," she said with conviction. "We should be down there by two, so by nine-thirty we'll have had seven solid hours of wild sex. I think we'll need a little rest!"

Ryan gazed at her with love-filled eyes as she stroked her cheek with her fingertips. "You can't imagine how much I'm looking forward to spending a full week exploring every little nook and cranny of your beautiful body."

"If it's half as much as I am, I'd say we're in for a treat."

"I don't doubt that a bit. Just in case you have any worries about tomorrow, try to remember that the only thing that matters is that we're together. We're partners now, Jamie, in life and in love. We can go as slowly or as quickly as you want. No matter what, I'll never put pressure on you, or push you further than you want to go. You're my one true love, and I intend to treat you like a priceless treasure for the rest of your life."

"Duffy," Martin called, as he was getting ready for bed. "Duffy boy, come on, lad, time for a trip to the yard." His call was greeted with silence, so he started to search for the reluctant pet. His first stop was the most logical one and after walking halfway down the stairs to his daughter's room, he spied the pup, curled up against his mistress's back. She, in turn, was curled up against her partner, so thoroughly merged that a breath of air could not have passed between them. Martin immediately decided to let the threesome remain undisturbed. *It seems that the days of "no overnight guests" have ended*, the senior member of the O'Flaherty household mused, smirking to himself as he climbed the stairs.

# Chapter Three

Shortly after dawn on Monday morning, Ryan woke to the delightfully delicious sensation of being in her own bed, snuggled up behind Jamie. Spooning up against her partner's sleep-warmed back, she started to slowly stroke her thighs, not trying to wake her, but needing the contact. Jamie was a long way from consciousness, and she nestled up against Ryan in an automatic, and now familiar, instinct. Ryan felt so warm and happy that, after a few minutes, she let herself drift off to sleep again. She woke nearly an hour later to the sensation of gentle kisses being planted all over her face. She gave Jamie a broad smile as she stretched like a cat for several minutes. "When did you sneak down here?" Jamie whispered into her ear.

"I never left," Ryan replied languidly, stretching her arms over her head. "I was unable to move from your tempting embrace."

"Oh, that's so cute," Jamie grinned. "You jumpstarted our honeymoon!"

"Yeah, but honeymoons are much more fun when you're both awake."

"I couldn't agree more. And speaking of honeymoons, are you ready to get up and go, or do you want to cuddle for a little while?"

"I want to cuddle a lot, but I think I'd rather do it in Pebble Beach," Ryan said thoughtfully. "How about you? Are you ready to go?"

"Yep. I can't wait," she said, snuggling up against her warm partner.

"We probably shouldn't leave until ten or so, to avoid traffic. Would you mind if I do some laundry first? I hate to leave all of those sweaty clothes lying in my suitcase for a week."

Jamie sat up a little and gazed at her lover thoughtfully. "You know, that's one of the things I love about you. I know how much you're looking forward to this, but you still want to take the time to get organized and neaten up. You're so mature," she said, as she tickled her a little bit.

"So, do you agree?"

"Yeah, that's probably a good idea. Let's get some breakfast and I'll wash out all of our bike clothes in the sink. You can start a load of underwear in the washer. Do you mind doing mine along with yours?"

"I think it's about time that our underwear got used to spending time together," Ryan said.

Jamie threw on some sweats and they sorted their dirty clothes. They only had three loads, besides the bike clothes, and Ryan trotted upstairs to get started while Jamie made a phone call.

When Jamie went upstairs, Ryan was hard at work making a huge breakfast. Conor had left for work already and Martin had eaten with him, so Ryan made oatmeal for just the two of them, and a big omelet with ham and cheese for herself. She was toasting a bagel and chatting with her father when Jamie appeared. "Did you sleep well, Jamie dear?" he asked brightly.

"I slept like a baby," she replied. "I don't know if it's the room or the bed, but I always sleep great down there."

"Jamie, Da and I were talking about our plans for the summer. I just finished telling him that we plan on staying at your house during the week and then coming back here on the weekends."

"How do you feel about that, Martin?" Jamie asked.

He let out a deep breath and looked down at his hands. "Do you want the unvarnished truth?"

"Yes," they replied in unison.

"I hate the thought of my baby leaving home," he said. "I know it had to happen sooner or later, but it doesn't feel like home without you here, Siobhán. Conor and Duffy and I bumped around here all week waiting for you to come back. We're quite hopeless on our own, you know."

Ryan walked over and put her arms around her father, hugging him. "Oh, Da, I hate to leave you, too, but Jamie and I need some time alone. This is gonna be quite an adjustment for both of us, and I think we need to focus on each other for a bit."

"Siobhán, I know exactly what you mean, and I agree with you. When your mother and I were first married, we hardly knew anyone else existed," he said with a laugh as he shook his head. "Still, I want you to know how I feel about this. I know this makes sense for now, but I want you to consider living here after you're finished with school. Nothing would make me happier than coming home at night to see your smiling faces."

"We'll seriously consider that, Da. There's nothing to hold us in Berkeley after we graduate. There's no reason that we couldn't live around here." She walked over to Jamie and slipped her arms around her shoulders. "Besides, I wouldn't want to have to drive all the way over here to drop the kids off with their babysitter."

Martin's eyes lit up at the thought of grandchildren. "Are you two serious about that?" he asked with unabashed glee.

"Definitely," Jamie said. "We both want to have a child, and you've done such a marvelous job raising your kids, I'd feel blessed to have you help us raise ours."

"So, darlin'," he said to Ryan with a grin. "This sounds suspiciously like you're past the dating phase and into the commitment phase."

"We're definitely into the commitment phase." Ryan grinned in return as she hugged her partner. "This is it for me, Da. 'Til death do us part."

"I feel the same way." Jamie gazed up into her partner's big blue eyes.

Martin wiped a tear from his cheek as he got up to wrap the two of them in a hug. "You couldn't have chosen better, Siobhán. Your mother would be so happy for you." He brushed a tear away as he patted Jamie on the cheek, "I'm so glad you're a part of our family, sweetheart."

Both women wiped the tears from their eyes, and each kissed Martin. "Thanks," Jamie finally choked out. "That means more to me than you'll ever know."

"So, Siobhán," he said after a moment. "Do you need anything for your honeymoon suite?" Then he added with a twinkle in his eye, "Besides a sturdy lock on the door?"

"No, Da. The room is perfect. I'm a little concerned about the boys, though. Do you think they'll mind having Jamie here?"

"Mind?" he asked in amazement. "They're thrilled about it! I spoke to Rory before he left, and both he and Conor are very excited to have you here, Jamie. And they both agree that we should make an exception to the house rules since you can't formally marry."

"That makes me feel a lot better," Ryan said. "I don't want to do anything to make the boys feel slighted."

"Not a worry, sweetheart."

After a quick breakfast with Martin, and a bit of ironing, they took all of their clean laundry downstairs and started to pack. "Do you think I should go get the Range Rover?" Jamie asked teasingly as Ryan assembled her gear on the bed. She had her Rollerblades, running shoes, running shorts and tank tops, swimsuit, wetsuit, sweats, slacks, blouses, a heavy jacket, and golf clubs, and she was still debating whether or not to bring her boogie board.

"Well, the Boxster is a little small for all this stuff," Ryan admitted, scratching her head as she stared at the enormous pile. "Do you think I'll need everything?"

"I think you could get by in your birthday suit," Jamie cooed into her ear as she wrapped her arms around her tightly.

Ryan tilted her head down to peer into her partner's eyes to gauge her seriousness. "Aren't you going to let me out at all?"

"Nope. You're gonna emerge on Saturday like a possum coming out of its den. It'll take you a day to get used to sunlight again. But seriously, sweetie, you could borrow my father's clubs, and we have lots of sports equipment for the beach. You just need to bring some clothes. Oh, and that reminds me," she added. "I want you to have Conor come down on Saturday and play Pebble Beach with you because I'll be at the graduation almost all day. It starts at one, so I have to leave by ten-thirty. Also, if

Conor comes down, he can give you a ride home and we can meet back here in the evening."

"That sounds great. He'll be thrilled." Ryan did her best to disguise her disappointment at Jamie's plans, but she couldn't help but rue the day she had agreed to them. *At least one O'Flaherty will be happy about the plans for the day. Hmm … I wonder what the penalty is for calling in a bomb threat …*

Ryan continued to pack her clothes, musing about various forms of mayhem she could conjure up to stop Jamie from going to the graduation. She was deep in thought when her partner emerged from the shower.

Ryan looked up and spent a moment gazing at Jamie, a slow smile spreading across her face. She wore a pair of deep rust-colored shorts and a cream-colored cotton polo, with a braided belt and a pair of woven leather loafers that matched the color of her shorts. Her hair was even blonder than normal, due to the sun, and her skin was a beautiful golden color. She looked fresh and clean and absolutely beautiful to Ryan's appreciative eyes. "Wow," she said as she wrapped her in her arms. "You look fantastic." A moment of nuzzling her partner's neck led to a few gentle nibbles, and Ryan smiled as she pulled away. "You taste great, too."

"Thanks," Jamie grinned. "Now you go get ready, because I've got big plans for you today." Her tone was stern, but underneath, it held a great deal of promise. Ryan nearly ran for the shower in her haste to comply.

Jamie, with Martin's help, was already upstairs packing their things in the car when Ryan strolled out fifteen minutes later, wearing a pair of bright white pleated shorts that fell a few inches above her knee. An oversized black linen camp shirt hung out over the crisply ironed shorts, and black leather loafers and her favorite backwards black knit driving cap finished her look. Her long black hair hung loose and her skin glowed bronze from the recent time in the sun. She still had some pink in her cheeks, though—partly from sun and partly from anticipation. Jamie's mouth went dry when she saw her, and Martin couldn't help but tease, "I hope Siobhán's going to drive today, darlin'. You don't look like your mind could focus on the road."

She hugged him to avoid having him see how deeply she knew she was blushing. "I hate being so transparent," she moaned into his chest.

"It's one of your most winning traits, little one," he said. "It's altogether adorable, Jamie. Don't you change a bit."

As Ryan draped an arm around her partner, she had to agree with her father. "It's not possible to improve on perfection, Da." The elder O'Flaherty smiled at his daughter and her mate, pleased beyond measure at their obvious joy.

Duffy had bounded down the porch stairs right behind Ryan, and she spent a few minutes petting him and whispering last minute instructions. Duffy looked terribly sad, knowing that his mistress was leaving again. "I don't know if I'll be able to keep him happy without you here, Siobhán. You may have to take him with you when you go to Berkeley," Martin said as he cast a loving glance at the pair.

"I'd love to have him, but I think you two need each other." Ryan stood and dusted off her knees. "We'll see how it goes for a while, and if he's unhappy, I'm sure we could take him."

Jamie kissed Duffy's head and gave Martin a hug and a kiss before she hopped into the passenger seat of the little yellow car. Ryan spent a long minute hugging her father. They both had their eyes closed, and Jamie was deeply touched by the tenderness of the moment. Finally, he released his daughter, giving her a kiss on each cheek. Obviously struggling with his emotions, he turned and strode back up the stairs and into the house before Ryan even got into the car. Duffy sat looking at them sadly for a minute, until Ryan ordered him back into the house. He gave her another baleful look and slowly climbed the stairs, giving her one last, disappointed glance before entering the open door.

"They don't make it easy, do they?" Ryan asked, as she sniffed a little and slipped her dark sunglasses on.

"They certainly don't! They can't help it though, honey. They're both mad about you." She squeezed Ryan's thigh in a comforting gesture and asked, "Would you really like to have Duffy in Berkeley?"

"Oh yeah, I really would. We could go for our long run in the mornings, which we both really enjoy. Duff challenges me to go farther and faster than I do on my own. Da doesn't like to have to exercise him before work, so it's asking a lot to expect him to take over. In a lot of ways, it'd work out better if he was with us." She looked at Jamie, her expression showing a little confusion. "Should I have checked with you before I said that? I—"

"No, Ryan." Jamie looked at her and patted her leg to reassure her. "I want you to think of it as our house. I want you to do whatever you need to do to feel at home there. If that means having Duffy, I'd love it."

"Our house," Ryan said as she tried the concept on. "That sounds kinda cool, doesn't it? It's kinda nice to have a house and a home, isn't it?"

"It certainly is, sweetheart. It certainly is."

Traffic was relatively light on this clear, warm Monday morning. Jamie knew Monterey Bay would likely be fog covered when they got there, so she enjoyed the warm sun as it beat down on them. They were making good time, playing some of Ryan's favorite CDs and just enjoying being together.

Their musical tastes didn't complement each other and they could never find a radio station they both enjoyed, so they'd reached a compromise. The driver got to play whatever music she liked. In practice, that meant that Ryan always played her CDs, and over time, Jamie eventually took her own music back into the house so she could hear it occasionally. Still, she had to admit that even though she would never choose the music her partner favored, it was well worth listening to it to watch her favorite body move sensually to the beat. She was often gifted with Ryan singing along, and few things made her happier than listening to her partner's deep, sexy voice. Jamie had her hand on Ryan's thigh, watching her drive and listening to her harmonize with some Jamaican singer. She felt so totally content, soaking up every sensation, she thought she would burst with happiness.

Three hours later, they drew near their destination. Ryan looked at Jamie and mentioned, "You know, I've never been to Monterey."

"Are you serious?" Jamie was a little shocked at the revelation, assuming that most Bay Area natives would have made at least one trip to Carmel.

"Yep. I've been to Half Moon Bay to surf, and I've been to Santa Cruz, but I've never gone any further down the bay. I never really had a reason to. Until now, that is."

"Well, I guess we're both in for some new experiences this week, aren't we?"

A very sexy smile lit up Ryan's face, and she shot a glance at her partner, one waggling eyebrow poking up from the frame of her dark glasses. "I certainly hope so," she purred, laughing gently at Jamie's wide-eyed response.

As they neared the heavily populated areas, they slowed down to about forty miles per hour. Jamie still had her hand on Ryan's thigh, and when they hit a stop light, she leaned over and gave her a deep kiss. She couldn't keep from running her hand up the leg of Ryan's shorts until the driver firmly grasped her hand and pulled it out, returning it to its former resting place. "I wanted to see what you had on under those." Jamie played innocent even as she tried to slip her hand under again. Ryan's vise-like grip stopped the intrusion.

"You're just gonna have to wait and see. I'm not going to wreck your car so you can feel my underwear. Especially since you can pull them off me with your teeth in about a half hour."

Even with the top down and the background noise, Ryan could hear her partner's audible gulp.

"Hey," Jamie said after a beat. "Did you say you surfed Half Moon?"

"Yep," Ryan said smugly. "Mavericks," she added, naming the famous surfing spot known for having the biggest waves on the West Coast.

"Long boards?"

"Yep."

"Uhm, Ryan, I hate to tell you, but no woman has ever successfully surfed Mavericks."

At the next stop, Ryan pulled her blouse away from her chest and peeked inside. "Well, you can tell me later after you've made your inspection, but I'm pretty sure I'm a woman."

"But surfing there is a really big deal for a woman," she insisted.

Ryan stuck her jaw out and said, "I didn't want publicity. I wanna blend in as much as possible. I bet nobody even noticed I was a girl."

"I didn't know you could surf if you were blind," she replied with her own grin, as she let her eyes linger on her partner's obviously womanly curves.

"To be honest, I try to look as masculine as possible when I surf. Guys hate to share with women. It's the most sexist group of people I've ever been around, and I've worked construction!"

"Could you surf a little for me? I'd really love to see you in action."

"I think I could rip a few for your viewing entertainment," she said. "And to be honest, I'm a decent surfer, but I'd never take Mavericks on if the waves were really breaking. I like testing myself, but I'm not suicidal. Too many excellent surfers have been killed there for me to think I'm in that league. Besides, I've done most of my surfing in the city. It's fun, but it's no Mavericks."

"I don't care if the waves are only six inches. I wanna see you in a wet suit!"

The signs indicated that they were nearing Seventeen Mile Drive, and Ryan knew it wouldn't be long before they reached their destination. A very strong physical pull urged her to keep on going, but she'd been planning a little something, and her heart told her that she needed to follow through with her plan.

"Is there somewhere quiet and private where we can stop for a few minutes?"

"Stop?" The look that accompanied Jamie's exclamation questioned Ryan's sanity.

"Yeah. I know we're both in a hurry, but today is really special for me, and I want to stop for a little while to commemorate it."

"You are such a romantic," Jamie mused as she graced her partner with a luminous smile. "I know a really nice place not too far ahead. I think it'll be perfect."

They were driving right along the ocean when Jamie indicated they should stop. Hopping out, she went to the trunk and rooted around in her suitcase for a few moments. Finding what she was looking for, she quickly tucked it into the pocket of her rust colored shorts. Ryan waited patiently, lifting an eyebrow at the delay, but Jamie shrugged and gave her a look that said, "*Don't ask.*"

Jamie took her hand and led her along a rocky path through the scrub that covered the harshly beautiful landscape. Around a bend they saw the spot and it was, indeed, perfect for Ryan's purposes. Very well hidden by the rocky boulders was a lone cypress tree that looked out over the wild ocean. The roar of the surf was muffled by the height of the cliff they were perched upon, but they could feel the violence of its crashing waves through the earth as they sat down under the sturdy branches of the huge old tree.

"Have you been here often?" Ryan broke the silence after they had stared out at the sea for a few minutes.

"Yeah," she said softly. "When I was a teenager, I used to ride my bike down here, just to be alone. I'd bring a book or sit and think for a while."

"Did you always come alone?"

Jamie nodded briefly. "This was my most private space. Up until now, I've never wanted to share my special spaces with anyone." She gazed up at Ryan as she said this, her eyes filled with love. "It's different now. I want to share everything with you, Ryan. Everything I have is yours. All of my dreams and hopes and plans mean so much more when I think of sharing them with you."

She raised her head just a bit, and Ryan simultaneously lowered hers until their lips met in a soft, tender communion. "I love you with all my heart, Ryan," she whispered when they parted.

Ryan lifted her hand and traced the features of her lover's face with the kiss of her fingertips. "There's nothing I wish more than that my mother could know you," she said, with a slight shadow of grief overtaking her features. "She loved me so much, and I know that nothing would make her happier than to know what peace I've found with you." Jamie scooted closer and pulled her lover into a tender embrace, holding her close for a long while.

"I wish that, too," she murmured softly. "I'd love to thank her for the gift of your love. She helped make you the woman you are, and for that, I'm eternally grateful."

Lifting her head to stare at the sky for a moment, Ryan took a deep breath and reached into the rear pocket of her shorts. She removed a small packet of tissue paper and grasped it firmly in her hand for a moment. Taking another breath, she unwrapped it and said, "You know that things generally don't mean a lot to me, but this …" she paused to compose herself for a moment, "is my most treasured possession." A brilliant beam of light filtered through the leaves onto the object, illuminating the simple gold ring. "This was my mother's wedding band." Silent tears fell from her eyes. "I'd … I'd be honored if you'd wear it."

"Oh, Ryan." Jamie gasped as her hand reached out to cover her lover's shaking fingers. "Are you sure you want that? Shouldn't you wear it?"

"No, I'm sure I want you to wear it. It's far too small for me, and I'd ruin it if I tried to have it enlarged to fit. Besides," she locked her clear blue eyes onto her partner, "my mother's always with me. It feels like wearing her ring will make her a part of you, too."

Jamie rotated her wrist, turning Ryan's fingers up to expose the ring. She extended her left hand and slightly raised her ring finger, waiting patiently as her partner slipped it on. "Forever," Ryan said in a strong, confident voice. Jamie draped her arms around her neck, holding her tightly as she slowly moved her finger, exposing the shiny band to the filtered sunlight.

"It fits perfectly," she marveled. "Like it was made for me."

"I think it was." As she pulled back, she gazed at her partner with a long, thoughtful stare. "I've been thinking about this a little bit, and even though this doesn't make a lot of sense to me, I have a theory. I don't believe that our lives are pre-ordained. I think the choices we make and the way we behave is because of our free will. But something about you has called to me from the day we met," she said. "I have no choice but to be with you for the rest of my life. I don't know what's behind this, but it's a pull I'm absolutely powerless against."

A gentle laugh floated up from Jamie's diaphragm. "You think it's a powerful pull for you? It yanked me out of a relatively happy engagement, and threw me into a whole new sexual orientation!"

"Any regrets?" Ryan asked, blue eyes twinkling.

"None. I've never been happier with any choice I've made in my life. I wish I had a ring for you," she said with a hint of regret. "Could I have a matching one made?"

"Absolutely," Ryan smiled. "I know that now isn't the time, but I'd love to stand up in front of all of our friends and family and publicly proclaim my love for you. I'd really like to exchange rings then."

Jamie graced her with a beatific smile, heartily agreeing with the wish. "I would love that, sweetheart. Until then," she bent her head to kiss the finger where she would one day place a ring, "this space is reserved." A tender kiss sealed the vow, and they rested in each other's arms for a few minutes, with Jamie occasionally holding out her left hand to gaze at her ring.

"I'll never take this off," Jamie murmured as she leaned in for another kiss.

"Luckily, it's already engraved," Ryan informed her with a sad smile. The smaller woman immediately slipped the ring off and stared at it for a minute, turning it a bit to allow the sun to hit the letters on the inside of the band.

"Mmm, I'm having trouble with this. Fighte fuaighte," she said haltingly. "Is it Latin?"

"No," Ryan said. "It's Gaelic." She pronounced the words properly, in her soft Irish accent.

"What does it mean?" The smaller woman stared at the inscription.

"It's an expression that roughly means 'woven into and through each other.' You'd use the expression to refer to things that are inextricably intertwined," she said softly. "Like my parents … like us."

"Like us." Jamie echoed Ryan's commitment as she lifted her head again to kiss her partner for several long minutes.

"Ready to go?" Ryan asked, her twinkling eyes turning dark with longing. "I think it's time you officially changed that sexual orientation thing."

Jamie's gentle laugh was accompanied by a smirk. "I think we've been putting a pretty good chink in the armor of my supposed heterosexuality already." Ryan returned her smile and nodded her agreement. Jamie leaned over and gave her another gentle kiss. "Before we leave, I've got a little something for you too."

Ryan looked down at her quizzically as Jamie reached into the front pocket of her shorts and extracted a small black velvet box. Smiling broadly, she handed her partner the gift. Ryan reached out to accept it with a slight tremor in her hand. She lifted the top to find two perfectly shaped round brilliant-cut blue stones set in simple platinum collars.

It was obvious that Ryan didn't quite know how to respond, so Jamie helped her out. "These mean a great deal to me. My great-grandmother Smith owned them. She wore them in a really ornate setting, and when I was little I really loved them. I loved the blue color. They looked so nice next to her blue hair," she laughed. "Anyway, she left them to me when she died. I never knew what to do with them, but when I look at them now, all I can think of is your eyes." She leaned over to kiss each closed eye in turn. "Maybe that's why I liked them so much. Maybe I somehow knew that eyes that looked like these would one day belong to my mate."

Ryan's voice was rough with emotion. She was deeply touched at the sentiment, but a little hesitant to accept the gift. "Jamie, these are a family heirloom. You can't give them away."

"Ryan, I've given you something much more precious than diamonds. I've given you my heart. Let me commemorate that gift with these."

"These are diamonds?" She stared at the crystal clear, ice blue stones.

"Yeah, they're rare, but diamonds are sometimes blue. Something to do with the type of carbon or something."

"They're gorgeous, Jamie," she murmured as she moved them slowly in the sunlight.

"Now you know how I feel when I look into your eyes." Jamie draped her arms around her partner and pulled her close for a few tender kisses. When she pulled away, she removed the gems from their box and delicately placed one in each perfectly shaped earlobe. "Perfect. Just perfect," she whispered.

They sat in silence for a long while, watching the crashing waves beat against the shore. Their hands were laced together and their heads touched lightly just above their temples. Finally, Ryan broke the silence. "Are you ready to go?"

"Yes, I am." Jamie chuckled as she stood and extended a hand to her partner. "I'm ready to have you make a woman out of me." Ryan grinned up at her as she was pulled to her feet. "You know, this is a much better way to get married," Jamie mused as they walked to the car, hand in hand. "Just the two of us, pledging our love to each other. As soon as we finish, no fancy party, no long reception lines—it's time for the honeymoon! This is clearly the better alternative—for our first wedding, at least!"

"I agree completely," Ryan beamed. "Let the honeymoon begin!"

As they drove along, Jamie could feel the restraints she had placed on her libido start to loosen. By the time they reached Seventeen Mile Drive, her hand was running up and down Ryan's thigh, and both women could feel their hearts starting to beat faster. Scenes from their weeks together began to play in Jamie's head and she could almost taste Ryan's luscious lips as they drew closer to her home. Thinking of the rabid desire she saw radiating from Ryan's eyes when they were at Mia's caused her heart to skip a beat, and she turned to say something to her partner. Ryan's head turned simultaneously and even behind the dark glasses Jamie could see that her partner's thoughts were headed in the same direction. Suddenly speechless, both women sighed deeply as they shared a smile that promised their desires would soon be sated.

Jamie called out the turns and right after they passed the Cypress Point Country Club, she indicated that Ryan should slow down. They pulled up to a gated driveway and Jamie gave her the entry code, which just happened to be her birthday. Ryan shot her a little grin as the massive gates swung open. She drove up the curved drive, through lush landscaping, finally arriving at a lovely covered carriageway that led to a crushed gravel courtyard. Jamie curtly instructed, "Leave it right here," scrambling out of the car while it was still slowing to a stop.

Ryan got out and started to stretch her back, only to be stopped mid-stretch by a hand that grasped hers and pulled her insistently up to the front door. Jamie lifted the cover of a small touch pad and pressed her thumb onto the device. A disembodied voice said, "Welcome home, Jamie," and then the door latch clicked open. Ryan gasped in surprise and tried to take a look at the device but was pulled roughly forward. She stumbled a bit as she fell over the entryway, regaining her balance only to have the air knocked out of her lungs as she was thrown back against the massive oak door with an audible *thud*.

Before she could open her mouth to protest, Jamie was on her with a fury. She started to unbutton her linen shirt as she ground her mouth onto Ryan's. In seconds, the shirt was hanging loosely from Ryan's shoulders and she was frantically working on the zipper of her shorts. Ryan was desperately trying to catch up, but she was stunned by Jamie's behavior. She was well aware that a very wild woman was hidden beneath the normally placid exterior of her partner, but she hadn't counted on that side appearing so dramatically. She desperately needed to feel some sense of control, so she tried to slow Jamie down a bit by lightening the intensity of the kisses raining down on her.

Undeterred, Jamie roughly grabbed the back of her head and held on tight, intent on maintaining the frantic pace that she had set. Now her hands dropped to grab Ryan's rear, pulling her forward as she ground her hips against her. Ryan's heart was beating loudly and she felt a little weak as Jamie attempted to devour her. She summoned every ounce of her composure to finally rasp out, "Can't we go to a bed?"

Jamie looked up at her and paused for a moment, a look of total confusion quickly replacing her fervid groping of moments before. Her face was flushed and her forehead was a little damp from her exertions. She looked as though that option hadn't occurred to her, but finally nodded her approval. Ryan wasn't sure what she was supposed to do. She had no idea where the bedrooms were, but Jamie just stood there, looking blank. She chose the only course of action that she could think of. She tossed her hat off, picked Jamie up in her arms and, after kicking off her shoes, started walking. She heard Jamie's shoes drop as she carried her toward a winding staircase. They climbed the lushly carpeted stairs, with Jamie latching onto her mouth again, forcing her to grab onto the railing with a free hand to guide their progress. Ryan passed two bedrooms and, as she neared the third, an arm shot out to grab onto the doorjamb. *This must be the place*, she thought, then gently lowered Jamie to the king-sized bed. She realized she was still wearing her sunglasses and carelessly threw them over her shoulder as she lowered herself to cover her partner with her body.

Jamie was waiting for her with a look of unbridled lust in her eyes. Ryan was a little tentative, not knowing what to expect and still amazed by the suddenness and ferocity of this neophyte's attack. Jamie rolled over onto her, straddling her hips as she sat up and ran her hands up and down her chest. Since Jamie had often expressed a preference for unhindered breasts, in lieu of a bra Ryan wore a tight black cotton knit tank top with delicate straps and a small lace inset at the neckline. While Jamie's hands feverishly trailed over the nearly bare mounds, her green eyes grew wide and unfocused. Slowly, her hands stilled completely and she gave Ryan a near-panicked stare.

Ryan sat up and pulled her down to the bed, embracing her tenderly. She trailed her fingers through Jamie's soft blonde hair, saying, "It's not as easy as it looks, is it?" Jamie shook her head, burying her face in Ryan's neck as her partner added, "That's why we tell newcomers not to try this at home without an experienced member of the club to guide them along."

When she lifted her head to meet Ryan's understanding gaze, the green eyes were still clouded by doubt. "I'm … I'm a little freaked," she whispered with a quavering voice.

"Hey, there's no rush here. Let's regroup a little, okay?" Even though Ryan was throbbing with desire, she didn't mind slowing down. She'd been dreaming about this day for months, and she didn't really like the idea of treating each other with the urgency of dogs in heat—at first, that is, she amended with an internal smirk. She had dreamed of making love with her partner for hours their first time and she hoped that a little break might allow them to slow the pace down considerably. She rolled off the bed and re-fastened her clothing, which now looked like she'd slept in it for several days. Extending her hand, she pulled her partner to her feet and held her tenderly for a few minutes. "What's your favorite room?"

"Uhm, I have a couple, but on this floor I like my old playroom."

"Come on," Ryan suggested as she held out her hand. "Show it to me."

"Uhm …" Jamie held back, hesitation evident in her face. "Do you want to uhm … in there?"

Ryan beamed a gentle smile. "I wanna regroup a little. Let's take this slow."

A quick nod, and she gripped Ryan's hand and led her down the hall.

As they walked along the thickly carpeted hallway in their bare feet, Ryan wondered about the need for a quiet, only child to have a "playroom". The O'Flaherty children could have really used a place to keep the toys and games that littered every square inch of their tiny house when they were small, but she couldn't imagine what went on in the playroom of Jamie's house.

At the end of the rather long hallway, they came to an exceptionally sunny room that looked more like a solarium than a playroom. The rear wall was nearly all glass, allowing a stunning view of the ocean. As Ryan looked up she saw that the majority of the sunlight came in through the narrow skylights that ringed the chamfered ceiling. The room was so big that there were twenty of them, each about three feet long by a foot wide. They allowed a great deal of light to enter but, since they were at the edge of the room, the early afternoon sun did not shine directly on them. "Boy, this must be a great place to curl up with a book on a winter afternoon," Ryan mused as she surveyed the wall of books that flanked an attractive fireplace.

"Yeah, it really is. Mother had this converted to a sun room/library combo when I was in high school. It's one of my favorite places down here. I used it as a study room." Ryan looked around and noticed a beautiful writing desk set on an angle in the corner of the room. The very comfortable looking upholstered chair that was snugged up under the table was obviously an office chair, now that she looked closely at the casters on the bottom. A laptop computer sat on the desk and Ryan had a vision of her young lover sitting at the desk, working on some term paper for school.

"Very nice setup," she said with approval as Jamie showed her the printer and other various office supplies hidden in the armoire behind the desk.

"Mother uses this as her office now." Ryan couldn't for the life of her figure out why a woman who didn't work outside the home needed an office at her weekend getaway, but she didn't think now was the time to ask.

As Ryan walked around to the front of the table, she noticed one solitary ornament besides the pencil holder—a beautifully framed picture of Jamie as a baby, no more than Caitlin's age. She was wearing a navy blue dress covered by a white eyelet pinafore, and she was gazing up at the photographer with the calm, interested gaze that she so often gave Ryan when she was trying to understand something. "God, this is precious." Ryan stroked baby Jamie's face through the glass as she held the frame in her hand.

Jamie chuckled at the tone of her partner's voice. "I've got a million of 'em if you want to look at pictures."

"No, there's something about this one that captures you. You hardly look any different than you do now. I've seen that look a thousand times."

"Hmm," Jamie speculated as she looked around Ryan's shoulder to view the photo. "I don't think I've seen that one before. Mother must have dug it out when she redecorated last."

Ryan placed the picture on the desk and looked around again. The room was mostly unstructured and was clearly meant to be a place to relax and read or contemplate, rather than entertain. There wasn't much furniture, just a pair of upholstered wing chairs that flanked the fireplace and a large, wide fainting couch in a delicate looking cream colored silk that faced the wide expanse of glass.

Taking Jamie by the hand, Ryan led her to the couch and sat down. "We can use the furniture, can't we?"

"Well, sure," Jamie agreed as she flopped down beside her, puzzled that Ryan would ask such a question.

"Wow, this is awfully comfortable." Ryan bounced a little on the piece.

"Yeah, one of mother's many indulgences. This bottom cushion is made like an innerspring mattress and covered with down. And the back cushions are all down."

"Wow, I always wanted a down pillow," Ryan said rather wistfully. "Sar … my … ahh … best friend in high school had down pillows on her bed, and they seemed so luxurious." Ryan mentally slapped herself for almost bringing up Sara's name. The last thing she wanted was to dredge up those painful old memories, and she was sure that Jamie didn't want the past to intrude on their honeymoon.

Jamie was struck by her partner's wistful expression, and she briefly considered the disparity in their upbringings. "All of this stuff doesn't bother you, does it?" she asked, gently placing a hand on Ryan's knee.

"Hnh-uh, not at all," Ryan said decisively. "It's kinda like being in a really elegant hotel. I mean, I know it's kinda your house, but it's not really yours, so I can just observe rather than feel overwhelmed."

"I think I understand," Jamie agreed, as she leaned against the gracefully curved back of the couch. "It'd probably bother you if my house in Berkeley was like this, and we were gonna live there, but since this is my parents' place you can be a little bit removed."

"Exactly." Ryan tossed her head back against the squooshy pillows. Sticking her arm out, she motioned for Jamie to curl up against her. "Come here, sweetness."

Only too happy to comply, Jamie cuddled up against her side. "Uhm, better than down," she muttered as she rested her head upon Ryan's chest.

"And hypo-allergenic."

"Mmm, I don't know about that," Jamie mused. "I think I had an adverse reaction in the bedroom."

"Hey, don't give it another thought. We've got the entire week to get comfortable with each other. There's no rush, Jamie. I really mean that."

"Really?" she asked, in a most fragile, childlike voice.

"Honey," Ryan soothed, trailing her fingers through her soft hair. "If we go back to the city on Saturday having done nothing more erotic than this, it'll be completely okay with me." *Well, that's the biggest lie I've ever told her. But after going so slow these past weeks I'm not gonna blow it now!* "I want you to go as slowly as you need to, Jamie. I figure we've got a good sixty years ahead of us. That's 3,120 weeks. What's the big deal about spending a few of them getting to know each other?" *Please make it not take weeks*, she silently begged.

A delighted smile beamed up at Ryan as she said these words. "Do you really mean that?"

"Of course I do! I'm here for you. To love, honor, and cherish you. I wouldn't dream of rushing you into anything you didn't feel comfortable with." As she said that, Ryan realized that she meant every word. As much as she wanted to consume the woman in her arms, she realized that their emotional connection and the trust they shared were the most important elements of their relationship.

"I love you, Ryan," Jamie whispered. "It's so wonderful how you constantly show how much you love me." She pulled the dark head down and spent several minutes kissing the soft pink lips.

"This is enough for me," Ryan murmured into her clean, floral scented hair. "To hold you and kiss you just makes me so happy." She gave her a strong squeeze, feeling her heart fill with the emotion that often overwhelmed her when she considered the love she felt for her partner.

"I … I don't know why I got so scared before," Jamie muttered in confusion. "I know you so well, and I've touched you so many times. Why do you think it bothered me?"

Ryan considered the question carefully before she answered. She finally postulated, "I think we were forcing it a little."

"Forcing?"

"Yeah. Normally we start out kinda slow and let our emotions and our hormones take us where they may. Today it seemed like we came here for the purpose of making love, and I think the pressure got to be too much for you. I think we just have a little honeymoon anxiety."

"We?" she asked uncertainly, having seen no evidence of anxiety from her partner.

"Sure," Ryan said. "I was a little freaked too. This is your first time with a woman, but it's my first time with you." Glittering blue eyes that held just a little mirth looked down at Jamie, and for the thousandth time she thanked God for the precious gift of this wonderful woman.

A heavy, contented sigh left Jamie's lips. She was feeling much better, but she wasn't sure how to get past the confusion that had befuddled her. "How do … we … get through our discomfort?" She knew that Ryan was toying with her a little bit, but she was grateful for the levity.

"Don't worry about it. It's not a race. If we act naturally, it'll happen. Let's not make it our destination," she offered. "If our bodies lead us there, it's fine. Try not to put pressure on yourself to go there if you're not ready."

"Okay." She lay her head back down on Ryan's chest. "I'll chill out a little." Looking at her watch she said, "It's nearly two. Don't you need some lunch?"

Ryan pursed her lips together, appearing to consider the idea. "I could eat," she finally conceded.

"There's a news flash." Jamie got up and pulled her perennially hungry partner with her. "Let's get a little something in that tummy." As they walked back down the hall, Jamie suggested a division of tasks. "If you bring in the bags, I'll make you a sandwich."

"Is there stuff here?" Ryan asked.

"Yep. I'll make some lunch, and we can eat on the patio."

When Ryan returned from lugging their bags upstairs, she noticed that the huge wooden doors in the living room were wide open, the ocean breeze causing the heavy drapes to flutter. She poked her head out and saw her lover sitting at a rectangular glass-topped table that could easily seat ten. The table and the matching chairs were a natural wrought iron with tan and cream striped cushions covering the seats. Several lounge chairs and chaises were placed around the granite patio, all covered with the same fabric. The patio faced the ocean, but the three-foot-tall, dry-stacked stone wall that surrounded the space was topped by equally tall Plexiglas panels that effectively blocked the near-constant wind. Jamie had set the table with placemats and linen napkins and was sipping a glass of lemonade, looking out at the ocean, when Ryan arrived.

"You really look like you belong here," Ryan mused, appraising her lover in her native habitat.

"Uhm, is that a compliment?"

"No, but it's not a criticism either," Ryan said as she pulled out a chair and sat down. "It's just an observation. I meant that you seem comfortable and self-assured in this setting."

"Well," she said thoughtfully. "I've spent a lot of time here, and I do feel comfortable. I actually feel more comfortable here than I do at my parents' home," she admitted. "When we were down here we acted more like a family, so I guess it feels more like home."

"What … do you mean?" Ryan asked, not sure why the change of locales would affect the family dynamics.

"Well, we were usually all together here. Daddy couldn't go to the office, and he almost never brought clients down. Mother was away from her friends and activities, so they both paid some attention to me," she said softly. "We'd play golf or just hang out. It was nice."

Ryan felt the stab of anger that often overwhelmed her when her lover talked about her childhood. Jamie had such a sad and wistful expression on her face that she wanted to hold her and make all of those lonely days disappear. Still, she knew that even though her wish was genuine, there was nothing that she could do to make the old pain go away. All that she could do was help prevent her lover from ever having another lonely day.

They ate their turkey sandwiches in a companionable silence. The brisk wind and the still warm sun made Ryan's appetite greater than usual and, after a few puppy dog looks, her partner went back into the kitchen and emerged with another complete lunch. Jamie sat and watched her demolish the second sandwich, hands laced together with her chin resting upon them, grinning the entire time. "I gotta put that weight back on," Ryan smiled, as she gobbled down another forkful of creamy coleslaw.

"Uh-huh," her lover agreed with a smirk.

When the second entrée was finished, Jamie went into the kitchen once again and returned with a plate of huge, dense cookies. "What are these?" Ryan asked as she took a big bite.

"Snickerdoodles."

"Wow," she drawled, nearly swooning with pleasure. "These are fantastic."

"Thought you might like 'em." Jamie smiled as she ate just one of the treats. Ryan didn't disappoint, consuming the other three cookies in short order.

"Anything you wanna do this afternoon?" Jamie asked as Ryan leaned back in her chair, looking very satisfied.

"Hmm, not really. I feel like lazing around a little bit. That chaise longue looks pretty good right now." Ryan indicated a wide chaise resting under a big umbrella.

"Let's do it," Jamie agreed, taking her hand.

# Chapter Four

Both women were still emotionally and physically exhausted from their strenuous week and they were nearly unconscious by the time their heads hit the cushion of the chaise. Even though the breeze was brisk, the glass barrier kept most of the wind at bay, and the filtered sun streaming through the umbrella proved to be a very effective sedative.

Waves crashing on the shore and the snapping of the fabric on the umbrella were the only noises that serenaded them, and the stillness allowed them to sleep for nearly an hour. They had reclined the chaise fully so they could cuddle, and when Ryan's eyes lazily blinked open, she had to crane her neck sharply to see what was going on under her shirt.

During their nap, Jamie's hand had wandered beneath the black linen, and her delicate fingers were splayed across Ryan's now firm nipple. Even though Ryan had decided that she didn't mind waiting for sex, she hadn't convinced her body of that fact, as a persistent throbbing between her legs reminded her.

She reached down and was about to remove her partner's hand when a sleep-roughened voice protested. "I like it there," Jamie murmured, as she leaned a little harder against her partner's warm side. "Do you mind?"

"I like it there, too." Ryan turned her head to kiss the golden locks.

"Kiss me," Jamie begged, her voice a little rough with desire.

Ryan complied, spending several minutes thoroughly tasting her partner's mouth. She didn't try to escalate the contact, though, deciding to let Jamie move on if she wanted to.

The next instruction was clearer, and more demanding. "Kiss me like you want me," she breathed softly into Ryan's ear.

"I do want you," Ryan murmured, her eyes half lidded with her own rising desire. "I want you more than I've ever wanted any woman." She slowly dipped her head and let her mouth and tongue communicate the rest of her thoughts. They kissed slowly and softly, unhurried in their passion. After endless minutes had passed, Ryan lifted her head and gazed deeply into Jamie's eyes. A small smile curled just the corner of her mouth as she began her exploration once again. The response from her partner was immediate and unequivocal. Soft, breathless moans escaped from her throat, each one more erotic than the last. Few things turned Ryan on more than hearing the effect her touch had on her lover, but today the sounds were positively incendiary.

Trying to control herself, she paused again, pulling her head up just enough to be able to focus. The look of wanton desire on her partner's face let her abandon her control and dive right back into the conflagration. This time her mouth started at her lover's eyes. Her warm tongue delicately licked at the achingly soft skin of her lids, pausing to tickle the dark blonde lashes. Her mouth followed the curve of her brow and slid up to her hairline, offering an incredibly soft touch all along the fine, nearly white blonde hairs. Perfectly shaped ears were next and they were treated to the same intense examination.

Ryan had learned that Jamie's ears were incredibly sensitive, and that knowledge increased her enjoyment of the exploration. Her partner didn't disappoint, gasping in delight as she felt the warmth of Ryan's breath tickle the side of her neck. Ryan's tongue languidly traced each indentation and depression, each ridge and hollow, breathing into the sensitive organ in time with her rapidly escalating pulse. Fine soft hairs covered the lobe, so tiny as to be nearly microscopic, but Ryan wanted—needed—to know each of them. She sucked the tender flesh into her mouth, running her tongue over it lovingly. Pausing to catch her breath, she lifted her head and again locked eyes with her lover. Matching smiles formed as each pair of eyes trailed down to gaze at soft, moist lips.

The beckoning of those lips proved too much for Ryan, and she returned to them again, this time intent on exploring each millimeter of skin. She started at the corner of the mouth, licking at the juncture of her lips with just the tip of her tongue. Jamie sensed that Ryan needed to explore her without interruption, so she willed her own lips to be still. Savoring the sensation was harder than she would have thought, however. Her mouth desperately wanted to consume her partner, but she controlled her body, even though she had no control over her groans of pleasure or the wild beating of her heart. Those beautiful deep pink lips moved along her mouth at a painfully deliberate pace. Ryan's tongue and lips lovingly investigated each little portion of the coral tinted skin. As each segment was sucked into her mouth, Ryan greeted it with a warm, sensual tongue bath that was quickly driving Jamie absolutely mad.

When Ryan was finally finished, she lifted her head once more, blue eyes sparkling with need. A feral smile curled the corner of her lips as she grasped Jamie's head with both hands and held her steady. Ryan finally lifted the bonds on her passion. Her touch was still filled with love, but the intensity and fierceness of the kisses that rained down upon Jamie ratcheted her desire to astronomic heights. Shifting slightly, the small hands pressed against Ryan's chest, pushing her away forcefully. "Stop!" she cried, breathless and dizzy.

"Wha …" Ryan gasped, shocked at the force of her lover's cry.

"I'm sorry," she moaned, burying her face in Ryan's shirt as she struggled to breathe.

Large, warm hands trailed along her back, the touch reassuring and gentle. "Tell me," Ryan urged. "Tell me what's wrong."

"God! Nothing's wrong! I … I felt out of control for a minute. I need to slow down a little."

"I'm sorry," Ryan murmured regret clouding her eyes. "I got carried away."

Jamie corrected her immediately. "No, baby, don't you dare apologize for that. I want you to show me what you need." Grasping Ryan's face with her hands, she looked deeply into her eyes, saying, "We've got to be as honest with each other as we can, okay?"

"Okay," Ryan agreed. She took a few deep breaths and finally looked at her partner with a stoic smile pasted on. "I think I'm okay now. We'll have to go a little slower next time."

"Next time?" she shrieked so loudly that Ryan's ears rang. "What do you mean, next time?"

"I thought you …"

"Oh, honey, did you think I was telling you to 'stop' stop?"

"Well … uhm … yeah," she admitted, her wide blue eyes showing her confusion.

"God no, Ryan. I felt like I was about to come! I needed a pause, not a stop."

"Well then, why didn't you yell 'pause!'" Ryan asked, then chuckled a little, the deep sound rumbling in her chest. "Whew, that's a relief," she mumbled, falling back onto the cushion. "I was willing to stop, but I don't think I could've walked for quite a while."

"You!" she laughed in reply. "I honestly almost had an orgasm just from your kisses!"

"Wanna try again?"

"Uh-huh," she purred as she forced Ryan onto her back and sat astride her hips. "I wanna be on top for a while."

"I'll flip for you anytime, babe."

"I told Mia that sitting on your hips was like being astride a panther." Bolts of desire shot through Ryan as Jamie wriggled a little to get comfortable. Ryan uttered a deep growl in a very close approximation of said animal. "How did you do that?" Jamie asked as she dropped down so that her face hovered above Ryan's grinning mouth.

"It's all in the tongue," she murmured as she wiggled one eyebrow.

Jamie grasped her chin and leaned down so that her eye was right at Ryan's mouth. "Do it again," she ordered. Even though Ryan complied, she couldn't get a good view. "I can't see far enough in there," she groused. "I know," she said as her eyes twinkled. "Give me a second and then do it again." She rested her mouth a millimeter from Ryan's but this time she slid her tongue deep into her partner's open mouth. She tapped her on the side to indicate her readiness, but this time the growl sounded much more like a panther gargling. "Nope. One more time," she instructed as her tongue slid in again. This time the poor panther seemed to be coughing up a hairball, and Jamie sat up and scolded, "You don't perform well under pressure, do you?"

"Give me that tongue back and I'll show you exactly how I perform," she growled in her own inimitable voice.

"It's all yours." She leaned over and presented her with the little pink gift. Seconds later, they were moving against each other furiously as Ryan felt her arousal once again spiral quickly out of control. She focused on pulling back, determined to let Jamie control the flow of their lovemaking, but she was having a devil of a time doing so. It helped quite a bit to close her eyes and feel the overwhelming sensation without the visual enticement of Jamie's voluptuous body.

Jamie pulled away forcefully, her lips expelling a small, disappointed sigh as she did. Focusing on her target and willing her hands to not shake, her fingers started to work at the smooth black buttons of Ryan's wrinkled shirt. As the last one released, she grasped the fabric and pushed it to the side. Now the only thing covering Ryan's breasts was the thin cotton of her tank. As Jamie surveyed her heaving chest and gazed at her parted moist lips and heavily lidded eyes, she nearly ripped the material from her body. But it was important to her to savor this moment, so she forced herself to move deliberately.

Her hands dropped to cover Ryan's breasts, her eyelids fluttering closed. "Ah," she cried involuntarily, her mouth remaining open as she struggled to breathe.

"Yessss," Ryan hissed as the determined fingers circled and pinched the rock hard nipples hidden beneath the thin fabric. "Oh, yeah," she cried again, her dark head tossing back and forth on the striped fabric of the cushion. Her hips lifted involuntarily, and the woman astride them remembered her description of the sensation of riding that wild beast.

"Slow down, Tiger," she soothed, running her fingers through the dark hair splayed out over the cushion.

"I … I'm so turned on," Ryan moaned as she sucked her bottom lip into her mouth and gently bit down in a failed attempt to control herself.

"I'll take care of you," Jamie soothed tenderly. "I promise, baby." To seal her vow, she leaned over again and tasted the nearly bruised lips. Hands automatically returned to the sensitive mounds of flesh, gently kneading them, while her mouth attacked Ryan's.

Now their groans and moans merged until it was impossible to distinguish what sound came from which body. Pulling up sharply, Jamie yanked her partner into a sitting position and pushed the abused black linen from her shoulders. Taking a breath for courage, she dropped her hands to the hem of Ryan's tight tank top and lifted it to her shoulders. Their mouths were locked together so tightly that she nearly had to break the suction to completely remove the garment, but the inch of separation she created allowed her to toss the tank onto the patio.

Ryan's mouth claimed hers again immediately, and they shifted back down to the cushions. When Jamie broke the kiss and sat up, she gasped in surprise and pleasure.

The months of fantasizing had not nearly prepared her for the perfection that was displayed before her. From their months of play, she knew that Ryan had full, heavy breasts. However, her most imaginative dreams had not prepared her for the absolutely adorable mounds of flesh that pointed up at her. The shape was perfect … full, ripe, and incredibly lush, the nipples surprisingly small and delicate looking. They were a beautiful rose color, just the shade of Ryan's lips when she was excited. The areolas were small, and the erect nubs were relatively tiny given the substantial size of the breasts themselves. The entire package was massively appealing and Jamie's hands reached for them immediately, a contented smile gracing her face at what she knew was only the first of thousands of such touches. Jamie's first touch caused her heart to skip a beat, and her eyes fluttered closed in pleasure. She hefted the weight in her small, cool hands, pleased beyond measure at the sensation. Her thumbs trailed over the nipples smoothly, causing Ryan's eyes to close as she sucked in a breath.

It was difficult for Jamie to control her hands or her voice, but she finally sighed and murmured, "Sometimes my imagination is just not vivid enough."

Ryan placed her own hands over her partner's and squeezed them gently. Her smile was sweet, but her eyes glittered with desire.

Jamie furrowed her brow in concentration and began to explore the tender flesh with renewed vigor. Her mouth curled into a delighted smile as she caressed each breast in sequence, watching for Ryan's enthusiastic response. "I think I finally understand why so many men are obsessed with these," she muttered, as much to herself as to her partner. In fact, she did now understand the fetish. There was some primal pull to the swells of flesh that she didn't even claim to understand. She immediately put the matter out of her mind, deciding that it didn't matter why she was so attracted to this particular part of Ryan's body, she was just going to enjoy it.

As she delighted in her experimentation, she noticed that Ryan's entire torso was covered in goose bumps. Looking up, she saw that the fog bank had now obscured the sun, and she acknowledged that it was too cold to stay outside any longer. She hated to break the mood but realized that it wouldn't get any easier later, so she smiled down at her lover and seductively issued an invitation. "How does a nice big bed sound right about now?"

"Perfect," Ryan agreed. "It sounds perfect."

As they walked through the living room and entered the foyer, Ryan used her bare foot to catch the edge of her hat that was still lying on the floor. Deftly, she kicked it into the air and managed to catch it in her free hand.

"Talented tootsies," Jamie teased.

"Wait till you see my hands in action," her dark haired lover leered.

Jamie's heart skipped a beat at the thought and her pulse raced a little faster. Once they reached the bedroom they came together for another tender hug, rocking slowly in each other's arms for a long while. Jamie was the first to pull back, looking up at her partner with a small smile while her hands dropped to unbutton her white shorts. The zipper followed and she eased the fabric from her body by sliding her hands down Ryan's ass. "Let's go to bed," she purred, seemingly confident now that she led the dance.

"You're a little overdressed," Ryan reminded her by teasing her fingers deep into the placket of the polo shirt.

Jamie replied with one wiggling eyebrow, and Ryan immediately accepted the challenge. She unfastened the rust colored shorts and quickly dropped them to pool onto the floor. The cream colored polo was next, and it was swiftly lifted from her body and tossed down to join the shorts. "Now you're ready," Ryan whispered while her hands roamed over the peach toned satiny bra and bikinis that barely covered her lover.

"Are you ready, baby?" the smaller woman asked softly.

Ryan replied with a small nod as she grasped Jamie's hand and led her to the bed. She sat down and wrapped her arms around her still-standing lover, burying her face into her satin covered breasts. "I've been ready for you all of my life," she vowed in an emotion-filled voice.

Jamie crawled onto the bed and tugged her lover up with her. Holding her gently, Jamie conceded, "I'm not sure where to begin. Will you help me?"

"You don't need any help. You know how to please me. All you have to do is let your body express what's in your heart."

"Are you sure?"

"Positive," Ryan replied decisively. "This isn't about technique. It's all about love. And no one has ever made me feel more loved." She tilted her head and captured Jamie's waiting lips in a few tender kisses. "Just love me, and let me love you," she whispered.

Her lover nodded slowly as she felt the unease disappear. She banished her doubts about her inexperience and decided to follow her partner's directions. All she had to do was show her love through her touch, and she knew that was an incredibly easy task. Once again she began by exploring her partner's mouth. Within minutes they were both throbbing again, but Ryan could sense Jamie's indecision about what to do next. Rather than try to reassure her, she decided to take matter into her own hands. Literally. Sliding one hand down between their bodies, she popped open the tricky "S" hook of her partner's bra with negligent ease. The full, firm breasts that had been straining against the satin poured out of the material and into her waiting hands. "Oh, sweet Jesus!" she gasped when her hands slid over the satiny soft skin.

Jamie's head fell back against the mattress as she hissed out a sigh of pleasure. Shifting slightly, Ryan climbed on top of her and delicately moved over her, allowing the slightest contact between their bare breasts. Softness slid over softness for a few long moments until Jamie grasped her partner's hips and pulled her down to increase the pressure. Now one set of breasts ground into the other, causing both women to moan at the delicious sensation. "Oh God, this feels wonderful," Jamie gasped as her legs slid open to lock around her partner's hips. She started to rock gently to increase the intensity of the feelings that the contact between them was generating.

Ryan knew that neither of them could last much longer, so she shifted her hips to break the hold of her partner's legs. Sitting back on her haunches, she slipped a thumb under each side of the tiny waistband of the bikinis and slid the garment down her partner's firm, muscular legs. Jamie helped by kicking both legs into the air, and as Ryan tossed the panties to the floor, those legs locked around her once again and flipped her onto her back before she could even blink.

Jamie stared at Ryan with wild passion as she grasped the black lacy high cut panties, shifting her body to slide them down Ryan's legs. Once more Ryan asserted control, grasping Jamie by the waist and tugging her down, positioning her so they were lying on their sides, face to face. Now their hands roamed at will, each touching the smoothness of the other, moaning in pleasure as new territory was explored.

As if it had been choreographed, each top leg bent simultaneously. Questing fingers slid into slick folds as each mouth gasped in ecstasy before they sought connection once again. Darting tongues, kissing lips and warm wet mouths devoured each other as slippery fingers moved in lightning quick patterns over swollen, velvety skin. Their moans indistinguishable, the sounds grew louder as their hearts thumped heavily in their chests.

Ryan's breath was coming in ragged pants, and she was forced to pull her head away to suck in a huge lungful of air. As soon as she could breathe again, her lips automatically sought out their tempting target, and their mouths locked together once again.

Now both chests began to heave and strain as they struggled to stay connected while their bodies moved against each other's. It was unclear which woman began, but within seconds both were groaning and gasping for air as a powerful climax exploded through both bodies. They shook and rocked together, vulvas spasming, nipples tightening, hearts racing. Hands blindly sought out the other's face, grasping gently, two mouths murmuring, "I love you, I love you," again and again. The salt of tears anointed the still merged mouths as they slowly calmed in each other's arms.

The emotion flowing through and between their still entwined bodies was far too great to process. A deep wave of physical and emotional exhaustion washed over them, but with her last bit of energy, Jamie lifted her hand to her mouth and delicately kissed the ring that she would always wear, and murmured, "Forever."

At around five o'clock, Jamie slowly emerged from her stupor. She blinked her eyes open and was richly rewarded by the sight of her lover, completely naked, splayed out across the bed, various parts of her anatomy inadequately covered by the once crisp pink sheet. A sly grin crossed her face and she indulged in the somewhat guilty pleasure of watching her sleep. Ryan's left arm was tossed over her head, and her right was jutting straight out from her shoulder. She was mostly on her back with one leg drawn up slightly. Jamie soaked up the sight of her beautiful body, watching her chest rise and fall in a strong cadence. She had an overwhelming urge to scoot over to her and nibble on those gorgeous breasts, but she had no desire to wake her sleeping lover. She was enjoying watching her in this unguarded moment and didn't want to break the spell.

Ryan's glossy black hair tumbled over her shoulders and across the pillow. Jamie loved to run her fingers through the silky threads, but she satisfied herself with imagining the sensation rather than experiencing it. Unable to resist, she slowly scooted nearer to be able to observe the beloved face more closely. Ryan's thick black eyelashes were another of Jamie's favorite things. She loved the way they framed her dark blue eyes, curling up to nearly touch her eyelids. The lashes were so long that they actually touched the lenses of her sunglasses, a chronic complaint on the ride.

Her moist full lips were slightly parted, and Jamie had to restrain herself from leaning in and capturing them with her own. Moving down with her visual tour, she again stopped at the perfect breasts. With Ryan fully on her back, the delightful flesh had flattened a little. The nipples still pointed up at the ceiling but the weight had shifted a little to the sides. She decided that she liked this look equally well, as she smiled in anticipation of seeing every permutation of shape in the years to come.

Now she focused on the tight belly that Ryan had insisted was not very "cut" when they began to work out together. Jamie had to admit that her own abs were more defined, but she actually preferred the thin layer of softness that covered her partner's rock hard belly. It was terribly exciting for her to feel beneath the softness and dig her fingers into that muscle and, much to Ryan's amusement, she did so every chance she got. As she gazed at the concave belly, she made a silent vow that she'd do her best to help her lover put on a few pounds. Even though she looked fabulous at this lower weight, it was probably not wise for her to keep herself so lean. She demanded so much of her body that she needed a little in reserve for times of stress.

Moving her gaze down a little lower, she smiled as she gazed thoughtfully at the generous triangle of jet-black curls. Ryan had almost no body hair to speak of, and the shock of springy curls was quite a contrast to the rest of her smooth body. Jamie shifted again to get a better look and smiled as she gazed at the shiny, matted curls that guarded her delicate flesh. Jamie had discovered that there were many lesser-known facets to making love than she'd been aware of. She had never stopped to consider how women might be different from one another, but she'd quickly learned that lubrication levels varied widely—even though her sample size was just two. Ryan's slightly parted legs revealed a glistening coat of moisture that extended several inches onto her thighs. She had actually been so wet that Jamie was afraid she wouldn't feel her fingers through the cushion of lubrication. Her worry on that point had been groundless, she smirked wryly, remembering with a shiver how quickly Ryan responded to her gentle touch.

Shifting her body once again, she moved back up to face her partner. She smiled over at her when her mouth moved slightly as her jaw clenched, and she began to regain some muscular tension. She turned her head slightly to face Jamie as she slowly batted those beautiful eyes open. Her face immediately broke into a crooked grin when she spotted Jamie's radiant visage just inches from hers. "How long have you been awake?" she asked, beginning her series of obligatory stretches.

"About ten minutes," she answered as she started to run her hand up and down the arching torso.

When Ryan had finished her stretch, she turned onto her side, mirroring Jamie's position. They were actually a little shy with each other after the explosion of emotion that had overcome them earlier, but Ryan broke the tension by trailing her fingers over the smooth planes of her partner's face. The dark blonde lashes fluttered at the sensation, then closed softly. Her mouth curled up into a little grin as she soaked up the luxurious feeling. Ryan's deep voice finally whispered, "Do you feel okay, up here?" She clarified by tapping her lover's temple.

A gentle nod was the unequivocal reply. "Up here." She grasped Ryan's hand and placed it on her forehead. "And definitely down here!" She grinned as she brushed the fingers across her still damp curls. "Never better down here," she emphasized with a giggle.

"I feel pretty good down there, too." Ryan chuckled as she now grasped Jamie's hand. "But I've never felt better here," she whispered, as she placed the hand over her heart. "I thought I'd made love before, but that was definitely the first time for me."

"Now I finally know what the big deal is." Jamie laughed gently. "I mean, I've enjoyed sex at times, and I thought I knew what love felt like, but I didn't really have a clue until now. Now I get it," she enthused as she hugged her lover tightly.

They lay entwined for a long while, moving gently against each other and soaking up the sensation of being so completely loved. Ryan's soft voice broke the silence. "I promised you something a while ago."

"What's that?"

"I promised I'd sing to you when we were lying in bed after making love," she reminded her.

"Oh, Ryan," she cried, terribly touched that her partner would not only remember the request, but would immediately fulfill it. "I'd truly love that," Jamie whispered.

"You asked me to sing something from *West Side Story*," she said. "Do you remember?"

"Of course I do."

"This is one of my favorite songs from the play," she said. "It's during the scene where the lovers have a little ceremony—a bit like we did this afternoon. They couldn't be married because of their familial animosity, so they pledged their love to God before they made love for the first time."

"I'd love to hear it," Jamie murmured as she sat up and crossed her legs. Ryan followed suit, scooting over so their knees touched. They held hands and gazed into each other's eyes lovingly.

In a strong, clear voice Ryan began,

*Make of our hands—one hand.*
*Make of our hearts—one heart.*
*Make of our vows—one last vow.*

*Only death will part us now.*

Lifting their joined hands to her mouth, she kissed the ring that graced Jamie's small hand. The emotion in her voice and on her face was too much for Jamie, and she couldn't stop the tears from flowing. Ryan brushed them away with her thumbs as quickly as they fell, smiling down at her with a knowing look.

When her lover had regained some of her composure, she began again.

*Make of our lives—one life.*
*Day after day—one life.*
*Now it begins, now we start.*
*One hand—one heart.*
*Even death won't part us now.*

A single tear fell from Ryan's clear blue eyes, but that one drop caused Jamie to release the torrent she had been trying to hold back. "Nothing will part us, Ryan," she pledged with a quavering voice. "In this life—in the next. I'm yours eternally."

They held each other for a very long time, crying and soothing each other. The room had gotten a little chilly, so Ryan pulled the sheet and light blanket over their bodies. She held her partner in a tender embrace until she could feel her skin warm. "Better?" she asked after a few minutes.

"Perfect. When you hold me like this nothing can harm me."

"I'll always try to make you feel safe. Safe, and warm, and loved. Very well loved."

Reaching up with her hands, Jamie guided her partner's head down to paint her face with kisses. She lingered on her lips, darting her tongue into the warm cavern of her soft mouth to languidly explore. It didn't take long for Ryan to become a very willing participant, offering herself up to her lover without reservation.

Jamie loved her slowly and thoroughly, her tender touch falling like a gentle rain on Ryan's overheated body. She let her hands speak of her love, discovering dozens of tender and sensitive spots on the long, lean body. The most amazing thing for her about this journey of discovery was the softness of her lover's body. She had imagined that Ryan's body would feel completely different from Jack's, but the difference was not so much in the size or weight. It was the softness—the absolutely silken feel of the skin under her hands—that stunned her into silence. She touched her so lovingly and so thoroughly that she could have recreated her body perfectly if her artistic talent had matched her sensory memory.

Ryan placidly traveled this sensual path with her partner. Since some of her ardor had been bled from her body earlier in the afternoon, she was able to relax and let Jamie build her passion back up to its previous height. Even though she was relatively calm, her heart began to beat faster when her partner bent her head and took her tender right breast into her mouth. Jamie now examined both mounds of flesh with the same intensity she had lavished on the rest of her body, and before long Ryan was humming with desire. Her legs spread involuntarily as she sought some form of relief.

Taking pity on her, Jamie moved closer and slid her fingers between the excessively slick folds, smiling as Ryan's breath caught in her throat, coming out in a low sibilant hiss. She started to move her fingers slowly, touching her partner as she herself liked to be touched. With her hips and her hands, Ryan guided her to move quicker and with a much firmer touch. Fearing that she would hurt the tender skin, Jamie tried to lighten up a bit, but Ryan was having none of it. "A little more, baby. I need a little more." She clamped both of her hands over Jamie's and roughly ground them into herself, demanding the touch she needed.

Jamie's fear of causing her lover pain disappeared and her own desire began to rise when she gazed at the look of rapture that suffused Ryan's beautiful face. Scant seconds after the larger hands joined Jamie's, Ryan threw her head back and cried out loudly, the air forcibly propelled from her lungs in a burst of sound.

Small whimpers and moans continued to spring from her lips for several minutes. Every time Jamie tried to remove her hand, Ryan's still-tight grip refused the request. It seemed as though the dark-haired woman needed absolute stillness to recover, and once Jamie realized this, she willingly complied.

Finally, Ryan released her hand, her own arms dropping to the bed with a thud. "Is it safe?" Jamie queried with a chuckle, as she moved her fingers a micrometer.

"It's safe." Ryan's exhausted voice replied weakly, and she grimaced a bit when the small hand was removed from her still-throbbing flesh. "Wow! I might need twenty-four hours of bed rest before I can walk again."

Sitting up quickly, Jamie placed her hand on Ryan's chest. "Did I hurt you, sweetheart?"

"No. All self-inflicted wounds," she said with a grimace. "I need a pretty long time to rest after an orgasm. If I don't have it, I need to have a lot more pressure to stimulate the next one. But I was so turned on, I couldn't resist another tumble."

"Will you be okay soon?"

"Oh, yeah. This is very temporary. It's nature's way of stopping me from being an orgasm glutton."

"You poor baby," she soothed, as she patted the body part in question very lightly.

"Not a problem. Now that my own fun parts are out of commission, I can concentrate on yours."

The leer that met Jamie's eyes caused her heart to skip a beat. "Have at me, Tiger," she offered as she stretched out before her lover's sparkling eyes.

"Just what I like … a willing victim." Ryan grasped Jamie in a rough embrace and wrestled with her playfully for a few minutes.

They giggled and laughed together, rolling around on the bed wildly. Slowly the laughter ebbed, and Ryan was left sitting on her haunches between Jamie's outstretched legs, gazing at her with undisguised pleasure. She lowered her hands and began to slowly massage Jamie's legs. She started with the toes, and as she rubbed and kneaded the soft pink flesh, she would occasionally pop one of the digits into her mouth for a gentle suck or a delicate little lick. "Oh … sweetheart." Jamie's eyes rolled back in her head as she felt her toes being sucked into that warm, wet mouth. "My God, that feels good," she gasped in a shaky voice. The massage continued up her instep, past the ankle, finally up her calf to her knee. Delicate, tender kisses and licks followed up her leg, finally stopping at the hip. Ryan grinned at the look of pleasure dancing across her partner's face as she grasped the other leg and began the same treatment. Small sighs and faint moans fell from Jamie's lips as the assault continued. Again Ryan halted her progress at the same spot.

Jamie felt herself being rolled over onto her stomach. The passionate massage continued on this side of her body, proceeding past the earlier stopping point. Ryan kneaded her firm cheeks, pressing deeply into the flesh with her thumbs. She used both hands to probe the muscles, finally ending up near her waist. She covered Jamie's body with her own, allowing her breasts to rub sensually against the smooth back. Jamie gripped the sheet with both hands as she struggled to control her movements. She pushed up with her hips, trying to grind against Ryan with her sensitized bottom. Ryan gripped her around the hips and rubbed against her for a few long seconds, finally rolling off as she placed hot, wet kisses down her back and onto her buttocks.

Ryan began to nibble on her neck, slowly moving up to the always-sensitive ears. She licked and kissed and sucked until Jamie was nearly frantic in her movements. Then Ryan backed off again, moving on to gently rub down her back, going lower and lower until she was past her waist again. When that movement caused reactions that were too intense, she backed off again, turning Jamie over onto her back once again. She was quivering with desire but Ryan refused to provide her release. She had waited all these months, and she was going to wring every ounce of pleasure that she could out of this experience.

Ryan sat back to gaze with open desire at the tantalizing body displayed before her. "My God, you're so perfect," she murmured as her eyes widened in amazement. Jamie looked up through half-lidded eyes and felt her heart swell at her lover's obviously sincere appreciation of her body. She felt a little exposed, but Ryan's open look soothed any thoughts of discomfort.

Reaching forward with both hands, Ryan touched the mounds of flesh that peeked up at her. A delighted smile crossed her tanned features as her eyes slowly closed to luxuriate in the sensation of feeling the weight and texture of the incredibly smooth flesh. "So perfect," she breathed in such a soft tone that it was as if she were talking to herself.

After an eternity of slow, steady exploration she moved her head down to one pert breast. Lying down next to her lover, mouth mere millimeters from a rose tinted nipple, she blew warm breath across the sensitive flesh. Jamie tried to force her breast into Ryan's mouth, but she firmly resisted, moving her head back just enough to elude the thrusting nipple. The smaller woman let out a frustrated moan but Ryan grinned at her, taunting her with her warm breath. "Lie back and let me take you where you want to go, baby. I promise we'll get there." The confident look on her lover's face assured Jamie that her compliance would be rewarded so she fell back onto the bed and tried to follow instructions.

When Jamie forced herself to stop thrusting against her partner, Ryan calmly dropped her head and took the nipple into her mouth. She slowly drew the taut little nub in, sucking firmly as it slid past her teeth. Jamie began to twitch her hips in time to the sucking motion, willing Ryan to continue the pressure. But Ryan was not to be dissuaded from her script. She knew how she wanted to love Jamie; she'd been dreaming about this day for months and she was going to continue at her own pace. This was her pleasure, and she was going to enjoy it to the fullest.

She released the sensitized nipple and began to touch the skin of the other breast lightly, using just her fingernails. The light scratching lit a fire in her partner, and Jamie again tried to push her breast against Ryan's hand, needing the increased pressure. Again her efforts were futile. Having learned her lesson, she lay as still as she could, unable to stop the constant moans that sprang from her lips.

Ryan reverted to another slow, gentle massage, this time starting at her fingertips. She pressed her fingers firmly against Jamie's hands, feeling the individual tendons, muscles and bones beneath her touch. She took each finger into her mouth, one at a time, locking eyes with her partner as she uttered a low, deep moan at the sensation. She loved each little digit in turn, licking, biting and sucking. Jamie lay in a limp heap, moaning continuously. She no longer struggled to increase the pace or the pressure. She knew that she had to let go and let Ryan control their sensual journey together. Nevertheless, she could not control her near constant sighs, moans and little gasps. These soft, involuntary sounds were music to Ryan's ears. She loved being able to wrest a particularly deep sigh or grunt from her lover's throat. She reveled in the power of providing such blissful stimulation to the woman she loved.

The massage continued for a very long while, finally ending after Ryan had returned to thoroughly rub and knead her tender breasts. Jamie lay still, almost unearthly still, as she waited for the next bit of torture to begin. She was panting shallowly, trying to focus, but she had lost that ability a long while ago. Now she lay there, waiting, open to Ryan's touch.

Ryan sat back on her heels and regarded her lover. She was still not ready to bring her to climax, yet she realized that she had to soon to avoid being cruel. A variety of options flew through her head, but she knew what she needed to do. Ever since the possibility had been presented, she had dreamt of tasting the luscious woman who now lay before her, and she could no longer resist the urge. She began at Jamie's sternum, creating a moist trail down her belly, pausing at her navel. "So beautiful," she murmured as her fingers ran up and down the gentle curves. She lowered her head and continued to trace the path down the center of her lover's constantly undulating body, but as she grazed the perfectly shaped triangle of dark blonde curls, she was alert for the clear sign that came from her love. Jamie had not only stopped moving, she had stopped making her little sounds of arousal. Ryan noted, with concern, that her body had also stiffened, and she quickly realized that this sensation was too overpowering for her partner.

Looking up and locking her eyes onto Jamie's, she gently soothed her. "I won't touch you if you don't feel comfortable. But I've been dreaming about your body for months. I need to look at you. Can I do that?"

Almost of its own volition, Jamie felt her head nod slowly and tried to relax her body as Ryan gently spread her legs.

The long, slender fingers slipped between her legs and slowly, delicately, spread the thoroughly wet lips. Her face was inches from the apex of Jamie's thighs, and the smaller woman gazed down at the intelligent blue eyes that worshipped her. "So lovely," Ryan whispered as her hand moved forward. "May I touch you?"

"Please. I … I need you to touch me."

The hand moved closer until one caressing finger moved slowly over every inch of skin, searching, seeking, and memorizing each furrow and fold. Jamie's eyes had fluttered closed, despite her attempts to watch her partner. The touch was so delicious that she could feel her whole body shiver with the sensation.

Finally the dark head tilted and beamed a smile at the reclining woman. "You are absolutely flawless," she pronounced, and the tone of her voice combined with the conviction on her face made Jamie believe her completely. For the first time in her life she felt that the elements that made her a woman were not only arousing—they were appealing. She truly felt that the woman who rested between her thighs found her body to be beautiful, and she was overjoyed with this gift of love that was already making her feel more comfortable with herself.

Ryan knew that her lover had taken a risk to allow her to touch her in such an intimate way, and she decided to make her touch very reassuring to bring her to climax. She rolled over and scooted up the bed until she was able to slide her arms under Jamie's back and knees. One swift move and the smaller woman rested on her lap, her back snug against Ryan's strong right shoulder, her legs spread and draped over Ryan's legs. As the warm hands began to tease her body again, Jamie began to respond freely, moving her body sensually as she lay cradled in Ryan's lap. Ryan brushed her nipples with the palm of her right hand as she probed her mouth with her tongue. She held her chin steady with her left hand and moved deeply in her warm mouth. Jamie began to sigh and moan in an unbroken string of incoherence, and Ryan finally relented and moved her left hand down to touch her wetness. She slid through the folds with just her index finger while she sucked on Jamie's tongue, drawing it into her own mouth. Their tongues danced slowly as her finger slid through the wetness. Jamie moaned right into her mouth as a second finger joined the first and found her secrets with unerring accuracy. After a moment, she shifted her hips a bit to guide Ryan to the perfect spot. The questing fingers began to rub lightly over the swollen clitoris, just as Jamie indicated. It was clear how difficult it was for Jamie to forestall her climax as she wrenched her mouth away from Ryan's lips to be able to breathe more freely, opening her mouth wide as her hips began their final thrusts. She grabbed Ryan's hand and pressed it against herself, grinding it around in a taut circle as she let out an explosion of air. She shouted out unintelligible cries as she gasped through the powerful waves of sensation rolling through her body. Finally spent, she released her grip on Ryan's hand but continued to move her hips, swaying them back and forth in a slow sensuous beat.

"Oh, God," she moaned languidly, the words barely falling from her mouth.

Ryan slid her to the bed and gazed down at her lovingly. Her arms were tossed over her head, forcing her breasts to ride up her chest wall. The flesh was still taut from the powerful climax, and the nearly mauve nipples were so rigidly erect that they looked as though they were perching upon the pink areolas rather than an actual part of them.

The view was so stimulating to Ryan's unquenched libido that she found her mouth heading for the alluring mounds once again, guided with laser-like precision to latch onto the enticing nipples with her warm, wet lips.

A shocked gasp caused the smaller woman to jerk, and her hands immediately flew to Ryan's head. Warring impulses fired simultaneously in her brain. The moderate, temperate part of her personality urged her hands to push Ryan's mouth away. But her throbbing need overrode that impulse and demanded instead that her hands grab the back of the dark head and mash it against her breast.

The force of that move took Ryan by surprise, but she was undeniably pleased by her lover's enthusiastic reaction. She took as much of the breast as she could manage into her wide-open mouth, and sucked it in as firmly as she could. Her right hand shot out to pinch and tug at the second nipple. After a few seconds of this rough assault, Jamie began to push her away, but instead of pushing Ryan off her body she was instead guiding her lower and offering herself once again. Her legs were so wide open that Ryan briefly wondered if she was double jointed. But now was hardly the time for that conjecture. Her partner needed some immediate attention, and she was more than happy to tend to her needs.

She rested her head on Jamie's belly, partly for the view but mostly to breathe in her intoxicating aroma. Her swirling fingers found their target and moved the moisture all around the swollen flesh, responding immediately to the subtle movements of her partner. As soon as she established a strong pace, Jamie's hips started to thrust upwards, her mouth falling open to groan out a low cry as another orgasm rocked her body.

Ryan tenderly petted her thighs, offering soothing words of love as her partner's pulse calmed to its normal pace. She was aware that her lover, surprisingly, had made no move to evict her from her intimate position. Guessing that she might still be receptive, Ryan scooted over until she was lying on her stomach between Jamie's legs. When she was confident that the aftershocks of the last orgasm had faded, she softly placed her thumbs alongside the shiny inner lips. When her partner made no move other than to hold her breath for a moment, she slowly began to slide her thumbs up and down the silky flesh.

Weak little sighs and faint moans were the music she loved to hear, and both richly rewarded her as she continued her gentle movements. After a scant few minutes, she felt her partner begin to spasm once again. She kept her thumbs right where they were, riding out the waves with her lover as she continued her feather light stroking.

Casting a glance up at the lovely face of her lover, she saw that Jamie was lost in Nirvana. She decided that as long as she wasn't pushed away, she would keep going. This time she scooted even closer, so close that her mouth actually watered when the arousing aroma of her lover's excitement suffused her senses. Using the tips of her fingers, she played with the tender flesh, achieving a steady pace in a few strokes. Her fingers never actually touched the tip of the over-sensitive clit, but the skin gliding over it was obviously incredibly pleasing to her partner. Her cries and gasps of pleasure did not cease the entire time that Ryan gently manipulated her, but when the inevitable climax began at last, her soft moans became so strong and rough that she began to cough and gasp for air. "Enough!" she gasped, as Ryan finally pulled her hands away.

Ryan climbed up beside her to hold her gently in her arms. Her hand slid through the damp blonde hair, pushing it off her face. "Have I finally reached your capacity?" she asked softly, a teasing grin on her face.

"The French call orgasm the 'little death'," Jamie murmured in response. "One more little death, and I'm gonna have a big death! My Lord, I've never been so weak!"

"Let's rest for a while," Ryan suggested, tugging her limp body up against her side.

"Rest. Good," Jamie managed to get out, before sleep claimed her once again.

When they finally woke from their third nap of the afternoon, Ryan grinned down at her lover, her blue eyes clear and sparkly. "Wanna go again?" she asked with an eyebrow wiggle.

"Sure," Jamie replied with feigned nonchalance. "I could have three or four more orgasms before dinner." She laughed uproariously at the look of shock on her partner's face. "You've gotta be on drugs to even ask me that!" she roared as she tickled Ryan unmercifully.

Once Ryan had Jamie's arms pinned, she chided, "You've never told me how fast you recover from an orgasm, you little minx. Were you testing me?" The deep flush that colored Jamie's cheeks surprised Ryan, and she dropped the teasing and quickly asked, "What's wrong, babe?"

"Uhm, I didn't know I could have orgasms that quickly," she admitted. "Surprised the hell out of me!"

"Really?" she said, shocked that her partner hadn't learned this fact about her body.

"No idea," she admitted with a wry smirk. "There could be all kinds of secrets hidden down there that I don't know about," she said, glancing down her body.

"It'll be awfully fun to discover them together," Ryan promised with a kiss.

"So … you can't do that?"

"Nope. Not possible. I shoot one round and have to reload. But it's clearly a blessing that I can't," she said with a laugh.

"How come?"

Ryan sat up on one elbow and looked at her with amazement. "Do you know how little time I would spend in a vertical position if I could come that often?"

Jamie giggled as she considered the ramifications of that capability. Then her brow quickly furrowed as she asked, "Do you know other women who can do that?"

"Do you really want to talk about this?"

The golden head bobbed in affirmation. "I think I need to understand all I can about how my body is responding."

"Okay, then, sure, I have. My friend the assistant D.A. could just come and come and come. I always got tired before she did. She told me that she spent a solid hour coming once when she used a vibrator."

"Wow," Jamie mused. "That seems like a little too much of a good thing."

"Yeah, once is really enough for me."

"It always has been for me too," Jamie said. "Do you think I'm gonna need a bunch of orgasms to be happy from now on?"

"No, I don't think so. Most of the women I've been with only want multiples when they're really turned on, or if they have a lot of time to play. I think you'll be perfectly happy with a singleton most of the time." She leaned over for a gentle kiss. "But you might want a bunch. It's no big deal. I think it's nice to know there are a few more lurking under the surface just waiting to be released."

"We'll see how my vulva feels about this development tomorrow," she said with a slight grimace. "I hope this isn't like getting sunburned on the first day of vacation. I don't want to have to miss a day."

"You know," Ryan whispered into her ear. "Some of my best sexual experiences have been when I was a little sore. It can be like scratching a really bad itch."

Jamie looked up at her with a huge grin on her face. "We're gonna have a ball together, aren't we, Tiger."

"Grrrroooooowl," was the smirking panther's reply.

# Chapter Five

To avoid temptation, they rinsed separately in the shower, and then slipped on the terrycloth robes that Jamie pulled from the closet. Jamie took her by the hand and started to walk towards the door, but Ryan wasn't ready to leave quite yet. "How long have your parents owned this place?" she asked as she looked around the large rectangular room, trying to get a feel for her lover's mark on this home.

"I think Mother bought it not too long after I was born."

"Mother?" Ryan asked quizzically.

"Yeah, Daddy would never have bought a place like this. But he's really smart about things like that. He knows she wants this type of thing, so he doesn't interfere. I really admire how he deals with her money. I don't think they ever have issues with it, and that's saying a lot."

"Are you worried about that with us?" Ryan asked as she turned to lock eyes with her lover.

"A little bit," Jamie admitted. "We haven't talked about it at all. It's a big issue, and I think we both need to feel comfortable with it."

"Why?" she asked plaintively. "It's your money, and you can do whatever you want with it. Why does it have to affect us?"

"It will, Ryan," she insisted as she wrapped her in a hug. "Trust me. This kind of money changes everything."

"Okay, sweetie. I don't want to talk about it now, though. Let's enjoy our honeymoon without getting into that, okay?" Ryan turned to look around the room again, but she stopped and looked at Jamie with a little grin. "Why am I doing this now? I'm starving!"

Jamie laughed and grabbed her hand, pulling her toward the door firmly. "You can take a tour later; let's get you fed."

They descended the stairs, hand in hand. They passed through the two-story foyer, where they stopped to pick up their discarded shoes, then through the huge living room and a formal dining room on the way to a gleaming gourmet kitchen. Ryan stood with her hands on her hips, surveying the massive room. "This kitchen is bigger than our living room and dining room put together."

Jamie looked around, slightly embarrassed by the opulence of her family's second home. "I guess it is a little ostentatious."

"It's not ostentatious at all. Opulent, yes. Grand, yes. Elegant, yes. Lavish, yes. But not ostentatious." She looked around the huge space as Jamie poked in the restaurant-style double refrigerator. The house was styled as an English country estate, and the designer had done a masterful job. The kitchen was a marvel of both design and utility. Large leaded glass windows looked out over the interior courtyard, but not much of the waning twilight came in through the heavy fog. Ryan walked over to the wall panel and flipped switches until she found the proper lights for the room. The soft halogen glow accented the room perfectly, and in the flattering light the room looked even more perfect. The walls were roughly divided in half, with the upper half covered in buff-colored wallpaper with a small print of dark green and maroon. The lower part of the walls was finished in rich tan stones, about nine by fifteen inches each, set horizontally. The stone looked a bit like limestone, and she noticed that it also covered the floors. Its rough, uneven surface felt surprisingly good on her bare feet, and she noticed that it was slightly warm. "Hey, Jamie?" she said, as she got down on her hands and knees.

"Yeah?" Jamie she took her head out of the refrigerator. "Hey, where are you?" She looked around the apparently empty room, seeking the owner of the voice that had called her.

Ryan's head popped up from behind the large center island. "Why aren't my feet cold?"

Jamie laughed at the way the question had been framed. "Because there's an under-floor heating system that goes on automatically."

"Cool," Ryan said as she got back to her feet.

Jamie smiled at her and asked, "What are you in the mood for?"

"What are my choices? Is there much in there?"

"Just about anything that your little heart desires."

"But how ...?"

"I called a service from your house this morning and had them stock the place. I didn't wanna have to leave in case we were unable to move," she said as she gave Ryan a sexy look.

"So you let strangers come into a house like this and fill up your refrigerator?"

"Yep. Pretty much."

"That's so odd," she mused. "A multi-million dollar place like this, and you treat it kind of casually. Yet with our little house, we don't even let the meter reader in unless somebody escorts him. It seems kinda backwards."

"Well, we are insured," she said with a tilt of her head, wondering why this arrangement bothered her partner.

"Yeah, but how do you prove the delivery boy stole your ... I don't know," she said in a frustrated tone, looking around for something that was obviously expensive. Her eyes settled on a lovely small painting that hung on a nearby wall. She jumped up and strode over to it, pronouncing, "your Monet … your *Monet!*" she cried, looking from her blushing partner and back to the painting several times. "Is that real?!"

"Uhm … yeah," Jamie gulped, feeling very uncomfortable.

"You have a Monet in the kitchen?"

A small nod was Jamie's reply. She fervently hoped that Ryan didn't ask the obvious follow-up question and that her shocked partner wouldn't wish to investigate the rest of the collection. To her relief, Ryan sat down heavily on her stool.

"This is … this is … different," she mumbled, obviously trying to come to grips with the Evans's lifestyle.

Jamie went over to her and put a hand on her shoulder. "Let's back up here for a second. We don't let just anybody in. We've used the same service to stock the fridge since we moved here. The owner of the company is the only one who has access to the house. As a matter of fact, we trust him enough to have his thumbprint entered into the security system, same thing for the maid. The gardeners and the pool man can't come into any of the residence units, they only have access to the grounds."

Ryan was shaking her head, trying to understand her partner's point.

"Does this all bother you?" she asked carefully, rephrasing the same question she had asked earlier in the sunroom.

"No. No. It really doesn't. It's gonna take some getting used to, but it's a real learning experience for me, and it's actually kind of fascinating."

"I know it's a lot, but you just let me know if you want to talk about any of it, okay? I don't want to you to be uncomfortable." She turned to go back to the refrigerator, stopping abruptly on the way. "Before I forget, let's decide how we want the security system set up for the week."

"Uhm, what are the choices?" Ryan asked, unfamiliar with security systems of any kind.

"Well, everything is alarmed now, but since they put this new system in, the keys don't work if it's turned on. Only my thumbprint will work, so if we leave it on you won't be able to go into the various buildings without me."

Ryan's chin was resting on her hands, and she blinked up at Jamie ingenuously. "I'm not gonna let you out of my sight, hot stuff, so that's not a worry."

"Not so fast. You don't know what else we have around here."

"Tell me!" Ryan cried, always interested in investigating potential new playgrounds.

"Nope. One thing at a time," Jamie insisted. "I think we should turn off the alarms for the places that I know we'll want to visit this week. You can protect me, can't you, Buffy?" She gave her partner a helpless smile, blinking her eyes coquettishly.

"If somebody tries to break in, I'll toss 'em that Monet," Ryan laughed. "That oughta hold 'em."

"You do that," Jamie laughed. She walked over to the display and pushed buttons for several minutes. "I hope I did that right."

"You said this was new?" Ryan walked over to the large display as Jamie went back to the refrigerator. Most of the labels for the zones were self-explanatory. She noted and understood "main", "gar", and "pool", but she was confused by "gst" and "surv." "What are gst and surv?" she asked, pronouncing the zones phonetically.

Jamie had her head deep in the refrigerator, and she called out, "Probably guest house and servant's quarters. I've never worked this keypad before, but that's my best guess."

*Hmm, how can you have this much money and not know how to abbreviate servant?* Ryan thought to herself. She quickly put that thought into the file she was mentally preparing concerning the idiosyncrasies of the very rich.

"You know, you still haven't answered me. Doesn't 'the beast' need to be fed?"

"Yeah," Ryan agreed as she rubbed her empty tummy. "Dinner or snacks?"

"Let's do both," Jamie said decisively.

"I knew there was a good reason that I love you so much." Ryan sighed with pleasurable anticipation. She sat on a tall stool next to the center island and continued to look around while Jamie removed items from the fridge. She spent some time trying to figure out what the counters were made of, finally asking, "Are these concrete?"

Jamie looked over and nodded, "Yeah, Mother had the kitchen redone last year. Those are polished concrete. There's a guy in the city who's a real artisan. He was down here for weeks making sure they were perfect." The counters really were perfect. They were about the same color as the floor, but they were polished to a very smooth finish. It was cool and welcoming when Ryan rested her cheek on it. "Hey, do you know what would be kinda cool on a hot day?" she asked with a leer.

"I think I have an idea," Jamie smiled. "But I don't think that's what Mother had in mind for her precious counters."

"You never know. If she's anything like her daughter …" Ryan left the thought for Jamie to finish as she cocked her head slightly.

"That's an image I'd prefer to flush from my memory bank, thank you."

"Does it bother you to think of your parents being sexual?" she inquired, genuinely interested. She assumed that Jamie didn't know that her father was having an affair, but she wasn't certain. She'd debated with herself long and hard before deciding not to tell her partner about seeing her father in the apartment, and she was still not one hundred percent sure she'd done the right thing.

"Uhm … I guess not. I mean, I don't think about it a lot. Obviously I'm not around them much, but when I was younger, I got the definite idea that they enjoyed sex."

"What makes you think they enjoy sex?"

"I don't think I noticed anything before I started to be aware of sex myself, like during puberty. Once I started being able to read the signals, I'd notice that sometimes in the mornings they'd be all sweet and tender with each other. Daddy would touch her a lot, and they'd kiss a little longer than normal before he left for work. Mother would be humming or singing a little bit while she ate breakfast. She looked happy and satisfied," she said with a shrug.

"Do they still do that now?" Ryan asked, having reason to be skeptical about their continued ardor.

"Again, I haven't spent a lot of time with them in the last three years, but the dynamic seems to have changed. Mother doesn't get up for breakfast anymore, and Daddy seems to work a lot more than I ever remember." She looked at Ryan thoughtfully and said, "It seems like Daddy's married to his job more than to Mother. I don't think sex is a big deal for them anymore. Maybe it's because they're getting older."

"How old are they?" Ryan asked, now regretting pursuing the subject since she knew that Jim Evans still had a healthy, if misdirected, sexual drive.

"Mother's forty-one and Daddy will be forty-six this year."

"You'd better still be throbbing when you're forty-one!"

"I'll be hot for you when I'm ninety-one," she promised with a grin. "I can see you now, with a big shock of pure white hair and those clear blue eyes. You're gonna be the hottest nonagenarian around."

"With you keeping me young, I think we'll both be pretty spry," she predicted. Her attention was diverted as her hands ran over the wooden pedestal that the concrete counter sat upon. "Hey, what do you call the finish on these cabinets?"

"That's bleached oak."

"Boy, Conor would love to take a look around this place," Ryan said. "Oh, I forgot to leave him a note asking if he wanted to come down on Saturday."

"Call him."

"I'll call him tomorrow. He's probably not home from work yet, anyway," she said as she started to fidget in her chair.

"You look like you need to get rid of some energy," Jamie said, recognizing the signs.

"I didn't *do* anything all day."

"You certainly did me!"

"Yeah, I guess I did, huh?" Ryan blushed a bit at the frank appreciation that lingered in her partner's expression. "I mean I didn't do anything really strenuous."

"My answer still stands, Tiger. I've got an idea. You munch on these, and then go get some exercise while I make dinner." She indicated the cheese, fruit and bread that she had assembled.

"Okay. Should I blade or run?"

Jamie's face began to cloud with worry. "I don't think you should do either in this fog. Don't you see what it's like out?"

Ryan walked to the window, unable to even make out the courtyard in the diffuse light. "Your point?"

"You big goof! Like I'd let you Rollerblade when you can't see the hand in front of your face. The road is about ten feet from a sheer cliff, you know!"

"Again, your point?" A smile began to curl her mouth.

Jamie shook her head and chuckled in frustration at her foolhardy lover. "Do you swim well enough to get your cardiovascular workout in the pool?"

Her face broke into a smirk as she laughed at a private joke. "Yeah, I can swim well enough. But isn't it a little cold?"

"Nope. Finish your snack, and I'll solve all your problems."

Ryan wolfed down the entire plateful of food, allowing Jamie one segment of an orange and a cracker. Together, they walked out through the butler's pantry, past a mudroom, exiting through a Dutch door. Ryan could hear the surf pounding in the background, but it was too foggy to see a thing. They followed a steppingstone path towards a soft glow, making their way across the lawn. As they drew near, Ryan assumed they were going to a greenhouse of some sort. The building was made entirely of glass, and she noted that it looked to be about sixty feet long but only twenty-five feet or so wide. Jamie opened the wide sliding doors, and Ryan was stunned to see that there was a long lap pool, a Jacuzzi and even a sauna tucked into a corner. Neither end of the building was glass, which struck Ryan as odd. "What's on the ends?" she asked, pointing to the nearest solid wall.

"Oh, there are separate apartments on each end of the building."

"Apartments?"

"Yeah. For guests. They each have two bedrooms, a kitchen and a small sitting room. It's really kinda cozy. When I had Jack down here, that's where we stayed." This revelation caused her to look a little embarrassed.

"Jamie, don't be embarrassed to talk about your relationship with him. It's part of you."

"I'll try," she said. "But it feels funny to talk about sleeping with someone else. I just wish you were the only person who'd ever touched me that way."

"Don't think like that, sweetie. Every experience prepares you for the next one. Jack was an important part of your life. If you hadn't had sex with him, you might not have been open to having sex with me."

"I guess that's true, but I still wish you were my only." Walking over to a door that led to a tiled bath and shower, she extracted a big fluffy bath sheet and placed it next to the pool. "You don't mind swimming nude, do you?"

"Mind?" Ryan asked incredulously. "I'd never wear a suit to swim, if I didn't have to." She dropped her robe on a rust-colored wrought iron chaise that was covered in a buff-colored cotton duck material and jumped into the pool, being careful to tuck her legs up after she judged the water to be about four feet deep. "Wow!" she said with glee, stretching out in the water. "This feels absolutely fantastic!"

"The water should be about eighty degrees. That's another big fight around here. Daddy likes it at seventy-seven, and Mother likes it at eighty-two. So they've finally compromised," she said with a smile. "Since we're alone, you can change it if you want to."

"Nope. It's perfect." Ryan turned over and started to swim. She smoothly stroked across the length of the pool, stopping at the end to execute a perfect racing turn. She came up near Jamie and popped her head out, shaking the hair out of her face as the water cascaded down her body. "This is absolute heaven," she enthused, as she tried to stay afloat.

Smiling at her friend's pleasure, Jamie turned her thoughts to more immediate, practical concerns. "I didn't ask you what you wanted for dinner," she said. "I could roast a chicken or grill some steaks, or I could make roast beef or …"

"You really did buy everything," Ryan laughed. "Chicken sounds good to me. Can you make mashed potatoes?"

"Of course I can make mashed potatoes," she said rather indignantly. "Would you mind if I did something a little creative to them?"

"Nope. I've yet to see you do anything creative that I didn't like. You're not gonna let me down now."

"Uh-huh," she nodded. "Now will you be safe out here all by yourself?"

"Yep. I'm very careful, and the water's not very deep. How many laps to a mile?"

"Well, the pool's fifty feet long, so …"

"So, about a hundred and five laps," Ryan said immediately.

Jamie stared at her open mouthed. "How did you do that?"

"Do what?" Ryan asked, perplexed.

"How did you do that math so fast?"

"I don't know. It seems obvious to me. Doesn't it to you?" she asked ingenuously.

"No, Ryan. It is not obvious to me, or to most of the rest of the world. You, my sweet, are a little savant."

"I'll take that as a compliment." Ryan grinned happily. "Even though I have no idea what you're talking about," she added as she dove under the water to begin swimming her laps.

Jamie had to stay and watch her for a minute. *She can swim all right*, she marveled. The sleek body slicing through the water mesmerized her, barely creating a ripple as she moved effortlessly. Ryan ran through her whole repertoire of strokes, moving from crawl, to breast, to back and finally to butterfly. That was the one that Jamie loved the best. Ryan would burst through the water with a powerful surge, creating a massive explosion of sound with each stroke. As her dark head exploded from the roiling water, she shot upwards just high enough to cause her breasts to peek out before she ducked under again. Jamie loved to watch the water sheet off of her head and shoulders as she shot upwards and slammed back into the clear blue water with a crash. Reluctantly, she tore herself away after she watched Ryan finish her butterfly laps.

Ryan returned to the house nearly an hour later. Her cheeks were bright pink and she glowed with vitality. Her skin smelled vaguely of chlorine, but Jamie knew she had showered by the scent of her hair. Burying her nose in Ryan's tresses, she thought of her Mother, who always used the wildflower scented shampoo that she kept in the pool house shower. "Did you bring any other shampoo?" she asked as she pulled away.

"Yeah, I brought my usual stuff."

"Good. You smell like my Mother, and I don't think I need that psychological scar."

"Do you want me to go wash it out now?"

"No, I'm teasing. My Mother smells pretty good, actually. It just caught me by surprise."

"You're really no fan of hers, are you?" Ryan asked quietly as she sat down on a kitchen stool.

"It's … it's not that. I've spent a lot of time talking about her in therapy, and I've finally come to realize that I don't feel much love from her. I think that I snap off sarcastic little remarks about her because it hurts me so much to feel that she doesn't care for me all that much. I wish she loved me like I love her," she muttered softly, as she turned to the sink.

This information hit Ryan like a blow to the chest. She immediately regretted bringing the subject up as she saw the look of sorrow on Jamie's face. Rising from her chair, she crossed the kitchen and wrapped her arms around Jamie's slight frame. "If she doesn't know how to love you, it's her issue. You're one of the most lovable people I know, and any emotionally healthy woman who was blessed to give birth to you would feel nothing but joy. If she doesn't realize how special you are, I feel nothing but pity for her," she said fervently, squeezing the woman in her arms.

"I'll probably overcompensate like crazy, but I've vowed that if I have a child, he or she will never wonder if they're truly loved." She sniffed as a few tears escaped.

"That will never be an issue for our children," Ryan promised as she made eye contact with her partner. "And it will never be an issue for you. I promise to show you every day how much you're loved."

"I'm completely confident about that," she agreed, as she hugged her one final time.

They broke apart, and Ryan went back to sit down, "Wow!" she said as she saw the chicken roasting on a spit in the huge stone hearth. "This is like being in the manor house, isn't it?"

"Yeah, I guess it is."

"But I'd be the one cooking for you, Ma'am," Ryan said with a thick Irish brogue as she joked to lighten the mood.

"Oh, I love that accent. Can you do that for me when we make love?"

"Sure. I'll be the Irish scullery maid, and you can be the lady of the manor. You can take me into the butler's pantry and make me do unspeakable acts that'll have me in the confessional for weeks."

"My, but you have a fertile imagination," Jamie purred as she came over to slip her arms around her lover.

"You bring out my wild side," the low voice rumbled in response. They spent several minutes kissing lightly until Ryan's nose began to twitch and she asked, "What is that delicious smell?"

"I'm caramelizing onions." Jamie jumped up and dashed to the oven to keep an eye on her sauté pan.

"Can I help?"

"Nope. Just sit there and watch me work. Would you like some wine?"

"Sure. That'd be good."

"The wine cooler is behind the island. Pick something out for us."

Ryan hopped off her stool and walked around the big island. She noticed as she passed that there were doors on the other side of the island, right under the prep sink. She leaned over and pulled open a door, quite surprised to find that it was a small refrigerator. Next to that door were two drawers, also food chillers, obviously for vegetables. "Pretty cool," she said, almost to herself.

She turned and opened the glass door of the wine cooler, getting down on her haunches to turn the bottles. "Do you have any suggestions?" she asked. "There's some Chardonnay, some white Bordeaux, some Ge … Ge …"

"Gewürztraminer?"

"Uhm … yeah, I think so," she said as she pondered the label. "German's indecipherable for me."

"Yeah," Jamie smirked. "This from a woman who can read Gaelic." Thinking about the wine for a minute, she chose the Gewürztraminer. "I think that'll go well with the potatoes."

"Okay by me," Ryan said. "I know as much about wine as I do about brain surgery. No, check that. I know a lot more about brain surgery than I do about wine."

Jamie smiled at her, privately thinking it adorable that Ryan really wasn't very worldly. "Hey, do you want to do our own cleaning while we're here? My parents usually arrange for a woman to come in every morning and clean, but I didn't know if you'd be comfortable with that."

"I don't think I want someone in here while I'm making you squeal," she said with a twinkle. "I think we can clean up our own mess."

"I thought you'd say that. I like it when I guess right."

Ryan had opened the bottle of perfectly chilled wine and went through the glass doors into the pantry to choose wine glasses. The pantry was a marvel of efficiency. Upper and lower cabinets lined the walls, and two full sized dishwashers bracketed a deep, wide sink. A long gooseneck faucet hung from the wall, obviously so that deep items could be washed with ease. All of the glassware, cutlery and china were kept in this narrow galley. Long, wide drawers held the family sterling in felt-lined safety. There was another small, waist-high refrigerator in here, filled with olives and cocktail onions and other ingredients for mixed drinks. A large commercial icemaker hummed in the corner. Ryan looked inside and saw that it had two separate compartments, one for cubes and one for crushed ice, and she smiled at the thought of indulging her penchant for chewing crushed ice. She finally chose two wine glasses decorated with an elaborately etched "S" and picked up the matching silver ice bucket, placing the bottle inside. Then she filled the remaining space with crushed ice and wrapped a bar towel around the neck of the bottle then she returned to the kitchen to take her place at the island and watch Jamie cook.

"Where do you want to eat?" Jamie asked.

Ryan looked around again. The island was large enough so that at least six people could sit around it and be comfortable. However, there was a more traditional eating area at the far end of the kitchen. Six barrel-style wooden chairs upholstered in deep, warm brown leather surrounded a round table. The table lay right below a wide bay window with a window seat decorated in a bright green print. The other wall hosted a large, deep fireplace stacked with split firewood. This area appealed to Ryan immensely, and she indicated her preference to Jamie.

"Why don't you start a fire?" Jamie asked. "Do you know how?"

"Harrumph!" Ryan muttered. "What kind of scullery maid can't start a decent fire?" she asked in her Irish accent. "My people have been lighting fires with nothing but peat for a thousand years!"

Jamie laughed at her antics and watched her place some kindling at strategic points between the logs. She stuck her head up inside the hearth to check the flue, satisfying herself that she'd opened it properly. She lit one of the giant matches lying near the kindling and watched the fire slowly flicker to life, then stood watching the flames for a few minutes, thoroughly satisfied with her accomplishment.

After a bit, she walked back over to her stool and sat down to watch her partner finish dinner. Jamie was starting to roughly mash the potatoes. She hadn't skinned them, and when they were the consistency she wanted, she added some chopped arugula and the caramelized onions. She stirred it all together and spooned them into a serving bowl, adding a handful of the onions to the top of the dish. Ryan's mouth watered as Jamie set the bowl in front of her. "Would you put that on the table, please?" Ryan did her bidding as Jamie removed the chicken from the rotisserie. She placed it on a carving platter and handed it to Ryan when she returned.

Jamie then went into the pantry to fetch plates and silverware. She brought everything over to the table as she stopped to compliment Ryan on her fire-lighting prowess. Ryan grinned up at her as she removed the plates from her arms then quickly set the table as Jamie poured the wine. When everything was set, Jamie carved the chicken, piercing a breast for Ryan and setting it on her plate. She took the other half breast for herself, knowing it wouldn't last long with her lover at the table. Ryan spooned generous helpings of mashed potatoes on each plate, and when she finished, she grasped Jamie's hand. "Thanks for making such a nice dinner. It's hard to believe that with all of your other talents you're such a good cook, too."

"I like to cook for you. It's another way of expressing my love for you." That merited her a kiss, which Ryan tenderly delivered.

They sat up and began to eat, with Ryan reverting to her usual histrionics. Jamie absolutely loved to watch her eat. It was like watching a microcosm of her entire personality. She was thorough, inventive, playful, and sensual all at once. She used all of her senses to their limits, and this caused Jamie to put extra care into both her cooking and the presentation of the meal.

To say that Ryan loved the potatoes prepared in this manner would be a significant understatement. When she had finished her first helping, she spooned another very generous portion onto her plate. Jamie hurriedly grabbed a small extra bit for herself, as she could see where the trend was headed. Ryan was working on her second leg and thigh when she smoothly moved the serving bowl next to her plate. "Saves time," she said with a grin as she began to eat directly from the bowl. When she had thoroughly cleaned the bowl, she eyed the tiny spoonful still resting on Jamie's plate. One raised eyebrow caused Jamie to relent. She scooped it up with her index finger and popped it into Ryan's mouth, receiving a sensual little suck as payment.

"You are such a delight to cook for," Ryan said appreciatively while they cleared the table. Ryan was eyeing the one remaining wing as Jamie began to toss the carcass away. "Sweetie, you'll be sick if you eat any more," she cautioned.

"Okay," Ryan agreed glumly.

"I'll make it up to you by making you a really special treat for dessert."

"What?" Ryan's eyes went wide with the thought of dessert.

"You're gonna have to wait and see. I couldn't think of eating dessert yet, and you're not going to get all of this."

"Okay, I'll wait," she agreed. "But you have to sit right there and let me clean up."

Jamie took up her post and watched Ryan methodically clean the entire kitchen. When she was finished, every utensil had been returned to its home, every bowl and plate was clean and every gleaming pot was hanging from the pot rack. They walked back to the dining area and sat down on the window seat. Ryan leaned back against the side wall of the unit with one leg raised so that her foot rested on the cushion. Jamie snuggled up between her legs with her head resting on Ryan's chest. They sipped their wine as they sat in peaceful silence for a long while.

Jamie broke the stillness when she quietly said, "I can't begin to tell you how wonderful this afternoon was."

"I didn't notice any complaints," Ryan teased. "Tell me how it felt for you."

"Well, the physical part was incomparable. I've never had more than one orgasm in a day, much less an hour," she said as she turned her head to smile at her lover. "You seemed to know my body so well. Clearly better than I do," she admitted wryly. "You knew how to touch me. It almost seemed like I was touching myself, it felt so right. But that element of surprise that you get from someone else made it obvious that it wasn't my hand." She lifted Ryan's left hand and kissed it gently, pausing a moment as she detected a lingering scent. "Is that me?"

Ryan lifted her hand up and sniffed it. Her voice turned seductive. "Nice, isn't it?"

Jamie fumbled for a response, but Ryan intercepted her. "Hey, does that embarrass you?"

"Uhm … yeah, I guess it does," she admitted. "I guess I've never smelled my scent on anyone before."

"Well I absolutely love it," Ryan intoned solemnly. "I almost didn't want to go swimming because I thought it would all get washed off. It's like I've got you with me every moment." She lifted her hand again as she moved her fingers in front of her face. "I must have done this twenty times while you were cooking dinner," she admitted.

"That's what you were doing!" Jamie laughed. "I saw you keep closing your eyes and sniffing your fingers. I didn't have a clue what you were doing!" She shyly lifted her own hand and tried the experiment. But no matter how hard she tried, she couldn't pick up Ryan's scent. "Why doesn't it work with you?"

"You didn't have your fingers in me for as long," she said softly. "But we can rectify that later."

"Oh, don't worry, Tiger. I'm gonna have your scent on me from head to toe."

Now it was Ryan's turn to gulp audibly as Jamie burst into laughter.

The fire crackled in the background, and both women stared at it for a few minutes, the silence companionable. Jamie shifted and took in a breath. "The most amazing thing about this afternoon was the way I felt inside." She searched for words for a few seconds before she continued. "I felt like I was home. Finally at home." She turned her head slightly as Ryan found her lips and painted gentle kisses on them.

"Welcome home, sweetheart," she whispered, her heart swelling with joy.

After a long while Jamie sat up and said, "Dessert?"

Ryan nodded enthusiastically, scooting off the window seat to join her partner in the kitchen. Jamie began to assemble all of her required components. A copper double boiler, various mixing bowls, graduated measures, spoons, a copper tea kettle, sugar, corn syrup and rum were soon lined up neatly. She looked around the pantry and finally found the critical ingredient—Scharffen Berger unsweetened chocolate. Passing by the refrigerator, she pulled out the sweet butter then set everything on the counter by the stove.

She handed Ryan the block of chocolate and instructed, "Use this heavy knife and shave off some chocolate. I need four ounces." She handed Ryan a precision scale and went back to preparing the rest of the ingredients. When she turned back around, Ryan was about done, but a sour look clouded her face. "You ate some, didn't you?" she asked.

Ryan wrinkled up her nose as she nodded her head. "That's like letting a baby play with a gun! You know she's gonna pull the trigger."

"I'm sorry, sweetie. I should have told you it was unsweetened."

"Blaaach," was all that Ryan could get out.

Jamie went through the process of preparing the taste treat, working quickly until it was at the boiling point. Ryan leaned over and inhaled the rich scent, looking like she was going to stick a finger in to taste it. "That's boiling hot, honey," Jamie reminded her.

"Is it ready now?" Ryan asked, looking up with hope-filled eyes.

"No, baby. We have to let it boil for nine minutes."

"Nine minutes!" Ryan cried in outrage. "I can't wait nine minutes!"

"You're gonna have to," the stern cook insisted. She picked up Ryan's hand and looked at her watch. "Tell me when it's nine o'clock. And not a minute before."

Realizing that arguing would do no good, Ryan ran hot water in the sink to clean up while they waited. At precisely nine, Jamie pulled some vanilla bean ice cream from the freezer and scooped it into bowls with an ice cream blade. She poured a tiny tablespoon of rum into the fudge and stirred it thoroughly, then spooned the fudge over the ice cream as Ryan watched from inches away. Her playful partner constantly nudged her pouring arm, and she wound up putting more sauce than ice cream in her bowl. With her first bite, Ryan moaned and groaned and generally made more noise than she had when climaxing. Her face was deep in the bowl, licking every molecule away as Jamie laughed at her. Finally she lifted her head and said seriously, "Do you mean to tell me that making the best hot fudge in the world is that easy?"

"Yep."

"Is Scharffen Berger a publicly traded company?"

"I'm not sure," Jamie replied. "Why?"

"Buy! Buy! Buy! Cause their sales are gonna skyrocket now that I know about them."

After Ryan cleaned up the few remaining dishes, they went back to the window seat. This time, Jamie reclined on her side, still nestled up between Ryan's legs. They chatted and kissed and reveled in the joy of being together.

"Babe," Ryan spoke up after a while. "I've been thinking about these earrings," she said contemplatively.

"Are you uncomfortable wearing them?"

"No, not at all, but I hate to take them from you since they have so much family meaning. Tell you what," she offered. "I'll make you a deal. I'll wear one, if you'll wear one." She fastened one perfect diamond in her lover's ear.

"I'll make you a deal back," Jamie negotiated. "Let's go have another piercing higher on our ear lobes. That way I can still wear another pair of earrings."

"Deal," Ryan said. "But are you sure you want the piercing to be in our ears? We could get a little more creative."

"I'm positive! Having my ears pierced is a stretch for me!"

After a few more minutes of slow kissing, Jamie had to stifle a yawn. Ryan laughed softly at the sight of her partner's droopy eyes. "Somebody looks tired."

Nuzzling against Ryan, Jamie nodded. "Sleepy. The day's really caught up to me."

"It'll take a few days to feel normal after the ride. You really stressed yourself."

Jamie stole a quick kiss. "Then we'd better get to bed."

"That's an idea I'll never argue with," Ryan said. They held hands and went through the house, turning off lights as they walked.

Standing in front of her dresser, Jamie asked. "Do you need anything to sleep in?"

"Just your arms," Ryan said, smiling. "Is that okay?"

"Yeah, sure. I … usually wear a T-shirt, but …"

"Whatever makes you feel comfortable," Ryan said. "I'm pretty sure I can keep you warm, but if you like clothes … no problem."

She closed the dresser drawer and turned to Ryan. "Let's see how well you keep the chill off me."

Ryan's confident smile made it clear that she knew she was up to the task. They were facing each other, and Ryan pulled at the tie on her robe, keeping her gaze on Jamie as the garment opened. "Your turn," she said, stepping closer.

Jamie looked a little hesitant, but she mirrored Ryan's actions and took in a sharp breath when Ryan's hands slid inside the open robe and pulled her close. Ryan's body was so warm and her breasts seemed even warmed than the rest of her body. They stood there for a few moments, letting their bodies acclimate to this new intimate exposure.

Maintaining her grip on Jamie's body, Ryan bent and kissed her, reveling in the softness of her lover's lips. "Let's go to bed."

Jamie pulled the sheet and blanket back and climbed in. She lay on her back and Ryan slid in and pressed up against her side, placing soft kisses upon her cheek.

"Today was … everything, Ryan. You managed to surpass all of my hopes and my dreams. Thanks for being so patient and loving with me."

Ryan gazed up at her fondly, then grasped her lover's hand and placed it on her breast. "I love you with my heart, and with my body." She pulled her head down to place a deep kiss on Jamie's parted lips, "and most of all, with my soul. Here's to the first night of our marriage. May every one be half as special."

# Chapter Six

Years of habit urged Ryan's senses to come to life just after six, and it took a moment for her to orient herself to the strange environment. The light in the room was wrong, there was no window over her head, the bed felt much more firm than normal, and the air smelled funny. The strangest sensation was that the entire front of her body was chilled while her back felt overly warm. Nevertheless, a peaceful lassitude seemed to permeate her entire being. She was lying on her right side, and her left hand slid down her body to confirm that it was cool to the touch, unclothed and uncovered. Reaching behind her, she immediately identified the source of both her external discomfort and her internal peace.

Her beloved was snuggled up against her back, their bodies touching from shoulders to toes. A turn of her head confirmed that Jamie's head shared her pillow, golden hair mussed attractively against the sweet-smelling cotton pillowcase.

As her eyes acclimated to the dim light, she realized why her chest was so cold; her greedy partner had stolen every thread of sheet and blanket during the night, and the majority of both were now lying uselessly on the left side of the bed. *How did she manage that?* Ryan smirked as she realized that only the far right edge of the covers was wrapped around her small partner. *I'm gonna have to lay down the law pretty quick on that little quirk. It's bad enough to steal them—but to steal them and toss them aside is unacceptable!*

She spent a moment reveling in the sensation of having her naked partner touching her so intimately, and then realized that she was too cold to enjoy it. So she reached across Jamie's body and tugged both sheet and blanket back to their rightful places. *Mmm, that's better*, she sighed peacefully.

A sense of warm satisfaction flowed through her body, but a tiny little voice asked if she should not be up preparing for her morning run. *Yeah, right*, she scoffed. *I'm nuts, but I'm not that nuts! Besides*, she thought righteously, *I'm sure my heart rate will be up in my training zone before the end of the day*.

That thought caused her body to slowly begin to tingle, and she allowed her hips to twitch, creating a nice little tickle where Jamie's neat blonde curls met her always-sensitive butt. *Oh yeah*, she sighed. *As soon as that little vixen opens those green eyes, we're gonna get busy!* Once her body began to anticipate the contact, her mind couldn't relax.

Taking advantage of Jamie's sound sleep pattern, she slipped out of bed, thoughtfully tucking the covers around the small body to make up for the loss of heat. She stood by the bed for a moment to make sure that her partner didn't stir, and when she was satisfied that she was still out cold, she grabbed the robe from the previous day and left the room.

*I could shower in our room, but I don't want to wake Sleeping Beauty*, she thought, walking along the long hall. *One of these doors must lead to a guest room.* The first door opened to a large closet, then, a workroom of some sort, and finally, a spacious guest room, complete with bath.

The room was fully prepared for a surprise guest—fresh towels on the gold-toned towel bars, two more folded upon the counter, bath soaps, shampoo and conditioner—all awaiting use. Ryan slid the trackless glass door open and hopped into the fully tiled enclosure, adjusting the temperature to her liking. She spent several minutes letting the warm spray invigorate her, then cleaned her body and washed her hair thoroughly, adding some conditioner as well. When she was finished, she noticed a small plastic-handled squeegee that she used to clean the water droplets from the shower doors. *I bet the maid bought those with her own money*, she smirked. *It could take a woman all week just to clean the bathrooms this place must have.*

When she emerged from the enclosure, she looked in the mirror and noticed a professional quality hair dryer on a shelf behind her head. It took a moment to figure out how to use the monster, but once she got it hooked up, she decided that she needed one for herself as soon as possible. The powerful blower removed every trace of water from her long, thick hair in just a few minutes, at least five times faster than her home unit. The force of the air had been so strong that her hair was full and straight, even with the foggy, damp air that shrouded the house. *Got to get me one of them*, she mused, but then realized, *that probably costs more than I make in a day!*

*Well*, she said to herself as she left the guest room, *I'm clean and lookin' for love, but I'd better get a little something to eat before I indulge in that pleasure.*

Making her way downstairs, she spent a few minutes reviewing the foodstuffs that Jamie had ordered. *Awww, isn't that cute? She got McCann's Irish Oatmeal for me!* She wasn't in the mood to spend twenty minutes stirring the slow-cooked oats, so she opted for a couple of bowls of corn flakes, made more interesting with the addition of fresh strawberries, a whole banana and a handful of blueberries. A glass of fresh orange juice and another of milk had her fully prepared for whatever the morning would bring, and she was about to rise from her stool when a pair of arms encircled her waist.

"Good morning." A sleepy-sounding voice floated past her ear.

"Good morning to you," Ryan responded, as she turned and kissed the adorable face that smiled up at her. "Sleep well?"

"Yeah, I suppose I slept as well as most people who've been hit on the head with an anvil," Jamie giggled. "Ooh, I shouldn't say that around you," she amended as she playfully covered her mouth with her hand. "You've probably had that happen."

"Nah, I've escaped that one, but I'm still young … give me time."

Jamie was wearing her robe from the previous day, but she hadn't yet showered. "Want some breakfast?" Ryan asked, her hand dropping to undo the tie that held the garment closed. Her questing hand slipped into the robe and tickled smooth skin as her other hand tangled in Jamie's hair and pulled her close for a kiss that carried a clear message. "Or do you need a little love before you eat?"

"Uhm …" Jamie said, stumbling a little as she stepped away from the embrace. "I uhm … I actually thought that we might get an early start and play some golf." She refastened her robe and walked to the refrigerator, removing the orange juice from the door before turning back to Ryan for a reply.

*Golf?* Ryan's brain screamed. *She wants to play golf? One day of lesbian love, and she's joining the LPGA?* She was doing her best to keep her incredulity from showing, and she must have done a decent job because Jamie calmly asked, "Is that okay?"

"Ahh, sure … whatever you want," she heard herself say. "This should be a vacation for both of us, so we should each get to do what relaxes us." *I know what relaxes me!* she grumbled to herself, but prudently decided that she needed to tread carefully with her less experienced partner.

"Well, we can do something else, if you want," Jamie said with a little hesitation in her voice. "Is there something you wanted to do today?"

"Nothing that we can't do later," Ryan replied honestly. *Okay*, she reminded herself. *She told you that she didn't like it when Jack wanted to jump on her first thing in the morning. Maybe she's just not a person who wakes up horny. You did drain her tank yesterday, you know.*

"You sure?" Jamie asked again, now sounding less sure of herself.

"Positive. Let me make you some breakfast while you get showered, okay?"

"Okay. That'd be nice. I'll call and get us a tee time, and then go get ready. You're really going to love this course," she said, her enthusiasm beginning to grow. "It's absolutely lovely."

"You're the loveliest thing I'm gonna see all week." Ryan's usual lovesick gaze settled on her lover.

"I'm never short of compliments with you around, sweetheart." Jamie smiled as she kissed her on the cheek. "Make me a third of what you had for breakfast. I'll be back in a few."

Ryan chuckled at the departing form and proceeded to fulfill her partner's request. Jamie, however, was a little slow, so a major portion of her breakfast had to be re-made since the cook had consumed it.

"You're a bottomless pit!" Jamie laughed as her partner scrambled to replace the meal.

"Hey, you drained a lot of calories from me yesterday," Ryan said with mock defensiveness.

"Yeah," Jamie agreed without elaboration. "Why don't you get dressed? I made us a seven-thirty tee time."

"Okay," Ryan said as she left the room. *Something's up with my sweetie*, she thought as she climbed the stairs. *I'll give her a little time today to talk about it, but if she doesn't,*

*I'll pry it out of her when we get home. I need to clear the air, so we can get to my favorite relaxing activity!*

Since the day was warm and dry, they had both dressed in shorts. Ryan wore the white shorts from the day before, but with a navy blue polo shirt. Jamie had found some golf clothes in her closet and she chose a pair of black and white hound's-tooth shorts with a white polo shirt. The shirt had a small band of the checked material around the edge of the collar and sleeves. After she fetched her I.D. and the key to her locker, they grabbed the spare set of clubs that Jim kept for guests and took off for the very short drive to the course.

They pulled up in front of the links with a few minutes to spare, then ran into the pro shop where Jamie was greeted warmly by one of the assistant pros. After she chatted with him for a moment, she introduced her partner. "Ryan, this is Chip Mahoney. He's my favorite pro here at the club." Chip was just a few years older than Jamie, Ryan guessed. He was very cute, in a boyish sort of way, and he seemed quite fond of Jamie. They teased each other about their games, and when Jamie told him they were set to tee off, he ran over to check the log. "Hey, Jamie," he said quietly, when he came back over. "They've got you with some hotel guests. Why don't I slide them to the next twosome, and I'll play with you?"

"I'd really like that, Chip. Is that okay with you, Ryan?"

"Sure," Ryan replied, a tiny bit disappointed to have to share her lover with another person. "As long as Chip doesn't mind playing with a rank beginner."

"Most of the people I play with are rank beginners. Not many of *them* think so, of course," he laughed. "I'd be happy to give you some tips, if you'd like. Actually, why don't I just tag along and give you a playing lesson. I want to see how Jamie's game is progressing and I can't do that if I'm playing, too."

"Sounds great to me," Ryan said. "I can use all the help I can get."

Jamie noticed that Ryan had not brought her glove, so before they left the building, she went up to the register and asked for a cadet medium in navy blue. She came back over and tossed it to Ryan, giving her a subtle little wink. Ryan grinned as she caught it and winked right back. Jamie had to run to the locker room to grab her shoes, so Ryan and Chip went out to wait by the first tee. He spent a few minutes giving her some advice on good warm up exercises. She nodded and humored him by following his advice, stretching slowly with a golf club to limber up.

"So, you're a friend of Jamie's from school?" Chip inquired, somewhat absently.

"Yeah, we met at school last September."

"Uhm … I heard that she broke up with her fiancé," he said tentatively, stealing a glance at the clubhouse door to check for Jamie. "Is that true?"

"I don't think she'd mind my confirming that," Ryan said, waiting for him to get to the point.

"Uhm … do you know if she's ahm … seeing anyone?"

Fighting her urge to insert her driver into his gullet, Ryan said, "Well, I don't generally like to talk about my friends when they aren't present, but I think you could safely say that she's seeing someone seriously. Very seriously," she added with a warning glance.

"Ahh, darn," he said as he kicked a clod of dirt. "I knew if I waited for her to come down here, she'd be taken. I should have called her in Berkeley." He looked up at Ryan with his crestfallen face. "She's really great, isn't she?"

"She's extraordinary," Ryan informed him with a confident smile, feeling a tiny bit sorry for the poor fellow, knowing that he would never have confirmation of just how extraordinary her partner was.

He stood back for a second and really looked at her, seemingly for the first time. "You look like you're in pretty good shape. Do you work out?"

"Yeah, I stay pretty active."

"So, how often have you played?"

"Jamie took me once, and I've been to the driving range about six or seven times with my brother. I played a full course three times with him, so I'd say my answer is, not very often," she laughed.

Jamie came jogging over to them as they were called to the tee. Chip watched her run over and said to Ryan, "Jamie looks like she's in really good shape, too. What're they putting in the water up in Berkeley?"

"I'm not sure, but I'm betting there's a citizen's committee being formed to stop it."

He didn't really get her joke, as his attention was focused more on Jamie than Ryan by this time. He watched her warm up with a few practice swings, finally commenting, "Did you always have those muscles?"

"Which muscles are those?" Jamie inquired innocently, batting her eyes at the compliment.

"Well, all of them," he said as he looked her up and down.

"You can give Ryan most of the credit for these babies," she said, as she flexed a bicep. "She's my trainer."

"You're a trainer?" he asked, as he turned to look at Ryan.

"Uh-huh." She nodded, narrowing her eyes at the appreciative looks he was giving her lover.

"Well, you've done a wonderful job with Jamie. She looks great," he said with altogether too much enthusiasm for Ryan's tastes.

"I'd have to say that Jamie played a small role," she commented slowly, wondering how long this assessment would continue.

They flipped a coin for honors, and when Jamie won, she placed a ball on the tee and took a practice swing. She then addressed her ball, settled her weight evenly between her feet, and pulled the club back smoothly and powerfully. She whipped the club through the hitting zone with surprising speed, driving the ball a good two hundred and seventy-five yards, drawing it slightly to the left.

"Wow!" said Chip, clearly impressed. As a smiling Jamie walked back toward him, he reached up and squeezed her bicep, shaking his head as he said enviously, "I want a trainer."

Ryan was up next, and she, too, took a few practice swings before she felt loose. She teed the ball up and set herself. Following Jamie's advice, she tried to clear extraneous thoughts from her mind, focusing only on two: the feel of sweeping the ball off the tee, and the image of Chip's head resting in place of the ball. She did just that, hitting it straight and true. She landed well back of Jamie's big drive, but she was very pleased, nonetheless. "I'm glad I'm not playing," Chip admitted. "You two would beat the pants off me!"

As Ryan got in her cart she smirked to herself. *Dream on Chip. Nobody around here is ever gonna see you with your pants off.*

Chip had his own cart, and he drove up to Ryan's ball. Hopping out, he gave her a few pointers, and both were pleased with her second shot. "Excellent, Ryan," Chip enthused. "Are you sure you're just starting?"

"Yep. Wait 'til you see me putt."

She hopped back in the cart, returning Jamie's beaming grin. "You are such a stud," Jamie giggled as they drove to her ball.

"Look who beat me by ninety yards," Ryan replied, as she playfully felt Jamie's bicep. "This reminds me," she said, giving the muscle another squeeze. "If he touches you again, will you use this to pop him one?"

Jamie turned and stared at her partner, truly amazed that her gentle kidding with Chip would upset her. "Does that make you jealous?"

Ryan's face colored a shade darker as she said, "I'm not sure. I don't think I've ever been jealous before, but if the desire to impale him on a pitching wedge is any indication, I guess I must be."

"Oh, sweetie, don't let that bother you. I just kid around with guys. I don't mean anything by it."

"I know," Ryan conceded. "It just brings up some bad feelings." Images of Jack flooded her mind, and she realized that she was far from over that hurt.

"Honey, if this bothers you, I'll plead a headache, and we'll go home right now!"

"No, no, I've got to get used to it. I'm sure every guy you know would like to have a chance at you … I might as well learn how to deal with it."

Jamie laughed warmly, amused at her lover's exaggeration. "Will it help if I tell you that I'm more attracted to you than I am to every man I've ever met—all rolled into one?"

"Ahhh, I guess so … but that's a pretty scary image," Ryan mused. "I guess it helps that I get to go home with you and see you naked … and sweaty," she said with a seductive grin. "And I've got plans to do just that."

Jamie's eye widened perceptibly at that comment, but they were nearing Chip's cart, so she patted Ryan rather primly on the leg and got out.

*Hmm, so her discomfort is about sex*, Ryan mused. *I think it's time for a sensitive chat as soon as we hit the house. Damn, I hate sensitive chats!*

Since she needed to cover only about sixty-five yards, Jamie grabbed her wedge and lofted a delicate little shot over the guarding bunkers, landing less than a foot from the hole. She turned to Ryan and gave her a little eyebrow wiggle as she got back in the cart. Chip drove by, turning to look at Jamie suspiciously as he passed.

When they reached the green, Chip helped Ryan line up and gave her some basic advice on putting. Her first effort was way too strong. The ball shot across the slick green, nearly rolling off into a bunker. "Whoops," she remarked, as she walked across the green to try again.

"Use that same stroke," Chip told her. "You're going uphill now, and you'll need all of that pace."

She bent over and concentrated, trying to remember how the previous stroke had felt. She did a reasonable job of executing, and wound up about four feet away from the hole. After Jamie told her to finish, she lipped out with her next try. Safely home with a six, Ryan was pretty pleased with her effort. Chip complimented her on her play as they watched Jamie coolly drain her short putt. She had a massive grin on her face as she admitted, "I've never birdied this hole."

"When did you play last?" Chip inquired.

"I played Olympic with my father in May," she said. "Why?"

"When did you put this muscle on?"

"Over the last six or seven months."

"You've got a whole different swing, Jamie. You're hitting the ball very crisply, and your club head speed is much greater than it used to be. Why don't you play the blue tees and really air it out?"

"Blue tees?" she gulped.

"Yeah," Chip said. "The course is designed for the blues. You're gonna have to harness your driver if you stick with the whites."

"Okay," she agreed hesitantly, "but I've only got a dozen balls on me."

"If you run out, I'll buy you more," he promised.

Ryan stuck with the white tees, but Jamie took Chip's advice and moved back. The long second hole played five hundred and two yards from the blues and only four hundred and thirty-nine from the whites. Chip advised Jamie to keep her driver in the bag and hit a three wood. "There's trouble if you go more than two hundred and thirty yards off the tee," he reminded her. She followed his suggestion and hit her drive about two hundred and twenty yards, actually holding back a little to keep the ball short of the bunker. "Boy, you have the most beautiful, natural draw," he said admiringly when she walked back to sit in his cart while Ryan hit her shot.

"Thanks. I need some work on my fade, though. It's pretty tough for me to push the ball."

"How long are you down for?"

"I go back on Saturday," she said. "Why?"

"If you come over tomorrow, I'll work with you for a while. You can tell me to mind my own business, but I think you should work on your game and try to play at Cal this spring."

"Are you nuts?" she said a little louder than she should have. Ryan soled her club and shot her a look before she got set again. "Sorry," Jamie called out, more quietly this time. "Are you nuts?" she stated again, in a quieter tone.

"No, I'm not. You've always had a great short game. Your only real problem was length and strength. It's hard to compete when your best drive is only two hundred and twenty yards. But you nailed that sucker on one, and I could see you hold back a little with your three wood. Your iron play is so much crisper than it used to be. I really think you should give it some thought. I mean," he added, "can you imagine how proud your dad would be of you?"

That brought a smile to her face as she considered the thought, silently musing that she could use all of the brownie points that she could rack up. "What time are you free tomorrow?"

While sitting in the cart waiting for Jamie to walk over to her, Ryan was rather amazed by the large numbers of people who were walking around near the course. There were access ways across the fairways and behind some of the greens, and it was obvious that the hotel was full today. People crossed their path at every available opportunity, and she found that she liked the thought of people using the course to get to their destinations. *It's way too beautiful for just a few golfers to enjoy.*

"Can I confess a sin to you?" Jamie asked shyly as they finished the next hole.

"Yes," Ryan grinned. "Especially if I can help you commit it again."

Jamie playfully slapped her leg. "Not that kind of sin, silly." She looked at Ryan rather seriously and said, "I really like being able to kick your butt at something."

"Well, then you must be in heaven," Ryan laughed. "'Cause my ass is black and blue already."

"I feel kinda bad, though. Like I shouldn't feel that way about you."

"Jamie, you're an athlete. What we *do* is compete, usually against ourselves, but also against others. It's entirely natural to want to win. Didn't you see how much pleasure I got out of dusting you going up the hills on the ride?"

"Yeah, I guess I did." she admitted. "But you know, one thing I really love about you is that you don't get down on yourself when you don't do something well. You don't get all bothered when you miss a shot."

"You haven't seen me play one of *my* games poorly," she warned. "I think your opinion of me might change a bit."

"So you do get mad when you don't play your sports well?"

"Eh, yeah," she nodded. "You could say that."

The fifth hole was one of the most spectacular settings that Ryan had ever seen. The hole rested atop the rocky cliffs of the cove. The green lay only one hundred and sixty-six yards for Jamie, and with the wind at her back she could easily have reached it with a six or a seven iron. Today, as usual, the wind was blowing directly into their faces as they stood on the tee. Ryan's sunglasses fluttered on her face as she turned her head, and her hair was blowing so wildly that she had to search for something to hold it back. Luckily Jamie had some covered rubber bands in her bag, and Ryan dug one out as Jamie consulted Chip about club selection.

"Well, I'd say it's playing a good two hundred five today," he shouted over the wind and the surf. They agreed that Jamie should use a three iron and try to keep it low. She hit a ball that bored right through the wind and landed on the left center of the green, where it slowly rolled down toward the cup, which had providentially been placed on the lower right edge of the green. She turned and gave Chip a quick hug for his advice. He looked a little flustered, but recovered enough to give her a big smile as she pulled away. *She's gotta watch that*, Ryan thought as she watched Chip's reaction. *She doesn't know the power of those hugs.*

Ryan also played an iron, winding up in the right front bunker. This time Chip went in with her and showed her exactly what to do by hitting a few balls out himself. Ryan watched intently, while Jamie looked on, smiling at the way Ryan unconsciously imitated Chip as he was performing the motions. When it was her turn, she did a much better job than the previous time, beaming with pride as she softly landed the ball on the green after only one try. But the hazards of bunker play on Pebble Beach were made abundantly clear to her as she received a face full of sand on her follow through. She spat and rubbed her eyes and removed the band from her hair to shake out as much sand as possible. Jamie was still laughing when her partner finally jogged over to the cart. "I don't get this sandy when I play beach volleyball!"

"Aw … you looked so cute standing over there spitting. I think that's the first time I've ever seen you do that."

"You can mark that down in your diary later, you hopeless romantic," Ryan said with a laugh.

The eighth hole always gave Jamie fits. It was a magnificent hole, but she had always had trouble getting the distance she needed. She usually played for bogey and hoped for the best. Feeling bold and confident today, she decided to go for it. She hit a nice two hundred and fifty-yard drive, positioning it in line with the aiming rock in the distance. Her lie afforded her a fabulous view of a deep chasm, an enticing, watery graveyard for thousands of errant balls. She knew that staying away from the chasm wasn't her only difficulty, however. The next big problem was that the green was absolutely tiny, nearly postage stamp size. She had one hundred and eighty-five yards left, and she chose to go with a four iron, hoping to hit it low and drive it hard into the green. Chip drove by and suggested that she play it safe. "Play left and hope for a great putt, Jamie. I don't think you can knock down a four iron in this wind." He left her to drive closer to the green to watch the balls land in case of trouble. As Jamie walked back to her clubs, Ryan could see the conflicting emotions playing across her face.

"What's wrong, babe?"

"I wanna go for it, but I don't wanna be stupid."

"What'll it cost you if you go in the drink?"

"Two strokes and a ball."

"What'll it cost you if you don't try something that you think you can do because you're afraid?"

Jamie looked at her with appreciation in her eyes. "Thanks." She nodded as she took her four iron and struck it stiff. The ball stayed low and came to rest serenely on the lower tier of the green. She was still a good twenty-five feet away, but the shot had greatly increased her confidence. "So, you're a good golf coach, too?" she asked with a beaming grin.

"Nope. I just understand momentum and confidence levels. I say, play bold until you lose it."

It took Jamie two putts to bring the ball home, but she was intensely pleased with herself for taking a risk. Chip didn't say much, but she could tell he was impressed also.

After they finished nine, they passed a snack bar and stopped to buy some treats. Ryan bought three candy bars and a big bottle of Gatorade, while Jamie decided on a bag of pretzels and some water. They packed their goodies in the cart and took off again moments later.

As they stood on the tenth tee, Jamie marveled at the fact that she was still two under par. She felt absolutely fabulous: strong, fit, well rested and well loved. She didn't recall ever feeling better. She smiled over at Ryan, "I feel so totally good. Is this what being in love does to you?"

"So it would seem," Ryan replied with a chuckle.

They made their way around the course quickly, and Chip complimented Ryan repeatedly on how rapidly she played. Driving up to the seventeenth hole after another compliment, Ryan muttered, "That sounds like when I compliment someone at the gym on how well she's breathing. That's what you say when you've got nothing else good to say."

Jamie patted her leg reassuringly. "This doesn't happen to you very often, does it?"

Ryan knew what she meant, and she had to admit that she was being a baby about the experience. "I don't like doing things I'm not good at," she agreed a little sheepishly.

"And it doesn't happen very often, does it? Hmm? Come on, Tiger, tell the truth."

Ryan blushed deeply, suddenly finding the snap on her golf glove to be very interesting. "No. It doesn't."

"I don't know if this'll reassure you, but golf is one sport where success only comes from long hours of practice. I know you could be quite a decent golfer if we play once in a while, but to be really good you'd have to dedicate yourself to it."

"No, thanks," Ryan said quickly. "I like it, and I like doing something active with you, but I wouldn't give up anything else to do this."

"Agreed," Jamie said. She gave Ryan a shy smile and admitted, "I kinda hoped you didn't like it that much, to be honest. I really want to be better than you at something."

"Oh, sweetie! You're better than I am at lots of things! You're clearly a better golfer, you're a better cook, and even though I haven't read your stuff, I'm sure you're a better writer, yo ..."

Jamie patted her leg as they neared Chip's cart. "Thanks, hon. Just a momentary insecurity attack. All better."

Ryan leaned over and whispered, "You're better at making love to me than I am." Jamie's eyes became so wide at that comment that even Chip noticed.

"Hey, Jamie, are you okay?"

"Fine. Just fine," she said as airily as possible. As she exited the cart, she gave her partner a pinch and jumped out before even Ryan's quick reflexes could allow her to retaliate.

The seventeenth and eighteenth holes at Pebble Beach are two of the most stunning finishing holes in all of golf. When they stood on the eighteenth tee, they looked down the cove edge that ran all the way along the fairway. Two beautiful cypress trees waited near the landing area, and The Lodge beckoned in the distance. Waves crashed violently over the walls of the cove, and gulls cried out loudly, trying to be heard over the thundering surf. The hole was made for Jamie's natural action. Putting every ounce of her power into ripping a drive down the left side of the fairway, she was astounded when she drove to the ball and saw that it had landed almost two hundred and ninety yards from the tee. She pulled her three wood from her bag with such an intense look of determination spreading over her face that Ryan had to stifle the urge to laugh. Jamie gave the three wood all she had, and it traveled a good two hundred and forty yards, leaving her just a wedge to the green. She strode back to the cart with a deeply satisfied grin on her face.

Ryan matched her infectious grin, completely forgetting about her own struggles on this beautiful hole. She loved seeing her partner so full of confidence. After she finally reached the green herself, she watched as Jamie shut out all distractions to concentrate on her putt. She was lying about eight feet from the hole, and she looked at the putt from every angle, getting down on her haunches three times to eye it from all perspectives. Ryan was surprised with how she finally chose to approach the ball. It looked like she was aimed all wrong, but she kept her mouth firmly shut. Jamie drew the club back and smoothly rolled the ball directly into the hole. She let out a *whoop* and thrust her right arm into the air in exultation. Ryan went over and high-fived her, and Chip called out a compliment as well. After Ryan holed out, they drove the short distance to The Lodge, where Jamie offered to buy lunch for all of them. Chip couldn't stay, since he had a twelve-thirty lesson, so he bid goodbye to Ryan, again mentioning her quick play. "Now don't forget our date tomorrow," he said to Jamie with a very friendly smile.

"Oh, I won't."

"I could make room for you on Thursday and Friday, too," Chip added, turning to leave.

Jamie started to walk toward the grill, but she turned when she noticed Ryan was not with her. A dark look had come over the normally smiling face, and Jamie scampered back to see what the problem was.

Ryan's hands were shoved in her pockets, and she rocked back and forth as much as her cleated shoes allowed. Jamie knew these were obvious signs of upset, so she placed her hand on her arm and guided her back outside where they could speak privately.

"What's wrong, honey?" she asked quietly.

"Date," was the only word that came from Ryan's pursed lips.

"Date?" Jamie was at a loss, wracking her brain trying to decipher this code.

"Chip said you have a date tomorrow." The words came out crisp and clipped.

"Oh!" Jamie relaxed and laughed, finding it rather funny that Ryan would take the statement in that way. "We're just having a lesson tomorrow, babe. I can't believe you'd think I would date him, or anyone else!"

To her surprise, this information did not brighten Ryan's mood. Her face was still set and unyielding, her posture rigid. "I was under the impression that this was our honeymoon," she said, enunciating each word. "I don't think I would have signed up for the trip if I knew it included the golf package." With that, she strode back into The Lodge and made her way to the ladies' lounge.

Jamie resisted the powerful urge to follow her partner. She knew that Ryan tended to get angry, blow off some steam and was then able to have a rational discussion, so she decided to stay outside and wait her out, hoping that the storm would pass quickly.

*Four days. We have four full days for our honeymoon. We could have had seven, but no. We had to stay at Mia's, we had to do laundry before we came down here, and she has to go to Jack's—goddamned Jack's*, she quickly amended—*graduation. Fine ... just fine.*

Taking the band from her hair, Ryan used one of the provided brushes to remove as much sand from her hair as possible. She was yanking the brush through her locks so forcefully that a dark halo of statically charged hair floated around her head. Wetting her hands, she smoothed the flyaway hair into place and splashed some cold water on her face.

Still steaming, she grabbed one of the thin washcloths and used it to thoroughly clean her face and neck. As the suds slid down the drain, so did much of her pique.

*You wanted to stop and see Mia, too, ya big dope. And it was you who wanted to do laundry.* She folded her arms across her chest, staring at herself in the mirror. *Jamie offered to skip Mia's and come directly down here, so don't act like this is all her fault.*

Narrowing her eyes at herself, she added, *She asked you if you minded if she went to goddamned Jack's graduation. If you were going to pitch a bitch, you should have done it then. It's childish to agree to everything, and then cry about it.*

Her lids fluttered closed as she took in a deep breath, then let it out in a controlled stream. *Face it. You're pissed because she didn't want to make love this morning. You thought you'd be horizontal the whole time, but she obviously has other plans.*

Her eyes opened just enough for her to catch the amused grin that was tugging at her lips. *Married life is all about communication and compromise—now get out there and start compromising.*

It took about ten minutes for Ryan to reappear, and Jamie fought with herself as each minute ticked away. She was just about to go find her when Ryan came back out. To Jamie's experienced eye, her partner looked much more like her normal self. Her gait was easy and fluid, and her eyes once again were able to meet Jamie's.

"I'm sorry," she said quietly, coming up alongside. Jamie was leaning against the wooden railing that surrounded the clubhouse, and Ryan imitated her posture.

They looked out on the course together for a few moments, until Jamie finally spoke. "I'm sorry I didn't ask you if you minded if I took a lesson tomorrow. That was thoughtless of me, and I'm gonna cancel when we go by the pro shop."

"No." Ryan placed her hand on Jamie's arm and squeezed it lightly. "I was acting immaturely. If you want to do that, I want you to do it."

"Can we go inside and have a bite to eat?" she asked, knowing that Ryan had to be starving.

"Sure."

They were escorted to a nice table with a view of the eighteenth fairway and green. After they ordered, Ryan sat back and considered how to approach the issue. A few moments of thought, and she jumped in. "I guess I don't understand why you want to take golf lessons at all, much less on our honeymoon. I mean, it's not like you're not good enough already."

"Thanks," Jamie smiled, deciding to take her compliments as she found them. "I'm sure it seems that way, but there are some big flaws in my game. Chip thinks I've really improved, and he wants to work with me a little bit to develop a better fade. I like to work with him, and he's available, and I guess I just wasn't thinking." She started to reach for Ryan's hand, but remembered where they were and drew back. "I shouldn't have been making any plans without consulting you. I'm gonna cancel."

"No, no, no," Ryan insisted. "I'm clueless about this, but I want to understand. Why do you want to improve your game?"

"Well he thinks, and I stress the 'he', that I could maybe play for Cal this year," she said with an embarrassed smirk.

"Is that something you'd like to do?" Ryan asked.

"I think I would," she admitted. "I really didn't want to stop playing after high school, but I wasn't able to keep up with the guys by my senior year, so I didn't even try when I first got to Berkeley."

"Why was it important that you couldn't keep up with the guys? Didn't you compete against other girls' teams?"

"I wasn't on the girls' team," she said with a twinkle.

"You were on the boys' team?"

"Yeah, my school didn't offer golf for girls, so I played my butt off to finally make the team. I worked at it so hard—I was a maniac. I had calluses on my hands so thick, I looked like a lumberjack," she laughed. "My mother thought I was insane, but Daddy was so proud of me."

"But you liked it for you, too, right?"

"Yeah. I did it for me too. I really like to play, and I'm pretty good at it. I like the fact that you compete mostly against the course; there aren't any judges to make subjective decisions. I also like having to be mentally tough to accomplish something."

"Wow," Ryan muttered, "this never crossed my mind."

"I won't do it if you don't want me to, babe." Jamie tilted her head to make eye contact with her partner.

Ryan fixed her gaze and sat still for a minute, formulating her response. "Is Chip the right guy to give you this advice?"

Jamie nodded confidently. "He's known me for a few years, and I like his teaching style a lot. I don't think he'd lie to me."

"Then I think you should do it. You've only got a year of school left, so it's now or never. I think you'd regret not having tried."

"Thanks for understanding," Jamie said, now giving in to her need and tracing her finger down Ryan's hand. "It means a lot to me to have your support."

"I do support you, Jamie. I'm sure you can do this, if it's something you really want."

"Maybe." The smaller woman was not as convinced at her partner seemed to be, but she was willing to give it a shot. "I'll work with him for a while tomorrow, but I promise not to commit to any more time without talking to you first."

"Agreed," Ryan smiled, feeling fairly normal again.

"I really enjoyed having the AIDS Ride as a goal," Jamie mused. "I feel like I need a new goal now that it's over."

"That's a good point," Ryan smiled. "I might need to reassess my goals too."

"What do you mean?"

"You'll have to wait and see, cupcake," she said with a grin as their food was delivered.

# Chapter Seven

When they arrived home, Ryan immediately got into the shower to remove the sand that had hidden itself beneath her clothing. She emerged a few minutes later, hoping to find Jamie in bed, but no such luck. Tugging on a bright yellow nylon tank top and a pair of blue and white print running shorts, Ryan went in search of her partner.

A thorough scan of the house failed to locate her, so the dark-haired detective walked out the back door to search the grounds. She stood outside of the door and scratched her head for a moment, thinking that the grounds were large enough to make her task rather monumental. "Jamie," she called, in a slightly raised voice. Hearing no response, she started to walk around the building. Both outdoor patios were vacant, so she jogged down to the pool house, which also failed to pay off. Trying her voice again, she yelled, "*Jamie!*"

That did the trick as she heard a faint, "Up here, honey."

"Up where?"

"Up here," her elusive partner replied, shedding absolutely no light on the matter. Ryan looked around again, starting at ground level. The house was set back on the lot with a large expanse of lawn that led to the fabulous view of the ocean over a high cliff. The pool house was at a forty-five-degree angle to the house, fairly close to the cliff. Near the house, almost directly across from the pool house, she noted a possible hiding place. Built into a tall, gnarled cypress was an elegant little tree house. It was unlike any such structure she'd ever seen, which didn't surprise her in the least, given that the Evans family was unlike any she'd ever known. The house was sturdily built out of wood with real casement windows and a little Dutch door. The roof was shingled in shake and weathered a dull gray; the outside walls were clapboard and painted a complementary dove gray. The properly scaled casement windows were open, and the top half of the door was also propped open.

As Ryan walked under the tree house, she spotted the means of access—small rungs nailed to the tree at about nine inch increments. One had to climb around the circumference of the tree to reach the door, obviously so that a small child could maneuver up the height, but she managed it easily, even with her rather large feet.

She poked her head over the closed bottom door to see her lover, clad in madras plaid cotton boxers and a sky blue T-shirt. "Hey, little girl," Ryan said seductively. "Can I come over and play?"

Jamie regarded her pink face for a moment. "That depends," she answered quietly. "Do you play nice?"

"I haven't had many complaints. But I'd be happy to let you choose the games we play."

"Okay, come on in."

Ryan grinned as she clambered over the closed door. She sat down on the floor, imitating Jamie's posture and looked quizzically at her partner. Jamie didn't seem to be in the mood to explain herself, and it seemed that she was feeling uncomfortable again. Ryan was determined to draw her out, so she commented, "I bet you spent a lot of time up here as a kid."

A small smile lit Jamie's features as she recalled, "Yeah. It was one place that was my own. I could come up here with my dolls and toys or a book, and while away the afternoon."

"You know, it's funny," Ryan said. "I'd guess that I didn't have an entire afternoon to myself … well … ever. I mean, I guess I could have, once I was in college and the boys were working, but I was usually working or going to class. Being down here has made it clearer to me how differently we were raised." She kept a careful eye out for her partner's reaction to her next statement. "I think we're both going to have to make some adjustments."

"Like what?" Jamie asked, looking interested.

"Like having a need for quiet time, or alone time … those kinds of things. I'd guess that you need time alone every day, don't you?"

"Yeah, I guess I do," Jamie said thoughtfully. "I haven't thought about it much, but I am used to having time to reflect and write a little every day. I haven't been doing that much for the last few months, and I miss it a little bit. What about you?"

"I get my alone time in the morning, when I run. That time is pretty precious for me, you know."

"I'm not sure I knew that," Jamie said. "But it makes sense."

"Yeah, it lets me work out problems and plan my day. I've missed it a little in the last couple of weeks."

"I guess we have upset each other's schedules," Jamie mused. "How do we get back to them?"

"Let's start now," Ryan suggested. "I'm nearly dressed for a run. Let me go on a nice long jog along the water, and you can spend some time up here in your little house."

"You don't think my house is silly, do you?" she asked with an embarrassed laugh.

"Not at all. Any place that allows you to get in touch with your young self is a good place. I do some of my best thinking playing on a playground."

"Now that I'd like to see," Jamie mused, with a grin on her face.

"Well, they're hardly any fun since they took out all the jungle gyms. Darned personal injury lawsuits."

"Yeah, well, it was kids like you that caused all of those lawsuits, Buffy. Now get a move on, and come get me when you're done."

"Will do," Ryan promised, as she leaned forward for a kiss.

"Be careful on the road," Jamie warned. "It's clear now, but the fog can come in quickly."

After Ryan had limbered up, she took off down the driveway, let herself out the small door in the large gate, and began to jog at a slow pace. There was a fairly steady stream of cars on the Seventeen Mile Drive, but the sound of the traffic was barely noticeable with the pounding of the surf in the background.

*If she has some time alone, she might be able to snap out of her mood on her own. I'll see how she seems when I get back, and if she's still standoffish I'll try a more direct approach.*

She paid more attention to the pavement than the scenery, but she was aware of passing many beautiful estates as well as some more modest homes. *Trashy little million dollar bungalows*, she thought with a snicker, as she allowed herself to reflect on the tremendous wealth that Jamie's mother must have. *I'm not sure I was prepared for all of this*, she thought. *I hate to admit it, but I think Jamie's right—we're gonna have some issues about this. I hope I can be as easygoing about it as her father is. I wonder how he'd feel if he were in my position, though. I've got about twenty-five thousand bucks to my name, which is more than I ever thought I'd have, but I'll probably be in school for at least three more years. If I go to grad school, I might have a hard time working enough to be able to pay my own way, and I don't have any idea how we'll balance things so I don't feel like I'm being kept.*

She turned a corner and came upon a clear view of the majestic Pacific as the sun peeked out from a large cloud. *My God!* she thought, as she skidded to an abrupt halt. *No wonder the rich people live here*. The dark sea crashed violently against the massive rocks that lined this section of coast. The rugged shore precluded any type of beach, and no one with a lick of sense dared go out onto the rocks. Ironically, these multi-million dollar homes had absolutely no access to the sea, though it was so very close. She took off again, surveying the homes she passed. She admired the way that most of the homes snuggled in amongst the trees, trying to achieve a natural look. The homes were, for the most part, large and rambling, but they really were not overly grand. Even Jamie's home, while as large as any she'd seen, was quite tasteful. It was set back far enough from the street, and was covered in enough mature landscaping, that it really did fit in to the more natural theme of the neighborhood.

She had reached the guard station at the end of Seventeen Mile Drive, and since she had no identification with her, she thought it prudent to turn around rather than exit the compound. Crossing the street and running back up the other side of the drive, she stopped once again to gaze at the fabulous view for a few moments. Sea birds of all sizes and shapes were busily looking for food, their calls and songs just barely audible over the intense thrumming of the waves as they crashed against the cliffs.

She started up again, spending a few minutes saying her usual morning prayers of thanksgiving. *Little late for the morning prayers,* she gently chided herself. She realized with a laugh that she had so much more to be thankful for since Jamie came into her life that her prayers were taking up a lot more time. *Small price to pay*, she thought happily as she sped along the lovely drive. She thought about her mother and tried to imagine what she would think of Jamie. She was absolutely certain that her mother would love her, but she realistically assumed that there might be a little tension between them. Even though her memories of her mother were few, she had heard enough from her father and the boys to know how fiercely protective the small auburn-haired woman had been of her children. *I think it would have been hard for her to let me go*, she mused. *I can't imagine that mothers don't have mixed feelings when their kids give their hearts to someone. And boy, mine is gone for good*, she thought. She lifted her hand to touch the earring that Jamie had given her. *This was so sweet*, she thought. *I should have known that she'd figure out some way to make our honeymoon even more special.* A more practical matter shot through her mind as she mused, *I'd better make sure she has these insured.* Even as she considered that thought, she had to admit that the monetary value on the earrings was not the important issue. Just like her mother's wedding band, the sentimental value would be forever lost, no matter how much insurance money was received to pay for their replacements.

As she drew near the house, she debated as to whether she should go further or stop. It had been fifty minutes, and she knew she'd only done about seven miles, but she really wanted to go figure out what was going on with Jamie. She let her desires overtake her discipline, deciding that her honeymoon was more important than her fitness. After she punched in the code, the gate swung open and she trotted down the drive, taking in all of the beautiful plants and trees that graced the path. Looking up at the house, she wondered how many bedrooms it held. *I hardly got a chance to see much of the place*, she mused. *Oh well, what we did yesterday was a lot more fulfilling than looking at decorating schemes.*

She took a detour into the pool house and used a towel to remove most of the sweat from her body, then jogged over to the tree house. "Anybody home?" she asked.

"Come on up, love," Jamie called down.

Ryan hung her torso over the half-open door and said, "Do you welcome stinky guests?"

"I'd welcome you if you were covered in … well … anything," she decided. "You always perk up my day."

"Part of the job description," Ryan assured her as she climbed in. "Friend, lover, confidante, perker-upper."

"You do very well at all of them."

"Thanks, babe." Ryan placed her hand on Jamie's thigh, but the small twitch that greeted her touch was not the reaction she was hoping for. She decided to be a little more direct, and see if she could make some progress with her obviously uncomfortable lover.

"You know," Ryan said thoughtfully, "I think I need a confidante today. You in the mood?"

"Of course, honey, what's wrong?"

"It's not a huge thing. I wanted to talk about yesterday a little bit. Is that okay?"

"Sure … of course it is," Jamie said, looking like it was far from okay. "Tell me what's on your mind."

Ryan lay flat on her back and placed her feet on the floor, drawing her knees up in the process. She stared at the ceiling of the house, and was briefly distracted when she noticed that there were no cobwebs or other signs of insect activity. *God, don't tell me they make the maid come clean this place, too!* Mentally shaking her head, she forced herself to focus and began, "I want to talk about how yesterday felt for me."

"Okay," Jamie said, her voice now even quieter.

"I … I was a little surprised at how powerful my feelings were," Ryan said carefully. "I mean, I knew it would be intense, but I wasn't prepared for how overwhelming the emotions were." She turned her head and made eye contact with her partner. "Do you know what I mean?"

"Yeah, I do," Jamie replied, her voice no more than a whisper.

Looking at the ceiling again, Ryan continued, "I've had some great sexual experiences. None as great as yesterday, of course, but great, nonetheless. The thing is, I've never had sex with someone who loves me like you do, and it was pretty trippy."

"Trippy?"

"I've never felt that … exposed," Ryan decided. "I think that's the word. I felt like I'd been stripped naked emotionally." She turned again and locked eyes with her partner. "I actually feel a little bruised today … does that make sense?"

The relief that flooded Jamie's face was obvious as she nodded her head vigorously. "Yes, yes, that's it! I feel raw and exposed today. Like I let you see too much!"

"Yeah," Ryan said, "That's a good way to put it. It's like we each revealed ourselves so much, that it's a little scary to be vulnerable again."

"That's it exactly," Jamie agreed. "I feel kinda shy around you."

"Me too," Ryan said, lying just a little. "How do you think we can get over it?"

Jamie pondered the question for a moment before coming up with a suggestion. "Maybe we need to pull back a little. You know … act like we had been before yesterday."

"Okay," Ryan drawled, inwardly cringing, and feeling angry with herself for trying to play psychologist. "Do you still want to sleep together?" Her stomach clenched, hoping that Jamie didn't want to pull back that far.

"Oh, of course! I need to sleep with you."

"Okay." Slightly relieved, Ryan pasted on a smile and rocked a bit, trying to figure out a way into her partner's mind. "How about kissing? Do you still want to do that?"

A broad smile answered that query. "Always."

Ryan rolled over and got to her hands and knees, crawling to her partner like a puppy. Tilting her head, she placed a light kiss on Jamie's still-smiling lips. "Did that feel okay?"

"Of course. That's what we're used to. You can go a little further if you'd like, though. We weren't that sororal before."

"Good point," Ryan said, as she sat down and scooted next to her partner. "Refresh my memory," she requested, sitting patiently with an impish grin on her face.

Jamie smiled back at her, then did as requested. She leaned in and slid her hand behind Ryan's neck, tickling the damp skin as she did so. Pulling the grinning face forward a few inches, she placed a few light, but slightly hot, kisses on Ryan's mouth. "Thusly," she declared smugly, sitting up when she finished.

"Oh, I remember now," Ryan said slowly. "You have very good powers of recall."

"Uh-huh," Jamie smirked, getting the idea that she was being set up, but minding not a whit. "Do you wanna try it yourself, or do you still need help?"

Ryan scratched her head. "I'm not sure I have it yet. Maybe one more try."

"Glad to oblige." Jamie repeated the demonstration, but this time the lesson lasted a bit longer than the previous one, and Ryan was seeing stars when she pulled away.

"Woo," she breathed. "I'm amazed that I didn't remember that."

"Well, you are a little slow," Jamie reminded her. "But you have other attributes that make up for it." The dangerous right eyebrow twitched saucily, asking for specifics. "Hmm, these are very, very nice." Jamie trailed the tips of her fingers down Ryan's muscled shoulders. "And you're quite pretty in some lights." She tried hard to hold back a giggle. "You're a decent kisser, too," she added as an afterthought.

"Would you like a demonstration?" the deep voice, now filled with desire, asked.

"If you want to," Jamie said, acting as though she could take it or leave it.

"You don't mind a little perspiration, do you?"

Jamie filled her lungs as a blissful smile crossed her face. "It's positively mouth-watering." Ryan's body glowed with a thin sheen of sweat and, much to her surprise, Jamie found the scent heady in the extreme. The aroma reminded her of freshly turned topsoil, all rich and earthy, and she decided that she was overly fond of it.

Grasping Jamie's face with both of her hands, Ryan delicately nibbled on her lips, teasing every bit of skin until the pink flesh tingled with sensation. Her tongue traced all around the coral-tinted lips, causing Jamie's mouth to slowly open to receive more of the tantalizing caress. Ryan took a deep breath, trying to fill her lungs with her partner's sweet scent, then she let her tongue deliberately explore. In moments, Jamie was hungrily sucking on the deep pink visitor, pulling it into her hot mouth with unbridled lust.

Both women began to breathe heavily as their mouths ground together, and before she knew it, Jamie's hands were tugging at Ryan's tank, trying to remove it from her body while their mouths were still joined. Ryan pulled away woozily and choked out, "Are you sure? This feels pretty intima—"

Her question was cut off as Jamie grabbed the top and yanked hard, tearing it from Ryan's body in one move. The wet sports bra was next, and Ryan let out a yelp as the tight garment was drawn over her breasts, but her cries were effectively silenced when Jamie hurled her body at Ryan's, taking her down onto her back with a thud.

*Oh, boy*, Ryan's mind raced. *Now what do I do? If we have sex now, I'm afraid she'll be uncomfortable later. But if I tell her to slow down, I'm still serving as a member of the sex police, and I don't want to do that anymore. Shit*, she mused. *This could have some unpleasant ramifications later, but I think I've gotta risk it. Besides, it feels fan-fucking-tastic!*

The little dynamo pulled away slightly and sat up just enough to be able to pull her oversized T-shirt from her body. Lowering herself again, she paused just inches above her lover's supine body and started to move, gliding her breasts against Ryan's, reveling in the feel of their sweat-slicked skin sliding sensually against each other.

Ryan's head was tilted back so far that her eyes were gazing vacantly at the wall behind her head, her dark hair splayed attractively against the worn floorboards. "Oh, God," she moaned, her chest rising as she took in a breath. "Feels so good."

Jamie's head was resting back against her shoulders, her eyes aimed at the ceiling. She moved slowly, deliberately, and her pace was unwavering. Her nipples were so rigid that they occasionally caught on Ryan's equally firm points, and the resulting tugs made her grind her teeth in pleasure.

Suddenly, she needed to see all of Ryan, so she lowered her body and rolled off her partner. Grasping the print shorts, she tugged them gently off her lover's body and tossed them into the corner. The running shoes and short, thin socks were next, and Jamie's own madras shorts soon joined these items. As the shorts came off, Jamie felt the knot in her stomach once again. She took a deep breath and tried to reassure herself, running her hands over Ryan's body while she repeated the calming mantra. *This is just you and Ryan, loving each other. There's nothing to be scared about.* Looking down at her partner, Jamie saw nothing but love and support and desire reflected back in those deep blue eyes, and the anxiety began to lessen. *You can do this. Touch her like you like to be touched. Watch her reactions. Her body's telling you everything you need to know.* As her hands continued to move, Ryan's actions gave credence to her thoughts.

Her loving gaze was unwavering, and Jamie felt like she could peer right into her partner's soul. The large, warm hands covered hers, silently supporting, but never directing. As Jamie's hands began to roam once again, Ryan's eyes fluttered closed, seemingly involuntarily. She seemed to struggle to open them again, and Jamie realized that she was much more confident when their eyes were locked upon one another. Her touch became bolder, more assured, and she felt her excitement begin to build once again.

Climbing astride her partner, Jamie's soft blonde curls left a slick trail down Ryan's belly as she thrust her hips gently against the softly moaning woman. Sliding farther down, she captured a firm pink nipple, raking her teeth over the tender flesh as Ryan grasped her head with both hands in an automatic gesture. The dark-haired woman didn't guide the warm mouth that hovered over her—instead she offered the gesture to encourage Jamie, in essence showing her that her efforts were being very well received.

The support that she felt from Ryan allowed Jamie to assert control, and in no time she seemed comfortable once again. Her newfound confidence allowed her to experiment. She switched back and forth between the nipples, driving Ryan nearly mad with the sensation coursing through her breasts. Ryan felt every sharp nip shoot like a laser right between her legs, her thighs compressing rhythmically to enhance the feeling.

Ryan's head was lolling on the floor, her moans and whimpers driving Jamie to increase the ferocity of her attack. She drew each breast into her mouth, pulling on the tender flesh with firm suction.

Ryan couldn't stand much more teasing. Her moans slowly became words that caused Jamie's heart to race in response. "Touch me," she gasped out. "Please, baby, please touch me!"

Taking pity on the moaning woman, Jamie moved her hand between Ryan's legs and gasped as her hand nearly slid off the drenched flesh. "So hot," she breathed right into Ryan's ear. "So wet."

A shiver that ran from the back of Ryan's head all the way to her toes accompanied a tiny head nod. Her voice was weak and wavered a bit, but she managed to gasp out, "Please."

Felling a stab of uncertainly, Jamie sought her lover's assistance. "Show me, sweetheart. Show me how you like to be touched."

Ryan's hand flew between her legs and slid into her own wetness just as Jamie's had. Their hands worked together, teasing the soft skin simultaneously. In a matter of minutes, Jamie could feel her partner getting close as her breathing started to become labored, and before she knew it, Ryan was crying out loudly, startling the birds that had been peacefully nibbling from the birdfeeder attached to the side of the tree house. With the fluttering of the birds' wings in the background, Ryan's spasms began to still, until she was able to regain control of her body.

"You frightened the wildlife." Jamie giggled as Ryan nestled cozily in her arms.

"You've turned me into a noisy comer," she drawled lazily as her body tried to calm itself.

"We'll have to make sure the children's bedrooms aren't too close to ours," she decided. "I don't want them to think I'm hurting you."

"That's sweet to think about." Ryan sighed as she pondered the future. "Maybe we can tell them that we lift weights in the bedroom."

"Well, we'd better have a lot of iron in there with the grunts you make, Buffy."

"Oh, and you're just the demure little thing, aren't you?" Ryan teased, as she rolled onto her side and supported her head with her braced hand.

"Uhm … I don't know," Jamie replied, with a tiny flush creeping up her cheeks.

"Let's find out," Ryan growled.

Without hesitation, Ryan got to her knees and, grabbing Jamie around the hips, easily lifted her up so that her legs wrapped around Ryan's waist. She softly placed her on her back with her legs still tightly grasping Ryan. Jamie's open lust and obvious need propelled Ryan to be more forceful and decisive than she had been so far in their lovemaking while still remaining mindful of Jamie's earlier unease. It dawned on Ryan, as she covered her partner's small form with her still-damp body, that Jamie didn't seem reluctant to be sexual. It actually seemed that it was the intimacy that had frightened her. This thought allowed Ryan to unleash some of her control and show her partner a glimpse of her lust.

She glided over her slowly, hissing out a pleasured "yes" as she closed her eyes tightly to soak up the sensation. The layer of sweat provided slick lubrication allowing their bodies to slide smoothly against one another. Ryan's mouth was locked onto Jamie's, her tongue probing the sweet cavity in a slow, thorough manner.

Ryan felt her desire as a pulsing need deep in her belly. Without thought, she gathered her lover up in her arms, unable to resist the need to hold her tightly. Her body needed sensation, and as a low growl sprang from her chest, her partner held on even tighter and tried to toss Ryan onto her back. Ryan's innate need for control reasserted itself, and the two sweating bodies began to roll over and over again, fighting for dominance. Tumbling across the floor, they clung to each other with a passion-fueled intensity.

As their bodies crashed loudly into the wall, Jamie wound up on top. Taking a deep breath, Ryan calmed her dominant side and allowed her partner to test her own assertiveness. Gazing up at the flushed face that stared at her with a mixture of lust and devotion, Ryan's hands roved all over her lithe body, teasing, taunting, gripping, grasping, pinching and pulling. She opened her hands and rubbed her palms over Jamie's firm breasts, increasing the pressure when the smaller woman urged her on with small thrusts towards her. She closed her fingers over each breast, grinding them rather roughly against her body. Jamie reacted strongly, thrusting into her with her hips, tossing her head from side to side. She arched her back and pushed strongly against Ryan's hands, demanding more.

Ryan slid her arms around her partner's waist when she sat up. Looking deep into her eyes, she slowly tilted her head and began another tender assault on Jamie's desire-swollen lips. Ryan tried to convey every one of her dueling emotions with her lips and tongue. The need to toss her partner onto her back and take her was pulsing through her body, but she resisted the urge.

Without a word being spoken, Jamie seemed to sense the warring impulses thrumming in her lover's body. With a gentle, inviting smile, she lowered her body to the floor and held her arms out in invitation.

With a smile bright enough to light the tree house, Ryan dropped down to meet her partner's slightly open mouth. Her desire began to spiral out of control again, and she rolled onto her side, trying to force her mind to work. Deciding that she could focus better without the constant temptation of Jamie's luscious lips, she slowly turned her onto her belly. Grasping her around the waist, she pulled her up so that she was on her hands and knees. Ryan imitated her position, placing herself above, but slightly to the left of her partner, with her right knee between Jamie's. Her longer arms and legs allowed her to rub slowly over her lover's sensitive back, and Jamie gasped at the sensation of the hard nipples trailing smoothly up and down her skin. She twitched her hips seductively, trying to increase the sensation of the soft, crisp curls rubbing up against her ass.

When it became too difficult to breathe, Ryan lifted off her and sat back on her haunches, sucking in a lungful of the slightly humid air.

Jamie's head had dropped and now hung down towards the floor, her damp hair tossed forward, framing her face like a golden halo. Her eyes were tightly closed, and she was also having a difficult time getting control of her breathing. As Ryan watched her flushed chest deeply expand and contract, she felt another jolt of sensation shoot through her groin, and she had to struggle to control her aggression.

She began to kiss and lick every inch of skin, up and down her back and sides. Jamie was moaning continuously as Ryan slathered her with tender nibbles and warm wet kisses. Her arms finally gave out as she dropped down onto her forearms, her head hanging down loosely, small, soft moans tumbling from her mouth.

A delighted smile crossed Ryan's face as she paused for a moment to gaze at the overpoweringly erotic vision that her partner presented. Her mouth began to water at the thought of finally tasting the gorgeous creature that was so temptingly displayed before her. Ryan climbed between her legs and dropped her head as she leaned in to kiss the glistening flesh for the first time, but as her lips brushed the first dark blonde curl, Jamie moaned a short, firm, "No!" before falling limply to the floor. Ryan immediately dropped down beside her and took her into her arms, running her hand through the damp blonde hair in a reassuring gesture. "It's okay, baby, it's okay," she soothed, unsure of what had caused the reaction.

Jamie shook her head a few times, gasping with arousal as she said, "It's too much right now. Just a little too much."

"My touch?" Ryan asked, confused and still a bit stunned.

"No." Jamie shook her head slowly, trying to explain herself. "*That* touch. *That* touch was too much."

Relief flooded Ryan's body as she sought to calm her partner. "That's fine, love. No big deal. We'll do what feels good to you right now." Sliding her hand down the slick body, Ryan slipped the tips of her fingers between Jamie's overheated lips and started to stroke her with a very tender touch. "How's that?" she soothed. "Feel good?"

A rapidly nodding head reassured Ryan that her partner was still receptive to her touch, and the little grunts of pleasure that followed enhanced that impression. Jamie's legs spread wider as the touch increased in speed, and within a few moments she cried out loudly, "Oh God, oh Ryan, oh, don't stop, don't stop, *yes*! Right there, baby, Yes, Yes, *Yes!*" One final gasp of air, and Jamie collapsed in a heap, panting roughly. Her arms were raised over her head, and her legs were splayed apart as she continued to gasp. Ryan leaned over her and barely heard her whisper, "Hold me."

She gladly complied, lying down next to her and wrapping her arms around the limp body. Ryan fidgeted for a moment against the hard wooden floor until she could position Jamie's head onto her outstretched arm. She held the still panting woman to her tightly, until Jamie pulled away to roll over onto her back. She stared up at Ryan with largely unfocused eyes. "My God, what did you do to me?"

Ryan beamed down at her, gazing fondly at the look of total, spent satisfaction that graced her face. "I just loved you."

"Then I've clearly never been loved before," she said with a heavy sigh.

"You're going to be loved an awful lot, sweetheart," she cooed. "Do you think you're up to it?"

"I'm more than willing to try," she said gamely, as she gave her a bright but weary smile. Ryan continued to trace small patterns on her skin as they lay together in the afterglow. Jamie would occasionally turn to gaze at her or rise up to kiss her lightly.

"I love the way you respond to my touch," Ryan purred.

"Really?" she asked tentatively, seeking the reassurance that Ryan was happy to provide.

Ryan leaned over to rub her whole face against Jamie's neck, then slowly intoned, "I absolutely, positively, unequivocally love it."

Ryan was beaming such a happy smile that Jamie couldn't help but join her. "When I look into your eyes, I see such love and acceptance. It's wonderful, baby. Just wonderful."

Ryan wrapped her arms around her partner and nuzzled her head into the crook of her neck. "I love you so much that when you touch me it feels like an electric shock! I've never experienced the kind of pleasure that I've felt so far from making love with you. And it's only gonna get better," she promised with a big smile.

Jamie beamed a smile that equaled that of her partner in intensity. "I'm so happy that I've pleased you so far. I was worried that you'd be so experienced that I'd seem inept compared with your other lovers."

"You couldn't be more 'ept," Ryan teased, as she gave her a little kiss.

Jamie tossed her arms around her lover's neck and gave her an enthusiastic squeeze. "Will you always be this sweet and thoughtful?"

"No, of course not," Ryan laughed. "I was trying to get you hooked on me. Now that I've got you, my real personality can come out."

Rolling onto her side, Jamie held her head up on one hand while the other slowly trailed over Ryan's face. She spent a moment staring intently at the strong features, while she tried to imagine what her partner's real personality might consist of. Unable to determine where Ryan was going with her tease, she finally gave in. "So … tell me about this real personality," she asked with a fond smile.

Ryan appeared to give the matter some thoughtful consideration. She pursed her lips and mused, "Oh, I expect I'll come home late most nights … probably drunk."

"Oh, you drink to excess?" Jamie asked, tilting her head in surprise.

"Oh, yeah," Ryan agreed with a straight face. "I'm rarely sober. I figure I'll get back into the habit of hanging out with my friends at various strip clubs. I won't want to take you, of course, because you'll get in the way of the lap dances I like to get."

"Why would I get in the way?" Jamie demanded, getting into the game.

Ryan gazed at her for a moment with a thoughtful look. "You seem like the jealous type," she decided. "I can't have you cramping my style."

"Oh … okay," she agreed. "Go on, love, this is fascinating."

"Well, if I don't get lucky at one of the clubs or the bars we go to afterwards, I'll stumble into the bedroom around three in the morning and wake you up with a rough shove and say, 'Do me right, woman!'"

Jamie was laughing so hard at this inconceivable image, that Ryan couldn't maintain her poker face for long. "Okay, okay," she admitted, joining her partner in a hearty laugh. "That's not *exactly* how I'll be."

"Tell me how you'll really be," the smaller woman begged. "I want to know what I've gotten myself into here."

"Okay," Ryan said. "It'll be more like this. You'll come home from school, and I'll be in the kitchen preparing dinner. I'll have the laundry all finished, and the house will be spotless, as usual. I'll pour you a glass of wine the second you come in the door. After an artfully prepared dinner, I'll make sure you're comfortable, then I'll clean the kitchen and go get ready for bed. When you come up, I'll be clean and naked and ready for you, hoping that you'll want me. Of course, I'll never ask for you to touch me or make any demands on you. I'll just hope that you can find it in your heart to want me." Trusting, hopeful blue eyes blinked innocently at Jamie, and she couldn't resist the urge to grab her partner's nose and give it a tweak.

"Given a choice between the two," the smirking blonde intoned, "I think I'd prefer the first scenario. You'd lose most of your considerable allure if you became my little lap dog."

"Hmm," Ryan said, considering the alternatives. "Maybe we should come up with a compromise."

"Okay," Jamie said immediately. "How's this? We get drunk together, and then *I* give you a lap dance. We order carry-out food and leave the kitchen dirty, go upstairs and make wild monkey-love until dawn."

"I'm not sure I know what monkey-love is, but I'm more than willing to learn," Ryan grinned. "I think your idea is fantastic, Ms. Evans. You're obviously the brains of this partnership."

"That's only fair, since you're the brawn," the impish blonde replied. "Now let's go clean up, tough-stuff. I'm a little hungry, and if I'm hungry, you must be starving!"

"You know me too well. And that's just how I like it."

After their showers, they decided to have a cookout on the patio since the day was so nice. Ryan agreed to handle the grilling duties, while Jamie took care of the inside preparation.

"Do you like eggplant, squash, carrots or radicchio?" Jamie asked as she surveyed the contents of the refrigerator.

"Yep."

"Which would you like tonight?" Jamie clarified.

"All of them, actually," Ryan decided. "I'm a little low on my vegetable intake today. Let's split a steak and cook the veggies on the grill."

"Hmm, split a steak. Do you mean 'split' like—each get half, or 'split' like—you get it all?"

"Half," Ryan said, smiling. "Well … maybe a little less than half. I don't like to eat too much red meat."

"Okay," Jamie said warily, "but I'm gonna prepare all of the vegetables that we have. I need some food, too."

"That's my girl." Ryan beamed as she went outside to start the fire.

They hadn't spent any time on this particular patio, but Ryan had noticed it when she was searching for her partner earlier in the day. It opened off of the dining room and was obviously designed so that grilled food could be served quickly.

The large but cozy space was designed for both cooking and entertaining, so it had been built with a six-foot-tall, dry-stacked stone wall to protect the inhabitants from the wind. Wrought iron flowerpot holders were spaced frequently along the wall, and each was filled with a brilliant fuchsia or other tropical plant.

The ground was covered in a soft, buff-colored flagstone, the spaces between the stones planted with curly thyme that emitted a nice scent when walked on. In the far corner of the area stood a gleaming stainless steel grill, waiting for action. Ryan spent a moment figuring out how to turn on the flame before she finally got it going. There were separate gas burners on the far side that would allow for the cooking of an entire meal, and she wondered how often the Evanses used the massive contraption. *Boy, at our house we could throw the oven away if we had one of these.* Noticing a refrigerator tucked under the granite counter that flanked the grill, she opened it to find several kinds of beer and wine and mixers for cocktails. Snagging a beer, she sat down on one of the generous spring chairs and put her feet up on the handy ottoman.

"Don't you look like you belong here?" Jamie joked, when she emerged with a big platter filled with cleaned and cut-up vegetables.

"Do I really?"

"Yeah, you do." There was a note of hesitation in Jamie's voice as she added, "That doesn't bother you, does it?"

"Bother me? No, it doesn't bother me, but I guess I'm … surprised. I don't feel like I belong, and I thought that'd show through."

Jamie set the tray on the counter and went to the refrigerator for her own beer. She handed the bottle to Ryan since her partner had a much easier time with bottle caps than she did. Pulling a matching spring chair over to face Ryan, she sat down and kicked off her sandals, placing her feet on Ryan's lap. "Does it bother you to be here?"

"No, no, not at all. It's just not what I'm used to … in the extreme," she chuckled. "I've been thinking about what it must be like to take all of this for granted, and … I can't."

"You know," Jamie mused, "this is the first time you've seen me in my native habitat. Does it make you feel … different about me?"

Ryan gave that question the consideration that it deserved, spending several minutes thinking about it. Jamie was noticeably fidgeting, but Ryan was concentrating so deeply that she didn't notice it. Finally she looked up and said, "No, of course it doesn't change how I feel about you, but it's hard to get my mind around. I mean, I know that you don't judge people by their net worth, but I wonder if you ever think I'm a culchie."

"Culchie?"

Ryan chuckled a bit as she explained, "One of my granny's terms. That's what she calls the people who live in the hills. It's like a country bumpkin."

"Ryan!" Jamie cried, reaching out to touch her leg, "How can you even ask that? I feel inferior to you in every way except money! My God, I feel so incredibly lucky that you've chosen me to spend your life with … I can't imagine feeling that I was better than you because of money!"

Ryan winced, having been caught in an insecure moment. "Sorry, babe. I'm a little touchy about money. Let's get dinner started, okay?"

She was halfway out of her chair when Jamie placed a restraining hand on her leg. "Honey, wait … please." Ryan did so and looked at her attentively. "I think we need to talk about this."

"Can't it wait?" Ryan begged, trying to forestall the discussion.

"I guess it can wait, but it's gonna come up again and again. We need to set some ground rules."

It was obvious that Ryan didn't want to have this discussion—now or later—but Jamie also realized that forcing her to talk when she didn't want to wasn't the solution either. She was about to try a different tactic when Ryan said, "I want to get dinner started. We can talk after we eat."

Knowing when it was wise to back off, Jamie got up and took Ryan's hand, leading her over to the grill. "Okay, we'll talk about it later. Have you grilled veggies before?"

"Just corn and baked potatoes. I've never done anything this delicate before," Ryan admitted, holding up a baby zucchini with the blossom still attached.

"I'd start with the eggplant."

"What do I do with them?" Ryan asked suspiciously, poking her finger at each of the vegetables in turn.

"Well, we have this vegetable-insert that you put over the grill, like this," she said, placing the implement into the slot designed for it. "Then you put them flesh side down and wait until they begin to get soft. Then turn them, and let the skin side cook for a while. Put 'em face down again, until they're nice and soft, and you're done. They'll take about three times longer than the other veggies, so have at it."

"Okay, but you'd better stay here and supervise. I might need assistance."

"No place I'd rather be," Jamie agreed, pulling up a stool and perching on Ryan's left side. "Need another beer?" she asked, when she noticed Ryan's empty bottle.

"A bird can't fly with one wing," was her partner's glib reply. Since the comment was made in Ryan's Irish accent, Jamie knew that the game was for her to decipher the phrase and act accordingly.

"I get it!" she laughed, reaching into the refrigerator for a second beer. "A bird needs two wings to fly, and you need more than one drink to do the same." She was quite pleased with her ability to figure out Ryan's little phrases, and her pleasure showed brightly on her smiling face.

"Brilliant!" Ryan smiled in return and gave her a kiss for good measure.

As the eggplant cooked, Ryan stood behind Jamie, her chin resting on the smaller woman's shoulder. "Know what I like?" she asked softly.

The blonde head shook gently. "No, what?"

"I like how great it feels to touch you all the time. I've never been around anyone, except Caitlin of course, who I wanted to have my hands on all of the time. It's addictive."

"For me, too," Jamie agreed. "Oh, I touched Jack a lot, but most of his touches felt sexual. Yours feel warm and soft and make me feel connected to you. I absolutely love it."

"How do you feel when my touch *does* feel sexual, like this afternoon?"

Jamie furrowed her brow a bit as she considered the question. "It felt luscious," she said, speaking the word just above a whisper. "I loved it."

Ryan walked around to stand in front of her, checking the eggplant as she did. "Tell me why you loved it," she asked, lacing her hands behind Jamie's neck.

"Promise not to laugh?" Jamie asked, a hint of hesitation in her voice.

"Promise."

"Okay … I loved it because I felt in charge for a change. I only felt that way once or twice with Jack. Normally I felt like the passive one, taking what he had to give and hoping for the best. But today, I felt like … an adult. Yeah, that's it! I felt like an adult."

She had the most satisfied grin on her face that Ryan had ever seen, and her own grin quickly matched that of her partner. "I'm glad," Ryan said, wrapping Jamie in her arms. They stood that way for a few minutes, both enjoying the closeness. "This is really different for me," Ryan said. "I was usually the more active, controlling one when I slept with other women. It was nice to let you share in the decision making today."

"That makes sense," Jamie said, nodding her head in agreement. "I guess I always assumed you'd be the more dominant one, but I'm not sure you've told me that in so many words."

"I think I've told you that," Ryan said, as she turned to flip the eggplant. "But I'm not sure, since I've told you so many things about myself."

"You said it felt nice for you today. Tell me about that." Jamie was right next to her partner, and she unconsciously reached up to brush her bangs from her eyes. Ryan looked a little unsure of herself, but she did her best to explain her feelings. "Uhm, you might not be able to understand this, but people expect you to behave in a certain way when you're physically imposing. Most of the women I've been with were smaller than I am, and they always seemed to expect me to be in charge. That fits my personality—at least most of the time—so it wasn't generally a problem. Once in a while, though, I didn't want to be in charge, but I was still expected to be. That gets old after a while."

"I bet it would," Jamie said.

"That's one of the things I liked about being with Ally. She was always in charge. It was a nice break for me."

"Hmm, and you were bigger than she was?"

Ryan cocked her head for a moment, her eyes widening as she thought about the question. "No … no, I wasn't. She was the only woman I've been with who was bigger and stronger than I am. Jesus! I treated her just like people treat me! I assumed that she'd be in control!"

"Maybe that's what she wanted," Jamie suggested gently. "You must have meshed if you saw each other for five years."

Ryan was shaking her head, her lips pursed. "I wish we would have talked about it. Maybe she didn't want that all the time."

"Well, we're talking about it now, and I'm glad we are."

"Really?" Ryan asked, with a grin curling up the corners of her mouth.

"Really … partner."

By the time dinner was finished and the grill cleaned, it was after nine o'clock. They were both too tired to muster the energy to do much, so they decided to go to bed early.

"Do you think this is how most people spend their honeymoon?" They were climbing the stairs together, hand in hand, and Jamie's head rested companionably against her partner's arm.

"Most? That I don't know," Ryan said. "I'd guess that most people just relax and try to get over the stress of their weddings."

"Well, we didn't have that stress, but I bet most people didn't ride a bike five hundred and sixty miles right before their wedding."

"Good point. It's gonna take a while to feel rested."

"We'll have to spend more time in bed," Jamie said, grinning.

"You have the best ideas," Ryan decided, bending to place a kiss on the top of Jamie's head.

When Ryan emerged from the bathroom, Jamie was already in bed, wearing one of Ryan's T-shirts. "A little overdressed, aren't you?"

"Our experiment was short-lived. I'm guess I'm just used to wearing clothes. Even with you keeping me warm, I like to have my shoulders covered. You don't mind, do you?"

"Whatever you like, babe. As long as you don't mind my taking it off you regularly."

Jamie giggled at the thought. "I look forward to being undressed by your talented hands for many nights to come."

"The pleasure is all mine." As they snuggled together to get comfortable, Ryan snuck her hand under the shirt and placed it gently on Jamie's hip.

"You always touch me there as we fall asleep," Jamie mumbled through a yawn.

"It's one of my favorite spots. The curve of your hip is so womanly. And you know how I feel about women," she chuckled lazily.

"I'm beginning to understand. And share the passion."

# Chapter Eight

Ryan walked up the stairs bright and early on Wednesday morning, balancing a heavy tray loaded with food. It was filled with a big, steaming bowl of oatmeal covered with cream and brown sugar, several bananas, two bagels with a slab of cream cheese, a big bowl of sliced pineapple, two large glasses of orange juice and a pot of coffee. As she gingerly pushed open the door, she expected to find her sleeping lover spread out across the bed, just as she had left her an hour and a half before. To her surprise, she found Jamie sitting up with a happy smile on her face, freshly showered and very much alert. The grinning blonde was obviously naked, but the top sheet was pulled up to her armpits and neatly folded over. Ryan's heart skipped a beat when she considered the treasures hidden under that thin cotton barrier. "Well, well, well," she said, grinning, "My little princess has arisen."

"I guess I'd better either get used to waking up alone or learn to get up before dawn, huh?"

"If you want to start running with me in the morning, you'll have to. Otherwise, it doesn't make much sense to get up for no purpose."

"Would you like me to run with you?" she asked, perplexed by the statement. "I thought you needed your time alone."

Ryan thought about that for a while. "I'm not sure," she finally admitted. "Part of me would like you to run with me, because I like to be with you constantly." She cocked her head slightly and continued. "But I love the solitude when I'm alone just before dawn. I think about things, say my prayers and stuff like that. I don't know if I want to talk while I run."

"Are you implying that you don't think I could run and not talk?"

"Sweetie, you even talk in your sleep," she said with a grin.

"I most certainly do not!"

"You most certainly do," she insisted firmly. "Last night, it was something like, "Oh, yeah, that's it, harder, harder!" Ryan wiggled her eyebrows and laughed at Jamie's stunned expression.

"Are you really being serious?"

"Yeah, I am. You were obviously dreaming about having sex, and you were giving me a little color commentary."

Jamie raised her knees and crossed her arms over them, dropping her head to rest on her folded forearms. "Oh, God, I'm so embarrassed."

Ryan went over to the bed and sat down, running her hand over her partner's thigh. "Why?"

"It's not like I'm not getting enough sex; why do I dream about it, too?"

Ryan ran a calming hand through her hair, stroking her softly. "I don't think that's odd at all. This is a big change for you."

Shrugging, Jamie said, "I've spent enough time talking about how I feel about being a lesbian. I should be over it by now."

"No way! I think you're just discovering your sexuality. And I don't mean the lesbian thing. I think you're learning to be freer with how you express yourself. It's probably on your mind a lot, and you're working through some of your issues in your dreams. It's perfectly natural, sweetie. And darned erotic!"

"Really?" Jamie shyly lifted her head a bit to ascertain that her partner was being sincere.

"Really," Ryan said. "When you were sleeptalking last night, I … uhm … ran my hand down between your legs. You were really ready, if you know what I mean." She moistened her lips, then made her confession. "I really wanted to touch you, but it seemed kinda wrong, so I put my arms around you, and you quieted down."

Jamie dropped her eyes to stare at the sheets as she mumbled, "I'd like to wake up like that."

"With me touching you in your sleep?" Ryan inquired softly, lightly trailing her fingers up and down Jamie's leg.

"Yeah, I … think I'd like it … a lot."

Scooting over, she wrapped Jamie in her arms, "Then the next time that happens, and I hope it's soon, you will be thoroughly and lovingly touched." Getting back to the original topic, Ryan sat up and ran her fingers through Jamie's hair, fluffing the bangs away from her eyes. "Now, would you like to get up and run with me, or sleep a little longer?"

"I guess running doesn't really sound like that much fun if I can't talk," she admitted. "I think I'll stay in bed and give you a darned good reason to come home."

"That should improve my time significantly," Ryan said with a grin. She rose and grabbed the breakfast tray, placing it across Jamie's outstretched legs. "Start on this while I take a shower." Lovingly, she kissed her cheek, then issued a warning, underscored by the narrowing of her eyes. "But you'd better leave some for me."

"How could I not?" Jamie protested, as she looked at the feast.

Ryan emerged from the shower a few minutes later. Her hair was twisted up in a knot and secured to the back of her head with a large metal clip. She was still a little damp, and she dried her body briskly with a fluffy white towel as she came back into the bedroom, rubbing so thoroughly that her skin glowed pink under her bronze tan.

Jamie watched her with deep interest, musing that she watched her lover perform the most mundane task with a focus that she could rarely muster otherwise—even for topics that fascinated her. "I like your hair up like that," she said thoughtfully.

"Do you? You can play with my hair any time you like. I don't spend much time on it, but you can." She walked back into the bath to hang up her towel, casually mentioning, "Actually, I was thinking about getting it cut."

"*What?*"

"Uhm … I was thinking about getting it cut?" she said once again, but more hesitantly this time, unsure of the reason behind Jamie's outburst.

"You mean just the ends, right?" The look on Jamie's face was near panic.

"No."

Jamie's voice rose to a somewhat louder volume. "You mean just a couple of inches, right?"

"No."

"How much?" Jamie finally demanded, getting up on her knees and putting her hands on her hips.

Ryan knew it was her turn to speak, but her stark naked lover was proving to be too much of a distraction for her to consider her reply. She shook her head and gazed at the ceiling so that she could respond. "I was thinking a little shorter than yours," she admitted, flinching a bit at her partner's immediate reaction.

Jamie was off the bed in a flash. She grasped her lover's dark head in her hands, shaking her own in negation. "I can't let you do that, Ryan. I'm sorry, but I can't."

"Are you being serious?" Ryan asked, the demonstration taking her completely by surprise.

"Totally," Jamie said as she closed her eyes. "I always thought guys were nuts when they made such a big deal about long hair. But I really, really love it. I love to run my hands through it, I love it when it brushes against my breasts, I love how it settles around your shoulders and looks kind of wild, I love grabbing it with my hands to guide your head …" She shook her head slowly and looked at Ryan rather helplessly, "I really love it, baby. I know it's your hair, but I really, really love it."

"Okay! I won't get it cut unless you agree. I wouldn't want to deprive you of so much … love." Fond smile in place, Ryan leaned in and gave her a kiss to seal the promise. "You never cease to amaze me," she said with delight. Still smiling, she sat on the bed, pulled the tray over and dug in. Between bites of oatmeal, she looked carefully at her partner. "Come to think of it, I haven't seen you with long hair. Maybe I need you to grow yours out."

"Okay, okay, fair's fair." Jamie went and pulled an album from a large, built-in bookcase. They sat on the big window seat overlooking the wide expanse of lawn and started to look through the photos while Ryan continued to munch on the remaining breakfast.

Pointing at a photo of the family in what appeared to be a game room, Ryan commented. "Can I look around the house later on? You've had me locked in either the bedroom or the kitchen for two days. I haven't seen any of the other rooms."

Jamie laughed at the image of Ryan trapped as her love slave, shaking her head roughly when the image became too appealing for her comfort. "Yes, sweetie," she said, forcing her mind back to the topic. "We can do anything you want today."

Ryan thumbed through the album while she finished her breakfast, smiling at the pictures of her lover in her younger days. The photos were almost exclusively from her high school years, and Ryan was charmed by the youthful innocence in Jamie's face. "You looked so young in high school."

"Don't I know it! I looked like I was twelve until I was eighteen! Luckily, by senior year I started to mature a little bit. See?" She pointed out a picture from late in her senior year. "It's like I grew up all in one year."

"Mmm, you grew in more ways than one," Ryan said appreciatively, trailing a fingertip down the developing curves on the picture of her lover. With a sly smile working around the corners of her mouth, Ryan tilted her head and ran that same finger down the curves that had now fully developed and were so perfectly exposed to her tender touch.

"Yeah, my popularity increased in direct proportion to my breast size," she admitted, patting Ryan's cheek fondly.

"You must have been the most popular girl in the entire Bay Area," Ryan declared solemnly, bending her head to place a gentle kiss on the focus of their discussion.

Jamie giggled and pushed her partner away when the kisses continue to rain down on her. "Down, girl," she ordered through her laughter. "We don't have time to finish what you're about to start."

With a tiny pout now replacing her smile, Ryan mumbled, "I never get to have any fun."

"I know," Jamie said with her voice full of mock sympathy. "I'll try to make it up to you later." When Ryan's grin was once again restored, Jamie switched back to the previous topic. "When did you reach your rather impressive height?"

"Hmm, I'd say that, except for my last growth spurt, I looked about the same from eighth grade on. I could have gone into a bar when I was sixteen."

"And I bet you did," Jamie said teasingly, as she pinched her on the waist.

"Not until I was seventeen," she corrected, squirming away from Jamie's pinch. "I don't know. You look pretty good with long hair. I might enjoy wrapping my fingers in your locks, too, and feeling their silky softness as they brush over my …"

"If you really want me to, I'd grow it long for you," Jamie interrupted agreeably. "I'd had long hair my whole life, and I wanted a change."

"Do you like it short?"

"I like not having to bother with it. I don't have to blow it dry if I don't want to, and it is a lot cooler."

"I think you should wear it the way you like it. But if you did let it grow, I sure wouldn't complain." One of the last pictures was obviously from senior prom. A much more mature young woman was standing next to a tall, dark-haired young man who was quite handsome.

"Who's this lucky devil?" Ryan scowled slightly at the boy, feeling territorialism rear its ugly head.

"Scott Hastings," Jamie said thoughtfully. "We dated most of my senior year. When he wasn't two-timing me, that is."

"You stood for that!" Ryan cried.

"Yeah, I guess I did," she admitted. "In retrospect, I didn't care all that much. He was fun and didn't put a lot of pressure on me to have sex … probably because he was getting it from someone else," she added with a wry laugh.

"I guess we were both searching for something at this age," Ryan mused. "We just went about it in very different ways."

"Yeah, I guess that's right," she agreed, with a pensive look. "I'm just glad that our searching led us to each other."

"Me too. Do you have any pictures from when you were really little?" she asked as she flipped through the pages. "I want to see your mom when she was your age."

"Sure." She went back to the bookcase and studied the contents. "Jamie Evans, the early years," she intoned dramatically, pulling out a big binder and handing it to Ryan.

"I noticed at the AIDS Ride that your father is pretty tall," Ryan commented as she opened the binder.

Jamie, unaware that she was being set up, looked up at Ryan with the question in her eyes, then she said, "And?"

"Uhm … what happened?" Only Ryan's quick reflexes saved her from the firm swat that Jamie directed at her abdomen.

"Nothing happened," Jamie retorted with narrowed eyes. "I'm small gened. I'll have you know that my mother is more height-challenged than I am."

"It's not a challenge," Ryan said, the sincerity of her words mirrored in her eyes. "I think we fit together beautifully. I wouldn't change one thing about you."

"Me either," her beaming partner agreed.

Ryan closely studied all of the pictures of a tiny little Jamie being brought home from the hospital, shots of her being baptized by her grandfather, and some adorable ones of her covered in food while she attempted to feed herself. There was one poignant picture of Jamie's mother sitting by her crib, her arms crossed and resting on the top rail as she gazed lovingly at her tiny baby. She clearly didn't know that she was being photographed and, judging from her weary face, she'd been in that exact position for quite a while. There was something so familiar about her expression that Ryan felt like she was looking at her lover, even though their features were not terribly similar.

"You may have your mother's height, but you look a lot more like your father than your mom," she observed quietly, still staring intently at the photo. "Except in this one picture." Ryan tapped her finger on the image, a little furrow in her brow. "Here, she has the exact same expression I've seen so many times on your face. It's nice to see you in another person. Do you know what I mean?"

She could tell that Ryan was thinking about her own mother by the distant, bereft look that invariably clouded her face when she thought of her. "I do." Jamie scooted a little closer to her partner and snaked an arm around her waist. "Do you share any features with your mom?"

A short shake of her head signaled both her lack of common features and her desire not to talk about the matter any further. Jamie honored her wish, giving her a squeeze to let her know she understood.

Looking at the album again, Ryan turned to a photo of Jim at his law school graduation. "You've got your father's nose and his chin. And your grin is identical to his," she said fondly, turning her gaze from the picture to Jamie's grinning face. "He has green eyes too, doesn't he?"

"Yeah, mother's are a nice, deep brown. They look good with her blonde hair."

"So you get your hair color and your height from your mom?"

It seemed important to Ryan to learn more about her mother, so Jamie gave the question some serious thought. "Yeah, that's about it, physically, don't you think?"

Before giving her opinion, Ryan studied another photo, this one of both Jamie's parents. Catherine was a little shorter than Jamie, and much smaller boned. She actually looked a little frail, being quite thin and not very muscular. Her face was very striking, with a delicate nose and prominent cheekbones. She was a beautiful young woman, and she and Jim made a very striking pair. He was tall—about six foot three, Ryan guessed—with broad shoulders and a trim waist. He looked like a jock with his casual stance, appearing very comfortable in his body. His hair was a sandy brown and he had an easy smile and twinkling eyes, very much like Jamie's. "Your parents are a very handsome couple," Ryan observed as she looked up at Jamie.

"Yeah, I guess they are. Daddy looks his age now, I guess from how hard he works. But Mother looks a lot like she did then. She spends a lot of time on her appearance, and I guess it's paid off."

"Do you think they'll like me?" Ryan asked quietly, a small frown playing at her forehead.

Jamie thought about that question for a long while. She looked at Ryan carefully as she answered, "If they were to get to know you as my friend, I'm certain they would. You're terribly charming, you know," she said with a smile. "But if their first opportunity to really know you is as my lover … I don't know. I really don't know." She looked down at her hands, fervently wishing that she could reassure her partner, but being completely unable to do so.

"Are they open-minded about things in general?" Ryan's tone was gentle and reflective, but Jamie could still hear the longing in her voice.

"In a way they are. I'm sure that Mother has a host of gay men in her retinue. She has a number of people who cater to her needs, you know, her hairdresser, her interior designer. I'm guessing she doesn't know many lesbians, though. She's pretty straight, and really proper about things in general."

"Hmm, I thought she'd be kinda … I don't know … kinda laid back," Ryan said. "I mean, she's almost fifteen years younger than Da, and she was raised in the Bay Area during a pretty wild time …"

"She seems to have escaped the 60s unscathed," Jamie said dryly. "She was at Stanford, in a very conservative sorority, and I don't think she experienced a lot before she met my father."

"She's tolerant about homosexuality in general, right?"

"Yeah, I think so. I don't think she'll be bothered by the homosexual aspect of our relationship, per se. I think the issue will be that this makes me 'different.' She doesn't like me to stand out in a crowd, even for good things. I think it really bothered her that I was on the boys' golf team. I don't think she wanted me to call attention to myself like that."

"What about your father?"

"I don't know. He's changed recently, and that confuses me. He's a big supporter of the Democratic Party, so he's pretty liberal. He's close to Mayor Brown, and the Mayor is positively gaga about gay issues." Ryan nodded her assent to this assessment. "A year ago, I would have said that Daddy would be completely cool with my being gay, but he's said some things this year that've really bothered me. He made a big deal about one of the partners bringing his lover to a firm party. It really surprised me, and I think he said it purposely because he knew I was friends with you."

"Did you tell him that I was gay?"

"Yeah, I think I told him right after we started working out together."

Ryan breathed a small sigh of relief and felt muscles relax that she didn't know she'd been tightening. "That's not an encouraging sign. But, he was very friendly to me after the ride. He knew I was gay, and he knew we were together constantly for a week."

The look on her face was so filled with hope that Jamie felt her heart clench in her chest. She reached up and took both of Ryan's hands in hers. "Sweetheart, I want them to approve of us. I truly want them to like you. But if they don't, it won't change one thing between us. I promise you that."

Ryan graced her with a fond smile and tilted her head to place a gentle kiss on her lips. "I know it might be tough when you tell them, but one thing I've learned from working at the talk line is that you're usually surprised by your parents' reaction. Sometimes it's a good surprise, sometimes it's bad, but it's usually a surprise."

"Well, that's something to look forward to," she said with a wry smile. She got up and stretched, then put the album back. "So, what do you want to do today?"

"It's up to you, sweetness. You pick."

"Well, I've got a golf lesson at ten. Maybe lunch and some shopping after that?"

"Shopping?" Ryan repeated weakly, looking a little ill.

"Come on," Jamie urged. "It'll be fun."

Ryan sighed deeply and shook her head a little bit. "You know," she said slowly, "If you're gonna be a real lesbian, you're gonna have to stop the shopping thing."

Jamie's nonplussed expression caused Ryan to pull back from her teasing. "Hey, that was a joke, babe. There's room in the lesbian community for a shop-a-holic."

The absent nod that greeted that comment showed that Jamie was still bothered by the joke, though, so Ryan tried to draw her out. "Tell me why that upset you," she insisted. "'Cause I know it did."

Jamie patted her hand, nodding briefly as she tried to collect her thoughts. It took longer than Ryan was comfortable with, but Jamie finally got to the issue. "I'm … I'm not sure that I like that term."

"What term?" Ryan asked, trying to remember the exact terms she had used. "Shop-a-holic?"

"No, no," Jamie said quickly, "that one's accurate." She drew in a deep breath and turned to face her partner fully. "I'm not sure I like being called a lesbian."

"Okay, I promise I won't use that term for you again," Ryan said. Her stomach did a small flip, but she had a feeling that her partner's reaction was mostly a question of semantics.

Jamie looked at her plaintively. "But … what am I, if I'm not a lesbian?" The look on her face reminded Ryan of a four-year-old who has just discovered there is no Easter Bunny.

"You're you," Ryan assured her, as she took her in her arms and hugged her tightly. "You don't need a designation to be you. You're the same you that you were before we kissed for the first time. The term doesn't make you who you are, Jamie."

"But you have one," Jamie complained, her words muffled slightly by the skin of her partner's shoulder.

Ryan smiled and patted her blonde hair in an affectionate fashion. "That's because that's what I feel like. I've always been exclusively attracted to women. If I were stranded on a remote island with a hundred good-looking men and no women, I'd never have sex with a partner again. It actually feels wrong to me to even think about being with a man. When I was a kid, and people would tell me that I'd get married some day, I'd actually shiver a little at the thought. It seemed perverse!"

"Really?" Jamie asked, now fascinated by Ryan's vehemence. "You would honestly go without sex for the rest of your life rather than have a man touch you?"

"Yeah," Ryan said confidently. "I love men, as you well know. I feel completely comfortable being with them … but the thought of touching them sexually is actually repugnant to me."

"That's a pretty strong reaction."

"No it's not." Ryan gave her a quizzical look and tried to make her point clearer. "Take my brothers as an example. I'm sure they'd do without sex if the only option was other men." After a beat, she corrected her statement a bit as she added with a chuckle, "Well, Conor would find some way to rationalize it, but Brendan and Rory wouldn't."

Jamie laughed at her partner's comments, fully able to see Conor trying to find the most feminine looking man in the bunch. "Your point was what?" she asked, after removing the image of Conor and his new boyfriend from her mind.

"My sexual orientation towards women is just as firmly affixed as my brothers'. But because I'm a woman, and a man's parts fit into me, it's hard for people to believe that. Even you," she said with a flash of hurt passing across her face.

Jamie sat back and stared at her partner for a moment as she forced herself to admit that it did seem like an entirely different thing to her. "I'm sorry, babe," she said, trying to apologize, but not really knowing what to say. "I guess I have some preconceived notions that make this hard for me to understand."

Ryan's expression softened, and she wrapped her arm around Jamie's shoulders, giving her a good squeeze. "It's okay. It just bugs me sometimes when you don't completely understand me. It's no big deal."

"I just … I guess I assume that you could be with men if you chose to. But I couldn't imagine your brothers, or Jack, or my father having sex with a man. I guess it is a double standard."

"It is," Ryan said with a smile. "But this is complex stuff. We have to keep talking about it so we understand each other better."

"Well, I feel funny not to feel like you do," Jamie said added after a minute. "It's like I don't belong in the club."

"No, no, no," Ryan said. "You don't have to feel any particular way or call yourself any particular thing. You are who you are … with or without a label."

"Have you been with other women without labels?" she asked tentatively.

Ryan smiled indulgently and gave her a gentle squeeze. "You know I have, babe. You know I dated that woman who was in a relationship with a guy. I'm sure she'd never call herself a lesbian."

"Is she the only one?" Jamie asked, hoping that many others shared her feelings.

"Of course not. I've been with women who fall everywhere on the continuum of sexual orientation. It's hard for lots of women to pick a spot they feel comfortable with on that scale. It's much easier for a woman like me, who can't imagine being with a man."

"So it doesn't bother you that I've been attracted to men?" she asked in a timid tone.

"Uhm, honey," Ryan gently reminded her. "Something about that engagement thing gave me a clue that you liked men. This isn't a surprise to me."

"Oh, Ryan, you know what I mean," she insisted, a little flustered.

"No, babe, I really don't. Tell me what bothers you about this."

"What … I mean … uhm … what if I *still* like men," she asked in a very quiet voice.

"Well, why wouldn't you?" Ryan asked warily. "That doesn't mean that you want to sleep with them, does it?"

"No, of course not," Jamie said immediately. "I just …"

"Look, honey. I like women … a lot. If we weren't together, I'd probably still be dating as many women as I could get my hot little hands on. But I'm committed to you. So my attraction to other women stays strong, but my desire to be with them is almost nonexistent."

"Almost?" Jamie's brow arched severely.

"Hey, we're being honest, right?" she grinned, but her grin faded when she saw the hurt in her partner's eyes. "I would never want to be with another woman," she insisted. "But I still notice them. I'll *always* notice them. And I assume I'll always have a physical reaction when I'm with an attractive woman. Just like you might have a reaction to being around a good-looking man."

"That's a laugh," Jamie chided her gently. "All of the good-looking men I'm around look just like you!"

"That's all part of my evil plan to keep you focused on me alone," Ryan laughed. "But seriously, how does this sit with you?"

"Okay, I guess," she said rather unconvincingly. "I suppose I thought that I'd feel differently when we got together."

"Nope, being with a woman doesn't change who you are. You're exactly who you were before you fell in love with me. You're just discovering facets to your sexual orientation that you weren't aware of before."

"Well, one thing I'm sure of," she said with a smile. "My orientation is firmly and irrevocably pointed in your direction!"

The golf lesson with Chip was a success for both women. Chip worked with Jamie patiently and, after a solid hour of hitting balls, her fade was significantly improved. Ryan split her time between the putting green and sitting on the ground behind Chip and Jamie, watching her intently. She loved to watch her partner swing a golf club. She particularly liked the way she twitched her hips a bit right before she began her swing. After they were finished, Chip offered to give Ryan a few more tips on sand play. She gratefully accepted, and they spent a good half hour in the practice bunker. Jamie joined them, also offering some tips. After hitting at least a hundred balls, Ryan was making real progress, but once again she had sand in places that she most definitely didn't want it. They thanked Chip for his time and, after they made another appointment for Friday, Jamie went into the pro shop to sign the lesson chit.

"Are you going to play again this week?" Chip asked Ryan as they waited.

"I'm playing with my brother on Saturday," she replied, "but I'm not sure if Jamie and I will play again this week. I guess we could play on Friday if we have time, but we haven't discussed it." She mentally crossed her fingers, hoping not to set foot on the course until Saturday.

"Does your brother play well?"

"He's a lot better than I am, but not as good as Jamie."

"Would you mind if I joined you if I don't have a lesson then?"

"I'd love it, and I'm sure Conor would love a few tips, too. We've got a 10:45 time, so if you can make it, we'll see you then," she said agreeably.

Chip sauntered off, and Ryan looked after him for a moment. *He's not such a bad guy*, she thought. *He's a little too interested in Jamie for my taste, but he does seem like a patient and knowledgeable teacher. I guess I just need to get used to guys drooling over her. God knows I do!*

# Chapter Nine

It was just past one o'clock when they left the course. As the valet delivered the Boxster, Jamie asked, "Would you like to go out for a fancy dinner tomorrow night?"

"Let's see," Ryan replied, as she looked up at the clear blue sky as if seeking divine guidance. "Dinner, you … what could possibly be wrong with that?"

"Did you bring anything elegant to wear?"

"Hmm." She pretended to mentally review the contents of her closet, then shrugged. "Since I own nothing elegant, I guess the answer is no."

"Then turn left on the Drive. We're going shopping, sweetie."

Ryan looked askance, but did as she was told. They drove into Carmel and parked as soon as they found a spot. As they walked along the neat shop-lined streets, Ryan decided that she'd better issue a dirt-alert. "If I take off my clothes, I promise that I'm gonna leave a pile of sand."

"At the place I'm taking you, they wouldn't say a word if you left a pile of kitty litter in the dressing room."

"Sounds like the kind of place I can't afford," Ryan said hesitantly.

"My treat, babe. It's only fair for me to pay since the clothes aren't for you," she reasoned. "I'm buying them for me."

"But I thought you wanted me to get something elegant."

"Oh, you'll be wearing them, but they're for me." Jamie's sexy tone left Ryan no doubt that her role was to serve as eye candy for her partner.

Ryan grinned, pleased that Jamie felt comfortable expressing her desires. When they reached the store, Jamie led the way, telling the sales woman exactly what she was looking for. Both the clerk and Jamie eyed Ryan like a prized filly, deciding what style of garment would look best on her long, lean frame. The woman left to search through her stock, and Jamie ordered Ryan into the dressing room. "Strip," she said decisively. Ryan gamely followed instructions, smirking when, true to her prediction, a sizable pile of sand wound up at her feet. She danced around, yanking at her underwear, trying to get the rest out. It was tough to tear herself away from the completely entertaining dance, but Jamie took pity on her partner and went out to intercept the sales clerk, giving Ryan a minute to collect herself.

The clerk brought three outfits of different styles, but Jamie chose only one to take into the dressing room. It was a thin silk, patterned in a rather indistinct floral print of salmon, bright blue and dusty rose. The top was close fitting with tiny spaghetti straps, coming just to the waist, while the pants, of the same fabric lined in satin, were designed to fit loosely.

Ryan had to take off her bra to try on the top and Jamie marveled at how the shape of her breasts barely changed when she removed it. "You don't even need to wear a bra, do you?"

"Yeah, I do," she replied. "My chest muscles make 'em keep their shape, but my nipples get hard when fabric brushes up against 'em. It's kind of irritating."

"Maybe to you it is," she purred, as she wrapped her arms around Ryan's waist. "To me, it's stimulating."

"I hope they don't have cameras in here." Ryan's head swiveled on her shoulders, looking in every conceivable place that a camera could be hidden.

"This isn't K-mart, sweetie," she said, kissing her gently. "Eww, your lips still taste like sand."

"Other than my taste, do you approve?" Ryan did a little pirouette to let her get the full effect.

Jamie spent a full minute taking in her lovely partner. The clothing fit Ryan as though it were designed especially for her. The close-fitting top captured Jamie's attention immediately, and the flowing fabric that covered her legs made her look even taller and leaner than usual. "Very, very much," she said, as she nodded her head slowly. "Although, all I want to do is take that off you," she added seductively.

"We could jump ahead to that part and save …" Ryan looked down at the garment, pulling it here and there to get a better look. "There's no price tag," she said, cocking her head in question.

"It's not that kind of place, Ryan."

"What kind of place doesn't tell you how much stuff costs?"

"This kinda place." There was a hint of humor in her tone as Jamie helped Ryan take off the top.

Still shaking her head in disbelief, Ryan tendered a proposition. "Jamie, either I pay for this, or I buy dinner tomorrow. I can't let you pay for everything."

"Well, you could, but I know you won't, so—it's a deal." Having come to an agreement, Jamie walked out of the dressing room, garment in hand.

When she learned the price of the outfit, Jamie quickly whipped out her American Express card. She knew that Ryan could order twenty-five entrees at the restaurant and not come close to the cost of the garment, so she decided to let her to pay for dinner. Ryan approached the counter as Jamie was signing the receipt. Turning her body slightly to block the taller woman's view, she quickly handed the form back to the clerk. As she turned to leave, Ryan stayed behind to confess that she'd left a bit of a mess in the dressing room. She caught up with Jamie just as she left the store. "That was thoughtful of you," Jamie said.

"I didn't want the next customer to get that on her feet."

"Nonetheless, you're a sweetheart," she said firmly.

They continued down the street until Jamie pulled her into a vintage clothing store. Ryan looked around idly until Jamie called her over to a big rack full of leather. "Do you have a motorcycle jacket?"

"Yeah, I have that black leather baseball-style jacket."

"No, I mean a real motorcycle jacket."

"Uhm ... no," she said as she shook her head. "Don't you think they're kinda ... butch?"

"Yep," she said agreeably as she began to pull jackets from the rack. Ryan patiently waited while Jamie decided on her four favorites. She tried each one on, waiting for Jamie's critical appraisal. When she tried the last one on, Jamie's eyes lit up. It was very well worn, scuffed severely on the elbows. Big shiny chrome zippers slashed across the chest and up the sleeves. The coat fit snugly against her hips but was roomy across the chest, and the sleeves were the perfect length, stopping just below her wrists. Since it was a bit more modern than the traditional style jacket, the coat didn't have the big belt and buckle that most of the jackets had, but still retained the classic form. It truly did look wonderful on Ryan and, without further consultation, Jamie unzipped it and pulled it off of her. She marched over to the counter to pay for it, ignoring the $350 price tag, but Ryan snuck up behind her, spotted the tag, and practically exploded.

"How much?" she shouted.

"It's worth it," Jamie said defiantly, as she handed the clerk her charge card.

"Not to me!" Ryan pulled the coat from the counter, fully intending to replace it on the rack.

"It's not for you," Jamie replied as she pulled it right back. "I want to see you in this, Ryan. Now let me have some fun!" She scowled at the grinning clerk taking in the whole scene.

"I think we need to have that talk," Ryan said through gritted teeth, then stalked out of the store.

Jamie followed behind her as she strode purposefully down the street. It was obvious that Ryan was angry—very angry, in fact. She didn't slow down all the way to the car and, when she got in, she sat in the passenger seat rather than the driver's side, as was her custom.

Jamie slid into the driver's seat and took a big breath. "Ryan, please don't be angry with me."

Ryan also took in a deep breath and closed her eyes. She turned to Jamie and said, "I need a few minutes. Can we talk when we get home?"

Jamie nodded and started the car. Tears were trickling down her face by the time they arrived home, and Ryan felt her stomach clench at the thought of causing her lover pain. She got out and went around to the driver's side of the car where she opened the door and extended a hand to help her out. Jamie grasped her hand and pulled her into a rough embrace. "I can't stand it when you're mad at me," she sobbed into her chest.

Ryan patted her back soothingly for a few moments as her sobs grew deeper, cooing to her softly, "It's okay. I'm not mad. We just need to work this out."

"You are too mad," she mumbled into her shirt.

"Okay, you're right, I *am* mad, but we still need to work this out. We need to talk about it, or it'll get worse."

"I'm the one who wanted to talk about it yesterday … and the day before," she reminded her. "I knew it'd bother you to be down here, and I wanted to set up some ground rules."

"You're right, sweetheart. I should have listened to you." She bent down to look into Jamie's eyes. "Are you mad at me for not listening to you yesterday?"

"Noooo," she said with a quavering voice.

"Okay, let's go get something to drink and go down to the pool house. I think we need to relax a little bit." She wrapped her arm around Jamie's waist and they went into the kitchen, where they made a pitcher of lemonade. While Ryan placed the pitcher and some plastic mugs on a tray, Jamie ran upstairs and got some papers from her suitcase and returned to walk with Ryan to the pool house.

"You know, I read some advice on arguing once." Ryan was calm now, and there was a twinkle in her eyes. "It said you should always fight naked, since it makes you more vulnerable and lets you see your partner in a vulnerable position, too." She plucked at her partner's shirt by way of encouragement.

"Okay, I'm game," Jamie said, then she quickly stripped out of her clothes. She went into the bathroom to get some towels while Ryan rinsed off in the shower so she wouldn't get sand in the Jacuzzi.

They both slipped into the hot water, both letting out moans of pleasure as they sank up to their necks. Seconds later, Ryan hopped out of the water and trotted to the bathroom. She came out and shot Jamie a shy grin, saying only, "Warm water," as she shrugged and climbed back in.

Jamie gave her an indulgent grin and said, "Can you tell me why you're mad?"

Ryan took a long slug of her lemonade, trying to make sure she phrased her complaint properly. "I'm mad because I don't feel in control. You bought things for me and didn't even ask me if I wanted 'em. Actually," she said, her expression reflective, "my opinion didn't matter."

Jamie nodded slowly. "You're right," she said softly. "That was wrong of me."

Flashing a goofy grin, Ryan tapped at Jamie's nose with her finger. "We can't have much of a fight if you give in so easily."

"That's not what the real fight's about. The big issue is how to handle money in general, not today's little incident."

"Okay. Give me your view. Tell me how you see the problem."

"Okay, I'm used to a certain lifestyle. I don't indulge in it much in Berkeley, but there's a part of me that's comfortable with money, and I like the little comforts that it brings me. I don't want to make you uncomfortable, but I also don't think I'd be happy if we had to live on your salary. And I'd really rather not have to take a job this year."

"Okay, okay, I get your point. I know I make less than you're used to, but I was pulling in twelve hundred bucks a week, thanks to you. If I did that full time, and you matched that, wouldn't that be enough for us? I just can't imagine that we'd need more."

"Is that really how you want it to be, Ryan?" she asked seriously. "Will you always want our living standard to be twice what you make? What should I do with the rest of my money?"

"You can do whatever you want with it, Jamie." Her rising voice was beginning to reveal her frustration. "I don't want to depend on you financially, can't you see that?"

"Why not?!" she asked, starting to get angry again.

"Because it's *your* money. It's not mine. I don't want to feel like you keep me."

"Is that how you'd feel?" she asked, truly incredulous.

The volume of their voices, and the tension between them, had been rising. Ryan took a deep breath and made a conscious effort to de-escalate from argument back down to discussion. In a softer tone, she admitted, "Kinda."

"Ryan, you've done as much to deserve that money as I have!"

"What? I haven't done anything to deserve it."

"That's my point! Neither have I! I got that money by nothing more than an accident of birth. It could have been you or me or some child from Appalachia. It was an accident. The last person in my mother's family who really worked for money was her great-grandfather. He worked his ass off, but everyone else hasn't had to do a thing since then, except keep an eye on it."

"That doesn't matter. It's yours now, and I don't want to take it from you."

Jamie dropped her head back against her shoulders and watched the clouds drifting overhead through the glass roof. The contemplative mood lasted for several minutes without an interruption from Ryan, who gazed at her placidly. Finally she lifted her head and addressed her partner, "Have you ever dreamed about winning the lottery?"

A small furrow crossed her forehead as she shook her head in surprise at the unexpected direction of the question. Then a little smile came over her face as she recounted, "Rory and I used to dream about winning millions of bucks, and we used to talk about how we'd spend it. We always had Da quitting his job, and we had cool cars and toys—lots and lots of toys."

"What if we each had a regular job, and you won the lottery? Would you spend the money on us, or would you put it in the bank and buy yourself occasional luxuries while we lived on my $30,000 a year?"

"That's not really analogous, Jamie," she explained patiently. "I would've won the money from some small effort on my part. Anything—good or bad—that happens to me, happens to us both. Of course I'd share it with you equally."

"That's exactly how I feel! This is something good that happened to me, and I want to share it with you. I know there will be bad things that happen to us. I know you'll share any of my burdens. Why won't you share in my blessings?"

Ryan pursed her lips and lifted herself out of the tub. She sat on the edge of the spa with her feet still dangling inside. "I don't know, but it doesn't feel right. I feel like I'm taking something from you that isn't mine."

"Well, technically that's true, but not accepting my money punishes *me*."

"That's a stretch," Ryan scoffed.

"Okay," she drawled. "I haven't been to Europe for over a year. I like to go every year, and I was planning on going this summer. Would you prefer that I went alone, or that I deprive myself of something I enjoy because you can't afford it?"

"But, Jamie," she moaned as she rubbed her face with both hands. "Bringing me up to your lifestyle would involve a ton of money! It'd cost $100,000 to travel and buy me clothes and go out to nice restaurants all the time. I can't let you spend your inheritance like that!" Ryan was struggling to understand Jamie's stance on this issue, but it went against everything she'd been taught about fending for herself.

The smaller woman narrowed her gaze and stared directly into Ryan's troubled eyes. "I've seen you give change to the homeless. Do you even think about that money?"

"No, but it's just change, usually less than a dollar. What has that got to do with anything?"

"Ryan, the money I spend is barely pocket change compared to what I have. I earned more in interest today than the sum of all the money I've ever spent on you."

"Jamie," she laughed, shaking her head at the obviously ridiculous statement. "I know math isn't your strong point, but that can't be true."

Pursing her lips against the sting of the jibe, she asked defiantly, "How much do you think I've spent on you, in total."

"Gee, I don't know," she said. "Golf, dinners, some clothes, maybe three thousand dollars."

"Look at my most recent trust statement for the Smith trust." She held one of the papers out to Ryan, forcing her to focus on it. "Now look in the corner here and tell me what my average daily earnings were for the March quarter."

"Holy crap!" Ryan's mouth fell open in amazement. "This can't be accurate!"

"Ryan, not only is this accurate, it doesn't reflect the money I'll get from the Dunlop Trust when I turn thirty. That's where the real bucks are. Plus, because of wise investing, my mother has lots more than I do, and I'm her only heir."

Ryan sank back onto the tile, her feet still in the water. "This is kinda making me sick to my stomach," she said weakly.

"That's how I feel sometimes. It's way too much money for one person to handle."

"So, you're basically telling me that you could buy anything you want and never have to even look at a price tag." She spoke slowly as realization dawned and she came to an acute awareness of just how immense Jamie's assets were.

"Yes. And I could do the same for all of my friends, not just you. I could buy anything, and I do mean anything, that I wanted, and not even give it a moment's thought."

"God, when you look at it that way, you really *are* moderate."

"Well, thanks," she said, still smarting from the earlier barb. "I'm glad you noticed."

Ryan had the good grace to look slightly embarrassed. "No, really, I'm a spendthrift compared to you. Until recently, I'd been earning just enough to get by, and I still bought myself every new piece of sports equipment that came out. I've gotta tell you, I admire your restraint."

"That's exactly what I'm talking about. I think you're right. I've spent less than three thousand dollars on you over the nine months I've known you. That's less than a third of what I earn in a day. That's why it hurts my feelings when you won't let me buy you a few little things. It gives me such pleasure, and it's not like I'm always throwing money at you."

"You're right, you're right. I had no idea how much you had. I thought that what you spent on me could put a big dent in your assets. I'm sorry I didn't try to understand sooner."

"Do you also understand that I want you to share this burden with me?"

"I understand the words, but I don't really understand what you want me to do," she admitted.

"I'd like to die with next to nothing left, Ryan. I want to figure out some way to give this all away, but I want to do it in a way that really changes some lives." The earnestness in her voice left no doubt that she truly wanted others to reap some benefits from her money. "But first, I wanna prepare us for the future. I want to cover your expenses for graduate school."

"Oh, Jamie, I don't know if I can do that." Ryan shook her head, knowing that an outright refusal would hurt Jamie, but that an acceptance would undermine her own self-respect.

"Yes, you can. We can figure out a way for you to be comfortable. You could even pay me back if you needed to, but I don't want you to have to work the number of hours you'll have to work to afford to stay in school. I want to spend time with you. Don't you want that, too?" The look on her face was so plaintive that Ryan's heart skipped a beat.

"Of course I do, babe. But I'm working hard now to make sure I can concentrate at the next level. I've saved enough to cover my living expenses for a couple of years if we live with Da. I won't need any more money."

Suddenly, it dawned on Jamie that she wasn't just arguing with Ryan. She was arguing with the dozens of O'Flahertys and Ryans that had combined to instill the strict work ethic in her partner. "Honey," she soothed. "I agree that you have to make sacrifices to get what you want. But what sense does it make to make an unnecessary sacrifice? If you go to Stanford, you're not gonna want to live in the city. You'll want to work to pay for half of our living expenses. I just know you will."

Ryan didn't have a ready answer for that, so she blew out another frustrated breath and lay back against the tile, wracking her brain for a good argument.

"Sweetheart," Jamie cooed. "I hate to be selfish, but I think we need time together as much as any other thing. Grad school is harder than undergrad, and your schoolwork will take up a lot more of your time. I think we have to make our relationship a priority too, baby, and having time together is a must if we're gonna get along well."

Ryan could agree with some of Jamie's arguments, but not others. "Okay, the grad school thing is a separate issue. If I go for a doctorate I won't have to pay tuition. But the living situation could get dicey. Let's table that agenda item for a later date." A sincere smile assured her partner that her concerns were being heard. "For now, let's settle the little issues, like buying me clothes and things."

Jamie hated to let the issue go, especially since she felt like she had Ryan backed up against the wall. But she decided that she didn't want to win this argument as much as she wanted Ryan to agree to a compromise. "Okay, it's like this. I'm a very visual person. Visual stimulation arouses me more than my other senses. I've been dreaming of you in a big black leather jacket since the first time I put my arms around you that first night on your bike. Having this jacket really *is* for me," she said sincerely. "I know you wouldn't buy a jacket like that, so why deny myself the satisfaction of buying it for you, if I really want to see you in it?"

"Okay, you win that point. I'll play dress up for you. You can buy me as many outfits as your wicked heart desires. Police officer, fire fighter, construction worker, lumberjack, you name it. Now what about day-to-day things? Like dinners and golf and stuff?"

Jamie didn't want to be harsh, but she felt like she had to be honest. "I've spent nine months going to crummy little take-out joints in Berkeley. I don't mind it, because I'm with you, but I like to have an exquisite meal every once in a while. The last great meal I had was on my birthday, and you paid for that! Does it make sense to only go when you want to spend your money on the same thing? Or would you rather I went with someone else? I bet Chip would tag along …" she teased.

"I bet he would," Ryan said through narrowed eyes. "So either I go out for fabulous dinners with you, or you find someone else to go with?"

"Pretty much," Jamie admitted with a laugh, feeling confident that her partner knew she was joking about alternate companions.

Ryan decided it was time to swallow some of her pride. "All right, all right. Thanks to you, I now make a good living. I'm learning that I enjoy a good meal almost as much as you do. So, I propose that we go out for a nice dinner twice a month. You pay once and I pay once." She cocked her head and waited for her partner's reply.

A wide smile crossed Jamie's face. "I like your style, O'Flaherty."

Ryan extended her hand and they shook on the agreement, each feeling that their needs had been met.

"How about a swim now that we've had our financial consensus?"

"Sounds great," Jamie said. They swam in the warm pool for a while, frolicking like otters. Jamie spent a lot of time climbing on Ryan's back while she tried to swim. Then Ryan took advantage of her lover's greater buoyancy and forced Jamie to carry her all around the pool as payback. When they were tired and wrinkled, Ryan got out and sat down on the chaise, pulling over the phone and dialing home. "Hey," she said when Conor picked up the phone.

"Oh, it's the honeymooners," he laughed. "Did you call to give me a blow by blow?"

"I'll give you one word to sum up the entire experience," she teased. "It's … fine."

"Well, since you obviously won't share the dirty details with me, why are you calling?"

"How would you like to come down on Saturday and play Pebble Beach with me, and then give me a lift home?"

"Oh gee, Ryan, I'd love to, but I was going to wash my hair on Saturday," he drawled. "Are you nuts? When and where—I'm there."

"Jamie's got to go to a graduation on Saturday, and she's leaving at ten-thirty, so I thought we could play a bit after that."

"Hmm." There was a brief silence as he worked out the logistics. "How about if I come down after work on Friday? Then I don't have to waste four hours on Saturday morning to drive down there."

"Oh, gee, Conor, I don't know … that's our last night here …"

"Listen, you sex maniac, I don't want to interrupt your little party, I just don't want to drive that far in the morning. Leave the front door unlocked with a note telling me where to sleep. You can keep right on doing whatever you do in your bedroom, or the dining room or wherever you perform."

Ryan laughed at his teasing and told him to hold on for a second. "Jamie, could Conor come down on Friday night and stay in the guest apartment?"

"Sure, that's a much better idea. I'd like to see him."

"I wouldn't," she laughed. "That's why I want to put him in the guest apartment!"

She put the handset back to her mouth. "Okay, bro, it's all set. I'll leave a note on the door telling you where to sleep. Now get a pencil to take down the directions. Oh, and Conor, look sharp for golf. They're not used to our kind around here," she laughed as Jamie rolled her eyes.

After the call, Jamie went over and climbed onto Ryan's lap. She wriggled around a little to get comfortable, and finally satisfied herself with her position.

"Do you know what I want to hear?" Ryan asked as Jamie reclined on her.

"What's that?"

"I want to hear more about this leather fetish," she said in a low voice.

It took her a few seconds to reply, but Jamie finally did. "I wouldn't really call it a fetish. But that first night that you took me for a ride on your bike started my imagination working overtime. Every time I saw you on it, I thought of you in a big leather jacket, a white tank top and your ripped jeans."

"What did you have me doing in your fantasy?" Ryan was fascinated by this glimpse into Jamie's dream world and wanted all of the details.

"Well, at first it wasn't you in my fantasy." Ryan frowned in puzzlement at that, but Jamie was oblivious, lost in her vision. "I would think about some dark stranger in a bar, holding a beer, looking tough. It wasn't clear whether it was a man or a woman. I guess that should have been another clue, huh?" She laughed as she slapped herself in the forehead. "But as time went on, and it was clear that I wanted you, I'd imagine you as the dark stranger in that scenario. I'd come in, and you'd take me, right there in the bar."

Ryan's eyes narrowed and her pulse picked up as she envisioned herself in her assigned role. "Sounds pretty hot," she said with fervor. "Was there any conversation?"

"Not a word," Jamie said. "You'd look at me, and I'd melt into your arms. It was mostly about the force of your personality, and the way I felt drawn to you."

"Speaking about the force of my personality, I'm really sorry that I got angry with you this afternoon." Ryan placed an apologetic kiss on the top of the head resting against her shoulder. "It really bothers me when we argue 'cause I feel so close to you. It stuns me when we don't agree on major things, and I think that makes the fight seem worse than it really is."

"Yeah, I think you're right," Jamie agreed. She turned her head to look back up at Ryan with searching eyes. "It really upset me when you wouldn't talk to me. I felt totally shut out."

"I didn't want to say anything that I'd regret. I don't like to argue when I'm upset—it seems too dangerous."

"Well, we need to figure out some way to give you a little space, but have me not feel like you're really mad."

"I don't have a solution to that right off the top of my head, but I'll think about it, okay?"

"Okay. I will too." She gave Ryan a quick kiss, and discussion time was over. They got up and went to start dinner, walking through the warm afternoon sunshine, hand in hand.

Both women were in the mood for a little spice, so they decided to have mango chutney chicken for dinner. While the chicken was baking, they each grabbed a beer and went out on the patio next to the living room to look at the ocean for a while.

"So … day three is almost over," Ryan said. "How do you think it's going?"

"Hmm, I'd say it's been idyllic," Jamie mused. "I feel better than I have in years, to tell you the truth. I'm rested and satisfied, and I feel very well loved. I was really worried that things would be odd or uncomfortable between us, but that hasn't happened much."

"Nope. Not much at all," Ryan agreed. "But I did want to ask you about one little thing."

"What's that, babe?"

"I know this is hard for you, but the only way we're gonna be really comfortable with each other is if we can learn to be really, really open about expressing our feelings."

"I agree," Jamie said, with a look of concern crossing her features. "Tell me what's wrong."

"No, no, there's nothing wrong," Ryan insisted. "Please don't think that. I want to be able to have an on-going dialogue about things—and I don't want either of us to be tense about any topics. The more we can talk about it, the more comfortable we'll feel."

"Okay," Jamie said, and Ryan noticed the massive breath that she took to calm herself. "What's on your mind?"

"Well, yesterday, when we were making love, I was a little disappointed when you asked me not to ..."

Jamie covered her face with her hands and she mumbled, "Aaargh! Do we really have to talk about this?"

Ryan considered the question for a moment before she replied, "That depends on whether you want to have an open, trusting, sexual relationship or not."

Jamie's head jerked up. "Do you really believe that? You really think we can't have sex without over-analyzing it?"

The tone of Jamie's voice and her choice of words stung Ryan a little, but she didn't back off. This was as important to her as settling the money issue was to Jamie. "I think we could have a decent sex life if we just stuck to what we've done so far and left it at that. And if that's really what you want, I'll try to cut you some slack." She spent a moment considering how frank to be, and decided to tell all. "But that's not what I want. I want our sex life to be as open and honest and fulfilling as the rest of our life. It surprises me to think that you don't feel that way."

Jamie got up from her chair and knelt down in front of her partner, "You know that I do. This is hard for me ... very hard."

Ryan reached down and pulled her onto her lap. As Jamie's head rested on her shoulder, she tried to draw her out. "Tell me what's hard for you."

"It embarrasses me to talk about sex," she admitted. "I think it should just be something natural that happens between us. I don't see why we have to take the magic out of the whole experience by talking about it."

"You don't seem to mind talking about other facets of our relationship," Ryan reminded her. "As a matter of fact, you seem to enjoy it when we talk about things."

"I do," she conceded. "But sex is different. It shouldn't need to be analyzed. It should just ... happen."

"Okay," Ryan drawled. "I wanted to make a certain thing happen yesterday, and you didn't. Do I keep trying that certain thing until I wear you down? Or should I try something once and then never try it again?"

"Well," Jamie mused, "that depends on the thing. There are some things that I might never want to do, and I don't want you to keep asking. But some things might be okay in general ... just not that day."

"And how do I know which of those things are which?" Ryan asked with a guileless expression on her face.

Jamie knew she was trapped, but she tried to extricate herself. "You can … just tell," she decided.

"Okaaaay," Ryan said again, "there are things I'd like you to do to me that you haven't tried. How do I ask you to do them?"

"Umm," Jamie thought furiously, trying to come up with a good set of signals. "You could kinda direct me, you know, with your hands or something."

Ryan nodded judiciously before she said, "There are some things I'd like you to do that don't lend themselves to hand signals. Then what?"

The smaller woman's mind reeled, trying to imagine what in the hell her lover could possibly be talking about. "Ummm, I guess we have to cross that bridge when we come to it," she decided, knowing how weak that solution sounded.

"Umm-hmm," Ryan said, looking doubtful. "That sounds like it'll work."

Jamie's head hit Ryan's shoulder with surprising force. "I know this is silly, but I really feel uncomfortable."

"Babe, there's only one way to get over the discomfort. And I think you know what that is. We trust each other, Jamie. I think we have to learn how to be open about this stuff. Will you at least give it a try?"

A heavy sigh preceded her reluctant agreement. "I … I'll try."

Ryan gave her a gentle squeeze and said, "Thanks. I guarantee that your discomfort will go away eventually. Now, will you tell me why you didn't want me to taste you yesterday?"

Jamie groaned as she complained, "Did you have to start there?"

"Babe," Ryan said earnestly, "tell me why the mere topic of oral sex is so hard for you."

Jamie's head shook slowly against Ryan's shoulder as she considered the question. "It's so … I don't know," she moaned. "I don't have words for how I feel. It felt like something that I wasn't ready for right then. Can't we just leave it at that?"

The timer on the oven buzzed, and as Jamie hopped up to return to the kitchen, Ryan stayed in her chair and considered their conversation. She knew that she'd been pushing her partner past her comfort zone, and she also realized that it was going to be next to impossible for her to force the inexperienced woman to get through her discomfort. *I think I need to back off a little and see how things settle. She might feel more comfortable discussing things in smaller bits.* Sighing heavily, she followed her partner into the kitchen to help with the dinner preparations.

Ryan busied herself setting the table while Jamie put some rice on to cook. Ryan was concentrating on the simple task when she felt a pair of arms encircle her waist. "Mad at me?" a small voice asked.

Ryan turned in the embrace and answered honestly. "Of course not. I'd never be mad at you because you were having a tough time. I know this is hard for you. I'm only trying to make things great for us in the long run. We have plenty of time to work things out."

"But are you happy with what we've done so far?" Jamie persisted.

"Yes! Most definitely, yes!" Ryan insisted, hugging the hesitant woman to her chest. "Please don't think I'm disappointed, babe. I swear I'm not! I want our sex life to be all that it can be—and I know it will be, once we're comfortable. Just because we haven't done everything possible doesn't mean that what we have done hasn't been fantastic. It has, baby, it's truly been fantastic!"

"You sure?" the small voice asked again, begging for reassurance.

"Positive," Ryan vowed. "Our relationship is going to develop over time, babe. I only want to make sure we have a good foundation—and I firmly believe that foundation has to start with open communication. I swear that's all I'm trying to do. I want to make sure we both feel able to express our wants and needs."

"Okay," Jamie said as she went back to her cooking. "I'll do my best to make sure we have a good foundation."

As they relaxed in their chairs after dinner, Ryan spent several minutes praising her lover's cooking prowess. Jamie beamed at her, charmed as always by the effusive compliments that Ryan was so willing to offer.

"What would you like to do tomorrow?" Jamie asked. "We've spent far too much time doing things I like. I want you to have some fun, too."

Ryan shook her head, smiling the whole while. "We haven't done one thing that I haven't enjoyed," she insisted. "Not one thing."

"Come on," Jamie persisted, drawing patterns on the skin of Ryan's hand with her index finger. "There has to be something you want to do."

"Okay," Ryan said, as she blew out a breath. "I'd like to get some real exercise. I enjoy golf, but in terms of exercise, that's just a slow, halting walk."

"Name it," the blonde demanded. "Whitewater rafting, mountain climbing, rappelling down office buildings …"

"Jamie, don't be silly," Ryan cajoled. "There aren't any office buildings around here tall enough to make rappelling any fun at all!" She ducked the pinch that her comment elicited and said, "I think I'd like to play in the water. Are you up for that?"

"Sure. You name it. I was entirely serious."

"Okay," Ryan mused thoughtfully. "Surfing."

"Surfing?"

"Surfing … and shopping," the blue eyes twinkled.

"Shopping? You want to go shopping?"

"*My* kinda shopping," Ryan declared with a beaming grin.

While Ryan cleaned the kitchen, Jamie sat on a stool and watched her work. After a few minutes she found that she was becoming mesmerized by the languid movements of her partner as she gracefully moved around the kitchen. She was thinking about attempting to distract her for a little love when Ryan announced that she was going to take a quick shower to get the chlorine from the Jacuzzi off.

Jamie was a little unsure of herself at this point. She was still uneasy about their earlier talk, and she wasn't comfortable making the first move. In the past she could just wait until Jack made a move—since he made one nearly every day—then she could decide whether or not she was in the mood. But she didn't want it to be that way with Ryan, and it was clear that wasn't what Ryan wanted either. In the middle of her reverie, she heard the shower stop running and decided to go upstairs and rinse off, hoping to get up her nerve to entice her partner. Ryan was coming out of the bathroom, sparkling clean, when Jamie arrived. "Hi, sweets," the dark-haired woman said with a smile. Jamie gave her a kiss and took a moment to breathe in her clean scent. "You smell great," she said in her best seductive tone.

But Ryan didn't seem to notice the tone or the small hand sliding up and down her backside. "I'll go downstairs and see what I can rustle up for dessert, okay?"

"Um ... alright," Jamie said. "Will you come back up?"

"No. It's a little early for bed," she said as she looked at her watch. "It's only seven, hon." She laughed as she tweaked Jamie's nose.

Swallowing her disappointment, Jamie got into the shower and had a little talk with herself. *She isn't like Jack. Yes, she has a healthy sex drive, but you've told her that you didn't like it when Jack came on too strong. You've got to learn to make the first move—or you're not gonna get what you need.*

The warm water slid down her body as her mind continued to muse. *Why don't you go downstairs and tell her what you wan? You know she'll do her best to please you.*

She was still wrestling with her indecision when she went downstairs fifteen minutes later. Noticing that the lights in the kitchen were quite dim, she came around the corner and saw that only the under-cabinet halogen lamps were on. "Ryan?" she called, but received no answer. Coming fully into the room, she gasped aloud as she took in the scene that greeted her.

Ryan was sitting on one of the high stools, leather jacket hanging open, revealing a tight white ribbed cotton tank top. Worn, ripped jeans hugged every curve but, oddly, she was barefoot. Her hair hung loosely against her back, looking a little wild as it curled around her shoulders. Dark sunglasses covered her blue eyes, and she held a beer casually dangling between her open legs. Jamie's mouth went bone dry at the sight of her dark, untamed beauty, and her heart started racing as she took in the fantasy-turned-reality.

In the time it took her shaking legs to propel her across the floor, Jamie fell in love all over again. It wasn't just the way her gorgeous partner looked at the moment, although that alone was enough to do the trick. Rather, it was her willingness to work through any problem, fulfill any fantasy, provide any support, and, in every way possible, make herself the kind of mate that every woman dreams of that made Jamie's heart flutter. Once again, she thanked whatever force brought this precious gift into her life, and she prayed fervently that they would be blessed with many years in which to share their love.

She walked over to her love very slowly, watching her closely. Quickly considering her own long T-shirt and panties, she mentally scolded herself for not being more appropriately dressed. But she was certainly not going to leave now, so she decided to make the best of it.

As she approached Ryan, her lover's dark gaze shifted to meet her. It was impossible to see her eyes through the sunglasses, but she could feel them burning into hers. A tiny ghost of a grin played at the corners of her luscious mouth, and that little bit of playfulness calmed Jamie's anxiety immediately. She slid closer and stood right between Ryan's spread legs, then grasped her tanned face with both of her hands and tilted the dark head to kiss her.

To Jamie's surprise, Ryan responded in a casual, almost lazy fashion. She was clearly waiting to be seduced by her partner, and she was going to make her work for it. Jamie accepted the challenge, beginning to press into her as she kissed her deeply. Her tongue slid from her own mouth, and was slowly sucked into Ryan's. She probed all over the warm surface, running her tongue over the perfect white teeth, one by one.

She leaned back a bit to gaze at Ryan's impassive face. Determined to make that face reflect the passion that she felt, she dove into her task with gusto. Sliding her hands beneath the big jacket, she found the warm, firm breasts. No bra guarded them, leaving them vulnerable to her caresses. She leaned in and put her mouth on each breast in turn, sucking them through the thin material. Her muffled groan revealed her feelings, and Ryan's nipple grew rock-hard before the desire-filled sound faded. Continued sucking brought a slight hip movement from her prey, but it wasn't nearly enough to please Jamie. Lifting her head, she continued to squeeze the tender flesh, eliciting a small gasp when she firmly pinched each taut nipple.

Her head tilted again, and she began to slowly kiss and suck on Ryan's lips and tongue. She ran her tongue all around the dark pink flesh, pulling in the top lip and then the bottom for firm sucks and tender nibbles. It was clear that Ryan was trying to remain passive, but faint moans and tiny sighs began to slip through her lips, revealing her growing arousal. Jamie's hands had not stopped caressing the sensitive breasts as she hefted each mound in a hand. She pulled back and gazed at the perfect orbs, fascinated by their weight and softness. Her head tilted a bit, and as her eyes met Ryan's once again, the dark beauty did not try to hide the knowing smile that slowly crossed her face. It was a glorious moment for the less-experienced woman. She felt so perfectly understood by her partner that her heart swelled with emotion. It was clear that Ryan got a tremendous amount of pleasure from having her breasts loved, but equally clear that she received as much pleasure from the fact that Jamie loved them so. This mutual give and take was something that Jamie had never experienced, and she felt weak with elation as she took it in.

Taking a few deep breaths to center herself, she dropped her head and again sucked the swells of flesh firmly through the tank top. Ryan's response this time was much more enthusiastic. Her hips had begun to gently thrust in time with the suckling of her breasts, and a few moans now escaped her parted lips.

Trying to maintain her cool, Ryan slowly raised her beer bottle and took a few long slugs to relieve her parched throat. She sank down even lower on her stool as her elbows caught the edge of the counter. In a deliberate, tauntingly seductive move, she slowly spread her legs wide as her sexy smile grew. Jamie's eyes popped open and her mouth grew dry when Ryan's head lolled back against her shoulders and that lucky beer bottle was lowered and teasingly trailed up and down the seam of her jeans. As the edge of the bottle hit a particularly sensitive spot, a gasp flew from her lips and her chest swelled as a deep, wanton growl immediately followed.

The blatant display of her desire propelled Jamie to accept the unspoken invitation and slowly, teasingly, pop open the buttons of the fly, one by one. She grasped the waistband and started to slide the pants down past Ryan's hips which were wordlessly lifted just enough to aid in the process.

As the fabric slid down, Ryan's arms locked around Jamie's neck and pulled her close. The rough, almost bruising, kiss that followed caused Jamie's heart to thump loudly in her chest, and she had to struggle to maintain her composure. The denim rested about halfway down Ryan's shins, and Jamie bent to remove the pants. But in a move that surprised both of them, Jamie fell to her knees and dropped her face right onto Ryan's bright white boxers.

A startled gasp flew from both mouths, followed by a low, sexy moan from Ryan. As her pulse continued to thrum in her ears, Jamie felt her chest expand as she inhaled her lover's wild scent deep into her lungs, savoring the sensation. Her mind shut down as her body reacted to the heady scent. Unsure of why she was doing it, but needing the sensation more than breath itself, she began to move her head around in a small circle, grinding her entire face into Ryan's throbbing vulva. Ryan began to groan softly, and her cries rose in pitch and frequency as Jamie continued to rub her mouth all over her through the fabric.

Ryan felt that she was nearly out of control, and a nagging voice in her head warned her to temper her response. But the freedom of revealing herself so fully to her partner was too powerful an urge to resist. Her hands flew to Jamie's head, her fingers lacing themselves through her fine, golden hair. Gently but firmly, she began to guide her partner's head, moving her an inch or two, until a voice she barely recognized as her own murmured, "That's it, baby. Ohh, right there … yes … ohh, so good!"

Jamie began to pull back, but Ryan didn't want to let her go, and she held on a little tighter than she should have. Seeking to reassure her needy partner that she would be satisfied, Jamie ran her hands tenderly across her partner's firm abdomen, dipping one hand into the shorts, caressing the curls. "Patience love, patience." Looking into the green eyes and seeing a look of complete confidence, Ryan released her lover's head and let her own fall back limply as she let out a low, deep sigh.

Still in her kneeling position, Jamie gripped the hems of the pants and, finally, slowly pulled the jeans off Ryan's long legs and tossed them aside, leaving her in her shorts, tank top and jacket. She urged her up; Ryan looked a little confused behind her glasses, but she got the idea and jumped up onto the cool, polished concrete counter, bracing her upper body with her hands. Ryan offered a silent apology to Mrs. Evans as she slid across the surface and waited for her partner to make a move. Jamie climbed onto the stool and placed Ryan's bare feet on her thighs, grasped her knees and slid her thighs open wide, a devastatingly sexy smile gracing her face.

Ryan's heart was beating so loudly in her chest that she was certain Jamie could hear it. The determined blonde began to work on her breasts again, sucking on them through the now-transparent white tank. Roughly pushing the material up until it gathered just above the tender globes, she dove for them forcefully, sucking on each nipple, biting each mound, as Ryan moaned and writhed on the cool concrete, her hips never ceasing their sensual dance.

The scent of Ryan's arousal called to her, and without conscious thought Jamie once again dropped her head between Ryan's legs and nuzzled her face lovingly against her squirming partner. Ryan's deep voice now rose in pitch, as her moans became whimpers and gasps of pleasure. Jamie grasped and kneaded the heavy breasts with both hands as she rubbed her face over Ryan's heat in a tight little circle. "Ahh!" Ryan cried, as Jamie rubbed her nose straight up and down several times.

Jamie slowly sat up as her hands lifted to tenderly caress Ryan's face. Gently removing the dark glasses that covered the deep blue eyes, she allowed her gaze to linger for a minute as their eyes locked in a look as tender as an embrace. Maintaining the fervid stare, Jamie allowed the love flowing from her partner to calm her racing heart. Her hands moved to Ryan's waist, and she rested them on the smoothly muscled skin for a long moment, feeling the desire that passed between them and reveling in the intimacy of their connection. With complete confidence, she grasped the waistband of the shorts and pulled them down. Ryan assisted by once again lifting her hips.

Maintaining eye contact, Jamie slid to the edge of the stool and gently placed Ryan's feet on her shoulders. Her blonde head tilted, and she batted her eyes slowly and whispered, "Can I taste you?"

Blue eyes blinked slowly as Ryan realized that her partner actually needed an answer. Her entire body was shaking with desire, but she struggled to reach out and slowly guide her head. "Please," she gasped. "Please, Jamie."

Their eyes locked for an instant, sharing the intimacy of the moment. Smiling serenely, Jamie dipped her head and delicately tasted her partner for the first time. "Ohh yesssss! Yes!" Ryan gasped as the incredibly smooth tongue slid from one end of her wetness to the other.

Jamie paused for just a second, allowing the scent of her partner to fill her lungs. Her eyelids fluttered closed as her head dipped again to savor the powerfully erotic taste. Her touch was slow, so painfully slow that Ryan had to grip the edge of the counter to deny her need to grasp Jamie's head and force the pace. But she knew that

Jamie had to be allowed the time to acclimate to the sensation, so she clamped down with every fiber of her iron will to control her impulses.

As the moments passed, Jamie felt her confidence build as her lover's rabid desire continued to be evident. Ryan urged her on with every signal available—she moaned and whimpered, running her hands through Jamie's hair with a reassuring touch. She twitched her hips rhythmically, showing Jamie with her body that her touch was very welcome and very much needed.

Now that she felt comfortable, Jamie began to explore a little bit. She teased her partner with a feather light touch, then leaned in and nuzzled her roughly. To her surprise, Ryan seemed to enjoy every type of touch, so she continued to investigate. She slowly ran her tongue straight up the glistening, swollen lips, and then gently opened her partner with her fingers, exposing the soft pink inner folds to her searching tongue. Her delicate touch slid up and down the impossibly smooth skin as Ryan thrashed about on the counter. Unable to control herself any longer, Ryan placed her hands on Jamie's head and pulled her a little closer as the hot tongue began to focus on the smooth inner folds. "Yes, baby, ohh yes. Oh God, just like that. Just like that," she gasped out as Jamie continued to tease her. Ryan's hips thrust harder and more uncontrollably now, and Jamie had a tough time staying with her. She grabbed the thrusting hips with her hands and forced her to remain relatively still. Her actions seemed to increase Ryan's excitement, as evidenced by her grunts, so she held her even more firmly, standing and pressing down with her weight.

"*Yes!*" Ryan cried, as Jamie softened her tongue and moved her head back and forth quickly, covering her entirely with her warm, wet tongue.

Despite Jamie's grip, Ryan's hips began to dance once again as she shook violently. "Ohh God, oh God, *Oh, yes!*" she shouted as her orgasm ripped through her body. Her moans continued as her body shook and rocked so forcefully that Jamie had to struggle to stay connected. As soon as Ryan regained muscle control she grasped the blonde head firmly, and restrained her so that she could barely reach her oversensitive skin. Her legs fell from Jamie's shoulders as they splayed open lewdly, her hands dropping limply as she released her grip.

Jamie rested her head on Ryan's abdomen, luxuriating in the feel of the pulsating flesh under her cheek. Spasms continued to roll through Ryan's limp body for long minutes as Jamie slowly, tenderly and lovingly rubbed her hands across the still-heaving torso. When she felt that the tremors had slowed, Jamie finally gave in to an overpowering urge. She dropped her head, and watched Ryan's entire vulva contract rhythmically, placing several small kisses on the insides of her thighs. Ryan jerked a bit as she felt her lover's head so close to her over-stimulated flesh, but she relaxed when she realized that Jamie was going to be content to kiss and lick her thighs. The pale head stayed right where it was until she was certain that all of the contractions had passed. Then she sat up a bit, resting her chin on Ryan's pubic bone. As Ryan's head lifted off the counter, she stared at Jamie for a long moment, finally asking with suspicion, "Are you absolutely certain you've never done this before?"

"Scout's honor," she promised with a beaming smile.

The tightly corded tendons in Ryan's neck stood out starkly while she maintained her gaze. "If I wasn't sure of your integrity, I'd think you had at least ten years of experience. You have a God-given talent that shouldn't be wasted, and I'm just the woman to exploit your gift."

"I couldn't agree with you more." Jamie smiled up at her lover, still a little overcome by the passion they'd shared.

Ryan trailed her still-shaking fingers through the blonde hair as she lazily asked, "How was that for you, baby?"

As she leaned her head into Ryan's touch, the smaller woman considered the question for a moment. "I honestly had to think about what you meant," she said with a smirk. "It seemed like a totally natural thing to do. Told ya I didn't need to talk about it," she smirked impishly.

Ryan's laugh caused Jamie's head to bob a bit from its resting place on her leather-covered chest. "As usual, you were right."

Ryan's hand still trailed through her hair, and the soft touch made Jamie feel totally content. She nestled her head up against the caressing hand, shaking her head slightly in wonder at herself. "I would have never believed it if you'd told me that touching you that way would feel so natural, but it did, babe. It was just another way to love you." She shrugged her shoulders a little bit as if it were already commonplace.

"So you weren't put off by it?"

Jamie sat up abruptly and stared at her partner in shock. "Put off? Why would I be put off?"

"Well, it *is* a little different ..."

"Ryan," she said softly, "I've *never* made love before this week. I've had sex, and I've been emotionally connected but I've never made love before. The way I touched you tonight was just an extension of our lovemaking. I *needed* to taste you, honey," she said emphatically. "I need to experience every part of your body. I need to taste you and kiss you and touch you everywhere."

To show her complete agreement, Ryan sat up as well as her still-weak muscles would let her. She wrapped Jamie in her arms and gently kissed her glistening face, purring at the delicious sensation of tasting herself on her lover's lips.

The disparity of their positions and the distance from her lover's face was suddenly too much, and Jamie climbed onto the counter to continue the tender kiss. When they broke apart, she lay down until they were shoulder to shoulder, and rolled over slightly, then turned Ryan's chin so she could look deep into her eyes, her voice like a whisper of air against Ryan's skin. "The way I felt when my lips first touched you was almost mystical. I could feel your pulse beating through your soft skin, and I wanted to crawl right up inside." She shivered a little at the memory of the sensation, and Ryan blinked slowly as she stared at her for a long time.

The tanned face relaxed into a smile as Ryan whispered, "You have such a beautiful way of expressing your love. You touch me so deeply that I feel ... overcome with love for you." She maintained the deep eye contact as she leaned in and began to kiss her partner with a wild fury. In no time at all, Jamie was naked and squirming on the counter, weathering the assault from Ryan's hands and mouth and tongue.

Ryan was stretched out lengthwise on the counter, her torso supported by her forearms. Jamie's upper body was braced by her locked arms, her legs spread amazingly wide as Ryan scooted forward to rest between them. Ryan still wore her jacket, and as she drew close, the heavy metal zippers touched the insides of Jamie's sensitive thighs, and she let out a yelp.

Ryan slowly lowered her head and began to kiss and lick her way up the tender flesh. She worked her way up one thigh and down the other, Jamie's deep moans providing constant encouragement. As much as she wanted to lower her head and taste her partner, she was hesitant. Since Jamie had expressed her discomfort with being on the receiving end of the act, she felt like she shouldn't indulge her own desires until she received a clear signal that her partner wanted her to continue.

After she had lavished her attention on the deliciously smooth thighs, she had to acknowledge that no clear sign had been given, so she decided to bring her lover to orgasm in a slightly less intimate fashion. She used her thumbs to gently manipulate the slick folds as Jamie squealed and twitched her way across the concrete, thoroughly christening it with the evidence of their passion. As Jamie's cries calmed, Ryan rested her head on one quivering thigh, mesmerized by the twitching, spasming flesh.

As soon as she was recovered enough to express her wishes, Jamie tugged her partner up to her, and kissed her with a bold, confident, passionate need. Ryan responded immediately, dipping her fingers into the simmering flesh that ached for her touch, and providing all of the stimulation her partner desired.

Their lovemaking continued long into the evening without a pause, save for one short break for nourishment that immediately turned into a game of "paint the writhing woman with ice cream." After they were both totally spent, and more than a little sticky, Ryan used the last of her reserves to gently lift her lover off the counter and carry her upstairs. As they climbed the stairs, Jamie sleepily inquired, "Honey?"

"Yes, love?" Ryan's deep voice burred against her ear.

"Why were you barefoot?"

Ryan's low laugh echoed up through the huge entryway. "You didn't tell me what shoes your fantasy required. I figured I was better off wearing nothing than choosing the wrong thing. I really wasn't prepared for this," she chuckled. "I didn't bring my ripped jeans, so I had to take a sharp knife to these."

Jamie laughed as she nuzzled up against her neck and said, "It's so nice to have you so willing to make my fantasies come true."

"My pleasure," Ryan said with a chuckle. As she placed her on their bed, she leaned in to ask, "Should I wear it to sleep?" indicating her leather.

"Maybe next time. I don't want to fulfill all of my fantasies at once."

## Chapter Ten

Jamie felt the nuzzling of her neck for many minutes before she could force her eyes open. "Mmmmm," she mumbled, rolling over languidly to kiss her bright-eyed partner. "You smell good."

"I wish I could return the compliment." Ryan delicately sniffed various parts of her lover's body. "But you smell a bit like a brothel ... or an ice cream parlor." Her gentle laugh rang out as she scooted out of the way of Jamie's fingers, which were poised for a pinch.

"And whose fault is that?" Jamie asked petulantly, sitting up to offer a mock glare. "This is *your* scent all over me."

"I've gotta admit, sex smells a lot better before it cures overnight."

Ryan's grin was so infectious that Jamie couldn't maintain the guise of anger. "Okay, I'll wash it off, but only if you promise to reapply it later."

"I think the smell of sex is like sun block, 'apply liberally and reapply throughout the day'," Ryan agreed.

Ryan was sitting at the counter in the kitchen eating an enormous bowl of oatmeal when Jamie arrived. "I'll go fetch the car while you finish up," she announced, kissing Ryan's cheek as she passed.

"I can do that," Ryan mumbled through a mouthful of her breakfast.

"Relax, I've got it covered. You need to get a proper breakfast if you're gonna dazzle me today." Her waggling eyebrows showed how much she was looking forward to watching her partner perform.

Before Ryan could say another word, Jamie was striding out the back door, keys in hand. Several minutes later she pulled up to the side entrance in a huge white Suburban. Loaded on the roof rack was her father's longboard, which she had assured Ryan he would not mind lending out. After adding all of the "necessities" that Ryan insisted they take, they were on their way.

They stopped at the first Starbuck's they passed so Jamie could get an eye opener. Ryan came back out with two huge lattes, two scones and three muffins of various flavors. "Fifteen bucks for a little breakfast," she grumbled.

"Some people would think this was a big breakfast." Jamie patted her leg fondly, shaking her head a bit at Ryan's nearly insatiable appetite.

Ryan had a happy little grin on her face and she chatted away nonstop on the drive up. Jamie rubbed her leg as she grinned over at her. "You love this, don't you?"

"What, surfing?"

"No, not just surfing. You seem to love anything that's risky or hard to do, or that really stresses your body."

"Yeah, I do," she admitted. "It makes me feel more alive to do things where I really put myself out there. Do you understand that?" She cocked her head in question.

Jamie was silent for a moment, considering her answer. "I don't share that predilection, but I think I'm beginning to understand how important it is for you to satisfy that need. It seems pretty primal for you."

"It is. I *need* to do things like this. I don't think I'll ever be the kind of woman who can always take the safe road. Do you think you can live with that?"

"I can live with almost anything, if I get to keep you in the bargain," she said as she flashed her a fond smile.

"I'm yours forever."

The drive to Santa Cruz took a little less than an hour, and the surf report was absolutely correct. The waves were breaking just the way Ryan liked them: big enough to scare away beginners, but small enough to keep her safe.

Ryan pulled the car up to the shoulder of a surfing beach that she had visited a number of times. As she stripped off her navy blue sweatpants and white hooded "Cal" sweatshirt, Jamie had to stifle a laugh at the fight she had to put up to get into her wetsuit. Just before she zipped it all the way up, she twisted her hair up into a bun and stuffed it into the attached hood. Her tight sports bra/swimsuit top, and the absence of her long hair, actually did hide her sex very effectively, and Jamie now understood how people could fail to notice she was a woman when she was in the water. They worked together to get the board off the roof, and then Ryan hefted it over her head as they walked together to the shore.

Before she took off, Ryan squatted down to the beach chair where Jamie lounged and kissed her gently. "Promise that you'll be careful," Jamie demanded as she placed her hands on Ryan's shoulders. "I love every little piece of you, and I want them all back."

"I promise I'll be careful," Ryan said somberly, staring into her partner's eyes.

Jamie threw her arms around her and hugged her so firmly that Ryan had to gasp a little. "Now, go play," she said indulgently, patting her on the butt as a send-off. As

Ryan reached the water, she turned and gave her a little wave and a very big smile, flashing all of her teeth. Just then, and for reasons that she didn't fully understand, Jamie felt an overwhelming sense of sadness for Ryan's mother.

*My God, how unbelievably hard it must have been to see that sweet, trusting little face and know that you were going to leave her. How devastating to close your eyes for the last time, knowing that your baby would never feel your embrace again.*

She watched Ryan cavort in the surf, furiously paddling out to sea. *You did such a wonderful job in such a short time, Fionnuala.* A few tears slid down her face, and she wiped them from her chilled skin with the back of her hand. *You'd be so proud of the woman she's become. I hope you can see her and know how happy she is now.*

Staring out at Ryan, Jamie felt an odd sense of peace settle over her. For an instant, she felt an eerie connection to a woman she would never meet, a woman who would always retain a vitally important place in her partner's life. In that moment, she felt calm and centered, and she knew in her soul that Fionnuala approved of their union.

She realized that she was idly twirling the ring on her finger, and acknowledged that it had already become a habit. *I'll do my best to weave our lives together, just like you promised to do with Martin.* Against all reason, she felt like every one of her words was clearly heard. *I promise I'll do everything I can to love her as much as you did.*

As quickly as it appeared, the feeling vanished, leaving Jamie slightly confused but deeply relaxed. It took a moment or two to snap out of her reverie, but the sight of Ryan gracefully standing on the board and riding a couple of small waves did the trick. It looked like she was merely trying to get comfortable with the board and the waves as she took several short rides. Even though she got dumped numerous times, she looked blissfully happy, and Jamie was terribly pleased that she'd been able to satisfy Ryan's desire to come to the beach.

Ryan was in a group of about twenty other surfers, all jockeying for the same good waves. A really good set came along, but the guys to her right grabbed on before she could get in position. To avoid being left behind again, she paddled out a little farther and cut right, going to the far end of the group. When the next set came, she was ready. She hopped on the board and caught the leading edge of the wave, balancing gracefully on her flexed legs, right foot well forward of her left. The wave gained height and speed as it came towards shore, but Ryan hung on, riding it for every foot that she could pull out of it. Jamie was struck by the mixture of power, strength, grace and daring that this act required. Ryan's bold, confident style seemed to almost dare the wave to knock her off the board. But she won the round, and slid in towards the shore as the wave meekly ran out of steam.

Not willing to rest on her laurels, Ryan immediately paddled back out to begin the process again. She rode wave after wave—some large, some small—the size seemingly irrelevant to the graceful woman. A few tossed her forcefully off her board, and some lifted her gently and almost lovingly deposited her into the water. No matter the outcome of each little foray, the deeply satisfied smile never left her face. Most of the other surfers were either concentrating furiously, or trying to look bored, and Jamie was very grateful that her partner didn't feel the need to affect a "look". She considered that one of Ryan's most precious traits was her willingness to show her true feelings—in this case, abundant joy—even if it wasn't the cool thing to do.

Ryan had been in the water almost an hour, playing ceaselessly, and Jamie was tired from watching her. When the waves stilled for a bit, Ryan paddled out farther than she had been all day and just sat on her board for a while. It looked to Jamie like her lover was tiring, and needed a break. At that moment, a big swell headed right for her, and she shook off her fatigue and quickly jumped on the board and took off. She caught the wave just as it began to pass her, and it was a big one—a very big one, easily the biggest of the day. It rose dramatically as it raced towards the shore, and Jamie's heart jumped to her throat as another surfer cut right in front of Ryan. Jamie watched in horror as the scene played out in slow motion before her eyes. His board caught the edge of Ryan's, and they both flew skyward. Jamie's heart nearly stopped as Ryan's body flew end over end, resembling a rag doll more than a human. Her board flew off at an angle, safely out of the way, but the other board looked like it landed on top of her as her body and the board hit the water hard, almost simultaneously. Jamie's mind raced, trying to decide what to do. She knew that if Ryan was unable to save herself, she couldn't swim out to get there in time. Panic washed through her body as she stood, frozen in place, feeling completely powerless.

She felt a scream tear from her lungs but no one responded to her tortured cry. The lifeguards were not on duty yet, and none of the other surfers made a move to go towards the spot where Ryan disappeared. Without even knowing that she was moving, she ran to the edge of the surf, scanning the horizon frantically, searching for Ryan's dark head as she fought to focus through her tears. After seeming hours had passed, she finally spotted her much farther down the shoreline, swimming in without her board. Jamie took off and ran faster than she ever had in her life, her footfalls pounding so hard on the packed sand that her heels ached.

Ryan was about ten feet from shore when Jamie grabbed her with a force that surprised them both. The smaller woman held on for dear life, her head buried against Ryan's wet chest. Ryan soothed her and patted her back, giving up on her desire to try to keep her lover dry. After a long while, Jamie lifted her head and asked with a panic-laced voice, "W … w … what happened?"

Ryan tightened her hold, realizing how horrible the entire event must have been for her partner. She spoke in a soothing, low tone, trying to reassure her with her voice as well as her embrace. "You saw that kid cut me off?"

Jamie nodded emphatically.

"My board flew away, but his came right for me. I don't know how I got lucky enough to be in this position, but I was thrown onto my back and the board came right down on top of me."

Jamie stiffened at her words but Ryan quickly continued, "I grabbed it with both hands and stopped it from hitting me, but when I hit the water, I got the wind knocked out of me. Luckily I was strong enough to hold onto the board as I hit, but it took me a minute to be able to swim in."

"Where's your board?" Jamie asked, as she tried to control her shaking voice and body.

"The surf will bring it in if somebody else doesn't."

Jamie threw her arms around her again and squeezed her hard. "God, Ryan, I'm so relieved that you're okay. I didn't know what to do," she moaned as she continued to sob.

"I'm so sorry that I worried you, sweetie. I really was careful, but not everybody else was today," she murmured into her damp hair. "But I'm fine, Jamie, I'm really fine."

"But you could have been ki … ki … killed," she gasped out, as the tears continued to stream down her face.

"I wasn't hurt," she soothed as she dipped her head to make eye contact. "You can't let yourself imagine all of the bad things that could happen. That'll make you crazy. The fact is that I had a bad scare, but I got away without a scratch. You've got to focus on the reality."

It took a few minutes of struggle to gain control once again, but the fair-haired woman finally stood tall and took in a deep breath. "You're right," she said, with as much composure as she could muster. "I'm going to have to get used to watching you do things like this." She did her best to adopt a stoic demeanor, and looked up at Ryan with what little confidence she had. "I'm sure I'll toughen up over time."

Ryan felt a pang of regret for the pain her partner was experiencing. "I don't want you to be tough, sweetheart. I really love how you care about me and watch out for me. Don't ever stop that." She wrapped her arms around her lover a little tighter and nuzzled her face into Jamie's hair. "Please don't ever stop that," she murmured in a shaky voice. "I depend on it."

"I won't. I promise I won't." They stood in the shallow surf, hugging gently, and as the shock eased from her body Jamie realized how cold the water was on her legs. Breaking the embrace, she grasped Ryan's hand and started to walk back towards the car.

About twenty yards down the shore the errant board was bobbing around in the surf. Ryan dashed out to retrieve it, and as she tucked it under her arm Jamie could see her body tension change.

Sensing what the change signaled, she called in amazement, "Are you going back out?"

A stoic nod was her only reply. Jamie could feel her guts clench, but she tried to sound as normal as possible. "Do you have to, baby? I'm getting a little chilled." She was, in fact, freezing now that her clothes were drenched from her unplanned dip, and the fear that still gripped her wasn't helping one bit.

"Go on back to the car," Ryan said gently. "I have to take care of one little thing. Go on," she urged as she pushed her firmly in the correct direction.

Jamie was having none of it. She looked up at Ryan and begged, "Please don't get into a fight with the guy who cut you off. It's not worth it."

Ryan smiled and placed a gentle kiss on her trembling lips. "I have no idea who did it, babe. Even if I did, I wouldn't fight him. Surfing is dangerous and you have to learn to take your lumps. Now will you go back to the car?"

"No. If you stay, I stay."

From the set of her jaw, Ryan could see that she wouldn't be dissuaded. "Okay, I'll be as quick as I can." She was dashing along the shore before Jamie had a chance to say one more word.

As she ran along, she reached up and tugged off her hood. Since she had not affixed her hair with a band, it tumbled out and fell against her back, bouncing gently as she ran. Just before she lay on the board to paddle out, Jamie watched her inexplicably yank the zipper of her suit down far enough to expose her white sports bra. *What in the hell* ....

As soon as Ryan got back to the pack and readied herself into position, she adopted a radically different attitude than she'd previously shown. This time she didn't play nice with the other children. She paddled out to the edge of the group and jockeyed for position, sticking her chest out and tossing her hair back out of her eyes repeatedly. She seemed to be trying to make sure that everyone knew she was there. This demeanor was so markedly different from her previous attitude that Jamie had a hard time making sense of it. Ryan seemed roughly aggressive, like she was trying to not only attract attention—she was trying to annoy the members of the pack.

After about ten minutes of impatiently waiting, a monster of a wave began to build. Ryan got to her feet and aggressively cut to the front of the pack, catching the leading edge of the cresting water and dropping down to begin carving it like a pro. The other riders tried to get into position, but no one could match the show she was putting on. She was too far away for Jamie to see her face, but she didn't actually need to. She was absolutely certain that her lover looked cool, calm, cocky and oblivious to every other person fighting for position. When Ryan was really "into" something, she often looked like she was waiting for a bus. But Jamie had learned that the cool exterior was a mask that was easily misunderstood. She was, in fact, concentrating so hard and enjoying the experience so much, that she was no longer connected to the rest of the world. She transported herself to another place, a place that Jamie would truly love to visit, but she doubted she would ever be privy to the secrets that would lead her there.

Watching her lover masterfully carve the wave actually sent chills down the smaller woman's spine, and when Ryan had exhausted the wave and trotted over to her minutes later, she knew that she still wore a big dumb-looking grin. "Now we can go," Ryan said matter-of-factly.

"Were you getting hot out there?" Jamie teased her as they walked away, hand in hand.

"No," she replied with a furrowed brow. "Oh ... you mean because I unzipped?"

"Yeah, wasn't it cold?"

"Freezing!" Ryan laughed. "But I wanted to make sure every guy out there knew that a girl was dusting their sorry asses!"

Jamie stopped dead in her tracks. "You did that just to make a point!"

"Partly. That guy really dissed me by cutting me off. And I was really irritated that nobody paddled out to see if I was okay."

"Couldn't you have stood on the shore and taken off your wet suit?" Jamie couldn't imagine going out in the frigid water with that much exposed skin just to make a point to a bunch of strangers.

Ryan laughed at the wide-eyed look her partner was giving her. "Sure. That would have made my point. But I was pretty scared by the whole experience, and I refuse to let my last run of the day scare me. I really had to go back out to build my confidence back up. Unzipping let me kill two birds with one stone."

"Did it work?" Jamie asked unnecessarily, seeing the twinkle in the sparking blue eyes.

"Like a charm. I feel … electric," she decided. "My whole body is tingling."

"Mine too," Jamie revealed. "But my feeling is localized." Her own version of the wiggling eyebrow had Ryan in hysterics, and they walked the rest of the way laughing aloud.

Ryan opened the doors to the truck and sat on the bumper to remove her wetsuit. Jamie stood in front of her with a big beach towel to give her some privacy from passing cars. She peeled her wetsuit off and wriggled out of her wet bathing suit. As soon as she was naked, Jamie got a gleam in her eye and pushed her down onto the floor. "Oh-oh," Ryan said with a chuckle as Jamie crawled on top of her, pulling the towel over them both.

The Suburban's third seat had been folded down, providing a nice, flat surface about the size of a double bed for them to play in. It was still quite cool, and Ryan was pretty chilled from being in the water for so long. As she scooted up to pull her legs in the truck, Jamie closed the doors with a thud. She climbed astride her hips as Ryan gazed up at her serenely. "Why do I think you have more in mind than helping me dry off?"

Jamie gave her a knowing smirk as she crawled over her to put the key in the ignition, cracking the windows and putting a beach towel in each one. Privacy curtains now firmly in place, she rolled the windows back up, then opened the windows on the highway side a few inches for ventilation, and crawled into the back. She sat cross-legged on the floor next to Ryan as she pulled out two self-inflating air mattresses that she had stashed. She watched the smirk form on Ryan's face as their little bed became even more comfortable. When the mattresses were fully inflated, she motioned for Ryan to climb on top, which she willingly did. It was obvious that this was Jamie's game, so Ryan relaxed into the sensation and let her drive.

Jamie shucked her sweatshirt and then her sodden pants, and started to remove her swimsuit, but Ryan shook her head with a little grin. The blonde smiled back and left it on, letting Ryan decide when it would come off. She climbed onto her favorite place, astride Ryan's hips, and felt the cool body underneath her. Bending from the hips to kiss her, within moments they were grinding against each other passionately.

The scare of the surfing incident was fueling Jamie's desire, and she willingly threw herself into the maelstrom of her emotions. She wanted to consume Ryan, to prove to herself that her lover was right here with her and that she was whole and safe.

Ryan sensed that this was more than just sex. She could feel that Jamie needed to be reassured, so she did her best to do so. Jamie spent a long time kissing Ryan, starting at her mouth, then slowly working her way down her body. She tasted like salt and the sea, but her natural scent came through, and the calming power of her aroma slowly brought Jamie some comfort. She looked down at her lover, and the loving smile on her beautiful face broke some dam in Jamie's reserve, and she began to shed the tears that she'd been holding in. She fell onto Ryan's chest, sobbing and gasping for breath. Ryan patted her back and spoke to her in a low, calm voice. She reassured her that she was fine, that she knew how to protect herself. She pointed out that she was very strong and had very good instincts. Then she teased her a little bit by reminding her that even a lead pipe to the head hadn't taken her out for long, so a little surfboard certainly wouldn't.

Jamie looked up at her and gave her a small smile. "I get so scared, Ryan. You mean so much to me, that I can't bear the thought of losing you."

"I know, sweetheart, I know," she soothed. "I promise I'll try to take better care of myself. I know how much I scare you sometimes, and I'll try to be more careful."

"I don't want you to give up the excitement that you need. But I want you to be as careful as you can."

"I know, baby, and I do try to be careful. I need to keep in mind how much you need me to stay healthy."

Jamie slid off her hips and curled up next to her in a little ball. Ryan rolled their sweats up into a makeshift pillow and drew Jamie closer. She rocked her slightly and hummed a little lullaby to ease her into sleep, but she was too wired to join her partner. The near-constant hum of traffic and the calm, even breathing against her ear began to soothe her, but she chose to remain awake. The feel of Jamie in her arms was so satisfying that she often wished she didn't need sleep at all, and could just hold her for hours at a time. Her musings grew less focused and, before she knew it, she had joined her partner in a well-deserved nap.

When they woke, Ryan was pleased to see that the sparkle had returned to her partner's eyes. They spent a few minutes kissing while they awakened fully, and then Ryan ran over to the public shower to rinse off.

When she emerged, she was dressed in her running clothes, and Jamie gave her a startled look. "Ryan, you've been surfing since dawn! Don't tell me you want to run now!"

Giving a sheepish shrug in return, Ryan said, "I got agitated today. I thought the nap would calm me down, but I still feel antsy. A nice run will let me get my equilibrium back."

"Hard to believe we're of the same species," Jamie mumbled.

Ryan helped her partner carry their gear down to the shoreline, and Jamie sat down in her beach chair with a book. Bending to kiss her goodbye, Ryan lingered a bit as she grinned through the kisses. "There's something so sexy about kissing your sweet, sweet mouth," she said with a seductive tone in her voice.

"Do you need to go back to the truck for a little love?" Jamie asked when she noticed her sparkling eyes.

"No, I'm getting used to being aroused all of the time," she decided with a lopsided grin. Jamie watched her for as long as she could keep her in sight. Few things pleased her as much as watching her lover run. She mused that Ryan actually looked like running was her natural way of moving. She had a long, economical stride that ate up ground as she moved along the asphalt path. Jamie had a demure smile on her face, and she realized after a long while that she wasn't going to read her book. She was so totally content to sit and wait for Ryan, that she didn't need the distraction of reading. *My God, will it always be like this?* She shook her head a little to try to clear it, but realized that the image of her partner rarely left her mind. *How will I ever be able to concentrate on school? I can't even read a book while she's running!*

The sun was finally starting to peek through the marine layer, but it was still too cool to remove her sweats. She leaned back in her chair and watched the still-weak rays fight to break through the clouds, and let her thoughts drift back to her lover. *I still can't believe that I was naïve enough to believe that I was in love with Jack. What a mistake it would have been to marry him! Our relationship was actually more like a business partnership than true love.* Shivers chased down her spine at the thought of being married to him for the rest of her life. *I would have never known what love could be .Now that I know, I'm determined to hold on as tight as I can to this feeling. It's far too wonderful to ever let go.* She closed her eyes and let her thoughts drift inexorably towards her partner. A very satisfied smile graced her face as she relaxed into the reverie. *Now I just have to figure out a way to keep her alive*, she mused, as she shook her head at the daunting prospect. *It was a lot easier with Jack. With him I only had to worry that he'd get a fatal paper cut!*

It was nearly an hour before Ryan returned. She was wet, but the day was so cool and breezy that the perspiration was drying fast. Jamie insisted that she put her sweats back on, which Ryan did after removing her wet shirt.

"Guess what I am?" she asked with a big smile, leaning over her partner like a predator.

"Either hungry or horny, I'd say," Jamie replied with a laugh. "Which oral craving do you need satisfied?"

"I'd like to start with eating, but I could easily be convinced to partake of the other later on."

"I bet you could," she replied as she patted her tummy. "Let's feed the beast and then decide on the rest of the day."

There were still two muffins left from breakfast, and Ryan polished them off quickly. Now sated, she stretched for a minute and said, "I think I'm ready to shop."

Jamie was surprised by this suggestion, and she gazed at Ryan for a moment, trying to make sure her partner was serious. "You hate to shop."

"Hnh-uh," Ryan insisted. "I love to shop—I just like to shop for the things that I really like. Ready to go?"

"Okay, you're the boss."

"Don't I wish," Ryan teased as she patted her on the butt.

They moved the car to a parking lot near the Santa Cruz boardwalk, but instead of heading back to the beach, Ryan led Jamie to the little shops that lined the streets of the town. Both women had slipped back into sweats and sandals and they strolled along the busy streets, hand in hand.

After surveying the neighborhood, Ryan finally informed Jamie of her objective. "I need new wheels for my skates," she said. "I wear them out pretty fast, and I'm sure the sand will chew up my current ones." Given the choice of three likely looking stores, Ryan chose the one that looked the grungiest. The salesclerks were dressed in big, black, baggy jeans and huge black T-shirts with logos of various bands on them. They were heavily tattooed and pierced, and Ryan thought they looked like they knew how to skate.

After chatting with one of the clerks for a moment, Ryan had her wheels, but a new toy caught her eye, and she had a hard time leaving the store.

"You look like a kid in a candy store," Jamie joked. "What'cha looking at?"

"It's kind of cool," Ryan said with a crooked grin. She showed Jamie a shoe that had a steel-reinforced piece of plastic right at the arch. It sat horizontally in the thick-soled shoe, and looked like a piece of pipe cut in half.

"What in the world is the point of that?"

"It's hard to explain," Ryan said. "I'd have to demonstrate."

Their sales clerk heard the conversation and casually asked, "What size do you take?"

Ryan told him her size in both women's and men's, and he gave her a smile as he went in the back of the store. He came back out with a pair in her size that'd been returned due to a defect in the leather upper. "These have to go back to the company," he said as he looked her up and down. "You up to giving 'em a try?"

Ryan knew a challenge when she heard one. She figured the kid didn't think she would accept, but he didn't know Ryan very well. She yanked them out of his hands and sat down to lace them up. They were a tiny bit snug, but she wasn't going to let that stop her. "Where should I go?"

"There's a bank just down the street, and they don't patrol it very well," he said casually, jerking his head in the proper direction.

Jamie had no idea what was going on. With a very confused look on her face, she looked from the clerk to Ryan, trying to figure out what they were talking about. Ryan turned to her and said, "Let's go. I may need you to bail me out," she added with a grin.

Jamie trotted along behind Ryan, who was purposefully striding down the street. Grabbing her arm roughly to stop her, Jamie demanded, "Where are we going? And what are you gonna do that can get you arrested?"

"I was just kidding. I don't think I'll get arrested. I'm pretty fast when I have to be," she said with a chuckle.

"Did that answer my question?"

"Wait and see, Jamie. I'm going to show you how I whiled away the hours of my misspent youth."

When they came close to the bank, she could see Ryan gazing all around, sizing up the layout. The cool blue eyes glanced around carefully, trying to see if there were any guards present. As they went around the bank to a side entrance, her eyes lit up with delight. She turned to Jamie and said with a twinkle in her eye, "This could be kinda cool, or I could split my pants or my head open." When Jamie's eye widened, she added, "My insurance card's in my wallet," as she took off running up the stairs.

The bank was a big, impressive structure, probably seventy-five or so years old. There were about twenty steps up to a wide, graceful entry. This side entrance had obviously been modified to make it handicapped accessible, since there was a new ramp that curved up next to the stairs, making the incline less steep. When Ryan got to the top, she focused her eyes on the ramp, and Jamie saw her rock back and forth a few times, planning her attack. Finally, a small smile came over her face, and her posture took on an air of confidence. She went to the far end of the entrance, turned, and started running—first in small steps, and then in a few long strides—and finally leapt into the air with her feet tucked up under her body.

Jamie nearly passed out from shock and fear. Her heart was pounding in her chest, and her eyes were wide as she stared, open-mouthed, at the image of her lover, flying through the air.

When Ryan's momentum carried her to the ramp, she lowered her feet and caught the handrail with the plastic inserts in her shoes. She sank down into a crouch, and rode the rail just like a surfboard, but when she hit the first curve, she lost her footing and started to fall. Jamie's heart was in her throat as images of Ryan's broken body flooded her head. Ryan's momentum was throwing her towards the concrete stairs, but just when it looked like she would crash, she pulled her feet back under herself and did a tight somersault in the air, landing neatly on both feet with a small stutter step to bleed off some of the force.

As soon as her feet hit the ground, a massive grin broke over her face, and she raised her arms like a gymnast and took a bow.

Jamie was too stunned to move. Her mouth hung open and she tried to force sound from her lips, but nothing would come. Ryan gave her a quick look saying, "I almost had it, babe. Next time for sure!" as she bounded back up the stairs.

She repeated her little ritual, bearing that same confident look as she began her approach. This time she hit the railing with more force than her previous attempt. She got down lower in her crouch and leaned back a bit, centering her weight over her butt. As she hit the first curve she leaned into it like a racecar on a track. She settled her weight again as she careened down the straight section of rail. The next turn was at a ninety-degree angle and Jamie assumed she would jump down. But when she got close she jumped in the air, still in her deep crouch and made a half turn, coming down the next section backwards. As she slid off the end of the rail, Jamie saw a bank guard come huffing out of the side door. "Hey!" he called. "Get off that rail!" As he came running down the steps, he stopped for a second, and with a look of surprise he shouted, "How old are you, anyway?"

Ryan shot him a grin as she ran past Jamie. "Run like hell!" she shouted as she blew by. Jamie heeded her advice and took off down the street, running as well as she could in her sandals. When she trotted into the store, completely winded, Ryan was already sitting in a chair trying on the shoes in her proper size. "I gotta have these," she said, with a look in her eyes that reminded Jamie of Caitlin with an ice cream cone.

The winded blonde plopped down next to her and admonished her firmly, "You have to warn me earlier when there's chance we're going to be arrested." She pulled in another deep lungful of air, "I could at least have worn my running shoes." When her breathing returned to normal, she looked at Ryan with concern, "Are you sure these are a good idea? You know you can't take many more blows to the head."

"I'll be careful," she promised with a wide-eyed look of pleading.

"That's a laugh!" Jamie said with a shake of her head. "You don't have a careful bone in your body!"

Ryan gave her a little shrug, along with a sheepish grin, as she handed the shoes to the clerk to ring up. She insisted on paying for the shoes herself, reminding Jamie, "If I do break my neck, do you really want to be responsible for purchasing the instrument of my demise?"

As they walked back to the car with their purchases, Jamie stopped and turned to her, giving her a big smile as she shook her head. "What was that for?" Ryan asked as they resumed walking.

"You never cease to amaze me. I mean, I really don't like you doing things like that. I love you so much that it frightens me to death to think of you getting hurt."

Ryan started to interrupt, but Jamie placed both hands flat on her chest, stopping her rebuttal. "You *will* get hurt, Ryan. You have before, and you will again. Let's be realistic."

Ryan pursed her lips before giving her a reluctant nod. Jamie continued, "Despite that, your wild side is so much a part of who you are, that I can't ask you to give it up to keep yourself safe for me." She leaned in and gave her a small kiss on the lips, "To be completely honest, I think you look really hot when you do crazy things like that."

Ryan gave her a broad grin and hugged her soundly as people passed by, staring at them as they went. "Hot, huh?" she whispered.

"Very," Jamie whispered back. "You look all wild and untamed, and your face breaks into this sexy, confident smile that makes me want to ravish you."

"I'd love to be ravished," she hummed into her ear.

"Um … Tiger?" she asked as she felt her knees beginning to weaken. "We're kinda in a public place. Can I ravish you at home?"

"Well," she said with a grin as she pulled back, "I'd love to be seduced in public, but I guess home's okay too."

Jamie gave her a firm pinch on the butt as they started up again. Ryan casually tossed an arm around her shoulders as they sauntered down the street.

As they passed a good-smelling coffee shop Jamie looked into Ryan's eyes and begged, "Can we stop here for a jolt? Getting up at four-thirty is hard on this little body."

"Anything you want, babe. You run in. I want to check something out." Jamie did as requested and, just as she received her drink, Ryan sidled up to her, looking a little smug.

"Where've you been, sweetie? You look like the cat that swallowed the canary."

Shifting a paper bag from one hand to the next, Ryan pursed her lips and puffed out her cheeks, feigning the removal of something from her even, white teeth. She gulped audibly, and smacked her lips together, looking at Jamie with dancing eyes. "Got a feather stuck between my teeth," she grinned, unwilling to reveal anything more.

Seeing Ryan's purchase spurred Jamie on to buy a little something, so they walked around for a while, looking in the shops. Jamie finally decided on a cute pair of board shorts for her long-legged lover. They were quite a bit shorter than the men's style, and were a very bright red, with a white design of pineapples and palm trees, and a white waistband and lace that pulled steel grommets together to hold them up. She looked terribly cute in them, and Jamie was completely pleased with the purchase.

Heading back to the Boardwalk, Ryan decided she needed a little blow out to test her new wheels. She got back into her blades, kissed Jamie lightly on the lips and wiggled an eyebrow. "Back in a minute," she said with a twinkle in her eyes.

She took off down the path, heading away from the populated section. Within three strides she was bent forward at the waist, her extended arms crossing in front of her with each long stride. Surprisingly, she didn't use her knees much at all. She had them flexed, but her real movement came from her powerful hips. She propelled herself by pushing out strongly toward the side with long, deep strides. When she was whisking along at her desired speed, she placed her hands behind her back, grasping one lightly with the other. Jamie watched her with amazement. *Is there anything she can't do well? She looks like every sport was just made for her.* As she watched, she began to get a familiar tingling and she mentally rebuked herself. *If you get hot every time you watch her do some activity, you're going to spend your whole life turned on!* After a moment she gave herself a mental slap and thought, *What's the problem with that?*

Ryan returned after about fifteen minutes, winded and slightly sweaty, but content. Jamie couldn't help but give her a strong hug, smiling to herself at Ryan's puzzled expression.

Ryan was starving by now, so they stopped at the first place that looked non-lethal and loaded up on fast food. Exhaustion overtook them both, and without a word they agreed to head home. As soon as they reached the house they collapsed into bed, fully clothed.

When Ryan woke, she slid out of bed and stretched for a few minutes. She was rested and ready to do something, but Jamie looked like she'd be out for a while. Rather than leave the room to look for entertainment, she decided to investigate the bookcases of her partner's childhood room. There were a number of family portraits placed around the room, and Ryan spent a few minutes studying them. She was particularly taken with one of the whole family when Jamie was about a year old. The resemblance between her lover and young Caitlin was really astonishing, and Ryan barely moved for a few minutes, studying the photo closely. Jamie came up behind her and slid her arms around her waist, laying her head against Ryan's back. "You were such an adorable baby," Ryan said as she turned and wrapped Jamie in her arms. "Of course, given how adorable you are now, that isn't surprising."

"Flattery will get you everywhere," she replied with a crooked smile as she stood on her tiptoes to kiss her partner. She continued the hug, nuzzling her face into Ryan's chest for a full minute. "When do you want to start our family?"

Ryan stood stock-still and tilted her head before she asked, "Where did that come from?"

"There were a bunch of kids at the beach this morning, and it started me thinking. How do you feel about having kids? I mean, I know you want to, but I don't know when or how."

"Hmm," Ryan said, addressing the issue seriously. "Well, being with you has changed my mind about that a little bit. Before we got together, I was pretty sure I wanted to have a child right after I graduated. But now I'm not so sure."

"Why would you change your mind because of me?"

"I used to think that I'd raise a child alone, and it seemed like a good idea to do it before I started a career. With you, I'm not in as big a rush. I won't have the same worries about child care, being able to afford it, and things like that."

Taking Ryan's hand in hers, Jamie led her to the window seat, where Ryan leaned up against the side wall, extending one long leg and bending the other at the knee. Jamie sat between her legs with her torso resting against Ryan's chest. "Much better," she said when Ryan's arms encircled her body. "Do you think it'll bother you to let me pay for a lot of the expenses of child-rearing?"

Ryan's deep laugh rumbled through Jamie's body. "I'm sure I'll have a few issues," she admitted. "But if we're gonna have kids, my primary concern is to make sure they're well cared for. I think I'll be able to put my concerns aside to make that happen."

"That's good to hear," Jamie said. "I've been afraid that we'd argue a lot about things like that."

"Oh, we probably will," Ryan chuckled. "I have a sneaking suspicion that you and I have different standards about what constitutes the necessary expenses of raising a child. We're going to have to come to some agreement about things before going forward."

"Details, details," Jamie assured her. "I certainly don't need to raise our children in the style I was brought up, and I don't think we need to stick with your family's austerity, either. We'll come up with our own little model."

"Sounds like a deal," Ryan agreed. "But, I would like to give you one little piece of reality, babe. My youth was not austere. We were very average in our neighborhood, and I can't think of anything I ever really needed that I didn't have."

Jamie squeezed her partner's arms as she quickly apologized. "Oh, baby, I didn't mean that like it sounded. I just meant that your upbringing was austere compared to mine. I was given everything—far too much, really. I don't want to raise our kids like that. But I also don't want them to have to work like you did for every little extravagance."

Ryan returned her squeeze and leaned over to nibble on Jamie's ear, "We'll see," she murmured, closing the door on the money issue for the time being.

"Given that, when do you think you'd like to start?" Jamie asked, returning to her initial question.

"I guess it still depends a little on what I want to do professionally. And of course, on what you want to do. I'm not in this alone anymore," she said with a smile.

"Is it important for you to give birth?" Jamie asked, assuming that it was.

"As selfish as it seems, yeah, it is important to me. I know I'd love any child of ours the same, no matter which of us gave birth to it. I just feel that there's a connection to my mother that I can only have if I actually give birth. I want to feel that primal, instinctual connection that childbirth gives you."

"I can't imagine how cute you would be pregnant," Jamie mused, picturing her partner's perfectly flat tummy expanding to massive proportions.

"I feel the same way about you," Ryan replied, as she nibbled Jamie's neck. "You would be devastatingly sexy."

"Do you find pregnant women attractive?" Jamie asked in a surprised tone, turning to make eye contact.

"Totally. And I'm sure you'd be so completely hot looking that I'd be on you like flies to honey."

"So if our sex life gets boring, I could get pregnant to spice it up?"

"Well, that's one of the worst reasons I've ever heard of to have a child, but I bet it would work," Ryan conceded. "Is it important to you to give birth?"

"I'm certainly not averse to the idea," Jamie mused. "I always assumed that I would, since I would be married to a man, and they're not very good at doing that. Now that I have a built in baby-making machine, I'm not so sure. I think I'll have to wait and see if I have a real need to reproduce. There's a part of me that might prefer to adopt a couple of kids."

"I'd be more than happy with that arrangement," Ryan agreed. "Although I have a very strong desire to have a cute little Jamie clone running around the house."

"I'd love to give birth if I could actually have a child with you, Ryan. But my desire is much less strong if I just have to use some stranger's sperm."

"Well, there are a couple of near clones that you might be able to hook up with," she said.

"Do you mean your brothers?"

"Yeah. Conor and Rory have already offered. Conor told me years ago that he'd be happy to help out."

"Wow!" she replied excitedly. "That puts a whole different spin on the issue. That would almost be like having a child with you."

"It's as close as you can get without cloning," she said with a twinkle in her eyes.

"But I don't know, Ryan. Having Conor for a dad and you for a mom could be really dangerous."

"And why is that?" she asked somewhat indignantly.

"You're both so wild and full of energy! I don't know if I could keep up."

"Yeah, but your moderating influence would be important, too. Maybe the baby would take after you."

"Have you paid any attention to the dominance of the O'Flaherty genes?" Jamie demanded. "Everyone but Rory looks like they came from the same mold. Even your cousins don't look like their mothers. Those are some powerful genes, baby."

"I guess you're right, there. Maybe you'd do better to just go to a sperm bank."

"Hnh-uh," she said with a determined shake of her head. "I love every little O'Flaherty gene. I'd be pleased beyond words to bear a child that resembled you in any way at all."

# Chapter Eleven

They sat in the window seat for a long while, each silently musing about their future children. Ryan's libido woke up after a bit and she started to caress Jamie sensually. Her partner gave her a devilish smile and said, "Let's go somewhere else. We've done this room thoroughly."

Ryan gave her a crooked grin and asked, "Where to?"

"Well, first, you need to hop in the shower," she decided. "I want to munch on every little part of you, but you're still salty and sandy."

"Be right back." Ryan smiled as she hopped to her feet and scampered into the bath.

When she emerged, she noticed that Jamie had set out an outfit for her to wear. "Mmm, dress up time?"

"Yep," the green eyes danced. "I love having my own life-sized dress-up doll." Ryan was still drying her hair with the towel, and as she paused to comb it Jamie asked, "Did you play with dolls when you were little?"

"Yeah, but not much here," she mused, sliding the wide-toothed comb through her tresses.

"Here?"

"America," she clarified. "Aisling and I played mummies and daddies all the time in Ireland."

"Mummies and daddies?"

"Yeah. Playing house, you know?"

"Oh, right," she said. "Why not here?"

"Which of my cousins do you think I could get to play house with me?"

"Riiight," Jamie drawled, finally realizing the problem. "Didn't you have any little girl friends?"

"Nope. I didn't make friends with girls until I was in grade school. Sara was actually my first real girl friend in America."

"Sara?" Jamie interrupted. "You didn't have girl friends until high school?"

"No, no," Ryan laughed. "I think I told you that we were friends in grammar school. She was in third grade when I was in second, and we were on our school's pee-wee soccer team."

"I don't remember if you told me that," she said softly. "But it makes it even clearer why losing her friendship was so horrible for you."

"Yeah," Ryan nodded, unwilling to go into the incident again.

"So tell me more about this mummies and daddies thing."

"It was funny," Ryan recalled, apparently content to continue talking about her youth. "In Ireland, all of my friends were girls because of Aisling. But in America, it was all boys."

"Which did you like better?"

"Neither. I liked them both. They were just different. I did different things and played different games, depending on who I hung out with. I was actually quite good at playing mummies and daddies. Guess which I always was?" she asked with a wide grin.

"Hmm, how many guesses do I get?" Jamie teased, slapping her partner hard on her bare butt.

As Ryan stood surveying the outfit that had been prepared for her, she held up a tiny scrap of fabric and asked, "Is this a hankie?"

"Nope. Those are your panties."

"Panties?" Ryan asked as she held the fabric up, spreading it with both hands. The little elongated triangle of shiny black material would actually have been too small to be an effective handkerchief.

"It's a G-string," Jamie chided her gently. "Come on, let me help you into it."

Ryan gamely placed her hands on her partner's shoulders and lifted first one foot and then the other. "You know," Ryan said as she felt behind herself and ran her fingers up the string leading to the tiny waistband. "I never understood why it was called a G-string. But it's actually shaped like a G that's lying on it's back." She twitched her hips a few times to settle the material between her thighs. "I bet most women who put one of these on end up on their backs pretty quickly too," she mused, with a leer at her grinning partner. "So where do you want to take this off of me?"

"Not so fast," Jamie chided, as she handed her the rest of the outfit. Ryan looked at her with a puzzled frown as she accepted the tight gray ribbed tank and black Lycra boy-cut shorts.

"Are we going out?" she asked, not wanting to journey far with the G-string flossing her butt.

"Not really," Jamie answered rather enigmatically. She watched as Ryan added the tank and workout shorts, then handed her a pair of socks and her cross-trainers.

"Workout clothes?"

"Come on," Jamie urged. "Play nice, and I'll give you something good to suck on later." Her dark blonde eyebrows wiggled dramatically, causing Ryan to laugh out loud.

"I just bet you will. But first, I get to choose an outfit for you. If I'm gonna display my wares, so are you!"

When Jamie was dressed in a green and blue print sports bra and blue running shorts, they walked along the path to what looked like a large garage. Ryan asked, "How do you know none of the key-holders are here today?"

"The gardeners were here this morning, as you can tell." She indicated the overflowing green recycling bins near the garage. "The housekeeper only comes once a week when no one is home. I've gotta admit I don't know when the pool guy comes, but we're not going far," she said, leading Ryan to a door on the side of an enormous five car garage. There was an interior staircase just inside the door, and they walked up it, hand in hand.

Jamie opened the door at the top of the stairs and turned to see Ryan's jaw nearly hit her chest. The large room ran the length and breadth of the massive garage. It was carpeted with nice deep green plush, and floor to ceiling mirrors covered every wall. The room held the latest and finest weight machines and free weights that Ryan had ever seen. There were machines to work every part of the body, and racks of free weights neatly lined up along a wall. There was a treadmill, an elliptical cross trainer and a recumbent bike. A large screen TV sat against a far wall, and huge speakers hung from the ceiling.

Ryan turned to Jamie wide-eyed and said, "Why didn't you show me this before?"

"Because I wanted to hold your attention. I wanted you sweating over me, not over this iron," she said with a grin. "But now I want you to sweat *for* me."

Ryan pulled her head back slightly as she gave her partner an indulgent grin. "I've got to say that if I'd known what a little firecracker you were, I would have put the full court press on you that first day in class."

"Well, you know now, sweetie. So get ready to light my fuse," she breathed, right into Ryan's smiling face.

"Name your pleasure."

A slight flush grew on Jamie's cheeks as she said, "I need you to indulge me a little bit, if you don't mind, that is. I've been dreaming of this since we worked out together on our 'Gay for a Day' outing."

"Was that when you had really good sex with Jack?"

"Good memory, sweetie," she laughed. "Yeah, I still feel guilty about that. He was making love to me, but I was making love to you," she said with an even pinker blush. "My powers of denial even amaze me sometimes. I convinced myself that all of the women in the gym wanted you, and that it was perfectly natural to have those feelings. I just chalked it up to animal attraction."

Ryan was intrigued to find out some more facts about how this process had worked for Jamie. "Did you fantasize about me after that?"

"Not when I was with Jack. I really did feel guilty about it, and it took some of the pleasure away. But ever since February, I don't think I've touched myself without seeing your face or your body."

"I thought you said you didn't touch yourself very often."

"I didn't. I think that's a very big reason why I didn't. My denial is only so strong, Ryan. And masturbating while thinking about your lean little body was tough for even me to reconcile," she laughed. "So I think I tried to suppress my entire sexual response."

"Well it doesn't seem very repressed now," Ryan whispered into her ear.

"No, I would tend to agree with that diagnosis, Dr. Freud. Now, let's get busy." She led her smirking partner over to the machines dedicated to the shoulders and back. "I don't know if I've ever told you this, but I've found out that I'm a back woman," she said, kissing each exposed shoulder.

"I don't think you have," Ryan said. "As a matter of fact, I don't really know what about me turns you on, besides these," she added with a grin, as she placed her hands under her full breasts and lifted them tauntingly.

"That's because everything about you turns me on, silly." She gave Ryan a little squeeze as she added, "Looking at other women has shown me that some parts get my attention first."

"And where have you been looking at other women? Hmm?" Ryan's tone was light and she clearly was joking, but Jamie still flushed deeply.

"I … I … I don't really look …" she began, but Ryan cut her off.

"Everybody looks. Most people aren't honest about it. It's not a problem."

Jamie rolled her eyes in relief, happy that her partner was so low-key about these issues.

"So," Ryan urged, her playful grin back in place. "What works for you?"

"Well, as I told you, shoulders and backs are big favorites." She trailed her fingers down Ryan's back, feeling each individual muscle under the gray cotton. "And I like to go a little farther down, too," she whispered, as she placed both hands on Ryan's firm rear and palmed her cheeks. She turned her around and ran her hands all over her muscular thighs. "And these make me throb," she said, as she knelt to snake her tongue up one taut quadriceps. She looked up from her position to see Ryan's tightly closed eyes and small smile. "C'mon, baby," she said, as she stood and took her lover's hand and led her to the lat pull-down equipment. "Time to sweat."

Ryan pulled up short and asked, "So … the game is to have me work out and then make love?"

"Umm … well … I guess that's about it," she admitted. Looking up at her partner with a questioning gaze she quickly added, "That doesn't bother you, does it?"

"Ahh … no," Ryan laughed. "Combining two of my favorite activities is all good. But if I'm gonna work out to turn you on, it only seems fair if you do the same for me."

Jamie crossed her arms over her chest, striking a confident pose. "So … tell me what floats your boat, hot stuff."

"Pardon?" Ryan asked, blinking her blue eyes ingenuously.

"I told you about my favorite body parts. What do you like about me?"

"Hmm," the brunette mused, walking around her partner to study her thoroughly. "What do I like about your smokin' little body."

"Come on," Jamie urged. "We haven't got all day."

"Don't rush me," Ryan insisted, continuing her perusal. "I don't really focus on individual parts very much. I have more of a macro approach."

"Really?" Jamie asked, dropping her arms and cocking her head. "You don't have certain parts that always arouse you?"

"No, not really," Ryan said, shaking her head briefly. "I meant it when I said that I was most attracted to energy. Oh, I notice certain parts, if someone has an extraordinary something-or-other, but I wouldn't say that any part particularly arouses me."

Jamie sat down on a padded bench, staring at her partner for a long moment. "Do you think it's weird that I focus on … things?"

Ryan squatted down next to her, placing her hands on Jamie's knees. "Do you think it's weird that I don't?"

A quick headshake and a furrowed brow indicated that she did not. "That's not the same thing," Jamie said. "Not doing something is never as weird as doing something."

"Ahh … I'd tend to disagree, and I have hundreds of examples to support my case, but let me assure you that I don't think you're weird in any way, babe. My guess is that more people are like you than me."

Jamie leaned over and placed a quick kiss on Ryan's lips, then pulled her up to join her on the bench. "So, tell me how you get aroused," she asked.

"Okay," Ryan happily agreed. "Let me think … I'll tell you how it is when I'm with you, all right?"

"Sure."

"This is pretty simple actually. I'm always aroused when I'm with you." A goofy grin covered her lovely face, and Jamie couldn't help but laugh at her.

"Okay, smarty-pants, tell me how it is … I should say 'was' with other women."

"Alright," Ryan agreed once again. "It's sort of a 'what came first, the chicken or the egg?' with me. I'd be kinda horny, and I'd call someone or go to a club and meet someone. I'm kind of a self-starter."

"Surely that wasn't always true," Jamie admonished.

"No, of course not. Sometimes someone I knew would call, or I'd run into them. If they asked me to come over, I'd get aroused thinking about how we'd had sex before. If I met someone that I didn't know, I'd have to say that the thought of exploring someone new was always arousing for me."

"That's how you got in the mood," Jamie insisted. "I want to know how you actually get aroused once you're in the mood."

Ryan looked perplexed for a moment, staring into space as she tried to answer the question. "It's the same thing for me," she finally said. "Once I'm in the mood—I'm aroused."

"That simple?" Jamie gaped. "You're ready to go once you're in a receptive mood?"

"Yeah," Ryan nodded. "I'd have to say that's true. I get aroused really easily, babe. I can go from having no thoughts of sex to being completely aroused in a couple of minutes." She shrugged her broad shoulders as she turned to look at her partner. "It's not like that for you, is it?"

"God no! I have to work up to it pretty slowly. It feels like a slowly rising thermometer for me," she said reflectively. "But I stay down in the low range for quite a while most of the time. I have to touch and be touched to really get worked up."

"Hmm, let's test that hypothesis," Ryan grinned, standing and extending a hand.

"Name your poison," Jamie smirked, as she joined her by the lat pull down equipment.

Ryan adjusted the seat and sat down, waiting for Jamie to set the weight when she indicated her preference.

Before she began she said, "I'll do my normal routine, and you can tell me where you are on the scale. Give me a one to ten on how aroused you feel, and I'll do the same for you, okay?"

Staring at her partner for a moment, Jamie said, "You know, you could make millions as a trainer if you used this tactic on all of your clients."

"No way, babe," Ryan laughed. "This is private training in the best sense of the term."

Jamie stood back and watched her partner glide through a twelve-rep set of the back exercise. "Nice," she muttered, coming close to place a kiss right behind Ryan's ear.

"Scale?" the smirking brunette asked.

"I'm a ten for being in the mood, but about a one in arousal," Jamie admitted. "You?"

"Mmm, I'm not registering yet," she said. "Do you know what it is about working out that makes you hot?"

"Hmm," she mused as she considered the question. "I uhm … think my main goal is to get you all flushed and sweaty," she admitted, blushing as she revealed her secret longing.

"I like sweat, too," Ryan purred.

"It surprised the holy heck out of me when I discovered that I like to see you sweat, but I've fantasized about it often since that time you took me to work out at the football stadium." Ryan gazed at her curiously, so she continued. "You were leaning over me, and the sweat was dripping off your face and landing on my bare skin. I almost came right then and there!"

"Did you know you were attracted to me then?" Ryan asked, unclear as to the date.

"Nope. It was right before Christmas break. I was clueless … on many levels," she laughed.

"Well, I'll sweat for you any time now, love," Ryan promised. She gripped the wide bar with her hands spread about eighteen inches apart and began to smoothly move the weight, barely letting the plates touch the stack before she raised them again. She completed her second set of twelve repetitions without interruption, but as she paused, Jamie's hands began to trace over her back muscles, applying almost no pressure at all to the skin. As Ryan began the third set, Jamie's hands rested lightly on the flexing muscles, feeling each fiber as it strained and relaxed, strained and relaxed.

"This is so hot," she whispered into Ryan's pink ear. "Just keep going, Buffy."

Ryan pulled the bar down again and again, concentrating on her form, while Jamie rubbed her thumbs in a sweeping pattern, starting at her spine and fanning out. The small hands moved lower, inch-by-inch, until she had covered the entire surface of the back, continuing until Ryan began to tire and stopped to collect herself.

"Five!" Ryan gasped out with a laugh. "When you whispered in my ear, everything started to tingle."

"I'm about a two," Jamie said. "But it's moving in the right direction."

"You know, it's hard for me to concentrate if there's loud music at the gym," Ryan admitted with a smirk. "This is a whole new level of distraction."

"Do you like it?" Jamie asked, afraid that maybe she was pushing her too far.

"I love it. I absolutely, positively, love indulging your fantasies." She turned around to bestow a tender kiss on her partner's lips, lingering a little longer than necessary. "As long as we're gonna be here for a while, do you want to test my capacity?"

"Huh?"

"That's when I work from a light weight with many reps and gradually increase to the heaviest weight I can handle for just one or two reps. Wanna see?"

"Sure."

Ryan went to the seated cable row and set the machine at sixty pounds. She sat down on the long-padded bench and executed fifteen perfect reps, sliding the straight bar back to its terminus as she finished. She raised the weight to seventy pounds and started again, after a rest. This time she did twelve reps and Jamie could detect just a few drops of perspiration trickling down her neck and running down to her tank top. The cotton wicked most of them away immediately, but Jamie managed to snag one and rub it into Ryan's back with her index finger. "Three," the blonde whispered into a flushed ear. Chills ran down Ryan's back.

The next set saw another ten pounds added, and Ryan looked like she was really ready to stop when the tenth rep came. Another short rest allowed Jamie to capture a few more drops of sweat and chase them around the smooth skin.

At one hundred pounds, the eighth rep seemed like it was going to fail, but she managed with a deep grunt to pull the bar against her chest. This time the rest was a little longer, allowing Jamie more time to play.

When the weight stack was set for one hundred thirty pounds, Ryan took a few deep breaths and steeled herself. She gripped the bar and grunted heavily as first one, and then two reps were successfully completed. She slid down and collapsed against the long bench, dropping her arms to dangle off of it. "Wow, that's a bitch," she muttered, getting to her feet.

"Not for me," Jamie murmured as she slid her arms around her waist and leaned in for a sweaty hug.

"Like that?" Ryan smirked, looking down as her partner took in a deep breath.

"Uh-huh," was her enthusiastic reply. "Four ... in the express lane ... headed for five."

"I actually fell down a little," Ryan mused. "I really had to concentrate hard to do those reps right, and the blood must have been needed in my back muscles more than my love muscles."

"Oh, we'll get you back up," Jamie promised. "Just you wait."

"That's about all I can handle on my back," Ryan decided. "Now it's your turn."

"Name it."

Musing silently for a moment, Ryan decided on her pick. She rolled a large green exercise ball over and held it still with her feet. "Crunches," she announced firmly.

"On that?" Jamie cried.

"Yep. Put up or shut up, babe."

"Oh, all right," Jamie sighed. "How do I do 'em?"

"I'll hold the ball still, and you lie down with just your upper back resting on it."

"I can't do that!"

"Of course you can," Ryan admonished. "It's not that hard. Come on now." To make it a little easier, Jamie got on the floor and rolled onto the big ball, with Ryan stopping the progress with her feet when she was in position. All of the weight of her torso was resting on the ball, with her legs merely providing stability. "Looks good," Ryan decided. "Now fold your arms across your chest, but hold them away from your body ... good ... good," she said. "Now do a set of crunches just like you normally do them."

Jamie shot her a look, but complied with the instructions, getting through a set of fifteen with little difficulty.

"Excellent!" Ryan cried. "How did that feel?"

"It felt like I'll feel it tomorrow," she groused. "And my number went down, too!"

"Well, mine went up," Ryan decided. "Let's do another."

By the third set, Ryan's eyes were definitely twinkling, and Jamie decided that she didn't mind feeling a little pain to keep that fire in those blue eyes. After the fourth set, the fatiguing woman rested by sliding farther onto the ball, letting her arms dangle against the lime green surface. Even in repose, the muscles stood out in the bright halogen light, and Ryan got to her knees next to the ball and leaned in to raise her number a little.

She started to trace the protuberant muscles with the very tip of her warm tongue, gliding over the dips and raises as Jamie held perfectly still, soaking up the gentle sensation. "Back to five," Ryan murmured between swipes of her tongue.

"Right there with ya, babe," the smaller woman murmured languidly, willing the touch to continue.

"Time for another set," Ryan whispered, breaking the mood.

Her compliant partner crunched her way through an even one hundred reps, and as she collapsed against the ball, Ryan started to work on her tummy once again. By the time she was finished licking and sucking on the moist, flushed skin, both of them were cruising along at a six.

"My turn again," Ryan announced. "Would you rather see chest or shoulders?"

"Shoulders. Definitely shoulders," Jamie immediately replied.

Ryan chose the exercise that she knew would highlight her muscles to their best advantage. She pulled a weight bench right up next to the rack of dumb bells and picked up a pair of five-pound weights to begin. "What are you going to do?" Jamie asked.

"Back delt fly," she replied. "If you could hand me the next increment as I finish each set, it'd help."

"Love to."

Ryan sat at the very edge of the bench and leaned forward until her back was just a few degrees from parallel to the floor. She held the weights behind her knees and slowly began to raise them to shoulder height. She looked a bit like a very large bird, slowly flapping its powerful wings, but Jamie found this particular bird to be terribly sexy. She climbed onto the bench and sat directly behind her partner, trailing her fingers down the now slick skin.

Ryan eased through twelve reps and paused just a moment, while Jamie handed her the seven pounders. Just before she began, cool hands began tugging at her tank top. "I think this exercise would be perfect if it was performed topless," a soft voice hummed in her ear.

Lifting her arms immediately, Ryan smiled up at her partner as the smaller woman tugged the wet garment off. The reps fell, as the weight and Jamie's arousal number increased, until Ryan was visibly straining to lift the thirty-pound weights for just two reps. Jamie loved the little grunts and "oofs" that she made, most of the sounds reminding her of Ryan's cute orgasmic cries. For her part, Ryan loved the feel of Jamie's fingers gliding over her hot, wet skin as she strained with the weights.

The taller woman stood and stretched a bit when she was finished with the exercise. Her skin glowed pink under her golden tan, and the already-prominent muscles of her back stood out even more, evidently from the demands being placed on them. Raising her arms high above her head, she reached for the sky with one arm, then the other, smirking slightly at Jamie's fascinated stare.

Jamie was nearly drooling as she took in the vision that stood before her: sweat beading all over the smooth torso, muscles rippling, chest straining from the effort of the workout.

"Number?"

"Duh," Jamie replied vacantly. "I'll get back to ya."

Ryan leaned her head back and laughed heartily, her breasts bouncing against her chest as she did so. Just as Jamie's hands lifted to grasp the slick globes, Ryan stopped her advance. "Unh-uh, sparky, your turn to sweat. You've barely got a glow on."

"Ungh," the feisty blonde cried, trying in vain to wrench her hands from her partner. "Just one squeeze?"

"Nope," Ryan decreed, standing tall and crossing her arms across her chest to block access. "Work first, then play."

A frustrated sigh and matching scowl signaled Jamie's forced compliance. "Okay, what next?"

"Hmm," Ryan thought carefully. "I'm gonna choose … pull-ups."

"Pull-ups? That's cruel!"

"Play by the rules, babe. I wanna see those shoulders and abs straining."

Rolling her eyes skyward, Jamie allowed her partner to lift her so that she could grasp the pull-up bar. She stuck her legs straight out, and started to raise and lower her body, keeping her form tight and smooth.

The effort she was forced to expend to perform the reps properly caused her muscles to stand out vividly, and Ryan delighted as she watched the veins on Jamie's biceps bulge from the stress. Indulging her evil streak, Ryan stood behind her partner, and began to take long swipes of her tongue down the straining back.

"Oh, God," Jamie cried, as she fought to focus. "Gonna fall!"

Ryan caught her easily, and lowered her softly to the ground. "That might have been the worst set I've ever seen you do," she laughed. "But for being a good sport, I'll give you a little treat." Jamie batted her eyes and smiled seductively as her partner tugged the damp sports bra from her body. Her eyes fluttered closed as Ryan stepped a few inches closer and squatted a little. She grasped Jamie's hands to deny her normal urges, and then allowed their rigid nipples to brush lightly against each other.

"Ungh," the frustrated blonde cried as she tried to raise her hands to grasp the objects of her desire.

"Uh-uh-uh," Ryan insisted. "If I let you have your way, we're done for the day," she sagely predicted. "Let's keep going until we're both at ten."

"No fair!" Jamie cried. "When I work, my arousal drops, and the same thing happens to you! We'll never get there."

"Hmm, you have a point," Ryan considered. "How can we accomplish our goal …?"

"I've got an idea," twinkling green eyes decided, confidently taking Ryan by the hand. She led her to a bar, resting at chest height on a structure that allowed the bar to glide up and down on a track. "Some squats should do the trick."

"Squats don't normally make me hot," Ryan advised her.

"You haven't been doing them my way."

"As usual, I'm game," Ryan grinned, allowing Jamie to lead the dance.

"Okay," the thoughtful woman decided. "Do a warm-up set first. What weight do you need?"

"Give me fifty for the warm-up," Ryan said. Jamie did so and watched as her partner moved the bar to the highest position and stood under it. She released the locking hooks and let the weighted bar settle onto her shoulders, carefully spreading her feet shoulder-width apart. She bent slightly at the waist to secure the feel of the bar and then began a set of squats, her thighs and butt taking on all of the weight.

Jamie stood behind her, letting her eyes wander all over the powerful body. Even though Ryan's thighs bore most of the weight, her back muscles flexed and stretched nicely, providing the smiling spectator with a nice show.

When the set was finished, Jamie decided, "Now that we're both warmed up, let me make one small equipment change." Ryan stood and waited patiently as Jamie peeled the shorts off her, leaving only the G-string. "Gotta see the whole canvas," she chuckled, as Ryan smiled down at her. "Okay, sport, gimme another set."

While Ryan got the bar ready, Jamie pulled a short bench over and sat down right behind her. Ryan took a quick look over her shoulder, shaking her head at the prospective torture she knew was in store for her. Nonetheless, she hefted the eighty pounds and began her set. On the second rep, a pair of cool hands met her cheeks as she squatted into the exercise. Those questing little hands roamed all over her ass, sending tingles down both spines simultaneously.

The tiny little strap that bisected Ryan's butt was much more visually alluring than actual nakedness would be, and the smaller woman's heart thudded in her chest as she watched the performance. The halogen spots that illuminated the space were providentially positioned to send a pool of warm light right onto Ryan's ass. The sculpted cheeks glowed with a fine sheen of perspiration and, as Jamie leaned forward, she found that her mouth was actually watering at the sight. Her tongue automatically darted out of her mouth, and she found herself licking at the smooth, firm mounds as she would a delicious ice cream cone on a sizzling hot day.

Ryan's groan snapped Jamie from her focus, and she sat up, letting her partner catch her breath. The weight slid back onto the self-locking hooks, and Ryan stood for a moment, her legs shaking from the combination of fatigue and arousal. Without a word, Jamie rose and added ten more pounds to each end of the bar, making it an even one hundred.

Sparing a suspicious glance, Ryan got back down to work, lifting the bar onto her shoulders and flattening her back. On the third rep Jamie's hand slid between her partner's spread legs, sliding along her cleft in an intentionally incendiary touch. A low moan sprang from Ryan's lips as she shrugged out from under the weight, letting it drop and clang loudly against the padded floor. She turned in the same motion and pulled Jamie into her arms, carrying her onto a pair of exercise mats. As she lowered her to the floor, she leaned down close and growled, "Ten!" as her lips captured her partner's in a fiery kiss.

They rolled around on the thin mats, laughing wildly as they wrestled. Miraculously, Jamie won, tossing the larger woman onto her back, legs slightly spread, with the tiny piece of fabric just barely covering her vulva. Little black curls peeked out the sides of the material, beckoning Jamie to explore the ineffectively hidden treasures.

Jamie leaned back and gave her a cool appraisal. Azure eyes silently begged for relief, hips twitching with need. The tantalizing body was flushed from head to heel, hair damp with sweat, bangs stuck limply to forehead. She had a fine sheen of perspiration covering her completely, and little rivers of sweat ran down her sides. Besides the tangy aroma of exertion, Jamie was also rewarded by the scent of the arousal that flowed from Ryan, occasionally wafting up to reach Jamie's nose.

She began to run her hands slowly up and down Ryan's wet body. Her hands glided along smoothly, aided by the lubrication. Ryan's head tossed back and forth in frustration as she sucked in a deep breath. Jamie's hands were not idle for a moment, stroking her slick breasts and her belly. "God, I love your scent," Jamie growled into her ear, as she bent to cover her chest and belly with tender, emotion-filled kisses. The kisses became more heated and soon progressed to firm sucking and sharp nibbles. Ryan groaned and gasped for breath as Jamie continued to lick and suck all down her body. Her breathing was ragged and quick, and she was nearly beside herself with arousal. "You have to … I've got to …" Ryan shook her head roughly, frustrated with her inability to form a coherent sentence. She grasped Jamie's hands and forced them between her legs, locking her clear blue eyes on her partner. Her features were tense from the frustration that pounded through her body, and she managed to speak only one word, but her meaning was crystal clear, "Please," she moaned, shivering roughly. "Please."

"Please?" the intentionally obtuse blonde purred. "Please what, baby?"

Ryan's eyes were largely unfocused as she gazed at her partner in amazement. She knew that her request had been understood, and it dawned on her that Jamie actually wanted her to beg. *It's your own fault, Ryan*, she chided herself. *I think you might be biting off more than you can chew when this one lets loose. Ah well* … she thought with a mental shrug, *I've begged before, and I'll beg again.*

Her hands slid up her slick belly to cup her breasts, clearly Jamie's favorite spot. Her eyes fluttered closed as her hands grasped the tender flesh, now so slick with sweat that she had a hard time holding on. Her head tilted back as she squeezed firmly, the flushed skin peeking out from between her splayed fingers. A small gasp of pain flew from her lips as she grew a little too enthusiastic, and she bit down on her lower lip as she intentionally kept up the pressure. The throbbing between her legs increased dramatically, and her hips began to twitch of their own accord, as she continued to squeeze her now-tender breasts roughly.

It was impossible to open her eyes fully, but the heavy-lidded glance she spared her partner showed that the demonstration was working according to plan. Emerald green eyes focused on her hands like lasers, and the blonde licked her lips as she leaned in so close that her hot breath floated across the simmering flesh.

Ryan knew she had her at this point, and she reveled in the power she felt in being able to affect her partner so strongly. Her desire flared even brighter as their eyes locked together and she could see the stark need displayed in the verdant depths. The power had definitely shifted, and Ryan offered a knowing smile as she slid her thumbs into the tiny waistband of her G-string and slipped it from her body. Her legs splayed wide open as she made her final plea.

One elegantly shaped finger was slowly pulled into her mouth while Jamie watched in fascinated silence. Ryan's cheeks pulsed as she sucked deeply, wetting the lucky finger thoroughly. Withdrawing it with a "pop", she trailed a wet path down her chest, moving to one firm nipple, then to the other—leaving a thin trail of moisture as the finger passed. Pausing to replenish the lubrication, Ryan continued her erotic demonstration, heading further and further south. She gasped and thrust her hips sharply when her finger grazed the edge of her swollen lips, and her eyes flew open when Jamie let out a growl and dove for her. Before she could blink, determined small hands had slid under her thighs and pulled her forward just enough for Jamie's questing tongue to lave her throbbing need.

A deeply satisfied smile graced Ryan's lips as she relaxed into the touch, her hands coming to rest gently upon Jamie's fair head. *Two can play the begging game, my love*, she thought with a wry smirk.

Even the distraction of reflecting on her accomplishment could not hold off her fulfillment, and after mere seconds of this exquisite torture, Ryan felt herself cresting near the edge. She gritted her teeth, trying to hold off the inevitable terminus, since the journey had been so arduous. But she was powerless over the fantastic sensations radiating from the center of her body, and after a scant few moments, her head began to toss back and forth, a low, strangled cry bubbling up from her chest as she climaxed.

As the pulsing slowed, her fingers found Jamie's shoulders, and she pushed gently, forcing the determined woman away from her stimulated flesh. "No more," she moaned weakly. "No more."

In a heartbeat, Jamie was at her side, wrapping her in a loving embrace, holding her close until her rapid heartbeat had calmed. "I'm covered in your scent again," the small woman murmured, rubbing her wet face against Ryan's cheek.

Ryan chuckled, deep and low in her chest. "You seem to have warmed up to the scent thing pretty quickly. What happened to that innocent young thing I knew just a few days ago?"

Jamie looked at her, eyes slightly wide. "Do you like it?"

"Like it?" Ryan asked with an even bigger laugh. "I love it! I knew there was a hottie hiding behind that demure demeanor."

"Mia was right," Jamie mused, as she snuggled up against Ryan's chest.

"Mia? Where does she figure into this discussion?"

"When we were talking on the beach, she told me that oral sex was one of the most fantastic things to do with someone you cared for."

"Hmm, I'm not sure I'd agree if I were straight, but there's nothing I like better with a woman."

Jamie knew that Ryan didn't have a clue about Mia's dabblings, but she didn't feel that she should reveal the truth, so she merely agreed with her partner. They rested together for a few minutes before Jamie looked up at her lover and asked, "Uhm … why haven't you done that to me, if you like it?"

Ryan's low laugh rumbled through both of their bodies. "I tried to, hon, but you were having none of it. I decided to hold off until you showed you were receptive."

"Oh, I guess I did that, didn't I?" she asked with a little giggle. "Well, it's okay if you want to do it now."

"Unh-uh," Ryan smiled down at her. "I want you to tell me when you're in the mood."

Jamie sat up and stared at her. "Tell you?" she gasped.

"Yep," Ryan decreed. "You've been uncomfortable before, and I don't want to make you feel odd about it. When you wanna try it, I want you to tell me, or signal me somehow." Ryan's eyes danced with humor as she reminded her partner, "You said you'd rather signal me than ask for what you want, remember?"

"Oh, honey," she moaned, as she collapsed against her partner's side. "I don't think I can do that. Can't you be in charge?"

It was obvious that Jamie desperately wanted her partner to take responsibility for this decision, but Ryan was adamant. "Nope. I told you the other night that isn't how I want this relationship to be, and you agreed. We need to learn to ask for what we want, and be comfortable with our desires. It might take you a while, but I want you to ask me for what you need. I promise I'll satisfy every request, if I'm able."

A deep sigh expressed Jamie's unhappiness with this arrangement. "I don't like it," she groused.

"Humor me," Ryan insisted. "Own your desires, babe."

"Oh, all right," she grumbled, rolling onto her back. Quickly shucking her shorts, she held her arms open and demanded, "I desire to have you make love to me until I'm faint."

"Your wish is my command."

Within moments they were gliding against each other in a slick, sensual dance, warm, wet bodies moving with tortuously slow grace. Ryan had taken her partner's wish with the utmost seriousness, and she was determined to make Jamie beg for mercy.

Bit by bit she loved her squirming body, kissing every surface, nibbling and sucking on most. The small woman writhed under the loving assault, moaning softly as she tried in vain to quicken her partner's pace.

Ryan was moving slowly, investigating every spot that caught her interest. Making her way down her partner's shaking body, she was now lying between her lover's trembling thighs, dark head resting on a firmly muscled leg. The fiendish woman seemingly was trying to drive her victim absolutely mad, as she languidly teased the sensitive skin of the inner thighs that lay just within reach. Her warm, wet tongue had been drawing complex patterns on the baby-soft skin for long minutes, never drawing closer to the goal Jamie desired but was too shy to request.

Trying to lure Ryan closer was having scant success. Jamie's legs were spread as wide as was humanly possible, but neither her position, nor her moans and whimpers had the desired effect. *Come on, baby*, she urged silently. *You know I want it, and I know you want to do it ... come on ... just another inch!*

Ryan's head moved just a fraction of an inch, giving the silent woman hope, but the soft lips fell onto the skin just adjacent to the spot where they were so desperately needed. For one tantalizing second, as Ryan lifted her head again and hovered above the throbbing spot, Jamie was sure that her partner would take pity on her and continue on her path. Her warm, humid breath floated over Jamie's overheated skin, so close and yet, so far. The dark head tilted just enough for cerulean eyes to lock onto mist green as Ryan pursed her ruby lips and blew a small kiss at the slick flesh and began to pull back.

Realization dawned on Jamie, and before Ryan had traveled three inches, determined small hands grabbed her head and pulled it forward, forcing Ryan's face into her moistness. "Do it, Ryan! God! Please do it!"

Without hesitation, Ryan tilted her head and let her tongue travel in an unbroken path, trailing all along Jamie's need with a long, wet kiss. "Oh, my God!" the gasping woman cried, her legs impossibly sliding open even further.

For a moment, Ryan lifted her head and made contact with Jamie's heavy-lidded eyes. "This was worth the wait," she murmured, the sincerity of her words reflected in her ardent gaze. "You're absolutely magnificent."

Green eyes fluttered closed as Ryan bent to her pleasure-filled task. Small hands went to the back of her lover's head and caressed it as Ryan settled down to feed upon the nectar of her lover's arousal.

Quicker than either woman wished, the blonde head fell back, and Jamie cried out loudly, moaning and gasping as powerful waves of sensation washed through her body. Ryan stayed right where she was, watching in delight as a series of spasms rolled through her partner's coiled form. She gently stroked the trembling thighs, murmuring words of love as her lover's body slowly calmed.

When the pulsing seemed to have stopped, Ryan crawled up and cuddled her still-spent partner in her arms. After several minutes, Jamie rolled onto her back and smiled lazily. "You always know best."

"Another convert to the cunnilingus club?" Ryan gently teased.

"As soon as my hands stop shaking, I'll sign up for a lifetime membership," the satisfied blonde smirked, dropping her head onto Ryan's chest for a short, well-deserved nap.

## Chapter Twelve

Hunger woke the pair, Ryan, as expected, coming to first. "I'm starving," she complained, her voice muffled by her lover's skin. During their nap, Jamie wound up on her stomach, with Ryan's dark head resting on her smooth back. She rolled off to allow her lover to move, and each of them spent a few minutes stretching out the kinks. "You're gonna have to get some thicker mats in here if we're gonna do that very often."

"I'll leave a note for Mother," Jamie replied absently, trying to get her own kinks out. "God, I'm stiff," she complained. "My back's been funny since the ride, and that little nap didn't do me any favors."

"I'll throw something together for dinner," Ryan decided. "You go swim a few laps to loosen up, and then sit in the spa until you're nice and loose. By the time you get out, I'll have dinner ready."

"No arguments." She winced bending over to pick up her clothes. "I hate for us to be apart, even for a few minutes, but I know you're hungrier than you are stiff. So get going, Buffy, and don't eat everything before I get there."

Forty-five minutes later, Jamie was relaxed and rejuvenated. The swim had helped tremendously, and her back felt perfectly normal as she walked up the path to the house. Ryan had obviously found the stereo hidden behind an articulated door in the kitchen, because Jamie could hear the pounding beat when she was still a good twenty-five feet from the back door.

Ryan didn't hear her when she entered. Given the volume, she wouldn't have heard a 747 land in the back yard. She had put on her new red and white board shorts and a skimpy square cut white tank that stopped a good four inches shy of the low cut shorts. Jamie's mouth actually went dry at the sight, but when her partner began to dance, she had to grab on to the doorjamb to keep from falling.

Ryan was a fabulous dancer, all long legs and sexy hips. But she was usually dancing in public, or for Jamie. Tonight she was dancing only for herself, and there was something so incredibly sexy about watching her body move only to satisfy her own desire that Jamie felt transfixed with lust, despite their recent lovemaking.

The song was being sung in French, but Jamie didn't recognize the accent. She had spent a good deal of time in France and had journeyed through the countryside, but this intonation was completely unfamiliar. After a few more lines, she realized from the beat and the rhythm that the singer was most likely African. She knew that Ryan had a fondness for music from around the world, but she had never been in a position to watch her dance to her favorites. The song was obviously one of that group, because even though her partner could not sing the words, she moved to the beat as though she had heard it hundreds of times.

As the words drummed through the speakers, Ryan's butt twitched and jerked, the movement of her micro shorts hypnotizing Jamie. Her lover was grilling a steak on the stovetop grill, and simultaneously warming some tortillas. As she worked, her movements perfectly reflected the beat and tempo of the music, gliding around the kitchen as if the entire dance had been perfectly choreographed. She had something in one of the low warming ovens, and as she bent over severely to check the contents, her butt kept twitching to the beat. Jamie couldn't take any more, and she practically flew across the room to grab two handfuls of the twitching bottom. "You have the sexiest ass I have ever seen on a human being," she growled into Ryan's surprised ear, leaning over to cover her bent body with her own.

"Glad you like it," Ryan purred, as she squeezed the hands that now wrapped around her waist.

Jamie pulled her up and turned her around quickly, now grasping the cheeks as she nuzzled her head against the perfectly located breasts. "I love being short," she drawled, as her face rubbed against a now hardened nipple.

"Dinner's gonna burn," Ryan reminded her, as she turned in her embrace to remove the sizzling steak from the grill. Jamie let her go, but not before she snaked a hand up the tiny leg of the shorts and grabbed a handful.

"Grurf," she growled, as she forced her body to behave and let her partner finish cooking. She crossed over to the stereo and turned it down five notches, then went to the refrigerator and took out a Corona. "Want one?" she called to her partner.

"Absolutely," Ryan replied with a grin. "You've got my temperature rising again, chica."

"Ha! If I were wearing any panties, they'd be soaked after that little dancing exhibition." She handed her partner a beer, tapping the necks of the bottles together to toast. "Cheers," she said as she grabbed a full cheek, copping one more feel before dinner.

"Just sit down and relax for a minute there, hot stuff." Ryan smiled indulgently. "Let's get some food into our systems before we start munching on each other again."

"Oh, I don't think so, baby," Jamie said with a shiver as she gently placed her hand protectively over her own vulva. "I need to save some energy for our last full day together. I've got big plans for you, sweet cheeks."

"Okay," Ryan agreed. "We can take the night off."

They worked together to finish the impromptu, but delicious, meal. Sitting next to each other on the window seat they ate quickly, both too hungry to spend much time in idle chatter. As the meal progressed and their pace slowed, Jamie broke the silence. "Ryan?" she began hesitantly.

"Yeah?" Ryan asked, interrupting the progress of her fork to look closely at her lover.

Jamie looked up at her with a sidelong glance, failing to meet her eyes. "How did you feel about today?"

"What part of today?" Ryan asked neutrally, guessing what Jamie was getting at, but not wanting to speculate in case she was wrong.

"What did you think about the sex we had in the gym?" she asked, as she looked down at her plate.

"I think it was about as hot as anything I've ever done," Ryan said, a big smile on her face. "I can't tell you how great it is to have you share the little fantasies that you've had on your mind all these months."

Jamie looked completely flustered as she choked out, "So I'm the wildest woman you've ever been with?"

"No, no, that's not what I meant at all."

"But you said …"

"I said it was as *hot* as anything I've ever done, and it was. I don't think I've ever been more aroused than that. But it's certainly not the wildest thing I've ever done."

"What is?" she hesitantly asked, looking up shyly through her golden bangs.

"Unh, unh, unh," Ryan said. "I wanna keep a little mystery in my life."

"Why won't you tell me?"

"Because I might … no, I *will* want to do it to you and I don't want to spoil the surprise."

"Okay," she agreed. "But are you sure you don't think what we did is … too much?"

"Too much? Too much what?" Ryan asked, clearly puzzled.

"Do you think we're moving too fast? I mean it was less than a week ago that I was confessing to Mia how frightened I was of making love to you at all, and now I'm kinda acting like a dominatrix."

"Jamie," she said with a laugh. "You don't act anything like a dominatrix! And believe me, I would know," she added with a wiggling eyebrow. She took Jamie's hands in her own and squeezed them tight. "You are gentle and loving and open, and very, very sweet to me. You never try to cause me pain or discomfort … well, maybe a little discomfort," she corrected, with a twinkle in her eye.

Jamie lifted her eyes to see if Ryan was teasing her. When she saw that she was, she gave her a hesitant smile.

"You're experimenting with power. Everybody does that, honey. It's one of the most fun things about sex. I do it to you, too."

Jamie looked up to gauge Ryan's meaning.

"Honey, every time we've made love, I could have tossed you down and finished you off in two seconds. But it's fun to make you beg for more. That's what lovers do,

Jamie. It increases the sensation, it makes you want to be touched so badly you could scream. That's kind of the whole point of having a lover. If you're only going to do the expected, you could masturbate. It's knowing that your partner is in control, and that she can do whatever she wants to you that makes it hot."

"I just never, ever did things like that with Jack," Jamie admitted. "I guess it kinda scares me."

"What about it scares you?"

"I guess it scares me because I don't know where it'll stop," she confessed. "I mean, I think you're right, I'm just figuring out what I like and what turns me on. But, what if I find out I want to tie you up and walk all over you in spike heels?"

"Hmmm …" Ryan gave that some thought, trying to hide her sly grin.

"I'm kidding, Ryan!" she exclaimed, as she slapped her on the thigh.

"So am I," Ryan retorted as she leaned over to give her waist a tickle. "But I am serious about one thing. I want you to be completely free to tell me what pleases you. That doesn't mean that I'll agree to do it, but I promise I'll never make you feel bad for having a desire, no matter how wild."

"Will you do the same thing for me?"

"Of course I will," Ryan assured her, as she leaned over and gave her lover a kiss on the cheek. "I couldn't be happier with the way we've made love. I wasn't exaggerating when I said that this week has exceeded my wildest dreams. But no matter how much we love each other, and no matter how great sex is between us, we will always have to keep communicating about it."

"I … guess I'll get used to that," Jamie said. "It's easier—much easier for me to react when my lust gets the best of me. But talking isn't a bad idea. It's just embarrassing."

Ryan wrapped her arms around Jamie's waist. "I hope you change your mind about that. Sex is just an intimate form of communication. Some days I'll feel like being wild, but you might want something soft, and gentle, and very vanilla. We need to be able to talk about that, and not take offense if we don't mesh sometimes. I guarantee that we won't be in the same mood all the time, sweetie. The only way to make this great is to make it perfectly safe to express our individual needs and desires."

"So, did you really enjoy this afternoon?" she asked again, but this time there was a sexy grin on her face.

"I don't have words to describe how hot I thought this afternoon was." Ryan leaned in to kiss her partner on the lips. "I've waited five years to be able to taste a woman, and I can't tell you how happy I am that you were the woman I got to experience it with."

Jamie sat up straight and stared at her partner. "What?" Her eyes blinked slowly as she tried to process this information. "What are you talking about?"

Ryan smiled and reminded her, "I've told you that I've been practicing safer sex for five years. Unprotected oral sex is a no-no."

"God!" Jamie uttered as she allowed herself to consider what "safer sex" really meant. "That never occurred to me."

"It's been hard," Ryan admitted. "Luckily, my Pavlovian reflex adapted pretty quickly. Now I get aroused from tasting Latex." Her amused smirk caused Jamie to laugh, and soon they were both chuckling at Ryan's adaptability.

"Well, you never have to have your lips on another dental dam."

"Not so fast, sparky." Ryan was still grinning, but Jamie could tell she was serious. "I've gotten quite used to the little things. I'm not ready to give them up permanently. You actually might like them for a change of pace."

Jamie made a face. "I'm not aroused by the taste of Latex."

"No … but you might like to feel my teeth raking over your clitoris through a little barrier. You use a whole different technique when you have oral sex with a dam. It's kinda fun." Waggling eyebrows punctuated just how much fun Ryan was talking about.

"I am *so* lucky to have you, girlfriend," Jamie said, as she laid her forehead against Ryan's.

"I'm the lucky one, sweetie," she insisted, turning her head to nibble on her lover's tender lips. "I'm luckier than I ever thought possible."

After dinner they went into the living room to let their meal digest. Sitting next to each other on one of the tasteful print sofas, Jamie said, "You know, for someone who claims not to cook much, you do a darned nice job. I might have to keep you in the kitchen, barefoot and pregnant." Ryan paid her back for her comment by fiendishly tickling her for a long while. Jamie gasped and giggled wildly as she fought to push her demonic lover away. The pushing and grasping soon gave way to some rough kisses that quickly progressed to passionate ones. Ryan came up for air and said with a laugh, "I thought you didn't wanna do the wild thing tonight!"

"Who says I do?" Jamie queried with a smirk, leaning in for another kiss.

"Well," Ryan breathed into her ear. "When you do this …" she placed a slow, deep kiss on her lips. "Or this …" she slid her tongue into Jamie's receptive mouth and let it languidly explore for a minute. "Or this …" she ran her hands up under her sweatshirt to tease the sensitive skin around her breasts, "a girl can get the impression that you wanna get wet and messy."

"I'm testing your response time," Jamie replied. "Purely scientific inquiry."

"How'd I do?" Ryan whispered into her ear as she rolled her over and sat astride her hips.

"I'd say that you are quite responsive." She pulled Ryan's tank up to reveal her rock hard nipples. "But there's one more place I should check for evidence," she decided, sliding her hand up the leg of her shorts.

Ryan grabbed her hand and held it firmly, pulling it out of her pants and placing it on her thigh. "I can save you the trouble," she said as she bent to kiss her again. "All systems are go. But if you don't want to blast off, you'd better keep your fingers off the launch button."

"So I could interest you in a little love?"

A slow, sly nod was her answer.

"Do you ever say no?" Jamie smiled, shaking her head at her partner's constant receptivity.

Ryan cocked her head and thought about the question carefully, as was her fashion. "I guess I don't," she admitted. "I've been a little like a hunter/gatherer from prehistoric times."

"Hunter/gatherers were always horny?" Jamie asked, having missed that tidbit in history class.

"No, silly," Ryan laughed. "Hunter/gatherers were never sure where their next meal was coming from. When they killed a large animal or came upon some food that would perish quickly, they ate as much as they could to make sure they got all of the nourishment they could stand. It helped them weather the next dry spell."

"And?"

"And … when I didn't know where my next sexual experience would come from, I felt like I needed to take what was offered, when it was offered. I trained myself to always be receptive, because I didn't know when a dry spell would hit."

"But, honey," Jamie purred, "you're never going to have another dry spell."

"Tell that to her," Ryan said, pointing to her always-receptive vulva, a smirk covering her face.

"Oh, so 'Little Ryan' is the one I have to convince, huh?" Jamie asked, as she gently patted "Little Ryan".

"Yep. She's suspicious by nature."

"I'll make you a deal, baby. Let's play a game. If I win, I get to ravish you. If you win, we go to sleep."

"Uhm … how does that make me the winner?"

"Oh, don't worry, Ryan, you'll lose. You'll definitely lose."

She got up and offered her partner a hand, and led her into a room at the back of the house. It was a big, fully equipped game room, with a large green-felt pool table in the center of the room. Two large Tiffany-style lamps hung over the table, lighting it to perfection. The room also contained two poker tables, two dartboards and a big screen TV, with comfortable overstuffed leather chairs facing it. An impressive wet bar took up one corner of the room, and big leaded glass windows looked out over the lawn and the blackness of the sea.

"Wow," Ryan said in amazement. "Yet another room bigger than our whole first floor."

Jamie gave her a fond grin and asked, "Do you play pool?"

"Am I not a lesbian?" she asked rhetorically, giving Jamie a big grin.

"Yes, but are you any good?"

"Let's see, if I win, we go to sleep, and if I lose, you make love to me." She wrinkled up her forehead, seemingly deep in thought. "I totally suck!" she announced forcefully.

Jamie walked over to the rack where a number of nice cues hung. Ryan came over and picked up a couple, sighting down them with practiced ease. "Uhm, Jamie," she said as she picked up one particular cue. "This one has your name engraved on it."

"Oh my, so it does," she agreed casually as she snatched it out of Ryan's hand. "Imagine that." She looked up at her lover with an innocent smile.

"I think I'm in trouble."

"Deep, deep trouble." Jamie nodded with a knowing smile.

They flipped to see who would break and Jamie won. Ryan could have left the room after that, because she didn't get to pick up her cue until the game was over. She sat open-mouthed on a stool and watched as her partner ran the table, methodically stoking each ball into a pocket, one at a time. As the eight ball fell into the corner pocket, she came over and stood between Ryan's spread legs. "Pay up," she insisted lustily.

"Two out of three?"

"Are you really more competitive than you are sexual?" Jamie asked, as she placed her hands flat on Ryan's chest and gazed at her in wonder.

"Duh!" Ryan said as she slapped her forehead. "I forgot that losing was winning! Let's go!" She grabbed Jamie's hand and headed for the door.

"What's your rush?" Jamie's sultry voice purred. "We haven't christened this room, you know."

"Geez, you've got me so confused, I don't know what's going on," Ryan said, plopping down on her stool again.

Jamie gave her a throaty laugh as she stood between her spread legs. "Do you have any special requests?" she asked with a grin that was partly innocent and partly lascivious.

"Unh-uh," Ryan replied, shaking her head slowly. "You haven't disappointed me yet."

"Hmm ..." She looked Ryan up and down speculatively. "How would I like you tonight?" She ran the backs of her fingers teasingly over the pouty breasts and considered. "I could make these little beauties the focus of my attention." Ryan seemed to like that idea just fine as she threw her shoulders back to make her breasts even more available. Jamie stepped back and looked all around the room, considering her options. When she returned her gaze to Ryan, she had a smug smile gracing her face. "I'm set." She leaned in and started kissing her, signaling that the games had begun.

As usual, Ryan was putty in her hands as soon as she began to kiss her. In a few minutes, she was breathing heavily and leaning in hard. Her mouth opened wide to suck Jamie's wet tongue into the warm, welcoming space. Jamie gripped her face with both hands and held her steady as she delicately nibbled on her lips, teasing every millimeter with her teeth and tongue. Ryan groaned lustily as her lover forced her way into her mouth and explored her thoroughly.

Jamie loved the power she felt as Ryan responded to her so enthusiastically. The dark woman was truly limp, and this surrender served as a powerful aphrodisiac.

Ryan's total trust and complete submissiveness revealed the depth of her love, and this vulnerability made the gift of her body all the more precious to Jamie.

She grasped Ryan's hand and pulled her over to a low leather sofa, then pulled a cotton throw from a chair and placed it across the seat to provide a warmer place to lie. Turning to Ryan, she reverently began to remove clothing, kissing all of the warm skin as it was revealed to her worshipful gaze. She spent a few minutes loving both the exposed and the covered skin until she grasped the shorts by the bottom hems and slowly pulled them down. Ryan kicked them off as Jamie rose to her feet.

She slowly tossed off her own clothing, her gaze never leaving Ryan's sapphire blue eyes, now smoldering with desire. She stood close enough that they were breathing the same air and she carefully turned her head and rested it on Ryan's strong chest, her hands loosely clasped behind the small of her partner's back.

"I love you, Ryan," she said softly, as she tightened her embrace and squeezed her firmly.

"I love you, too, Jamie," came the husky reply.

Jamie sat down on the sofa and pulled her legs up on the surface. She raised her left leg until her foot rested on a cushion, and spread her right leg wide open so that Ryan could sit between them. As she slid in place, Ryan gave her a little smirk feeling the wet warm kiss that her back received from Jamie's vulva. She leaned back against her partner as Jamie slid each of her legs under Ryan's.

Jamie nibbled sensually on her neck as each hand cupped a heavy, lush breast. She kneaded the firm flesh, teasing Ryan's ears unmercifully with her tongue. She spent extra time running the tip of her tongue all around the blue diamond that Ryan wore in her left ear, whispering, "I love that you wear this sign of my love for you. I want everyone to know how much I love you, Ryan."

Her mouth captured the sensitive flesh of the tender earlobes, and she lightly nibbled and sucked each little bit of flesh into her mouth. Ryan was moaning softly as her hips began to sway slowly back and forth.

Jamie simply needed to show her love for her partner tonight, without teasing or refusing her entreaties, so she gently slid two fingers from each hand into her partner's wetness. Ryan's hips lifted off the sofa abruptly as she sucked in a very satisfied breath. She sank back down as her lover's fingers slowly increased her arousal, a bit at a time. The knowing fingers ratcheted up her excitement until she was tossing her head back and forth against Jamie's chest, gasping for breath as her hips thrust up and down insistently. Just a bit of firmer pressure sent her over the edge. Sighing deeply, she let out a small whimper, sinking onto the sofa, nestled securely between her lover's legs.

Her head rested limply against Jamie's shoulder, breath still coming in heavy gulps. She lifted and turned her head catching a glimpse of her partner's smiling face. "That was very, very nice," she said appreciatively.

"I needed to touch you gently tonight," Jamie admitted. "Do you like that as well as when I'm a little wild?"

"Absolutely," Ryan said firmly. "It's like when you want to go out to dinner. Sometimes you want spicy Szechwan food, and sometimes you want a nice turkey sandwich. They're each perfect if that's what you're in the mood for. But if you really want a turkey sandwich, and somebody gives you Szechwan green beans, you're not a happy camper. Tonight I think we were both in the mood for a little tenderness." She reached up to grasp the back of Jamie's head and pull her down for a gentle kiss. "How about you? Could you stand a little tenderness?"

"Hmm, I'm afraid that I'll be sore if I get much more friction."

"I guarantee I can give you a nice little sedative without much friction."

"Umm, I am feeling awfully aroused," she mused. "Sure you're up to it?"

"Double your money back if I fail to deliver," Ryan smiled down at her.

A short while later they lay in bed, snuggling as they relaxed before sleep. "As usual, you are a woman of your word," Jamie chuckled into her partner's ear.

"No friction?"

"Just the right amount," she murmured. "You're a virtuoso, babe."

Without warning, Ryan hopped out of bed, running to retrieve the bag her new shoes had been placed in. "What are you doing?" Jamie asked, sitting up and watching her partner dash around the room.

"I bought you a little something," the brunette informed her, holding the object behind her back. "I felt bad about buying that shirt for Ally, and I didn't want you to feel left out. So when you were buying coffee today I went on a little search and got a shirt so I could continue the custom with you. Now, it's not quite the same, since I'll never let you out of my sight, but when we go somewhere together, I'm going to buy you a shirt to commemorate the trip."

"Come over here, you big, sweet, gorgeous hunk of woman," Jamie ordered. As Ryan approached the bed, the blonde asked rhetorically, "How did I get so lucky?"

"Search me," Ryan joked, shrugging her broad shoulders.

"Later," the grinning blonde promised with a waggling eyebrow. "Now … show me my gift."

"Okay, but promise you won't be offended," Ryan cautioned. "It's a little joke based on a conversation we had … but it *is* a joke."

"Mmm, this I gotta see," the smirking blonde said. "Hand it over, babe."

Ryan did just that and grinned as Jamie held up the large black T-shirt. Big purple block letters proclaimed, "I'm not a lesbian, but my girlfriend is." Lifting her amused green eyes to Ryan, Jamie shook her head as she said, "My motto is: there are no straight women."

"What?" Ryan said, a frown covering her face. "What in the heck do you mean by that?"

"There are only women who haven't met Ryan O'Flaherty," Jamie decided with conviction.

They'd been asleep for just a few minutes when Jamie sat up as though she'd been slapped awake. Her eyes were wide with alarm, and she sucked in a deep breath, trying to calm herself. Ryan sat up quickly and her eyes darted from Jamie's shocked face to the surrounding room, returning to her face again when she noticed nothing amiss.

"What's wrong?" she asked, her own voice echoing Jamie's obvious alarm.

"Closed circuit cameras," she panted, turning a ghostly shade of pale.

The abrupt awakening and the late hour combined to cloud Ryan's usually perceptive mind. "What?" she cried, thinking that Jamie might be recounting a dream.

"My parents have closed circuit cameras ..." She began to almost hyperventilate as she gasped out, "in the gym!"

Ryan immediately understood the gravity of the situation. "Are you sure they're running?" she asked, more calmly than she felt.

Jamie nodded her head slowly. "They're only on when my parents are gone."

"Where are the controls?"

"I'm not sure. They just put this in last year."

"Do they keep the tapes here, or is there some service that does it?"

"I don't know," she said, starting to cry. "Oh, Ryan, if they find out about us this way, we'll never be able to have a relationship with them. This would kill them if they saw us having sex here. Like we did," she added with a deep blush, as scenes from their gym adventure flooded her brain.

"Jamie, Jamie," she said as she patted her heaving back. "We'll figure this out. I promise you." Staring into Jamie's eyes, she repeated sincerely, "I promise you."

Jamie clung to her tightly, her mind running through various scenarios, all of them disastrous. She looked up at Ryan, her tear-stained face reflecting shame and embarrassment. "It's making me sick to my stomach to think of someone watching us," she said as the sobs overtook her again.

"Jamie ..." Ryan slowly pulled back and lifted her lover's face with her fingertips. "I swear to you that we'll figure out a way to make sure your parents don't see that tape. No matter what we have to do, they will not see it."

"What can we do?"

"We'll do what we have to. I'll bring all of my cousins down here to tear this place apart brick by brick if we need to. We will absolutely figure out a way to make sure your parents do not *ever* see that tape."

Jamie still looked physically ill, and Ryan soothed, "There's nothing wrong with how we made love today. Nothing." She lifted her chin as her partner dropped it again in shame. "What we do together is intensely private, and I never want another soul to watch us. But whatever we do together is done with love, and trust and tenderness." She softly kissed her lover on the lips. "Always based in love."

Jamie curled up into her embrace and laid her head on her strong shoulder. "I do love you, Ryan. So very, very, much."

"I love you too, Jamie," she said as she nuzzled into her neck, "with everything that I am. I've never lied to you, and I'm not lying now. We *will* fix this, and no one will ever know."

As soon as her partner was asleep, Ryan slipped out of bed and went downstairs to find the keys to the gym. Walking down the path to the garage in the heavy fog, she got the key into the lock by feel alone. When she went in to investigate the workout space, she spotted a door in the corner that she'd not previously noticed, and she wondered if the equipment might be kept there. She tried the knob, but it was, of course, locked. There were no other potential hiding places, so she glumly walked back to the main house. She spent another few minutes looking all around the library and the kitchen, searching for a set of keys that might work for the door, but they all looked like the ones for the front door or were clearly for automobiles. She sat down on a stool in the kitchen and rested her head on her crossed arms, deep in thought. After a bit, an idea hit her, but she couldn't explore the thought until morning, so she turned off the lights and went back upstairs to slip back into bed, her temporary absence completely unnoticed by her partner.

# Chapter Thirteen

Anxiety over the cameras caused Ryan to rise even earlier than normal. She hadn't really slept that well, with thoughts of her partner's anguished face waking her repeatedly. *Jamie's depending on me to make this right*, she mused as she crept around the room, trying to successfully dress herself in the dark. *There has to be a way to find out how the system works and to stop the Evans's from ever seeing any evidence of our lovemaking. God, Da knows I'm gay, he knows I'm a horn-dog, and he loves Jamie. With all of that, even he'd freak if he saw photos or tapes of us together ... like we were.* She blushed a bit as she considered how they'd pleased each other in the gym. *That wasn't just sex*, she reminded herself with a sly grin. *That was ... that was ... I don't even know what that was. But I want to make sure we do more of whatever it was in the very near future!* After a stop in the kitchen for a small snack, she paused in front of the alarm display and shook her head at her own lack of imagination. *How in the holy hell did I not understand that "surv" meant surveillance?* She was angry with herself over her failure not to pursue her question about the various zones, knowing that if she had pressed the issue Jamie would likely have remembered the cameras. *Water under the bridge, Ryan. You can't change the past, but you can get your butt in gear and fix this problem as quickly as you can.* Grabbing the keys, she headed over to the gym to investigate her idea of the night before.

Bounding up the stairs, she walked around and looked carefully at the cameras, noting the manufacturer and the model number. Going to the locked door, she checked the lock manufacturer and then went to the phone located on the wall, making a quick, but productive, phone call. After checking a few more minor—but possibly important—details, she felt her anxiety begin to ease now that she was taking some action. Her mood lightened appreciably, she took off for her run, a bounce to her step, singing softly to herself most of the way.

After an hour she was headed back up the drive, but stopped short when she remembered that there was a very attractive alternative to cooling off in the shower. By the time she reached the pool house most of her clothes were off, and she reflected on how delicious it felt to be able to strip outdoors. She kicked off her shoes as she entered and immediately dove in, using a racing start. The water felt divine, and after twenty graceful laps she hopped out. She was about to grab a towel and dry off when a childlike grin crossed her face as a delicious sounding idea lodged in her head.

Leaving her clothes where they lay, she opened the door of the glass building and stood on the stone entryway for a few minutes, gauging the safety of her plan.

Since she had awakened so early it was only quarter to seven, and she was fairly confident that no one would be on the grounds that early, even if they did have business to attend to. Deciding the reward was worth the risk, she started to run across the wide expanse of perfectly manicured grass that separated the pool house from the oceanside cliff.

Naked as the day she was born, chlorine-scented water droplets covering her body, the lanky woman began to cover ground at a quick clip—no destination in mind. Her goal was not to reach a destination at all—it was to revel in the journey. And today's journey consisted of enjoying the delightful sensation of running on thick, spongy grass on a dark, foggy morning, completely naked.

One of Ryan's favorite sensations was to expose every inch of her skin to the great outdoors. When she was a small child, her parents fought a constant battle to keep clothes on her, and she had never lost the desire to feel the kiss of a breeze on normally covered skin. The dense population of San Francisco prevented her from indulging her wish very often, but this isolated, protected estate was made to order. She'd traveled only a hundred yards or so when the telltale hiss of an automatic sprinkler alerted her prior to erupting from the lawn and emitting a fine, cold spray in a wide, pulsing pattern.

The chance to experience this new sensation beckoned, and she found her body propelling itself towards the streaming water as one sprinkler after another kicked in.

The water was colder than she would have guessed, the fine, icy needles pricking her skin everywhere it hit. But she didn't let that detail deter her—instead it urged her on, and she picked up the pace until she was running at her limit. The sensation was so intense that she heard her own voice let out a joyous whoop of pleasure as she ran through the water. Not surprisingly, the fine, short grass, the foggy morning and the cold spray didn't provide a good running surface, and after a short while, she took a header—falling onto her belly, arms extended. She slid a good ten yards, grass tickling her chilled skin. But the fall did nothing to disrupt her enjoyment of the experience—instead it allowed her to create a variation on the game.

Getting to her feet, she took off in a mad sprint, and then intentionally flopped onto the ground, sliding as far as her momentum would take her. This wild romp continued for some minutes until she heard a gentle laugh floating up from the pool house.

Turning quickly, she spotted her lover, clad only in one of Ryan's T-shirts. The small, shivering woman smiled engagingly at her wild lover, shaking her head in amusement at the antics.

Ryan started to run over, waiting until she was about twenty feet away to launch herself again, sliding on her belly until she stopped a foot or so from her laughing partner.

"You obviously didn't get the memo, sweetie, but you ceased to be a three-year-old twenty years ago."

The dark head shook forcefully as Ryan returned the smile. "I never read memos," she declared. "And if you take that shirt off and join me, you can act like you didn't read it, either." Dark eyebrows twitched in challenge, and Jamie knew that she had made a tactical error in coming outside in the first place. Still, the luminescent smile on her lover's face compelled her to whisk the shirt off and grasp the hand her playful partner extended.

They took off together, Jamie screaming at the shock of the ice-cold water pelting her body. Ryan's joyful laugh caused her to forget the discomfort and revel in the experience—forcing herself to feel only the exhilaration of the moment.

They got up a good head of steam and dove across the ground together, hands clasped as they slid through the spiky blades of grass. Ryan grasped her lover's chilled, soaked body and wrapped her in a joyful hug, their joined bodies almost immediately creating warmth everywhere they touched.

"That was fabulous," Jamie cried, throwing her head back to let out a yell.

"That rocked!" Ryan released her partner and took off one last time, this time executing a stylish feet-first slide, then rolling onto her back and spreading her arms and legs out fully. "Race you to the spa!" she yelled, scampering to her feet and taking off.

Shaking her wet hair like a dog, Jamie ran after her mischievous companion, laughing the whole way.

After fifteen minutes in the spa, both women were warm and invigorated. Jamie had thoughtfully brought a set of sweats for each of them when she noticed her partner's antics, and they now each put the welcome outfits on.

"Got any plans in mind?" Jamie asked.

"Nope. Not a one," Ryan smiled. "You?"

"Let's drag a couple of chairs out by the cliff and watch the sea birds eat breakfast."

"Okay," Ryan warned. "But watching those birds eat sashimi is definitely gonna make me want a big breakfast."

It took a few minutes to drag a pair of heavy, wrought iron chaises from the pool house out to the cliff, but the view was worth the effort. It was seven-thirty now, and the fog, while still thick, showed signs of dissipating. The temperature was in the high 50s—brisk, but not too bad with the warm sweats covering their bodies.

They watched the surf crash and thrum against the rocks for a long while, each silently lost in her own thoughts. Jamie finally broke the silence, squeezing her partner's hand as she asked, "What goes through your mind to cause you to do wild things like that?"

"Wild?" Ryan laughed. At Jamie's nod she answered, "I don't know. I love to be naked outside—always have. Whenever I get the chance to be out in the elements I jump at it. Today was a perfect opportunity."

"But how do you feel when you do something like that?" Jamie asked, wanting to understand her partner better.

Ryan mused about her answer for a few moments. She finally turned and said, "I feel … alive. I don't have a better way to put it. I love to feel sensation—the cold, the wet, the sharp blades of grass tickling my tummy—all of those things remind me that I'm alive."

"Have you always been like that?"

Ryan's face darkened noticeably. She paused a second, then answered. "I had to make a decision about how I was going to live my life when I was young. I could choose to let the fear of death ruin my life, or I could consciously embrace every day. I try, with all my heart, to do the latter."

Jamie squeezed her hand firmly, then drew the hand close and kissed the warm palm. "It always hurts to think about that time, doesn't it?"

Ryan nodded, lips slightly pursed.

"I've uhm … been thinking," Jamie said. She'd been mulling an idea around in her head ever since the AIDS Ride, and this seemed like a good time to bring it up. "I might not have any idea what I'm talking about, but it occurred to me that you never talk about your mother or Michael without ending on a really sad note. Now, this might not help at all, but I thought maybe you could try to talk about the happy times with them, rather than just their deaths."

Ryan nodded again, lips still pursed, but a thoughtful look on her face. She ran her hands through her dark hair, fluffing it in the breeze to help it dry. Jamie was resigned to have the short nod be Ryan's only reply, but after another minute of silence, Ryan finally spoke. "Do I really never talk about them in happy times?"

Jamie shook her head, smiling briefly as she grasped Ryan's hand again. "Uhm … you might with your family, but … you never have with me," she said softly. "I think I understand more about your mom, but I really don't know what Michael meant to you when he was alive. I don't know about the good times you had together, baby."

Ryan turned her head enough to make full eye contact with her partner. "Do you really want to know?"

Jamie did want to know, not just to make Ryan feel better, but so she could feel more like a member of the O'Flaherty family. "Yes," she said, loud enough to be heard over the waves. "I want to know because he means so much to you."

"That he does," Ryan murmured, her gaze returning to the sea. "Okay, I'll make an attempt. I'll do my best to tell you about the fun we had together." Her face was set in a stoic grimace, and she looked like she was about to have a few important teeth pulled.

Jamie wasn't at all sure that this exercise would help, and she briefly regretted bringing it up. "You don't have to do it all at once," she cautioned. "I want to help you get some of the sadness out of your system. It might help to temper it with some good memories."

"It might," Ryan agreed. "I mean, I know that the family should talk about this stuff, but we really don't. We talk about my mother, but Michael is still pretty much off-limits."

"There's a lot of pain there." Jamie empathized, knowing that his youth, his devastating illness and the split with his father had to make the loss all the more traumatic.

"Yeah, of course there is, but there's a lot of joy there too, and I've ignored that for a long while. Let's give this a try, babe. Maybe we can chip away at some of this frozen grief." She gave Jamie her most winning smile, but Jamie could plainly see the sadness hiding behind the bright blue eyes.

"I'm game."

Ryan set her jaw and gathered her thoughts for a moment. "What did Michael mean to me ... Let's start with music. That's one of his biggest influences on me."

"Really?" Jamie was a bit startled by this revelation. "I had no idea ..."

"He got all of us started," Ryan said. "His life was music ... either playing, singing, or getting others to play. He played the piano, the guitar, the mandolin, the fiddle .... He could pick up almost any instrument and figure out a way to make something pleasant come out of it."

"Did he take lessons?"

"Yeah ... he took lessons in a number of things, but I think it was mostly his natural talent that shone through. We all wanted to be like him when we grew up, so we all started taking lessons in something as soon as we were able."

"That's so neat," Jamie said, green eyes twinkling. "What kind of music did he like?"

"Ha! Let's start with what he didn't like! He didn't like ... I don't think there was anything he didn't like," Ryan laughed. "I'd have to say his favorite was R&B and soul, but he was an aficionado of traditional Irish music, he knew a lot about African music, and he liked a lot of artists from Western Europe. He didn't know much about classical music or opera, but he probably would have gotten to them if he'd had time." She laughed gently, but the sadness started to show through again.

Trying to get back on the positive track, Jamie asked, "R&B and soul were his favorites? That surprises me."

Ryan laughed and agreed. "It was kinda funny. Here was this big, buff, white gay kid, totally into Otis Redding, Marvin Gaye, Al Green. I'm not sure how he was first exposed to those artists, but they clicked with him."

"I'm sure you realize this, but your tastes are the same as his."

Ryan laughed a bit at this. "I know, babe. I'm a female clone. If Michael liked it, I liked it. Who knows, if he'd been alive when I was developing my sexuality I might have been into guys!"

"That's a stretch!" Jamie laughed, confident that Ryan's sexual orientation was the narrowest part of her expansive personality.

"Yeah, you're right there," Ryan agreed. "Hero worship could only go so far!"

A happy smile covered Ryan's face, and Jamie gave her hand a squeeze. "Thanks for talking about him a little bit. This was helpful for me."

Ryan nodded her dark head, looking pensive. "It was for me too. We'll have to do this again."

"I'll hold you to that promise," Jamie assured her, leaning over to kiss the smiling lips.

After the chairs were returned to their rightful spot, the twosome walked back to the house, hand in hand. They were nearing the house when Ryan said, "I think I have a pretty good idea on how to solve the security camera issue."

"*What!* And you're just telling me this now?!"

"Uhm … yeah," Ryan laughed. "I'm not certain of the details, so I didn't want to get your hopes up. I think my expert might call soon, though, so I thought I'd warn you."

"Your expert?" Jamie blocked the entry to the house, standing with her hands placed firmly on her hips. "Ryan, what's going on?"

The phone rang in the middle of this exchange, and Jamie dropped her hands and led the way into the kitchen, where they heard Conor's voice over the answering machine, "Hey, Secret Agent, pick up," he demanded.

Ryan gave Jamie a crooked grin and trotted over to grab the receiver. "Hi, Conor, it's me," she said. She rolled her eyes at Jamie as she added, "Yes, it's really me." Another pause and a second bout of eye rolling had her providing further identifying information. "Siobhán Ryan O'Flaherty. October 30, 1975." Jamie giggled as Ryan shook her head at her brother's playfulness.

Ryan listened attentively for a few moments as a big smile spread across her face. "I owe you big time, Bro." Mere seconds later she shook her head violently, "I don't owe you that much, and it's kinda sick to even ask." She pursed her lips as she said sarcastically, "It wouldn't have the same impact if you cut me out, dummy." Her smile returned as she said, "I love you, Conor. You're the best."

She hung up the phone and sat on her stool with a self-satisfied grin on her face. She crossed her arms and grinned at Jamie, waiting for her to ask about the phone call. The blonde tried to wait her out, but was totally unsuccessful. She finally jumped at her and tried to tickle the information out of her. Ryan fought her off pretty well, finally grasping her around the waist and picking her up until she had her comfortably placed in her lap. Jamie wrapped her arms around Ryan's neck and kissed her a few times, pulling away with a big grin on her face. "Well, I can't tickle or kiss it out of you, how do I get you to tell me what that phone call was about?"

Ryan smiled down at her partner and batted her big blue eyes. "You could just ask, sweetheart."

"Where's the fun in that?" Jamie asked. "But if that's all it takes, I give. What was that call about?"

"I called Conor this morning before I went for my run. I told him the manufacturer of the cameras and gave him a description of the room and where they were located. Then I told him about the door and gave him the manufacturer of the lock. When he got to work, he made a few calls and found the company that makes the system. They gave him the name of the local distributor, and he talked to them, too."

Jamie was jumping up and down with delight. She couldn't bear the tedious recitation of facts, but she knew that she had to bear with Ryan's thorough style.

"Now, don't get too excited, cupcake." Ryan's face grew serious as she tossed a major problem into the mix. "Not surprisingly, the local alarm company wasn't willing to give out too much information to a complete stranger. They wouldn't even confirm to Conor that they had done the work here."

"What do we do now?" Her frustrated plea was accompanied by a frightened look that caused Ryan's heart to clench.

"Worry not, babe. We have other avenues. Conor's gonna work on finding out who put the lock on the door. If he can't find that out, he's gonna buy a new lock and replace the one on the door after he cuts it off. Then we can have the new lock re-keyed tomorrow to match your parents' original keys, but we do have to find those keys if we can't find the lock installer."

Jamie leaned back and gazed at Ryan with open-mouthed surprise. "I can't believe you two got all that done and it's only eight o'clock."

"Yep. Actually, the best time to reach a lot of these guys is between seven and eight. Most of them are in their shops during that time, so it worked out great. Plus, the alarm manufacturer is on the east coast, so it was normal business hours there."

The frightened look was beginning to disappear from Jamie's face, but she still didn't have any idea about what their next step should be. "What can we do on this end?"

"Do you have any idea where your parents keep documentation on work they've had done?"

"I looked around pretty carefully yesterday, but I didn't think to look for receipts for the work. Daddy is a real neat freak when it comes to paperwork, and my guess is that they'd keep all the bills and stuff for this property in the library. Let's look through it all and see if we can find the original paperwork from when the lock was installed."

They walked hand in hand to the library, both relieved that Conor was on the job. Ryan sat perched on the edge of the desk while Jamie sat in the big leather chair and sorted through the neatly labeled file folders. "Bingo!" she cried after a few minutes. "Here's the work order for the alarm company, and here's the receipt from Pebble Beach Lock and Key."

Ryan took the papers and quickly decided on her course of action. "Let's pursue the lock issue first." Her brow was furrowed with concentration as she slapped the receipts against her open palm. “I think it’ll be easier to get a duplicate key made than to have to call the alarm company and admit we don’t know a thing about the darned system. Let’s get that door open and hope for the best.”

“What will we do if that isn’t where the system is set up?”

“Conor thinks it’s the most likely place, and he’s quite knowledgeable about systems like this. The worst thing that’ll happen is that we have to stay here until Monday and come up with some ruse to get the alarm company out here.” Sliding her fingers through Jamie’s soft hair, Ryan added, “Staying here through the weekend isn’t the worst thing in the world, is it?”

Jamie finally smiled at that question. “No. It wouldn’t be bad at all.”

Ryan’s eyes held a hint of playfulness as she dialed the lock company. She explained that she was Catherine Evans and that she had lost the key for the door to her security camera room. After a few more minutes of discussion, the locksmith agreed to bring over a spare key later in the day. She thanked him profusely but remembered to ask, “What will the charge be for the key?” After a pause she said, “That’s quite generous of you, Michael. So there will be no bill or statement that comes to the house?” She paused again, then said in a conspiratorial tone, “My husband gets so angry when I lose things. I really don’t want him to find out about this.” Another pause. “You’re a dear! Thanks so much.” She hung up with yet another satisfied smile on her handsome face. “Mission accomplished!”

“My hero!” Jamie said, pulling her from the desk and enveloping her in a hug. “Hey,” she said as she sat up. “How did you learn to lie so well?”

“All those years of Catholic school have to come in handy for something,” Ryan said with a grin. Standing up, she looked around the room and asked the question that had been in the back of her mind since the previous day. “Are there any other cameras in the house, or are they just in the gym?”

Jamie looked up with a shocked expression on her face. “Shit! Shit! Shit!” she fumed as she furiously stomped her feet on the floor. “They’re in all of the public areas, like the foyer and the living room, and the main staircase. There might be one in the kitchen, too. And I’m sure there’s one outside the front and side doors. And probably one in the pool house.”

Ryan slid around her to pick up the paperwork from the alarm company, carefully reading the work order, since she knew plenty about contractor jargon. “This clearly says that the controls for everything are in the gym, so we should be able to figure out how the system works once we get that key.” She fell back into the big chair and let out a heavy sigh, “Jeez, Jamie, why did we have to be naked, or touching, or kissing, in every imaginable square inch of this house?”

Jamie climbed onto Ryan’s lap again, sitting sideways with her head resting against the leather chair back. “Do you regret being adventuresome?”

Ryan slid her arms around her and squeezed her tight. “Not at all! I think we’ve had one of the most memorable honeymoons on record. As a matter of fact, I was thinking of starting a journal, and writing down all of the fun we’ve had here. I thought it’d be nice to have a keepsake that we could save.”

"Beat you to it, baby," Jamie said with a smile. "I've been keeping a journal since I was in high school. I haven't had a lot of free time since we've been here, but I wrote the other morning when you were running, and I made a few notes when you were jogging on the beach. It would be cool to start a new book on our honeymoon, though. We could do it together if you wanted to."

"I would love that, sweetie. When you go for your golf lesson, we can stop at a bookstore and buy a new journal. Then we can spend some time this afternoon reflecting on the week."

"Hey, that reminds me, what was Conor giving you a hard time about?"

"You couldn't figure that out?"

"Well, I guess it was about the surveillance system. Did you have to tell him what we were doing?" She looked a little cross, and Ryan sought to defend herself.

"All I said was that there were closed circuit cameras that we didn't know were on. He asked why that was a big deal, and I said that your parents didn't know about us, and we didn't want them to see us being affectionate. I certainly didn't tell him how affectionate we'd been," she said, "but he's a sharp boy, and he knows me pretty well …"

"So he knows."

"He knows we were doing things that we don't want your parents to see. But I'm sure he doesn't have any idea exactly how important it is to prevent them from knowing what we've been doing."

Jamie nodded briefly, her worry ameliorated by Ryan's explanation. "I don't want Conor to think less of me."

Ryan began to laugh so hard that Jamie had to throw her arms around her to stay on her lap. "Oh, Jamie!" she said, after she caught her breath. "That's priceless!"

"What?" she asked, slightly embarrassed.

"He might change his opinion of you, but it wouldn't be in a downward direction!"

"What do you mean?"

"If he had any idea of how totally hot, and sexy, and wild you are, he'd hang himself!"

"But why?" Jamie asked, rather incredulously.

"He's not kidding when he teases you about having a crush on you, babe. He really likes you, and I guarantee he would've made a very big play for you if I hadn't asked him not to."

"Are you serious?"

"About which part?" Ryan's brow twitched in question.

"Start with you telling him not to make a play for me. Why did you do that?"

"Why?" she asked with a puzzled grin. "Would you rather he had?"

Jamie laughed heartily at the very idea. "Hardly. I love Conor, but even if I were straight, I wouldn't have gone for him. I've never been attracted to bad boys, and he is their poster child."

"But you seem to like bad girls," Ryan purred as she nuzzled up against Jamie's ear.

"Unh-uh," she said, shaking her head. "I thought you were a bad girl for exactly one day. When we met in class I thought you were a total bad girl, but when we went for our drive the next day, I immediately changed my opinion of you, and you've never given me a reason to go back to my original impression."

"That's fascinating," Ryan mused. "So you really don't think of me as bad?"

"Not at all! You're so sweet and thoughtful and kind. You care so much for other people's feelings, and you're so upstanding and moral. You seemed to use that bad girl aura like a shield, but for some reason you took the shield down really quickly with me."

"The truth is that Conor does the same thing. He's easily as sweet as I am," she admitted.

"He could be Mother Teresa with testosterone and I'm still glad that I got you. Now what was that other little thing you were trying to convince me of?"

"I was pointing out the obvious. You're one gorgeous example of womanhood, but I don't think you're even conscious of how attractive you are."

Jamie blushed deeply at this compliment. She looked up at Ryan shyly and said, "I don't think of myself as being very attractive. I feel like I'm kinda cute, but in a little girl way."

"No way, babe. I'm attracted to women, not little girls." She leaned in to give her a deeply passionate kiss, "You are a very sexy woman." Reaching up with both hands, she tenderly lifted Jamie's full breasts. "These are a woman's breasts." Then she trailed her hands down to her waist. "These are a woman's hips. Everything about you is full and ripe and sexy." She leaned in for another deep kiss. "Definitely a woman," she said as she closed her eyes and leaned in close for another hug.

"I'm your woman, Ryan. Always yours," she said fervently as she leaned her forehead against Ryan's.

After they had cuddled for a while, Ryan asked, "Does it bother you that Conor has a crush on you?"

"No, it doesn't. I think of him like a big brother, so it is a little disconcerting when he teases me, but it doesn't bother me."

"I can ask him to stop teasing you, you know. He'll stop if I tell him to."

"No, I actually think it's kinda cute. He's so obvious about it that it doesn't seem like any kind of a threat."

"Well, my guess is that he'll stop doing it when he sees us together for a while. Once they get used to you being their sister-in-law I think they'll feel funny about having sexual thoughts about you."

"What do you mean, 'they'?" Jamie inquired suspiciously.

"Oh, Brendan and Rory have a crush on you, too. And Padraig and Niall had a big argument about which of them you would prefer," she said with a hearty laugh at Jamie's shocked face. "I'm telling you, Jamie, you're a hottie!"

Jamie shook her head in embarrassment and leaned against Ryan's chest. "I'm reserving my heat for you alone, Tiger. For the rest of my life."

"So …" Jamie asked when they went back into the kitchen to plan their day. "What would you like to do today?"

"Oh, I don't know," Ryan said thoughtfully. "I'm kinda torn between taking you back upstairs and ravishing you until you scream for mercy …"

Jamie placed her arms around Ryan's neck and leaned her head down until they were nose to nose. "Or what?"

"Or having you take me upstairs and ravishing me until *I* beg for mercy," she replied with a crooked grin, as she kissed her partner lightly on the lips. "Do your plans differ from mine?"

"I've got that little golf lesson, and then I have a surprise for you that might take a while, but other than that …" she teased, eyebrows wiggling. "Would I be able to satisfy you this afternoon?"

"I'm completely unfamiliar with the level of desire I have right now," Ryan replied as she tilted her head and rested her chin on her lover's shoulder. "I've never been with anyone that kept me so constantly aroused. I truly feel like I could make love to you all day long."

"Believe me, sweetie," Jamie said as she kissed Ryan tenderly, "if I didn't feel the need to retain my ability to walk, I'd definitely want to be in bed all day. But I know what you mean about the level of arousal. It's a little overwhelming for me. How about you?"

Ryan thought about that for a minute before she answered, "Yeah, I guess it is. I'm used to a lot of sex, so it's not that part that's strange for me. It's the intimacy that overwhelms me," she said as she wrapped her arms around Jamie and held her tight. "I've never felt this connected to anyone."

Jamie was touched and pleased by this admission, knowing how close Ryan felt to her family. "I feel the same about you, baby."

She looked up at her partner with a very shy grin curling up one corner of her mouth. "I like it when you call me 'baby'."

"Well, you are my big, sweet, beautiful baby, and I love you more than words can ever say."

Ryan nuzzled her face into her partner's soft breast and sighed deeply at the comfort and warmth she felt in her embrace.

Since her golf lesson was at noon they had an hour to kill, so they decided to go into town to shop for a honeymoon journal. They found a small but well-stocked bookstore and decided on a clothbound book with spaces for pictures. They hadn't used their camera much but Jamie wanted some pictures, so they decided to ask Chip to take some at the course and then have Conor take some that evening.

While Jamie worked on her game with Chip, Ryan jumped into the sand bunker again and worked for a solid hour. Having learned her lesson from her previous experiences, she placed herself so that the prevailing wind blew the sand away from her body. She was actually quite successful, both in her improved bunker play and her nearly sand free face.

Chip obliged their request and took a few shots of them by the clubhouse. They didn't feel able to be too demonstrative, but did manage to drape their arms around each other casually. Jamie insisted on getting a few shots of Ryan hitting balls out of the sand, since she'd spent so much of her time there. Ryan retaliated by having Jamie hit some big drives while she clicked away, getting some very good shots of her big follow through.

It was a little after one and Ryan was starving as usual. To get nourishment into her body as quickly as possible, they chose to eat at the club. "I gotta tell you, Jamie, it's good to be rich," Ryan said with a big, satisfied grin as they relaxed at their table.

"I'm glad you like it, sweetie. Maybe I can make a hedonist out of you after all. Gosh, maybe you can join Mother on some of her shopping sprees!"

"Do you think I'll like her?" Ryan asked as she cocked her head slightly.

The earnest, nearly fragile look on her partner's face made Jamie tread carefully. "Uhm, I'm not sure," she hedged. "She has impeccable manners, and she's very good at making people feel like she's interested in them, so I guess you might," she said with a thoughtful expression.

"Gee, that was quite an endorsement," Ryan laughed. "Do you describe me in such glowing terms?"

"Of course not," Jamie said a little abruptly.

"Jamie," Ryan said slowly, "did that hurt your feelings?"

"No, not really." A small shake of her head and a frown preceded her answer. "I guess I'm just in a bad space right now about my mother. I'm really glad that I'm in therapy, Ryan, but I'm realizing things that I've ignored my whole life." She looked down at her plate and admitted, "I don't much like the person I'm uncovering."

Ryan stared at her partner for a moment as a realization dawned on her. She had always focused on how much she'd missed by losing her mother at such a tender age. Looking at the hurt in Jamie's eyes reminded her that even though her memories of her mother were few, they were uniformly positive. She had been spared the normal mother/daughter fights and the distance that naturally grew as a child matured. She didn't know one woman who had escaped adolescence without some major problems with their mother, and she briefly considered that she was happy that she had such loving memories. "I'm sorry, honey. That must be hard for you. You've told me a little bit about your childhood, and about how little time your mother spent with you, but you've never really talked about her. I've got to admit that I don't know a darn thing about her."

Jamie nodded at the truth in this statement. "I feel like a jerk talking about her like this. I know I shouldn't be so hard on her," Jamie admitted. "She was truly an awful mother in terms of caregiving, but as I got older, and lowered my expectations, we got along well. When I was in high school we spent a lot of time together, going out to dinner and the theatre and things like that. I'd have to say we act more like rather reserved friends than mother and daughter. All in all, she's really pretty interesting, Ryan. She's bright and actually kind of funny, in a reserved way."

"How are you like her?"

Jamie had to think about that for a long while. "I'm not really sure. I like to think that I'm a lot like my father, since I respect him more, but I know there are a lot of things I get from my mother, too." She pondered the idea for a few more minutes. "I've got to admit that I like to shop, and I really like clothes. I think I get my sense of style from her. I love architecture and art, and those are two of her passions. I also really enjoy classical music and opera, and that's purely from her. Come to think of it, I guess I got my love of language from her." She sat back in her chair with a smile as she continued. "When I was little, she spent a lot of time correcting my speech and grammar. I sounded like an English teacher by the time I went to grade school. You know," she said with a laugh, "I have to force myself to speak like other people my age. I actually try to dumb my speech down so I don't sound like I'm being pompous."

"You don't have to do that around me," Ryan said sincerely. "I don't mind sounding like a dolt compared to you."

"Ryan, you speak beautifully," she chided. "You actually speak more like a European than a Californian. You know, the first time I heard you speak I thought you might be foreign-born. Now, when I think about it, it was the way you pronounced your name. Did you know that your accent comes out when you say it?"

"It does?" Ryan gaped in surprise. "I had no idea."

"Yep," Jamie grinned. "It really does. You sound Irish when you say your name and when you talk about Ireland. It must be subconscious."

"Weird," Ryan mused. "I mean, in a way I was raised in Ireland, but in other ways I'm entirely American. It really surprises me that I sound Irish."

"Don't misunderstand, babe," Jamie insisted. "Your accent is very subtle. You sound European mainly because you speak more formally than most people your age."

Ryan nodded, now understanding her partner's point. "Da wouldn't tolerate us speaking like the other kids. When he went to school, he'd be beaten for poor grammar, and he wouldn't let us get away with sounding uneducated. I let myself fall into sloppy grammar in college. Funny, isn't it? The more educated we get, the dumber we sound!"

"Well, if you can avoid splitting infinitives or dangling any participles, my mother will love you!"

"Oh, not me," Ryan vowed. "That is the type of nonsense up with which I shall not put!"

Jamie laughed at her partner's borrowing of the famous Churchill quote. After a moment she became serious again. "I'm not sure how she'll feel about our relationship, but since she's never very genuine, I guess it really doesn't matter."

"Is she really that bad? I mean, is there nothing about her that you really like?"

She pursed her lips for a moment, deep in thought. "No, she's not that bad," she admitted. "I'm so down on her that it's hard for me to see her good traits. Let me try to focus on the things that I *do* admire." When another few moments passed, Ryan felt a pang of sorrow that her lover had such a hard time being positive about her mother. Jamie blew out a breath and began her list, "She spends a lot of time doing charity work—although I think she does it just to be seen by the right people," she added in a disparaging tone. "She's a devoted student of whatever little topic she's currently interested in. Of course, she has nothing else to fill her time, so she can spend hours and hours on minutiae."

Ryan shot her a glance and widened her eyes as she said, "I don't think this is a good time to talk about the things you like about her. You're really damning her with faint praise."

"You're right," she agreed, blushing a little. "Anna assures me that I'll eventually get my anger out, and then I won't have to spend so much time grousing about her. But that remains to be seen."

"I hope you get to a point where you like being around each other again," Ryan said. "I want you to feel closer to your family, if it's at all possible. But if it's not, you know you're fully accepted as an O'Flaherty."

"Maybe I'll change my name," she said thoughtfully. "Jamie O'Flaherty. It has kind of a ring to it doesn't it?"

"Not bad," Ryan agreed. "It's not all that easy to merge a lot of names with O'Flaherty, but yours is darned good."

"Don't I know it!" she agreed. "I've been thinking up names for our children, and you almost need an Irish given name for it to sound good."

Ryan flashed a high wattage grin as she asked, "Have you really been thinking of names for our kids? That's so totally adorable!"

"Yep. If Conor is the sperm donor, I'll name mine O'Flaherty, too. That way they'll feel more like siblings."

"That is so precious of you! You have to tell me what names you like." The nearly giddy look on Ryan's face made Jamie's heart beat double-time as she considered how much she loved this emotion-filled woman.

"Well," she mused. "I don't know many Irish names, but I think our first daughter has to be Fionnuala," she said softly, barely touching the tips of Ryan's fingers with her own.

Ryan immediately pulled her lips in between her teeth in what Jamie recognized as an effort to avoid tears. She closed her eyes slowly and whispered, "Thank you for understanding that's important to me."

"It's important to me too," she replied, as she battled her own emotions. "She's important to me since she gave me you. I'm forever in her debt." Their fingers moved on the table and gripped a little tighter in a totally unconscious gesture, ignoring all of the other patrons of the busy restaurant, seeing only each other.

The conversation reverted to a teasing game in which Ryan tried to think of the most awkward Irish names for their children. Jamie finally called a draw with Phelum and Fergal for a boy, and Dymphna or Gobnait for a girl. As they prepared to leave the club Jamie felt a brief flash of panic as she mused, *She's kidding, right? Please God, don't let her grandmother's name be Gobnait!*

## Chapter Fourteen

It was after two when they returned home, and to their extreme pleasure the key to the door that contained the recording equipment was in the mailbox when they arrived. Jamie kissed the envelope with a big smack, and they dropped off their purchases and raced each other to the garage.

Jamie slid the key into the lock, and smiled in satisfaction as the knob turned. "Whew!" she said, dramatically wiping her forehead with the back of her hand. They walked into the small room together and looked around at the array of monitors displaying images from around the property. Just as Jamie had suspected, there were cameras in the courtyard, near the rear and front doors, in the foyer, up the main staircase, in the pool house, the garage and the gym. There was also one located near the front door of each apartment, but none inside. There was no camera in the kitchen or any other living area in the main house, and Jamie sighed in relief, at the knowledge that, no matter what, at least her mother would not see them defiling her precious concrete counters.

The room contained four large recorders sitting on big metal racks. It looked as though one recorder captured still shots of the courtyard, the access doors, the main staircase, the pool house, and the apartment entrances. A separate recorder was dedicated to the foyer, another to the gym, and a third to the garage. As they sat and watched the cameras work, it became clear that the largest recorder captured shots of most of the property in sequence, showing a photo of the rear door, followed by one of the front door about thirty seconds later. The rest of the exterior followed, so that every three minutes there was a shot from every camera.

Regrettably, the cameras in the gym, the foyer and the garage were dedicated to just that area. The camera took a still about every thirty seconds, so the tape was a very choppy rendition of the activity occurring in that space. Nonetheless, as they rewound the tape from the foyer, it was obvious what was occurring on Monday afternoon when they arrived. The first shot was of Jamie pinning Ryan to the door. The next was of Jamie fumbling with Ryan's zipper as she tried to remove her pants. The third shot was of Jamie pushing her hips against Ryan while she grasped her butt firmly. The last still was of Ryan lifting Jamie into her arms, mouths locked together. They looked at each other with wide eyes. "Now what?" they said in unison.

"I'm really not sure," Ryan admitted. "Obviously, if it comes to it we'll destroy the tapes and hope they don't notice, or plead ignorance if they do. But I only want to do that as a last resort. Maybe we should wait for Conor. He's a whiz with electronics. And if anybody is an expert in getting out of trouble, it's Conor. He has years of experience!"

"Okay," Jamie agreed, a bit hesitantly. "But he won't have to look at these, will he?"

"No, baby," Ryan promised, wrapping her arms around her partner. "I guarantee no one will see these tapes. Except me!" she added with a leer, as she rewound the tape from the gym. "I bet this one is a scorcher!"

Jamie protested a bit feebly, but she secretly wanted to see their lovemaking also. She had to admit that seeing Ryan do squats was hot, even in still photos. But she was mortally embarrassed that the tapes showed just how in control she was. Ryan looked like putty in her hands, as she was guided around the room with a glazed expression on her face. "I hardly knew where I was," she admitted with a chuckle as they watched the images roll across the screen.

"You do look a bit blank," Jamie agreed, as yet another image of a stunned looking Ryan flashed by. "God, I hate to admit this, but I'm getting hot!" she said as she rested her head on Ryan's chest. "This is like watching porn!"

"It most certainly is not!" Ryan protested. "Porn is … it's … it's about exploitation. This was about love. The fact that it turns you on to fulfill some of your fantasies doesn't make it pornographic. It's still you and me, loving each other in different ways at different times. Just because it's a little wild doesn't make it any less loving."

"I … I … I guess you're right. It just makes me uncomfortable to see how in control I look."

"Jamie," Ryan cooed. "I thought we'd resolved this last night. You told me then that you were feeling okay about this. What happened, baby?"

"I don't know," she admitted glumly, shaking her head. "I guess the pictures made it seem worse to me."

"I think we need to talk about this a little bit," Ryan said, as she took her hand and led her out of the room. She sat down on a weight bench and pulled Jamie onto her lap. "You seem to feel that being in control is a bad thing."

"It feels like it is," Jamie confirmed.

"Let's start at the beginning," Ryan suggested. "I want you to tell me how you learned about sex. Did your mom talk to you about it at all?"

"Hnh-uh. Neither of my parents was very good at that kind of thing. My nanny, Elizabeth, was in charge of all of that stuff."

"Tell me about her," Ryan prodded, not having heard of this woman before.

"She was really a sweet woman," Jamie recalled. "She was probably close to sixty when I was born, and she came to work for us the day they brought me home from the hospital. She didn't have any duties other than raising me. I mean, she didn't have to cook or clean or anything. So we spent practically all of our time together. I'd guess that my character was formed by her more than my parents, at least for the first few years."

"Did she talk to you about sex?"

"Yeah, she did," Jamie admitted. "She was very English and very proper, always answered my questions, but in a clinical way. I do remember her telling me that sex was something that your husband was in charge of. She gave me the clear impression that it was something that women had to bear." Ryan didn't say a word, wanting Jamie to talk about as many memories as she could dredge up. "I remember when I first got my period. She told me that it was another trial that women were put through, like childbirth. I remember thinking that all of this stuff was tied up together, you know? Menstruation, sex and childbirth. They all seemed like mysterious and painful things."

"Did she have children?"

"No, she and her sister were spinsters. They live together now, back in England."

"What else do you remember?"

"I do remember when I first started to date boys. She sat me down and had a very long talk with me about how they would all want to touch me, but that I shouldn't let them. She really made it sound kind of scary, and I was kinda freaked when guys first started trying to touch me. I remember thinking that it was some sort of game, and that I'd lose if I let them do what they wanted."

"Wow!" Ryan said as she shook her head. "That's not a very sex-positive message to give to a young girl. Did you believe everything she said?"

"Yeah, I did," she admitted. "I might have doubted her, but from the first date I had, the boys *were* trying to get into my pants. I wasn't allowed to start dating until I was fifteen, and the boys in my school were really pretty wild. Most of them had already had sex by the time they took me out, and it was a constant struggle. The older I got, the worse it became; it was kind of a game for the guys to see who could get me to give it up. But you know me," she said with a chuckle. "There's no better way to get me to dig in my heels than to try to force me to do something."

Now that she finally knew how hot her lover was sexually, Ryan asked a question that had puzzled her for months. "Did you really not want to have sex?"

Jamie leaned against her chest and let out a heavy sigh. "It's hard to say. I probably would have if I'd gone out with someone who didn't try to force himself on me," she admitted. "I don't know why guys can't figure this out. If they'd act like they were casual about it and not push so damn hard, they'd probably get a lot more."

"Is that what happened with Jack?" Ryan asked, not wanting to pry, but genuinely curious about her lover's sexual development.

"Yeah, it is," she admitted with a small smile. "The first time we went out he tried to kiss me a little too intimately for my taste. I told him in no uncertain terms that I didn't do that kind of thing with guys I didn't know well. He's as stubborn as I am, and I think he took it as a personal challenge. He really backed off, and I was eventually the one who started going a little farther each time we went out. He would sit there with this smug little smile on his face while I was going crazy!"

"Smart man," Ryan said with a grin. "That's a very effective ploy." She had used the trick a time or two herself, and Jack climbed up a few notches in her estimation for being so crafty.

Jamie shot her a smirk and agreed, "Oh, yeah. He's pretty quick. I have to admit that's why I eventually trusted him enough to sleep with him. It felt safe since he wasn't pushing. After he asked me to marry him, I knew how committed he was, and I felt free to be with him."

"But even with that commitment you weren't free from those old warnings, were you?" Ryan seemed to understand her situation completely, and Jamie felt her unease about discussing the topic begin to fade away.

She shook her head, rubbing her head against Ryan's chest in the process. "No, all of those years of saying 'no' still hadn't gone away. I expected Jack to know what to do, and I thought I could lie there and have him make me feel good. I think it caught him by surprise since I was pretty aggressive when we used to just kiss and touch each other. But once we started to have intercourse, I got really submissive. The stupidest thing we did was that we didn't talk about it. I know both of us were disappointed, but we didn't try to work it out. I think we both had issues about sex that stopped us from really looking at the underlying problem. When we tried to get back together, things were better because we talked, but it was too late by then, since I was so in love with you."

"What do you think your issues about sex were?" Ryan asked gently. If the problems that Jamie and Jack had experienced were isolated within their relationship, Ryan didn't want to pry. But she had a strong feeling that whatever problems occurred in the past might crop up again, and she was determined to avoid that at all costs.

"I know this sounds crazy, but I never got over the feeling that sex was something Jack took from me. Do you understand what I mean?"

"Uhm ... not really."

"Well, I think I felt that sex was mine to give or withhold. He was always ready to go—kind of like you," she said with a little tweak of Ryan's chin. "I felt like I had to control how much sex we had because he would consume me if I didn't. It's like I felt it was a precious resource that I had to conserve."

"Did that make you feel like you couldn't express yourself?"

"Yeah, it did. It really did." She wriggled around in Ryan's lap trying to get comfortable, but she realized that must be even more uncomfortable for her partner, so she got up and tugged her over to a cozy chair that faced the large-screen television. "Better?"

Ryan grinned up at her and snuggled closer.

"It's like this, babe," Jamie continued. "There was no room for me to explore. Any time I gave him the slightest signal, he wanted to get horizontal. Not that that's bad, of course. But it didn't allow me to try little things and see how I felt about them." She smiled up at Ryan and added, "That's the most wonderful gift you've given me. Letting me play with you without you jumping on me really freed me up to explore myself a little bit. Obviously, that's an ongoing process, but I feel so much better now, it's really remarkable."

"Do I ever make you feel overwhelmed?" Ryan asked softly.

"Well … yeah," she said as her face curled into a smirk. "But I like it when you overwhelm me." Jamie's voice had taken on a sultry tone, and she snuck a little nibble of an always tempting and conveniently located ear.

"Not that way," Ryan chuckled as she pinched her sides. "Do I ever make you feel like I'm asking for too much? Do you ever fear me, or feel that I'm consuming you?"

An impish grin had settled on Jamie's face as she replied. "I think I've shown that I no longer have an issue with the consuming thing, either."

That comment earned her a serious tickle attack, and when Ryan had delivered her punishment she calmed down and answered the question seriously. "I don't ever feel that way with you, Ryan. I don't understand exactly why I feel so comfortable with you, but I really do. Maybe it's because you seem to get so much pleasure out of satisfying me. Sex with you doesn't just seem like it's all about you. I mean, it was really discouraging to Jack when I would fail to have an orgasm. But he wasn't really willing to do whatever it took to help me get there. He wanted to have intercourse and make me come that way. And that rarely worked for me. But with you," she said, resting her head on Ryan's shoulder, "I can feel how much pleasure you get out of my enjoyment. And I know it's not because you want to use my body to have an orgasm. You're really doing it for me. Just me," she said softly.

"I appreciate the thought, but that's not really true," Ryan whispered. "I get so much satisfaction out of watching your face and touching your body, that it feels like it's just as much for me. It's truly a toss up as to how I get more pleasure. If you never touched me again, I could honestly be happy just loving you."

Jamie kissed her cheek and reiterated her point. "Sorry, hon, but I've gotta insist. You're selfless."

"How so? I admitted that I get intense pleasure from touching you."

"Yes … but in my view of the world, there is a difference between using my body to have an orgasm and getting pleasure from giving me pleasure. I'm sure I would have felt differently if Jack hadn't been so centered on making me come the way he wanted to. It was a rare day that he focused on my needs."

Ryan leaned forward and nibbled on one sensitive earlobe. "It's gonna be a rare day that I don't focus on your luscious body, sweetness. I'm gonna study you from top to bottom. And when I finish, I'm gonna start all over again."

"You make me sound like the Golden Gate Bridge," Jamie laughed, joking about the never-ending task of keeping the edifice painted its deep rust color.

They shared a laugh at the image, and then Ryan framed another question that had been working around in her mind. "How do you feel about the way you respond to me? I know you're not used to really letting go." Twinkling blue eyes predicted that a tease was on the way, and Jamie smiled in anticipation. "You're about as much as I can handle, so if you haven't let go yet, I think you'd better warn me."

"Worry not. I'm giving you everything I've got." Jamie kissed her partner briefly, showing her that the gentle tease was well received. "Seriously, I think I feel great about my response. The only thing that still bothers me is stuff like this tape. It really freaks me out to see that I'm orchestrating the whole thing. I'd have to say that I feel a lot more comfortable when I'm responding rather than leading."

Ryan was running her fingers through Jamie's soft hair, and she smiled serenely when the golden head pressed into her hand, begging for more. "I feel very comfortable when I lead," she admitted. "I really do believe though, that we'll have a better relationship if we can step out of our typical roles and go out of our comfort zones occasionally. Over time, I think you'll get comfortable leading. We need to go slow and practice, practice, practice."

With a soft laugh, Jamie agreed. "I suppose I need a lot of reassurance from you right now. I need to know that I'm not being too forward or too demanding. Like when we were in the gym, would you have told me if you didn't want to do those exercises in the nude?"

"Yes, sweetie. I promise that I won't participate in anything that makes me feel uncomfortable or that makes me lose respect for you. I want you to know though, that you are a very, very, very long way from making me feel uncomfortable. I've done a lot of things in my life, and not very many of them have bothered me. Sexual arousal is a very complex thing, babe, and if something doesn't hurt or objectify me, I'm willing to try it."

The small list of things that Ryan mentioned gave Jamie pause, and her protective instincts came out immediately. Reaching out to turn her partner's face so she could look into her eyes she asked, "Has someone hurt you, baby?"

Ryan laughed gently, shaking her head to reassure her concerned partner. "I uhm … didn't mean that kind of hurt."

"Oh." Jamie blushed at the implication, but she was curious about the topic so she continued. "Will you tell me what kind of things did bother you?"

"Sure, but I have to think for a minute," she added as she furrowed her brow. After a while she said, "I don't like to have sex with more than one person at a time. One time a woman that I didn't know very well wanted a guy to join us. I wouldn't participate in that, since guys don't arouse me. But it wasn't just guys. When I was really young, I had sex with two women and I really hated it. So I decided to never do that again."

"What did you hate about it? I'd think you couldn't have too much of a good thing."

"I really have to concentrate when someone's touching me. Having four hands and two mouths on me at the same time was way too much stimulation. It didn't feel personal enough to me, if that makes any sense."

"Yeah, I think it does," she agreed, instantly knowing that she would hate to have anyone join Ryan in her bed. "But I've got to tell you that the voyeur in me would love to have seen your lithe young body being pleasured by two women. Whew!" she exclaimed as she shivered a bit in her lover's arms.

Ryan chuckled a little and said, "Would you still like to see it? I could call in a few favors …"

"I'll see it in my fantasies, thank you very much," Jamie declared, lightly tapping her partner's pink cheek with her open hand. "What else has bothered you?"

"Not a whole hell of a lot, to tell you the truth. I'm a pretty open-minded girl!"

"I'm aware." Jamie's dry tone reminded Ryan of some of the exploits Jamie had witnessed. "Continue, please, there has to be something … branding … caning …"

"Oh, right!" Ryan looked pleased that she had been reminded of another practice. "Well, through the years I've met a lot of people into bondage and discipline. Again, I've got no problems with people pleasing each other that way, but it's not for me. I like to play with power and control, but I have no desire to cause someone pain through sex, and nobody is going to do that to me, either. To be honest, I think the people who tried to play with me that way weren't very good at it, but I wasn't interested in finding anyone who really knew what she was doing. Now, that said, I'm not averse to a little restraint. In fact, I like that quite a bit," she said. "But tying me up and beating me is just not going to happen."

"That's a relief!" Jamie said with an exaggerated wiping of her brow. "I can't see you letting someone hit you. You weren't hit as a child, were you?"

Ryan's face clouded a little, and she looked a trifle uncomfortable. "My parents never hit any of us," she said quietly. After a pause she turned her head and asked, "How about you?"

"No, my parents weren't involved enough to know when I was being bad. I don't recall Elizabeth ever hitting me either, but once at the park she told another nanny that she should give the little boy she was watching a good thrashing. That freaked me out and made me wonder if she would ever hit me, but as I said, I don't remember her doing that."

"You'd remember," Ryan said quietly.

Sensing that there was a lot going on under the surface of her calm exterior, Jamie turned slightly and said, "Someone hit you, didn't they, baby?"

Ryan nodded her head briefly. She pursed her lips and said, "Is it okay if we don't talk about it right now?"

"Sure," she said, knowing that she needed to respect her wishes for privacy. Trying to lighten the mood she reverted back to her lover's favorite topic. "Anything else you haven't liked about sex?"

The smile returned as Ryan thought about her sexual history. "I have to feel that I'm an integral part of the act. One time a woman wanted me to only touch her from behind. I really like to do that, so I didn't mind a bit. But she could only touch me from behind, too. I turned around when she was touching me, and she freaked out. She said she couldn't go on because I had 'ruined the moment.' It made me feel like she wasn't connected to me in any way and that really made me feel used, so I never saw her again."

"That's sounds very strange," Jamie said as she shook her head with a look of distaste.

"Well, I don't really like to label sexual response. If it's consensual, go for it. People get off on different things, babe. If you had some unique need, I'd be very willing to work with you so that we could both be satisfied. But in this situation, she wanted me to follow the script and not screw it up. I felt objectified and I can't tolerate that."

"Is there anything that you like or want that I haven't done for you?" Jamie's voice was quiet, and she played with the ends of Ryan's hair, unable to make eye contact.

"Nope. Every one of my needs has been fully met," was the decisive reply. "I need to feel loved and honored and cherished and desired. And you are definitely an expert at every one of those things."

"You're very sweet, Ryan, but you know what I mean. Is there anything that you like that I haven't done for you … physically?"

"There are tons of things that I like that we haven't done yet, Jamie. But those are technical details. The things that make me feel connected to you are the important things. We're gonna be with each other for the rest of our lives. We have plenty of time to explore every position and technique known to womankind." Ryan paused for a moment, feeling that it was very important that Jamie understood exactly how she felt about this issue. "If you were only comfortable doing ten percent of what I liked it'd be enough because of how much I love you. What we do is far less important to me than the fact that we do it to show our love for each other."

Snuggling against her partner, Jamie felt her trepidation lessen. She sighed deeply and voiced her last insecurity. "I guess I'm still a little worried about my technical abilities," she admitted, turning a little so she could rest her head on Ryan's shoulder again.

Ryan fidgeted a bit, trying to sit up straighter in the chair. She was going to do her best to relieve Jamie of her doubt, and her delivery was forceful. "I must not be making myself clear, sweetie. I've been with women who have made love thousands of times. Not one of them could hold a candle to what you do to me." She placed her hand on Jamie's chin and tilted it up to make sure she could read her eyes. "I don't love making love with you only because of how I feel for you emotionally, Jamie. You make me absolutely crazy with desire, baby. I've never had orgasms like I do with you. I've never looked at a woman and gotten as turned on as I do with you. I swear, Jamie, that the sex we've had this week is more satisfying and more fulfilling than everything I've done up until now, all rolled into one!"

"Ryan," she said with her lower lip trembling, "that's the sweetest thing you've ever said to me." The tears started to flow, and Jamie cuddled against her partner tightly, reveling in the safety of her arms.

When Jamie was more in control Ryan asked, "Are you feeling a little emotional because it's our last night here?"

"Yeah, I am," she said. "This has been so blissful that I'm afraid of breaking the spell by going back into the real world." She looked up at Ryan and mentioned another piece of her emotional puzzle. "I think my PMS is much worse than normal this month too."

"Poor baby."

"I'm fine, hon. I'm just a little more emotional than usual. No biggie." Getting to her feet, Jamie extended a hand to her partner. "I need to get up and get my blood flowing again, though. You game for a little excitement?"

"Hmm." Ryan's cocked head showed her thoughtful consideration of the matter. "I'm just trying to remember the last time I refused a little excitement."

With a pinch on her side, Jamie encouraged her partner to join her. "I have a little treat that I've been saving for you." She looked up at a smiling Ryan and shot her a shy grin. "I've been keeping something very important from you."

"What's that?" Ryan inquired, immediately curious.

Jamie led her down the interior staircase and paused before another door. "Daddy has something in here that I know you'll love, but I haven't shown it to you yet."

Ryan put two and two together and knew they were talking about cars, one of her very favorite things. "What? What?" she asked excitedly. "What's he got?" Her eyes were wide with excitement and anticipation was flowing through her body.

"Well," she teased, intentionally prolonging the agony, "it's a five car garage and every bay is filled. Wanna see?" Ryan was jumping up and down, a wide smile covering her face in a perfect Caitlin imitation. "Are you sure Caitlin isn't your child?" Jamie asked with a chuckle. "She acts just like you!"

"No, we both act like infants," Ryan corrected her. "Now show me the cars!"

Jamie used her key to open the side door to the huge space. The Suburban was parked right by the door, obscuring their view of the rest of the cars, so Ryan dashed around the front of the big truck and sucked in a breath. She stood with her mouth wide open, staring at a fire-engine red 1968 Shelby Mustang Cobra. "Oh, my God!" she said as she walked around the car reverently. "It looks like it just rolled off the showroom floor!"

Ryan glanced at the other cars quickly, noticing that large canvas covers covered two of them, but the car next to the Mustang was revealed in all of its glory. The black Acura NSX was gleaming under the fluorescent lights, looking terribly fast even though it was standing still. Jamie thought she detected a bit of drool leaking out of Ryan's mouth as she took in the car. "You and your mother can go shopping," she said firmly. "I'm hanging out with your dad. He rules!"

Jamie was charmed by the childlike enthusiasm that Ryan showed for her father's little toys, watching with delight as her partner examined both cars from every angle, never touching their pristine paint. Luckily, the garage floor was spotless, so Ryan's clothes were not ruined when she got down on the floor and shimmied under both vehicles as far as she could.

The inspection over, the tall woman got to her feet and stared at Jamie, wide-eyed. "I don't think I wanna know what's under those other two covers. I don't think I can stand any more pleasure."

"Are you sure?" Jamie asked solicitously. "In that case, I'll have to do the little favor that Daddy asked you to do."

"Favor? What favor?"

"He likes to have the cars driven every couple of weeks, and since they won't be down here for almost a month, he asked me to drive them a little bit," she said casually. "But if you don't think you can stand the pleasure …"

"Jamie, I can't drive these! Your father wouldn't want a stranger driving these babies."

Jamie reached into her pants pocket and took out a handwritten note, which she handed to Ryan. It read:

*Dear Jamie,*

*I hope you and Ryan have a good time this week. Please make her feel at home and don't be shy about playing golf at the Club.*

*I normally ask the gardener to run my cars, but I would actually prefer that you two take them out for a spin. You've told me that Ryan is a car nut, so please ask her if she would mind taking them out and blowing some carbon off the plugs.*

*Feel free to raid the wine cellar. We've recently stocked up on some of your favorite white Bordeaux, and now that you're 21 you can enjoy a glass or two without threat of arrest!*

*We love you, cupcake. Take care and enjoy your week.*

*Love,*
*Daddy*

Ryan lost all of the color in her face as she read the note several times. "He's actually asking me to drive these beasts?"

Her look of incredulity was terribly charming to Jamie. "Yep. But if you don't feel up to it …"

"Keys! Gimme keys!" she demanded, right leg twitching perceptibly.

"Calm down, Tiger," Jamie said soothingly. "You don't want to unleash these monsters when you don't have your emotions under control."

Ryan took several deep breaths while Jamie ran back to the house to get the keys. When she returned, Ryan's color had returned and she looked considerably calmer, but her excitement was evident. Her eyes were still wide and her foot tapped impatiently on the gray concrete floor. "I can't decide what to drive first," she said as she looked between the Mustang and the Acura.

"Are you really not going to look at the other cars?" Jamie was stunned that her lover would delay a sensation that she got so much satisfaction from.

"Not yet," she said impatiently. "That's like having four beautiful women lined up in front of you and all of them want to have sex. You know you'd be thinking about the other three when you were with the first one. It's too much information! I need to concentrate."

Jamie gave her a big grin as she held out two sets of keys. Ryan continued her mental debate, looking back and forth between the two sets. Finally, she closed her eyes and opened her hands, silently asking her partner to make her decision for her. Jamie placed the Mustang keys in her hand and walked around to get into the passenger side of the car. Ryan slipped into the driver's side and sat quietly as Jamie leaned over and pushed the button to lift the garage door. As she did, she recalled the first time they'd been in a car together. "This reminds me of the first time you drove the Boxster."

Ryan turned and gave her a dazzling grin, showing that she recalled the drive as well. "It was all I could do to stop myself from putting a major move on you that day. I still remember smelling your perfume when you leaned over me to show me how something worked, and just wanting to take a nibble from your luscious little neck."

A heavy sigh and a seductive grin showed how things had changed. "Nothing's stopping you now, Tiger."

Ryan made up for lost time, pouncing on her partner and pinning her to her seat back. It was obvious that the excitement of the cars was spilling over into other facets of Ryan's determined personality, and after a few minutes of the gentle assault, Jamie regretfully pulled away to focus on the task at hand. "When we get home, baby, you can show me everything you wanted to do to me that day."

"Deal." Ryan added one more kiss to complete the contract. Mind back on business, she ran her hands all over the dash and the instrument panel, fingers tickling over the gear shift and the turn signals, seemingly trying to memorize the entire car. She turned slowly to her partner and said, "Thank you, sweetheart. This is really a treat for me."

"You're welcome. Now let's have fun!"

She graced her lover with her most winning smile, showing her even, white teeth, then turned the engine over, closing her eyes in pleasure as the car growled a low, throaty roar. "This is the epitome of the muscle car," she said, as Jamie smiled over at her.

She tossed her right arm over Jamie's seat back and turned around to carefully guide the car out of the garage. When they reached the street she turned and asked, "Which way should we go?"

"Let's take Seventeen Mile Drive and head south," Jamie decided. "It's slow this time of day, and we can mosey along."

"Sounds good," Ryan said happily as she turned left onto the drive. "So, tell me about your father's love affair with cars."

"Well, his family didn't have money for cars when he was growing up and I think it really bothered him. They lived in the city, and didn't need one anyway, but I think he really longed to have a hot muscle car to impress the girls."

"That's why I wanted one," Ryan teased, then tried to scoot out of the way of Jamie's pinch. "So when did he get these?"

"I remember him buying each one, so I'd say he got the Mustang about twelve or thirteen years ago. Everything else came after that."

"Does he drive them, or does he keep them only as a collector?"

"Oh, no, he's not that kind of guy. He likes things for what they are, and these are cars that are meant to be driven. He actually drives the wheels off of them when he's down here. His regular cars hardly leave the garage. I'd say the Acura is driven less than any of the others though," she said with a smile. "He really loves his muscle cars."

"What does he drive at home?" Ryan asked, wondering what one would choose as an everyday car if money were no object.

"He has a seven series BMW that he drives at home. But he gets a ride to work, so he really doesn't take it out much."

"Your father carpools?" she asked incredulously, turning slightly to gape at her partner.

"Uhm … not exactly," Jamie replied, a little embarrassed. "He has a driver who picks him up."

"Well, at least that makes sense!" Ryan laughed. "I can't see you father in the carpool lane with two other people in the car, talking about what they had for dinner last night."

"No …"Jamie agreed. "Even though he comes from a simple background, he's a bona fide member of the upper class now."

"You've got to admit the benefits are pretty awesome."

"Oh, I freely admit that," Jamie said. "And speaking of that, how are you liking your little drive?"

"This car is pure bliss," she said with a huge smile on her face. "I could drive all day."

"You've got three more at home, sweetie. Don't be a glutton."

"Hey, as long as we're out and about, why don't we find some place to have our ears pierced? I know we could wait until we get back to the city, but I'd really like to have it done while we're actually on our honeymoon."

"Sounds like a deal," Jamie smiled over at her partner, charmed that it was so important to her to perform this rite.

Jamie knew the area very well, and she suggested a few places that she was reasonably sure would do a good job. She was surprised when Ryan began to pepper her with questions about the establishments—questions that she could have no way of answering. "Uhm, honey, I don't really know if these places use an autoclave … whatever that is."

Ryan was adamant about her demands, causing Jamie to believe that her partner was being overly cautious about such a simple procedure. "We're not getting our nipples pierced, Ryan," Jamie argued to no avail. "Can't anybody do it?"

"You might be cavalier about someone sticking a needle through your body, but I'm not," she said firmly. "I need to make sure they know what they're doing."

"Okay," she finally conceded, recognizing that argument was futile against the firm set of her lover's jaw. "Let's check them out."

The first stop was an attractive little shop that sold jewelry and other small goods. Ryan decided in less than five seconds that they did not measure up.

"What was wrong?" Jamie asked, trotting behind her on the way back to the car.

"You just had a bench to sit on," she replied, as if the answer was obvious.

"And?" Jamie prodded.

"It's not professional. They should have a nice chair. If they skimp on that, they might skimp on keeping the instruments clean."

The second and third shops that they looked into were also unacceptable according to Ryan's high standards. Number two, because Ryan didn't like the guy's "attitude," number three, because there were very young girls waiting to have their tongues pierced, and Ryan found that objectionable. Jamie had a feeling that they were not going to get it done that day, but Ryan prevailed upon her to try the last place on the list.

It was a short drive and, to Jamie's amazement, Ryan immediately declared that it was a winner. It was clean, the woman who did the piercing was friendly to both of them, there was a dentist's chair in the private room, and they were the only customers.

Ryan told the woman what they wanted, and the heavily pierced woman asked them a few questions about where they wanted to be pierced. They agreed that the earrings should go just above the first piercings on their right ears. Jamie decided to go first, and Ryan asked if she could stay to hold her hand. "No problem," replied the woman. "Are you lovers?"

"Yes, we are," Jamie replied. "Is it obvious?"

"Probably not to most people, but I'm gay too, and you give off a lot of vibes," she said with a smile. "Did you just start seeing each other?"

"Uhm ..." Jamie looked at Ryan for help.

"We've known each other for a while, but we've just recently become lovers," Ryan informed her as she smiled fondly at Jamie.

The woman cleaned Jamie's ear with antiseptic as she said, "Congratulations! I hope it works out for you."

"It will," they responded simultaneously, as the woman laughed heartily.

"Could you two be any cuter?" she commented with a chuckle as she showed Ryan where she was going to shoot the stud. Ryan nodded her approval and gripped Jamie's hand. One little twitch from her hand, and the piercing was finished.

"That wasn't bad at all," Jamie said as she got up from the chair. "Your turn, sweetie." But when she looked at Ryan she noticed she didn't look quite right. "Are you okay?"

"Fine, let's do it," she replied curtly as she sat down in the chair.

The woman looked at Jamie, who shrugged. It was obvious that something was bothering Ryan, but equally obvious that she wasn't going to say what it was. The woman showed Jamie where she would put the stud, and Jamie nodded and reached down to grab Ryan's hand. To her surprise, she couldn't pry it from where it gripped the arm of the chair, knuckles going white. It dawned on Jamie that Ryan's demeanor reflected nervousness, so she placed her hand on her shoulder to reassure her.

The woman put the gun up to her ear and, as the steel went through her lobe, Ryan's eyes rolled up in her head, and she was out cold. The woman gave Jamie a stern look as she asked, "Did you know she was that nervous?"

"No!" Jamie said in alarm. "I had no idea!"

The woman handed Jamie a cold compress. As she applied it to the back of Ryan's neck, she gripped her limp hand. Within seconds, Ryan came around. "Did I pass out?" she asked groggily.

"Yes," Jamie replied as she leaned in close. "Did you know you were going to do that?"

"I thought I might," she admitted. "I really hate needles."

"Why didn't you say something? We didn't need to do this."

"You wanted to, and I knew if I told you how nervous it made me, you wouldn't want to do it anymore."

"You've got that right, baby. I would never ask you to do something that made you faint."

"I'm sorry I didn't tell you, but it means something to me to have to do something I'm really frightened of to wear my earring," she said earnestly as she reached up to touch her diamond, temporarily resting in her left earlobe. That merited her a sound kiss from her beaming lover.

"You are so sweet," she said as she shook her head. "I love you, Ryan," she said softly as she kissed her again.

The shop owner watched this whole scene with an amused grin on her face. "Young love."

After a short walk in the cool breeze, Ryan felt capable of taking the wheel again. They headed back to the house, chatting companionably the whole time. When they returned, Ryan kissed the steering wheel with a flourish as she got out. "Goodbye little Pony," she said with a fond wave.

Standing to stare at the Acura for a moment, Ryan said, "I need my sunglasses for this baby. Be right back." Waiting patiently, Jamie spent a moment to consider her lover's reaction to the unexpected gift of being able to drive the cars. The childlike joy that her partner expressed was, in Jamie's opinion, one of her most winning traits. Ryan acted like an enthusiastic five-year-old when she was given an opportunity like this, and Jamie fervently hoped that her partner would never lose that childlike wonder.

She was pulled from her musings when Ryan returned. Jamie tossed her the keys to the Acura and, in the blink of an eye, the child disappeared as Ryan's face broke into a sexy leer and she hopped into the low-slung car. Jamie joined her and studied her carefully, noticing how her entire demeanor had changed. A sly, sexy grin looked to be permanently embossed upon her face, and her moves were slower and more languid than normal. She exuded a bold confidence that radiated from her powerful body. *She looks like she used to look when she was stalking a woman!* Jamie thought to herself. *Just like she did that night at the bookstore ... all feral and predatory.*

Ryan brought the very powerful engine to life, narrowing her eyes as her smile turned up just the corners of her mouth. She turned to Jamie and slowly lifted one eyebrow until it popped out above the top of her very dark glasses, simultaneously kicking the car into reverse, sliding out of the garage a little faster than Jamie would have advised. The car eased into first and Ryan rolled out toward the street, failing to ask for advice this time. The top of the car was off, and her black hair blew wildly around her head as she sped off in a determined fashion for the nearest highway.

Moments later they reached the highway, and Ryan quickly brought the car up to cruising speed. She slid the big black beast between cars with ease, never staying in one lane for long. The game seemed to be a test of her own reflexes and those of the car, as she made one quick but graceful cut after another. Not a word had been spoken since they got in, and Jamie was too mesmerized by the aura radiating from her lover to break the silence. There was a discernable feeling of sexual tension in the car, an almost primal allure that seemed to snake from the dark beauty and wrap around Jamie's body.

When they had passed the heavy traffic, Ryan stayed in her lane for a while and pushed the car as much as she could. Dark head thrown back by the force, Ryan's hair flew around her, as the determined smile grew wider. Jamie recalled her partner's teasing comment on the AIDS Ride, asking if speed made her hot. There was little doubt at this point that speed most definitely made Ryan hot, but Jamie had to admit that the magic seemed to work for her as well as she became aware of a tightening in her belly.

She found her hand unconsciously running up and down Ryan's thigh, and after a moment Ryan lowered her glasses slightly, slowly turned to her partner, and gave her the sexiest, most openly lustful look that the smaller woman had ever seen. Jamie was shocked, but immediately aroused and ready to do something about it, all in the time it took to return that invitation. She gazed into Ryan's eyes for the moment that the dark woman could spare, then looked back to the road, nearly gasping in shock when she noticed a pale neon sign that announced, "Big Sur Motor Inn." *My God*, she thought to herself, *we've gone at least fifty miles!* But the throbbing between her legs demanded attention, so she ordered, "Pull over into that parking lot on the right."

Ryan raised her brow once more, and slowly nodded, acceding to Jamie's command. She rolled to a stop, kicking up gravel and dust as the car skidded a bit. Jamie cast a quick glance at her partner, lust and desire still permeating her gaze, "Wait for me."

Ryan leaned back in her seat, looking straight ahead in an almost bored fashion, while just underneath the skin her body appeared to be coiled for action. A few minutes later, Jamie came back to the car and adopted her own sexy grin as she dangled the room key right in front of Ryan's eyes.

The small woman had to dance out of the way as Ryan reached for the key with her right hand, her left smoothly opening the door. Quickly glancing at the number on the key, she grabbed Jamie's hand and led her to the stairs. When they reached the second floor, she seemed to instinctively know that their room was to the left, and she smoothly guided Jamie down the open walkway by placing her hand on the small of her back.

Sliding the key into the lock, she turned the knob slowly, and the big, rough wooden door creaked open. Ryan grasped her partner around the waist and, with practiced ease, picked her up and held her suspended in midair while Jamie wrapped her legs around her waist. The dark head lifted and latched onto Jamie's tender lips with a rough passion, her foot kicking the door closed at the same time.

Tossing Jamie onto the bed, she leapt on top of her in a single move. Mere seconds passed as she roughly tore at her partner's clothing, popping a few buttons off the cotton camp shirt, the tinkling of the plastic echoing loudly as they hit the Spanish tile floor. Ryan grasped madly at her own clothing, yanking her polo shirt over her head with Jamie's frantic help. Her jeans proved to be more troublesome, with the button fly not cooperating quickly enough for her need. She stood and yanked the jeans down, creating red marks down her hips from the friction of the tight jeans against her tender skin. Too impatient to get the jeans all the way off, she jumped back onto the bed with her running shoes still firmly attached to her feet, jeans and shorts around her ankles.

Jamie had pulled her own shorts off while Ryan was struggling, and had opened the front clasp of her bra, but she had no time to remove her panties before Ryan was back on top of her.

Ryan's sports bra was still protecting her breasts from Jamie's searching hands and mouth. Neither of them could wait for a proper removal, so Jamie yanked it up over the breasts and began to ravish the tender orbs. Ryan groaned deeply at the contact and spread her legs as wide as she could, then pulled Jamie's leg firmly between her own. She reached down with one hand spreading her lips open wide, her eyes closing slowly as her head tilted back in pleasure. Her hand slipped between her legs and she ran her fingers up and down her drenched sex for a few moments, spreading the moisture all around the throbbing flesh.

With a slow, achingly deliberate pace, she lowered herself onto Jamie's raised thigh. A gasp of pleasure and a satisfied smile signaled her pleasure. She sucked in a deep breath, holding it for long seconds as she acclimated herself to this delicious pressure, glassy eyes locked onto her partner's. With a grunt she placed her hands on either side of Jamie's face and locked her arms, carrying all of the weight of her torso on her hands.

Jamie was too stunned to speak, but she needed to somehow connect with her partner emotionally. The force of Ryan's need had caught her unawares, and she needed some reassurance that her gentle lover was still inside this wild woman humping her leg with abandon.

As though she could read her mind, Ryan reached up and removed her dark glasses. Her vivid blue eyes were dark with lust, but as she locked her gaze on Jamie, the love that they shared was starkly evident. She didn't speak, but a surfeit of emotion passed between them in that instant. Maintaining eye contact, Jamie lifted her hand and brushed her thumb across Ryan's lips, tracing their outline as hot breath passed over her skin. Ryan's eyes fluttered closed as she sucked the thumb in and laved it with her warm, wet mouth. The intimate touch kicked Jamie's desire up another notch, and she pulled her hand away as Ryan bit down rather sharply.

Determined hands grasped Ryan's hips and helped guide and steady her as she thrust. She slid up and down her lover's now slick thigh with a deliriously unhurried pace. Her breath came in gasps as the sensation shot through her vulva and suffused her whole groin. Her body rocked against Jamie's, back arching deeply as she slowly thrust her hips in a deep plunge. The pace began to quicken as Jamie roughly sucked and nipped at her breasts. The entire bed was pounding against the wall with each of Ryan's thrusts, and Jamie briefly wondered if there were guests in the adjoining room. Sweat dripped off Ryan's face as her pace quickened again. Her head was thrown back, and she sucked in a deep lungful of air as she gasped and groaned with each thrust against her lover's leg. Jamie forcefully sucked much of an entire breast into her mouth, causing a jolt of feeling deep in Ryan's center that was met with a sustained growl that grew louder and stronger with each thrust.

Jamie felt Ryan teeter on the edge of release, and she bit down sharply on the nipple in her mouth, shivering as the first rough spasms tore through her partner's body. Ryan coughed out a deep groan, still managing to hold herself up, but beginning to weaken. Jamie grabbed her, forcing her arms to relax and causing her to fall rather heavily. A small grunt escaped from Jamie's lips as most of the breath was knocked out of her, but she held on tight, comforting Ryan's sweat drenched body with her own.

Not a word had been spoken.

Without a pause, Ryan rolled onto her side and began to caress Jamie's wildly sensitized body. Surprisingly, Ryan's ardor had obviously not been sated, since she began to slowly twitch her hips in time to the caresses.

Her long, elegantly shaped fingers played over the swollen mounds of Jamie's breasts, tweaking the rock-hard nipples repeatedly. The bed bounced roughly as Ryan attempted to kick off the remains of her clothing without removing her mouth or her hands from her partner's breasts. It was a difficult task, but the determined woman managed the feat after a few minutes. Now that she was unclothed, she set about the same task for her partner. Exhibiting a gentler touch, she loving guided her partner into a sitting position and then removed the mangled camp shirt from her shoulders. The lacy white bra was next, and now the only clothing covering the writhing blonde was a pair of French-cut lace panties. Ryan decided to leave them on for a while, thinking that her partner looked even sexier with a tiny bit of clothing on.

The small woman was squirming on the bed, the demands of her desire forcing her body to move continually, silently begging for more contact. The image of her partner expressing her need so clearly caused Ryan's arousal to flare even higher, and she had to squeeze her thighs together to soothe her ache.

Jamie gazed up at her with glazed eyes and begged, "Please, baby, please touch me."

Unable to refuse her lover's request, Ryan rolled the smaller woman onto her stomach and slowly maneuvered her onto her knees. Jamie dropped down onto her forearms as Ryan knelt between her spread legs. She leaned over and began to place hot, wet kisses down her spine, stopping when she reached the waistband of the lace panties. Grasping the material with her teeth, she let out a feral growl as she tugged the material from her partner's hips, smiling in satisfaction when the smooth expanse of pale skin was revealed to her appreciative eyes. Her hands rose to remove the fabric from the quivering woman, and she sat back on her heels for a moment, taking in the lush curves of her partner's sexy body.

Leaning in close, Ryan separated the slick folds that glistened with the essence of her lover's need. Jamie froze at the touch, desperately willing it to continue, but Ryan had not finished teasing the flesh that beckoned her. She placed a thumb on either side of her partner's opening and rhythmically began to open and close the desire-swollen skin.

A low, need-filled moan escaped from Jamie's body, shivers concurrently running down her spine. Ryan continued with the teasing touch, stroking smoothly and slowly. Leaning in even further, she began to blow a warm stream of air all over the overheated flesh, reveling in the goose bumps that covered her partner's body. The pink flesh spasmed under her thumbs, a rough cry falling from Jamie's lips. "Please," she cried, her voice muffled by the pillow her face rested on. "Please, Ryan."

Ryan rested her head on her partner's smooth back, continuing to tease, as her deep voice vibrated against the pale skin. "Please what, baby?"

"Touch me," she cried, her voice low and rough.

"How would you like me to touch you, baby?" Ryan soothed as she trailed her fingers down a smooth white cheek. "Would you like me to touch you like this?" She placed the tip of her index finger at the entrance of her partner's slick opening and waited for a response.

The answer was unequivocal as Jamie groaned heavily, sliding back determinedly against the much-desired visitor. "Yes, oh, God, yes," she hissed as she paused for a moment to accommodate the feel of her partner touching her deep inside. After a few seconds, she let out a devastatingly sexy groan as her hips began to thrust.

Ryan sat back on her heels and reveled in the vision of her partner pleasing herself so thoroughly. Sexy moans and grunts of passion burst from Jamie's lips as she pumped against Ryan's braced hand, the thrusts becoming more forceful as the moans rose in pitch and frequency.

When Ryan felt the first spasms begin to pulse she placed her face between the shaking legs, laving the entire slick surface with her tongue. Jamie struggled to brace herself on her hands, her back arched deeply, as waves of pleasure flowed through her body. Without warning, she collapsed fully onto the bed with a rough grunt, and lay panting for several moments before she could breathe normally again.

Ryan climbed over her leg and snuggled up next to her, expecting to snuggle and soothe her while she recovered. But Jamie rolled onto her side almost immediately, and with a determined move growled, "I've got to do that to you—right now!"

Ryan's eyes flew open as the small hand forced itself between her legs and the questing finger sought entrance. The shock quickly gave way to a pleasured sigh as Jamie's finger slid inside. The smaller woman snuggled up next to Ryan's head and whispered into her ear, "This feels so unspeakably delicious."

Ryan nodded, a satisfied smile covering her lips. Her legs opened wider and her hips tilted as she softly moaned, "More, please."

Only too happy to oblige, Jamie slid another finger into the snug opening, leaning over to kiss her partner as the prone woman tilted her head back and gasped slightly, trying to accommodate the fullness. "Mmmm, perfect," she sighed, exposing her neck to Jamie's mouth as her hips began to move once again.

Jamie's fingers glided along the slippery walls, her lips repeatedly seeking to connect with Ryan's, relishing the closeness and the intimacy of the act. She loved the feeling of her lover struggling to catch her breath as her arousal spiraled inexorably upwards—the tiny gasps and sighs that formed on her ruby lips—the way the remarkably slick walls gripped her fingers as they slid in and out.

Jamie knew that her partner was close, but she was not sure that she was coordinated enough to be able to touch her with one hand while the other was inside. Ryan took care of her little dilemma by slipping her own trusty left hand into her wetness, purring like a panther as she stroked the sensitive skin.

After scant moments, Jamie felt the first strong pulse, smiling to herself as her lover's muscles milked her fingers up and down their length. Ryan's face was contorted in a pained-looking grimace as a strangled cry tore from her lungs. Her howl turned into a dry cough, her body shaking as it rode out the powerful orgasm.

Jamie wasn't sure of the correct protocol, so she left her fingers right where they were, enjoying the periodic spasms that continued to course through Ryan's body.

Ryan had an arm tossed across her eyes, and after a moment or two she murmured a quiet, "Wow."

"I thought you had a hard time having two orgasms," Jamie teased, whispering into Ryan's flushed ear and taking a gentle bite.

"Mmm-hmm," she mumbled, "and I thought you hadn't made love to women before, so we're even."

Jamie laughed gently at her partner's reply. "I never thought you'd buy my story. I knew it was just a matter of time before you found me out."

"Mmm," Ryan moaned as she raised her knees and gently removed Jamie's hand, her eyes closed as a small whimper escaped from her lips. "No hard feelings, babe. I'm looking forward to learning a few tricks from you."

"Ohh, I think you're going to be a very, very apt pupil," she decided, placing a kiss on Ryan's cheek. "But for now, you look like you could use a little nap."

"Take it or leave it," Ryan decided, her breathing settling into a peaceful cadence as sleep claimed her. As she watched her lover dream, Jamie decided that she would get more pleasure from watching her partner sleep than catching a nap herself. Her resolve stayed strong for scant few minutes before the lure of Ryan's slow breathing pulled her to join her in sleep. Half an hour later she blinked her eyes open and smiled at her partner, still slumbering contentedly in her embrace. She couldn't resist the urge to reach up and touch the sweet face, but that small movement caused those baby blues to open and blink for a moment before they focused. A huge smile broke out over that beautiful face, gleaming teeth flashing in the bright afternoon sun that streamed into the window. "Hi, gorgeous," she rumbled in a sleep roughened voice.

"Hi, yourself, Sleeping Beauty. Did you have a nice little nap?"

"Yes, I did, thank you for asking." She stretched languidly for a few minutes, yawning and growling deep in her throat as she did so. "Do you want to go home, or hang out here for a while?"

Jamie looked around the room and then glanced at her partner with a curious look. "Uhm … have you looked around here, sport?"

"No, not really," Ryan admitted. "My mind was otherwise occupied." She lifted her head and glanced around the nearly bare room, detecting a threadbare chair, a small, circular table bolted to the floor, one 1970s vintage television, and a small three-drawer chest, leaning a few degrees to port. "It's nice. Should we stay overnight?" Only her dancing blue eyes gave away her joke, but Jamie knew her well enough to recognize the sign.

"Sure," Jamie agreed. "But we have to switch sides so this damn spring sticks in *your* back!"

"Okay, okay, I'm up," Ryan proclaimed, rolling to the edge of the bed and getting to her feet. "Whoa … dizzy," she added, sitting down for a minute.

"Are you all right?" Jamie asked, crawling over to take a closer look.

"Fluid loss," Ryan grinned. "I'm fine." She stood easily and extended a hand, helping her partner up.

The sun was just about to set and since they had removed the hard top, Ryan knew it would be a cold ride home. Picking up Jamie's shirt, she noticed that only one button remained. "Whoops," she grinned guiltily, extending the shirt for Jamie's perusal.

"Now what, Wild Woman?" Jamie asked, not very happy about going home topless in the very cool evening breeze.

"You hop in the shower and clean up," Ryan instructed. "I'll figure something out."

When Ryan returned, the door to the bath was open. Jamie was trying to order her hair when Ryan squeezed into the small room, dropped her jeans and sat down to relieve herself. Almost in the same moment, Jamie scurried out of the bathroom, closing the door firmly behind her. Ryan shook her head as she finished up and came back out into the bedroom.

"Uhm, Jamie?" she began, but was cut off by her partner.

"I know, it's childish, but I don't like to watch."

"That's okay. There's no rule that says you have to watch. I'm wondering why it seems to bother you so much." After a pause she added, "Is this another Elizabeth thing?"

Jamie pursed her lips and nodded. "She was really proper and prim about things, and by the time I was three I had to go by myself. She always told me that what you did in the bathroom was private, and should never be shared with anyone else. The bathrooms at my grammar school were quite the adventure," she added with a grimace. "It took me forever to time it just right so no one would be in there with me."

"Are you comfortable with that, or would you like to change how you feel about it?"

"I guess I never considered that I could change how I felt about it. How would I do that?"

"You could probably desensitize yourself little by little. Your therapist could help you figure out how. But you should decide if it's something you want to change."

"Does it bother you that I want my privacy?"

"No, it doesn't bother me at all. It's a little awkward at times, like the night you and Mia got drunk, but other than that, it's not an issue for me."

"What happened when we got drunk?" she asked tentatively, having never gotten any details from Ryan.

"Don't you have any memory of that night?"

"Yeah, I do. But it's pretty hazy."

"Sure you want to know?" Ryan had a small smile on her face, but something about her tone made Jamie wonder if Ryan was hiding something.

"Yes. If I'm dumb enough to get that drunk, I should be forced to hear about what I did."

"It's not bad, Jamie. It just … well, you decide what it is."

"Tell me!" she demanded, wanting to cut to the chase.

"Well … before I put you to bed I asked you if you had to pee. Of course you did after all you drank, but you refused to let me stay in the bathroom. You kept saying, 'It's private!' Then I asked if you could go by yourself and you said 'No'. So I was in kind of a hard place."

"What did you do?"

"I convinced you to let me sit you down, and then I waited outside until you were finished. You were supposed to call me when you were done, but after about five minutes I went in and you were sound asleep, leaning against the wall, snoring your head off."

"Oh, God," Jamie said, covering her face with her hands. "I honestly think I've embarrassed myself in front of you more this year than I have with everyone else in my whole life!"

"But you were so cute," Ryan said as she took her in her arms. "You were so jealous when I kissed Mia that you really threw a fit!"

Jamie stood up and put her hands on her hips. "What do you mean you kissed Mia?" she demanded. "I thought Mia kissed you!"

"Well … either way."

Jamie jumped on her from behind and pushed her onto the bed. Ryan was sprawled across the lumpy mattress with her partner lying on top of her, covering her entire body. "You're not getting up until you tell me the whole story, Ryan. Now spill it."

Ryan could have turned over and tossed Jamie off, but she liked the feeling of having her lover on top of her. "Let me think," she mused. "Whose idea was it?"

Jamie started to tickle her sides, getting in under her ribs, a lethal spot. Ryan twitched and squealed under the assault, finally crying, "I give, I give."

"Now I want answers," Jamie threatened, "or there's more where that came from," she said as she twitched her fingers in front of her still squirming partner's eyes.

"Okay, when we got back to your house I called Cassie to help get Mia to bed. But Mia wouldn't go unless I kissed her. Cassie was fuming, and I knew if I didn't get rid of Mia right then she'd leave her and I'd have to carry you both up the stairs. So I gave her a tiny, itsy, bitsy, chaste kiss. More chaste than I give my grandmother."

"So why would that bother me?" Jamie demanded, knowing that there had to be more to the story.

"Well … that's how I kissed her … but that's not how she kissed me," Ryan said as she let out a deep chuckle.

"How did she kiss you?" Jamie demanded as she dug in for another round of tickling.

"I'm gonna have to turn over to show you," Ryan giggled. Jamie let her turn over but she stayed right on top of her. "I think I need to sit up to get the geometry right." She sat up with Jamie straddling her lap. "Okay, I'm Mia and you're me. Now, remember that I've got a big mouth, and I'm about to blab to Cassie about how you told her what a good kisser I was. Also remember that I'm blind drunk."

"Get on with it," Jamie mumbled.

Ryan did a very accurate re-creation of Mia's kiss, running her tongue over every surface of Jamie's astonished mouth. When she pulled away her partner sat in shocked silence for a moment, finally uttering, "That was so hot! I can't believe you let her do that! I can't believe she wanted to do that!" After a second she asked in a much quieter voice, "Did *you* want her to do that?"

"No!" Ryan cried, scrunching her face up in a show of distaste. "She was blind drunk, Cassie was watching, you were crying! Jesus! If I wanted to make out with Mia I'd opt for a little bit more privacy."

"Did you enjoy it? I mean did it … is she … uhm …"

"No, I didn't enjoy it, Jamie. Just because I've kissed lots of women doesn't mean I kiss just anyone. I don't have sexual feelings for Mia. I was actually kind of offended, and if Cassie hadn't been there, her determined little tongue would not have gotten past my teeth!"

"So when you kissed Mia, did I get upset?"

"You cried like a baby," Ryan informed her with a big smile.

"Well, I'd cry again if I ever saw you kissing another woman. Those pretty little lips are all mine now, Tiger."

"That's just how I like it, hon," Ryan insisted. She rolled off the bed and handed Jamie a stonewashed maroon sweatshirt that proclaimed in golden letters, "Big Sur Motor Inn."

"Nice," Jamie smirked. "Another memento of our honeymoon?"

"I told you I'd buy you a shirt every time we went on a trip," Ryan joked. "You may add this to your growing collection."

# Chapter Fifteen

Sliding into the car, Ryan placed her dark glasses on her face, once again lifting a dark eyebrow and giving Jamie a sexy leer. As her lover's eyes blinked in surprise, Ryan removed the glasses and allowed a goofy grin to replace the leer, her normal personality once again back in place.

"You are such a brat!" Despite her scolding tone, Jamie was charmed by her partner's ability to switch between her various personas so easily. A gentle squeeze of her leg showed Ryan as much, and the knowing grin that met her gesture gave silent affirmation of Ryan's understanding.

Deciding that Conor would get even more pleasure from the muscle cars than she had, Ryan decided to defer the other test drives until he arrived. "He's really gonna flip when he sees your home, Jamie," she mused as they neared Pebble Beach.

"How much does he know about my financial situation?" Jamie asked. They'd never discussed what the O'Flahertys knew of her family or their wealth, and she was curious as to how much Ryan had revealed.

"He only knows what you've told him." Ryan placed a hand on her thigh and gave it a squeeze. "I talk about you at home, but I would never talk about something as personal as your money. Of course, when we went to the Giants game I think he got a pretty good clue that you had some bucks, but I'm sure he has no clue how much."

Jamie looked over at her with a grin. "What do you say about me when you talk about me at home?"

Ryan gave her a sidelong glance as she drove along. "I don't know, just things like how sweet you are, or how good you make me feel. I've talked about how great you are with Caitlin, and I've told them about how you talk to strangers and make friends out of them in two minutes flat," she said with a chuckle. "I've told them how smart you are, and how I love the way your mind works. And I've talked a lot about your determination, and how you stuck with your training and workouts for the ride."

Jamie was charmed by Ryan's recounting of her talks with her family. "You are such a dear woman," she marveled. "I am so lucky to have you." Her head shook slowly as she counted her blessings once again.

"You're not half as lucky as I am, babe."

When they returned home it was fully dark, and as they walked across the crushed stone drive Ryan said, “I’m in dire need of a shower. You can spare me for a while, can’t you?”

“I suppose so. But I think it’d be more fun to get clean together, don’t you?”

Ryan stopped and gazed up into the night sky, deep in thought. “Hmm … I guess that’d be okay,” she said after a minute. A quick pinch to her side caused her to reconsider the enthusiasm of her response. “I mean, absolutely! You’re right as usual, dear.”

“Don’t push me, O’Flaherty. You know I have a short fuse!”

Ryan produced her most innocent look as she said, “I’ve never considered the length of your fuse, but if it looks like the rest of you, I would guess that it was short.” Her laughter rang out as she raced her partner to the kitchen door.

“Of all the women in the world, I had to pick the one with the smartest mouth and quickest feet!”

Entering the kitchen seconds after her partner, Jamie said, “My guess is that you need a snack before you can manage a shower.”

“Mmm … snack,” Ryan murmured, heading for the refrigerator immediately.

Jamie helped her to prepare a large platter of cheese, crackers, fruit and vegetables. Grabbing a chilled bottle of Pinot Grigio she took Ryan’s hand and led her down the stepping-stones to the pool house.

“I don’t believe I have my bathing suit,” Ryan commented innocently, batting her eyes at her partner.

“It’s a birthday suit kinda pool,” Jamie assured her.

Ryan set the platter down on a small table that she placed between two chaise longues. She looked up to see Jamie going to a series of controls near the main door and looked up in surprise as the huge, glass roof panels slid open, revealing the crystal clear black sky. “Wow,” Ryan marveled, smiling broadly as the scent of the ocean filled the space. “The enclosed pool was the only thing less than perfect about this whole place,” she commented. “And now you’ve even remedied that!”

“Told ya I was perfect.”

“No need to tell me that,” Ryan insisted. “You’re preaching to the converted.”

“So … do you want to swim first, or eat first?”

“Hmm … if you were really perfect, you’d know the answer to that question,” Ryan grinned. Her grin widened when Jamie stripped off her clothes, took a seat on the chaise, and began making a plate of tidbits for her partner. “Just as I suspected,” she beamed, happily accepting the plate.

They plowed through the plate in record time, with Ryan pulling more than her share of the load, as was her custom. A glass of wine accompanied the repast for each woman, and by the time the platter was clean, both were pleasantly relaxed and mostly sated. Neither felt like swimming after the wine and food, so they got into the hot tub to relax a bit further.

The water was hot—102 degrees—so they could only remain in the bubbling tub for a few minutes at a time. After about fifteen minutes of jumping in and out, Jamie got out and turned off the heat, allowing cool water to flow into the tub through the still-running jets. The temperature dropped quickly, getting down to ninety-eight degrees in just a few minutes. The relaxing water, the wine and the long day started to catch up with them and after another fifteen minutes of relaxing, they got out and went to lie on the double chaise that was set near the as-yet-untested fireplace.

Since the pool house shared a common wall with one of the guest apartments, the Evanses had the foresight to include a double fireplace in their building plans, and now both spaces had access to a cozy fire on a cold night. It wasn't particularly cold this night, but with the roof open, a little extra heat seemed like a perfect idea.

Jamie pulled the chaise even closer to the fire, while Ryan lit the artificial gas logs. "I've never seen a fake fireplace that didn't look silly," the larger woman commented as she watched the gas flame dance. "But this one is pretty darned good."

"Yeah, they didn't want the hassle of worrying about guests lighting too big a fire and burning the place down."

"You dad is always thinking about lawsuits, isn't he?" Ryan teased.

"I've never thought about it that way, but I guess you're right. He's … well, I guess I'd say that he's careful, and very protective of the things that mean a lot to him. He really loves this place, particularly the pool house. I'm sure he went out of his way to make sure it was well taken care of."

"Can't blame him," Ryan said. "I like to take care of my things too. Speaking of which," she asked, fingering her new diamond, "are these insured?"

"Of course," Jamie said. "I have a rider on my homeowners policy that covers all of my jewelry."

"Whew," Ryan said, wiping the imaginary sweat from her brow. "I'll be careful with it, but I know I couldn't replace it if it was lost or stolen."

"Honey," Jamie said with a look of serious concern. "These are yours now. You wouldn't have to replace them if you lost them. You could sell them if you wanted to. They're a gift."

"Unh-huh," Ryan nodded. "That sounds like me. 'Oh, I think I'll go hock these family heirlooms that Jamie gave me and buy some crack.'"

"You could do that if you wanted to," Jamie said. Noting Ryan's surprised look, she quickly amended. "Not the crack, of course. That's off limits. But if you wanted to sell them, you could. They're yours."

Ryan snaked an arm around her shoulders and gave her partner a squeeze. "They're ours, babe. And I'll treat them with the same level of concern that you would. They mean a lot to you, so they mean a lot to me."

"Like my ring," Jamie murmured, lifting the band to her lips for a quick kiss.

Ryan threaded her fingers through her partner's hair for a few minutes, smiling to herself when the pale head nudged against her, begging for more. "You know," she said softly, "I thought tonight would be a good time to talk about our week a little bit. Even though we have part of tomorrow together, Conor will be here and I don't think we'll be alone much. So in a way, this is the end of our honeymoon."

Jamie snuggled up against her chest. "Ohh, I hate to hear you even say that. Let's drop out of school and just live here."

Ryan knew her reply was fanciful, and she steered the conversation back to the subject. "Reality has to hit sometime. Tomorrow night, we're back in the city."

"In our new home," Jamie whispered.

"One of them," Ryan gently corrected.

"Hnh-uh," Jamie disagreed. "Tomorrow we'll be in our new home. On Monday we'll go to our new house. Big difference, babe, big difference."

Ryan paused a moment, letting Jamie's comment sink in. "Do you really feel like that … like my family's home is yours too?"

"Yeah … in a way I do," she admitted. "I feel so much a part of your family that it seems natural to feel like the house is mine too. When we go for Sunday dinner, I feel like I'm coming home."

Ryan turned and wrapped her in an embrace so tight that Jamie had to pull back to get a breath. "That means so much to me," she said fervently. "I never even dreamt that I could find a lover who would feel that close to my family … I thought it was hopeless."

Jamie pulled back severely to get a good look at her partner's face. "Hopeless? What do you mean, babe?"

Ryan took a breath and pursed her lips for a moment, then cocked her head and took a long sip of her wine, collecting her thoughts. "This is part of what I wanted to talk about tonight," she said. "I want to talk about our honeymoon, and how things have gone for each of us, but I also want to talk about what you mean to me, and how you've changed my life."

Jamie gave her a charmed smile and said, "I can't imagine anything I'd rather hear. Fire away, love."

"All right," Ryan grinned. "I'll start, but you need to join in, okay?"

"Like you could stop me from going on and on about you," Jamie teased, patting her lover's bare thigh.

Ryan tilted her head back, staring at the clear, black sky, noticing the first star of the evening. "I'm not sure where to start, so I guess I have to put this in context. As you know, I've known a lot of women." Jamie nodded her head, a small smile affixed to her face. "My motto was always that it was a mistake to date a friend. Now I realize that I would have been denied this gift if I'd stuck with that stupid idea. The whole reason that we were able to get together is because of our friendship. It's silly, Jamie. There have been two women in my life that I've loved. Two—out of all of the women I've known. And both of them were close friends long before I knew I was in love with them. Why was that so hard for me to figure out?"

"I don't know," Jamie replied. "But I'm glad you're a slow learner—otherwise, I'd just be a classmate that you encouraged to do the AIDS Ride. If you'd been open to love, you would have been snatched away years ago."

"I'm not so sure," Ryan said thoughtfully. "I don't think I was ready before."

"You must have been ready, since you were willing to try to be serious with Tracy," Jamie reminded her.

"Ahh, Tracy," Ryan said, considering the name. "She was actually very helpful to me."

"How so?"

Since they'd broken up, Ryan had rarely mentioned Tracy, and Jamie wondered if it was just to spare her feelings. Ryan quickly set her mind at ease when she revealed, "Without her, I don't think I would have seen the dichotomy between how I felt with you and with her. I still remember how I felt on New Year's Eve." Ryan smiled in remembrance. "I was on the verge of going to bed with her for the first time, but after you came over to say 'hi,' I spent more time thinking about you than her!"

"I didn't know that!" Jamie gasped.

"Yep. After you left it was like, 'Back to work, Ryan.' It's hard to explain, but it felt so easy and comfortable with you, and with her I felt like I had to play a role."

"A role?"

"Yeah. Actually, I almost always had to play a role with the women I knew. Most women knew one facet of my personality. A few knew me a little better, but no other woman … except Sara, of course, knows all of me." After a brief pause Ryan amended, "No, that's not quite true. Sara never knew the sexual predator."

"I sure got a healthy dose of that one this afternoon," Jamie laughed. "I want her to come out and play more often!"

"My pleasure," the sexy voice rumbled.

"I don't think I knew that you felt that way. I assumed that at least your special friends, like Ally or Alisa would know you well."

"Nope. Ally knows me pretty well, but she's never seen my 'baby side', as you call it. I didn't ever act childlike around her. With her, we were just sex-loving jocks—lots of wrestling and trying to show who was stronger and things like that."

"Mmm, that would be fun to see," Jamie mused. "I'd love to see two big, buff girls wrestling." Upon Ryan's twitching eyebrow Jamie added, "In my dreams, Buffy. I'll see it in my dreams."

"Just as well," Ryan agreed. "I'd lose face when you saw me get my ass kicked!"

"So tell me more about this role thing," Jamie inquired. "How were you with Tracy?"

"Mmm, I had to be a full-time adult with her. She was pretty serious, even though she had a decent sense of humor. Honestly, I don't think she was really very into me," Ryan theorized. "I think she wanted to have sex with me, and when I played hard-to-get she took it as a challenge."

"I got the impression that you two were getting pretty close," Jamie said. "We had that talk about falling in love ..."

"Yeah, but I learned that if you have to ask someone else's opinion, you're not in love. I didn't know how it was supposed to feel. I guess I'd say that we were getting pretty close, but there was a barrier there that we couldn't get past."

"What was it?" Jamie asked, very much wanting to know these details.

"I never felt like she wanted to know all of me. She seemed to like me quite a bit, but she wanted to know me just as I was ... She wasn't interested in how I got that way."

"Give me an example."

"Okay. The first time I was going to bring her to the house, she asked a few questions first. She asked about my parents, and I said that my mother was dead. There was a pause, and she said she was sorry to hear that. That was the only time the topic came up. To this day, she doesn't know when she died, or what she died of, or how her death affected me."

"Why didn't you tell her?" Jamie asked, stunned that Ryan wouldn't reveal the details of this momentous event in her life.

"That's not my style," the dark head shook rapidly back and forth. "I tell people the bare minimum. If you want more, you've got to ask for it."

"You don't do that with me," Jamie reminded her.

"I used to," Ryan insisted. "This is one of the primary reasons I fell in love with you. Early on, you made me feel like you were deeply interested in me. You wanted to know what made me tick. And I felt the same about you. That trust and openness went both ways. That had never happened with another woman."

"Now that you mention it, I guess I do remember you being pretty close-mouthed about a lot of things. But it didn't seem to last too long."

"No, it didn't," Ryan agreed. "I'm really very open with my family. It's how I feel most comfortable. Maybe since I can be myself at home, it's not a big deal to have a more reserved mask in public. But with you, I was able to take the mask off pretty quickly."

"I'm so glad that happened," Jamie replied, leaning over for a kiss. "I fell in love with your true self ... not one small part of you."

"You get the whole quirky package," Ryan agreed. "Now, I've blathered on long enough. It's your turn."

Jamie poured another glass of wine for each of them, taking a sip before she began to speak. "I'd have to say that one of the biggest ways you've changed my life is that you've given me another chance to be a child." Ryan smiled and squeezed her hand, encouraging her to continue. "I was thinking about this when we were running in the sprinklers and sliding across the grass. I never did that sort of thing when I was young. Elizabeth would not have stood for that type of frivolity! I got to play with other kids at the park, but if I got too rowdy we would go home ... immediately. She didn't like it when I yelled or ran around too much—said it wasn't ladylike."

Ryan's eyes were nearly bugging out of her head at this thought, but she held her tongue since Jamie seemed to have more to say on the topic. "I've got to admit, that was one of the things that most appealed to me about you. You seemed so casual and free—like you weren't listening to some inner voice telling you not to do things."

"No, I'm pretty free of inner voices," Ryan joked.

"Yeah, that comes across really clearly," Jamie nodded. "I remember when you broached the AIDS Ride to me for the first time. I thought you were nuts! It seemed absolutely fantastic that you would mistake me for someone who could do something like that. I doubted your sanity!"

"That really wasn't evident in the way you behaved," Ryan assured her. "You acted pretty happy-go-lucky."

"That was an act," Jamie declared decisively. "I always had some kind of tape playing in my head, telling me not to step outside of the rules."

"So why did you agree to do the ride with me?" Ryan asked.

Jamie thought of her answer for a moment, and then realized, "Because you assumed I could do it. You treated me like an adult, who could have a goal, work towards it, and accomplish it. I swear that you were the first person in my life who ever encouraged me in that fashion."

"Not even your grandfather?"

"No … not really. I think he was always very careful not to get too involved in voicing his opinion about a lot of things because he didn't want to contradict my parents or Elizabeth. He was always loving and supportive, but he wouldn't have encouraged me to be too independent."

"God, we couldn't have been raised more differently," Ryan mused. "It's truly amazing."

"I think it's amazing that our differences have allowed us to come together," Jamie said. "I can get a little dose of wildness from you, and you can hear the voice of reason from me."

"Yeah, I can use a little moderation every now and again," Ryan admitted with a big grin.

"So I guess I'm saying that, in a way, I think we give each other the same gift. You allow me to find that hidden child inside me and let her out. I allow you to be a child around me."

"You let me be vulnerable," Ryan added.

"You let me be wild," Jamie smiled.

"It's a pretty sweet deal."

"Indeed." Jamie leaned over and expressed her appreciation by giving Ryan several tender, gentle kisses. "Now do we get to talk about the honeymoon?"

"Go for it," Ryan murmured, looking like she could spend a lot more time on the kissing part of the discussion.

"I'm amazed with how quickly this all felt absolutely normal to me," Jamie said. "I know I was a little freaked out on Tuesday morning, but since then, it's been so easy. I swear I would never have believed it, but it really has been!"

"Tell me how you mean."

"It's hard to describe. When I was with Jack, sex was so much in my head! I thought about stuff the whole time—was this gonna work, was he enjoying himself, was I gonna have an orgasm. It was this constant running analysis. If I wasn't having fun, my mind would wander to school, or I'd think about my to-do list, or something like that. I know it sounds horrible, but I could disconnect really easily and be in a whole different world—while he was actually inside of me!"

"Yikes!" Ryan grimaced, a sour look on her face. "I take it that you don't do that now?"

"No! Just the opposite! I'm all about feeling now—it's really weird. I just react to your touch, and I touch you with that same instinct. I don't think about what you're doing, or worry about what I'm going to do to you. It just happens. It feels so free and natural. Do you know what I mean?"

"I think I do," Ryan agreed. "I mean, sex has always felt like that to me—I've never spent a lot of time thinking in bed. But you've shown me a whole new facet of lovemaking that I didn't expect."

"Tell me," Jamie urged, eyes shining.

Ryan took a sip of wine and let the amber liquid roll around on her tongue for a moment, collecting her thoughts. "Obviously, I've enjoyed having sex in the past," she began. "And some of those encounters were very fulfilling. But there's a whole new feeling I have when we're together," she mused. "It's hard to explain, but I'd have to say that my focus has changed."

"Focus?"

"Yeah. My focus," Ryan decided. "I'm more generous and more giving now. Even though I love being touched more than I ever did, I feel like I also love touching more than ever before. I know I've told you that I loved touching women—it was a very big deal for me. But in retrospect, I was touching them more to fill myself up, than for them. In a way, it was a power trip. I liked to see what my touch could do … how I could make a woman respond." Taking another sip of wine, Ryan continued, "It's not like that with you. When I touch you, I'm trying to give you pleasure, and I'm trying to show you how I feel about you. It's not a huge difference, but it's a very important one."

"It's important to me," the smaller woman murmured, tilting her head to kiss the wine-flavored lips. "I can feel how you put yourself into our lovemaking—it feels like you're giving me everything you have."

"I try to. I'm always going to try to show my full self when we make love."

"Me too," Jamie whispered, smiling as Ryan leaned down to kiss her several times. As the dark head lifted, Jamie asked, "So … is there anything you're unhappy with about our honeymoon? Did you get everything on your list?"

"I did not have a list!" Ryan cried. After a pause she gave her partner a sly grin and revealed, "Well … maybe I had a short list." She laughed softly and added, "You fulfilled every wish on Monday afternoon."

"Tell me what was on the list," Jamie begged, eyes intent on her lover.

"Well … I'd say that my biggest wish was that by the end of the week we'd be comfortable with each other." She turned a bit, lay on her side, and trailed her hand down her lover's body. Starting at her collarbones, she traced a path that included every erogenous zone, and as she finished she looked up and said, "I think we've done pretty well on that score."

"That was all that you wanted?"

"No, I desperately wanted you not to be afraid of me," Ryan admitted. "I thought you might have a very hard time being open to me." Leaning in for another kiss she added, "That didn't happen either."

"Come on … there's more."

"I hoped that we'd be able to talk about little problems and concerns that came up about sex," Ryan said. "And I think we did great on that."

"Yeah, we did, didn't we?" Jamie smiled. "It's actually been fun talking about sex … who knew?" After a short kissing break, Jamie asked, "What about the sex itself? Didn't you have any expectations?"

"Mmm, not real specific ones. I mean, I did consider every possible permutation of how to touch you, during these past weeks, but it wasn't like it was a wish list."

"Well, no matter what was on that list, I'm sure we've done it," Jamie mused.

Ryan paused for a moment, expecting Jamie to laugh but when she didn't her own laughter bubbled up from her chest. "Oh … that's rich!" she cried. "Do you really believe that, babe?"

"Well … uhm … yeah," the embarrassed blonde replied. "I mean, there are only so many things you can do, and it seems like we've done them all."

"Whoo! You're in for a treat, sweetness. We've just begun to explore each other!"

"Really?" Jamie asked, her voice now hesitant. "But … what … uhm … there are only so many … I mean …"

"Relax, babe," Ryan soothed, wrapping her in a hug. "We've got all the time in the world."

"But Ryan," she complained, sitting up a little bit. "How much more can girls do?"

"Trust me," Ryan said, a crooked grin covering her face. "We have barely scratched the surface … but that isn't what matters. What matters is how we make each other feel. And you are an expert at making me feel loved."

"You are too," Jamie assured her, snuggling into her arms.

They sat in front of the fireplace for a long while, sipping their wine, each lost in her own thoughts, and plans, and dreams. Some time later, empty wine bottle on the table next to them, they drifted off to sleep, holding each other in a warm, love-filled embrace.

At nine o'clock, the huge, black Dodge Ram crunched along the drive, pulling up to the rear entrance of the house. Conor hopped out and rang the bell, patiently waiting for his sister to answer. After a few minutes, he tilted his head and looked around the property, spotting the Boxster next to the garage. *They've got to be here*, he mused. *Probably passed out from too much sex!*

He followed the path to the front door and rang again, now a little impatiently. *Come on, you two! I've gotta go to the bathroom!* After a few tries at rapping sharply, he kicked the door in frustration, and began to peer into every window that he could see into. No signs of life were apparent, so he placed his hands on his hips and started to look around the grounds.

The stepping-stone path to the pool house was lit with graceful tulip-shaped verdigris metal lamps, and he followed the stones to the main door of the glass house. Conor's big blue eyes scanned the space, stopping first on a pile of clothes dropped haphazardly onto the floor. Turning his gaze to the flickering fireplace the big blue eyes got even bigger when he spotted the tops of a blonde and a dark head—the two women obviously reclining together on the wide chaise longue. *Shit! I finally get a chance to see Jamie naked, and my stupid sister is with her! Doesn't that just ruin everything!* He fought with his conscience for a moment, finally deciding that the pleasure of peeking at Jamie was not worth the guilt he would feel for spying on his sister. *Maybe I could create a diversion*, his always-mischievous mind mused. *Ryan would get up to see what the noise was, and then I could get a good look at Jamie.* He smiled evilly, but quickly quashed his plan. *It's not the same anymore*, he had to admit. *Now that she's with Ryan, it's almost like I've got two sisters … just what I always wanted*, he groused. *There's finally a hot woman in the house, and my sister gets to sleep with her!*

Deciding to avoid embarrassing them, he went back to his car and honked the horn a few times, smiling to himself when Ryan came barreling down the path a few moments later, wrinkled clothes hanging haphazardly from her long frame. Jamie was nowhere to be seen, but he figured that she didn't have a lot of experience in getting dressed quickly like his sister did.

"Nice key and set of directions you left for me, Sis," he shouted when she was within earshot.

"My bad, my bad," she admitted. "I'm sorry, Con, you haven't been waiting long, have you?"

"Nah," he lied. "Just got here. You didn't answer the bell so I thought I'd announce myself."

"Well, I'm glad you're here," she said, wrapping him in a fond hug.

"Where's Jamie?"

"Oh … ahh … we were in the pool house … swimming … and she needs to close it up."

"Nice …" he mused, looking around. "Uhm … is she Bill Gates' illegitimate daughter or something?"

"No," she laughed. "She knows who her parents are. This place is unreal, though, isn't it?"

"I'll say. I've worked on some pretty nice places, but this one is sweet, and I haven't even seen the inside."

"Come on in," she urged. "Have you had dinner?"

"Nope. I got in the truck and drove. I got a snack right before I left, but it's long gone."

Jamie ran up the path just as the O'Flahertys were entering the kitchen. "Hi, big guy," she smiled, giving him a kiss on the cheek.

"Hi yourself," he said. "Wow, you look great, Jamie," he added. "You both look really healthy and happy. The honeymoon must be going well."

She batted her eyes at Ryan and enthused, "I think it's the best one on record."

"Conor hasn't eaten, babe. Can I make him something?"

"I'll make you both something," Jamie decided. "How about a frittata?"

"Sounds good to me," Conor said, smiling broadly. Turning to Ryan he asked, "Do I like frittatas?"

"Yes, goofball, you'll like it," she laughed, rolling her eyes. "That sounds good. I'll get Conor set up in a guest room, okay?"

"Fine," Jamie replied. "I think Conor should stay in the main house, don't you?"

"Okay, come on, Conor, I'll give you the nickel tour."

After his bag was placed in the guest room most distant from her and Jamie's, Ryan said, "You in the mood to work on our little problem?"

"Yep," he agreed. "Show me the scene of the crime."

An elbow to the ribs kept the comments to a minimum as Ryan led her brother to the gym.

"So … the honeymoon went well?"

"Conor, I had no idea what I was getting myself into," she said with a chuckle. "I plan on being with Jamie for the rest of my life, but at this rate, that might not be very long!"

"I'm really happy for you, Ryan," he said as he leaned over to give her a kiss. "I'm happy for you both, actually. She's pretty lucky to have you, too, Sis." As they climbed the stairs he cocked his head a little and asked, "What do you mean, you had no idea what you were getting into? Was this your first time together?" he asked incredulously.

"Yep. It was truly our honeymoon," she said with a big grin.

"*You* waited this long? *You?*"

"Believe me Conor, she was worth waiting for," she said, sliding her arm around his waist.

Conor's eyes nearly bugged out of his head as Ryan opened the door to the gym. "Holy crap!" he shouted as he looked around the lavishly appointed space. "Ryan, how much money do these people have?"

"They've got plenty," she said succinctly, leading him over to the control room.

"And this is just their weekend house? What does their main home look like?"

"I don't know. I'm a little afraid to find out, to tell you the truth," she admitted.

"Have you even met her parents?"

"Hnh-uh," she said as she shook her head. "Well, actually, I briefly met her dad after the AIDS Ride. He came down to L.A. to see Jamie, but he was only able to stay for about five minutes. I had dinner with her grandfather, though. He's a real sweetheart. To tell you the truth, I'd like to meet her nanny. She's the one who really raised Jamie."

"Boy, that's weird," he said. "I guess your family backgrounds couldn't be more different, huh?"

"We're not from different worlds, we're from different solar systems!" she agreed.

She opened the door to the control room and Conor spent a few minutes looking at the equipment with Ryan anxiously looking over his shoulder. "This isn't a problem, Sis. These tapes are easy to erase."

"But they're electronically marked with the date and the time. It'll be obvious that we edited them," she argued.

"Obvious to whom?"

"To whoever reviews them."

"Oh, that's the problem," he said with a smile. "You obviously don't know how these systems work. Here's the deal. The security company installs these as a part of their total home protection system. The cameras take a still shot every so often, depending on how you set it up. When the tape is full it rewinds to the beginning and starts over."

"But who looks at the tapes?"

"No one, unless an alarm goes off. Then the monitoring company comes out to investigate. They go through their normal procedure, and then they enter the house and review the tape to see what triggered the alarm. Usually it's just a malfunction or some foliage that brushes against a door. But if there really was a security breach, they have pictures to help identify the intruder."

"But the homeowner can review the tapes if they want to, right?"

"Yeah, and most of them do so for a couple of weeks, but the novelty wears off really quick. So if you just leave this alone, it'll rewind itself and start over."

"Can you tell how often they rewind?"

"Yeah, give me a minute." He looked at his watch and timed the cameras. "They shoot every thirty seconds. These are standard videotapes and they hold six hours of pictures. Can you do the math?"

"I think I can handle it," Ryan smirked, her math abilities legendary in her family. "They rewind every seven and a half days," she said after thinking for a few seconds. "I don't want to take the risk of an alarm going off before they've rewound themselves. Is there a way to erase them?"

"Yeah, we can rewind the tape, hit this erase button and scroll through the whole thing. It'll only take a few minutes. Which tape are you worried about?"

Ryan blushed to the roots of her hair, "All of them," she mumbled.

"Jeez, Ryan!" he laughed. "Even the garage?"

She mutely nodded, still blushing.

"What about this one?" he asked pointing at the machine that recorded the perimeter of the buildings and the front entrance.

She gulped noticeably, "That's one of the worst ones," she admitted, thinking back to their arrival.

"The gym?" he asked incredulously.

"That's *the* worst one," she declared as she stared at the floor, thoroughly mortified.

"Well, well, well, you girls have had a gay old time, haven't you?"

"Conor, don't make this worse than it already is, and please don't tease Jamie about this. She's embarrassed to talk about it with me, and I was the one doing it with her!"

"Hey," he said as he wrapped his sister in his arms. "I'm sorry, Ryan. I didn't mean to upset you. I think it's great that you two are having such a good time together. And I promise I will never mention this whole thing in front of Jamie."

"Thanks, Conor. You really are the best," she said as she stood on her tiptoes to kiss his cheek. "Now go play in the gym while I erase these babies."

He left the room with nary a teasing comment, for which Ryan was eternally grateful. She erased the tapes one by one, but the one that captured the scenes from the gym caused her to pause and consider whether she wanted to erase it. Scanning through it with Jamie had aroused both of them, and she considered that the tape could be just the ticket for a little spice when they hit a sexual lull. She was fairly confident that Jamie wouldn't approve, and she knew she'd have to tell her if she kept it. *Knowing Jamie, she would agree to keep it, even if she was opposed, if she thought it was important to me. Hmm, my sweetie would be mortified if anyone else ever saw this tape. No matter how safe we think it is, there's always the chance that it could be discovered.* Deciding that her partner's feelings were worth more than the thrill they could get from watching the tape, Ryan popped it in and erased it, rewinding and playing it again, just to make sure. *We can always re-create the scene,* she mused. *That'll give us a good excuse to come down here again.* When she exited the room, Conor was playing around with the exercise equipment while he watched the Giants on the big screen TV. "This is some sweet setup," he said as he shook his head.

"You ain't seen nothing yet, Bro," she assured him as they left the gym.

When they returned to the kitchen, the table was set, the wine was chilled and dinner was being served. "I was just about to come and get you two," Jamie said as Ryan came up and gave her a little kiss.

"Mission accomplished," she said in a low voice.

Jamie gave her an anxious look, but Ryan shook her head a little. "It's perfectly all right. Don't worry about a thing."

They sat down at the table after Ryan and Conor spent a few minutes arguing about the proper way to light a fire, finally managing to get a roaring blaze going using a combination of their techniques.

The siblings agreed that the vegetable frittata was a perfect bedtime snack, and Conor was effusive in his praise of Jamie's culinary talents. "Jamie, it's not fair that you can cook, too," he whined. "You truly are the perfect woman. I know you don't have any sisters, but do you have any cute cousins?"

"Yeah, I do have two cute cousins. One of them is sixteen and the other is fourteen. Can you wait a few years?"

"Hey, if they're gonna turn out like you … except for that one little thing … I'll gladly wait."

"No guarantees, Conor," she laughed. "And I didn't find out that 'one little thing' about myself until I was twenty-one. I'd hate to see you waste all those years waiting, only to be disappointed."

"Good point," he admitted. "I guess I'll have to find a woman on my own. Now that Ryan's off the market, the pickings should be easier."

"Hey," she warned, "I didn't date many straight women."

"You had your share," he reminded her with a smirk. "But it's not fair that you got the best one in the whole Bay Area," he complained with a grin as he patted Jamie's hand.

That got him a kiss from Jamie as she stood to collect the dishes. "Not so fast there, Jamie. The cook does not clean," Conor said firmly, pulling Ryan to her feet. "The O'Flahertys will have this place shining in no time."

"Did you make dessert?" Ryan asked hopefully.

"No, but we've got another bar of Scharffen Berger chocolate," she replied with a grin.

"Excellent!" Ryan said. "Conor, you're going to get a hot fudge sundae the likes of which you will never forget."

By the time they finished dessert and clean up it was ten-thirty, and Ryan was fading fast. Conor was still wired from his drive, so they showed him the game room, and within moments he was racking the pool table while watching the Giants extra-innings game on the big-screen TV.

When they were alone in their room, Ryan provided some details about the tape erasing procedure. "I erased each tape myself," she assured her anxious partner. "Con knew how the system worked and he walked me through it, but he stayed out in the gym while I did the work."

Shy green eyes peeked out through golden bangs. "Did he tease you really badly?"

"No, he didn't because I told him it was off limits. We all respect each other's boundaries if we know what they are. I think he'll drop it after today."

"Whew, that's such a relief," Jamie said dramatically, falling to the bed.

"I agree. The next time we come down here, we're sticking to the bedroom."

"Will you come again?" Jamie asked.

"I love it down here," Ryan assured her as she stood in the bathroom doorway, brushing her teeth. "I'd certainly hope we can come down often. Especially on our anniversary," she added with a gleaming smile.

"I thought you'd enjoy it," Jamie replied as she ducked under Ryan's outstretched arm to grab her own toothbrush. "It feels like you're really away from people, even though Carmel is full of tourists."

"I like the whole lifestyle down here on the coast. Partly, I think I like it because it reminds me of the Atlantic coast of Ireland. I like the fog and the rocky cliffs, and I really love the wildness of the ocean. And I could sure get used to playing golf at Pebble Beach."

"What do you think of golf? Is it a game you'd like to play?"

"Don't you mean play better?" she teased. "I do like it. I usually pick up sports really easily. But golf doesn't come naturally for me. I'm going to really have to work at it to get better, but I don't want to be a golf widow, and if you're going to try to play for Cal, you're going to have to really work on your game. So if you don't mind my slowing you down, I'd really like to play with you."

"Let's figure out our schedules sometime this weekend so we can play together once or twice a week. Would you mind playing with my father on Sundays?"

"No, I think that'd be a good opportunity for him to get to know me a little bit. I do like to have dinner with my family on Sunday, though."

"So do I, Ryan. I'll never ask you to give that up."

Ryan gave her partner a toothpaste enhanced kiss, silently thanking her for understanding and sharing in the pleasure of her family dinners.

"Speaking of kissing," Jamie murmured, "let's get into bed and give our lips a little workout. You didn't kiss me nearly enough today."

"You know, you're right," Ryan said as she helped Jamie pull the covers back and climb into bed. "We had sex today with hardly a kiss."

"That is pretty rare, isn't it? You got me so hot, so fast, I couldn't waste any time with the preliminaries. I had to have your mouth on me right then."

"Today was fun," Ryan agreed, "but I enjoyed last night just as much. It doesn't really matter what we do, or how we do it. What matters is how much we love each other, and how clearly we express that love."

"You are such a romantic, Ryan O'Flaherty. I love your little Irish heart," she said as she dipped her head to kiss over her left breast.

They spent a few minutes kissing, not increasing the pace or the intensity. They just enjoyed the closeness and the intimacy for a while. Ryan was lying on her back with Jamie resting against her side. As Jamie placed a few more soft kisses on Ryan's lips, she felt her body begin to lose its muscular tension. She snuggled up tighter and laid her head on the broad shoulder. "Goodnight, sweet baby," she whispered to her sleeping lover. "I love you."

# Chapter Sixteen

Ryan woke relatively early on the final day of their honeymoon and decided that she needed a nice, big breakfast. Eschewing her normal morning run, she prepared a six-egg ham and cheese omelet, two bagels with cream cheese, a big bowl of green grapes, a sectioned orange, a pot of coffee and two big glasses of juice. She carried her loaded tray up the stairs, setting it down on the floor as she slowly opened the door. Tiptoeing into the room, she could hear her lover begin to stir. It was just quarter to seven, but the sunlight was streaming through the big windows, creating lovely patterns all across Jamie's body.

The smaller woman had kicked the sheet off in her absence, and Ryan stood and stared at her for a long minute. The unguarded beauty of her lover caused her to reflect on how blessed she was to be able to spend her life with a woman who attracted her so strongly. She knew that she would love Jamie no matter what kind of a package she came in, but she was not unaware of how the strong, firm body called to her in some elemental way that she was powerless over.

Jamie's eyes slowly blinked open and locked upon Ryan's for a few moments. She caught the desire reflected in those deep blue eyes, and she responded with a slow, sensual smile, silently welcoming her lover to proceed in any way she wished.

Ryan beamed at her as she placed the tray on the window seat and crossed over to sit next to her on the bed. "Sometimes I'm so struck by how beautiful you are that I really have to struggle to keep my wits about me," she admitted as she ran her hands lightly across Jamie's smiling face.

"If I tried for a year, I couldn't think if a better way to wake up," Jamie said sweetly. "Your loving face, that gorgeous body, a wonderful compliment and a big breakfast waiting for me." She shook her head slowly. "Heaven's gonna have to pull out all the stops to top this."

"This is just one woman's opinion," Ryan mused as she fetched the tray, "but I think *this* is heaven." A small smile accompanied her words, but Jamie could see the grain of truth reflected in the vivid blue eyes. Ryan took a big bite of the omelet and closed her eyes in pleasure. "Boy, I sure can cook," she said happily. "You've done pretty darn well for yourself, Ms. Evans. I get up early and make a fabulous breakfast, and you don't have to lift a finger."

"I know how well I've done, Ms. O'Flaherty," she agreed with a big grin. "I thank my lucky stars every morning that you're my partner."

"I don't know if the stars have anything to do with it, but I give thanks for you every day too."

"Ryan?" The tone in her voice let Ryan know that a serious question was headed her way, and the dark woman paused to give her partner her full attention. "Do you think we knew each other in a past life?"

"Pardon me?" Ryan shot her partner a skeptical smirk, but when she saw that Jamie's question was sincere, she tried to control her reaction.

"You heard me, silly. Do you think it's possible? I just feel so close to you that it's hard to believe we've only known each other since September."

Ryan grew pensive, giving the question the thought that it deserved. "I agree that we have a bond that seems to predate our meeting, but I think that past lives stuff is a lot of hooey. I believe you get one bite at the apple, Jamie. That's why I try so hard to jam my days with lots of activity. I don't believe you get a second chance at life. It's a precious gift that leaves us all too soon, and I believe we need to savor each moment."

"I suppose you're right. I guess it just scares me to think that our time together is limited to this one lifetime."

"Sweetie, we don't know what comes after this life. But I'll tell you one thing: if it's possible to be reunited after death, we'll be together. Nothing could keep me from you if there was any possible way to be together." Her pledge was whispered softly into pale fragrant hair as she wrapped her arms around her partner and nuzzled her head into her neck. "Even though I don't believe in past lives, I do think that some force brought us together. I like to imagine that my mother had something to do with it," she said with a shy smile. "That might be a lot of hooey too, but it's a way I keep her involved in my life." She traversed Jamie's neck in sweet little butterfly kisses from her ear to her collarbone. "And I know she would love you, Jamie." she said solemnly. "She'd see all of the beauty you possess, both inside and outside. She'd be so happy for us, honey, I'm certain of that."

Jamie wiped a tear from her eye with the corner of the sheet and gazed up at Ryan with a look of pure love. Making a quick decision, she decided to share a very precious moment with her partner. "When we were at the beach the other day, I was suddenly struck by this really powerful feeling," she said as she shook her head a little, still trying to make sense of the incident. "I had this visceral reaction to watching you run and play in the surf. You acted like such a little girl, and I suddenly felt how your mother must have felt, knowing that she wouldn't see you grow up." She struggled with her emotions and eventually gave up the fight when she felt Ryan's tears rolling down her shoulder. "It's odd, Ryan, but I felt like she could hear me, so I thanked her for the marvelous job she did in raising you. I swear that as soon as I did that I felt an overwhelming sense of peace. I think she sees us, Ryan. And I think it does make her happy," she said as the tears rolled down both of their faces with abandon.

Ryan lifted her head and began to kiss the tears from Jamie's cheeks. Jamie's searching lips captured Ryan's tears, and as the minutes passed, their kisses became more heated and more insistent. Within moments they were moving against each other sensually as they sealed their love with a sweet, tender communion. Their intimacy reached a new height, though it didn't progress to intimate physical contact. Instead of touching each other sexually, they shared their raw emotions, holding nothing back, revealing all of their most fragile hopes and fears in the deep merging of their souls.

They were both shaken by the overpowering feelings that their connection had brought to the surface, and they held each other for a very long while, letting the feelings seep into their bones. It was almost eight o'clock when Jamie mumbled, "I should get up soon. I've gotta look like an adult today."

"Is that such a hard task?" Ryan asked softly, her voice a little rough from disuse.

Jamie chuckled lazily and began to stretch out her muscles. "Not usually, but I've gotten used to being naked for almost a week. It's gonna take some time to get into nylons and a dress."

"Let me help you," Ryan offered. "We can make the time in the shower count."

"Okay," Jamie said brightly. "If we're gonna do that though, I've got a good idea."

"You have yet to have a bad idea," Ryan decided, tweaking her partner's nose.

Handing Ryan a robe, Jamie led her into her mother's bedroom.

"Uhm, are you sure this is okay?" Ryan asked hesitantly.

"Absolutely," Jamie replied. "Mother loves it when people enjoy her bathroom. It's her favorite part of the house and she's always offering it to guests."

Ryan was rather stunned when they passed through the bedroom and into a massive walk-in closet. Neatly organized clothes covered three walls, with the fourth containing built-in cabinetry that functioned as chests of drawers and a generous dressing table with professional lighting for applying make-up. A large oak door led to a bath, the likes of which Ryan had never seen.

The first thing she noticed upon entering the room was that the floor was a beautiful, highly polished tan marble. The floor dropped off into a sunken tub, located beside a massive leaded-glass window that provided a stunning view of the wild, roiling ocean. Across from the door, two graceful pedestal sinks flanked a large oak armoire. Open shelving on the top half of the piece held decorative soaps, fluffy towels and other little knick-knacks.

To her right, Ryan noted a short wall with a wide marble top with a TV/DVD combination rested on an articulating arm so that the picture could be seen from any part of the room. Behind the wall, a commode with a very strange looking seat was visible. Jamie crooked a finger, and Ryan followed her over to the far wall. Turning to her right, Jamie led her partner into a large tiled shower with a curved seat that extended all along the back of the enclosure. A large skylight provided a clear view of the gray, foggy morning sky. Ryan rocked back on her heels and let out a low whistle through her teeth. "I … I … I've never seen anything like this," she said as she shook her head. "I can see why your mother likes to share this place."

"It is pretty neat, isn't it?" Jamie asked, a little embarrassed at the opulent display. She removed her robe and asked for Ryan's, placing them on the marble counter.

"I'll say," Ryan remarked. "Do we really shower in here?" She indicated the tiled enclosure. "Where's the door?"

"There isn't one. It's sloped just enough so that the water doesn't flow out. This took a lot of time to get right, but Mother loves the open feeling you get in here."

Ryan's face was covered by a wide smile. "Are you going to join me in this den of pleasure? We've never showered together, you know."

"I'm all yours, precious," she smiled.

"Let the games begin!" Ryan decreed with a laugh as she turned on the overhead rainfall shower, unexpectedly drenching her partner.

Sputtering the water out of her face, Jamie cried, "You are such a brat, Ryan O'Flaherty! I've got half a mind to leave you here all alone."

"I'll be good," she replied with her most innocent expression firmly pasted to her face. "I'll make it up to you, baby," she cooed, running her hands all over Jamie's wet torso.

"Hey!" Jamie said sharply. "Where are those hands?"

"But I'm just helping to dry you off," she replied with a hurt look on her face.

"Yeah, right!" Jamie replied, already too familiar with her lover's tricks. "You wait right here while I get a few things, you naughty girl." Moments later she was back, and after adjusting the water temperature, the twosome got under the water. No sooner were they wet than Jamie turned off the flow, instructing, "Don't go away," as she scampered out of the enclosure.

Ryan heard the water running in the tub, and she sat on the wide seat in the shower and patiently waited for her lover to return. Jamie peeked in a few minutes later and beckoned her partner to join her. "Come here, sweetie," she instructed. "Climb into the tub. You can grab the railing in the back so you don't slip."

Ryan did as she was told, letting out a huge sigh as the warm water came up to her knees. Jamie sat on the edge of the tub and motioned Ryan to come closer. She did so, rising from the water to sit on a ledge that surrounded the tub. Facing the wall, Ryan closed her eyes in pleasure as Jamie started to brush her hair with a round wooden hairbrush. She brushed it thoroughly, pulling all of her hair away from her face, and when she was satisfied with the look, she began to braid it into a thick rope. She put a covered band around the bottom to hold it together, and then clipped the braid up against the back of Ryan's head to keep it out of the water. She slid into the water right next to her partner and sat on her lap for a moment. "You look too tasty to pass up," she whispered as she wrapped her arms around Ryan and spent several minutes kissing her tenderly.

She slid off Ryan's lap and gently splashed some water on her face. Then she slowly spread a dark, gritty substance on Ryan's face and neck. It looked a lot like mud and had a rich, deep earthy smell. When she was finished, she handed the jar to Ryan and splashed some water on her own face. Ryan mirrored the application for her, and a few minutes later they each sat back in the tub and soaked in the fragrant water.

Ryan was feeling deliciously relaxed after fifteen minutes in the tub. Just when she was about to nod off, Jamie stood up and pulled the stopper, allowing the tub to drain. They climbed out together, then Jamie led her back to the shower where she unclipped her hair and pulled the braid apart, letting her hair hang loose down her back. "Sit," she commanded as she pointed to the bench and turned on the handheld shower that the lower set of fixtures controlled. She let the warm water run over Ryan's legs for a moment, then she squirted out a generous amount of shaving cream onto her hands and started to lather it onto one long leg. She rinsed her hands and sat beside and slightly behind her partner, then took a disposable razor and started to stroke smoothly up those strong legs, stopping just above the knee as was Ryan's habit. The very fine blonde hair that grew on her thighs was one of Jamie's favorite things, and she was loath to remove the downy covering. She worked all around the leg, getting up to pull the foot up into the air so she could reach the back of her lover's leg properly, then she followed the same procedure for the other leg, caressing each silky leg to test for perfection.

"Nobody has ever shaved my legs before," Ryan dreamily murmured as she leaned against her partner. "I guess it's your turn, huh?" She grasped the razor and the cream and, catching the amused grin on her partner's face, gave her a puzzled look. Following Jamie's gaze, Ryan slid her hands up the smooth legs and muttered, "You have hit puberty, haven't you?"

"Yes, Ryan," she smirked, slapping her on the shoulder. "I don't have much hair on my legs."

"Hmm," the playful brunette mused. "Maybe you'd like to get rid of this little bit up here," and then playfully tried to remove the blond curls as Jamie slapped her hand and backed away.

"No way, baby," she laughed. "I'm keeping every one of those!"

Ryan leaned over and placed a kiss on the springy curls. "I swear that you have the most perfect little triangle that I've ever seen," she marveled. "You could wear a thong and not have one little curl stick out."

"Just another example of my perfection."

When Ryan was finished ogling her, Jamie pulled her to her feet and washed the masque off her face, using a soft cloth to help the process. When the masque was completely removed, she squirted a generous amount of fragrant shampoo onto her hands and guided Ryan under the rainfall showerhead. When her hair was properly wet, she jumped onto the seat and worked the shampoo into the ebony locks, giving her a thorough scalp massage in the bargain. Ryan let her head rest heavily against her partner, enjoying the unfamiliar sensation. When the temporarily taller woman was satisfied with her efforts, she again used the handheld fixture to rinse every bit of soap residue out of her partner's hair. After she ran her hands through the tresses several times to remove excess water, she applied some conditioner and sat Ryan back down to let it work.

Jamie started to scrub off her own masque, but Ryan divined her intentions and insisted on returning the favor. Next, she washed and rinsed Jamie's short tresses, applying some firm pressure to various spots on her head and neck to relieve any lingering stress. An application of conditioner for Jamie preceded the thorough rinsing of Ryan's head. By the time all of the product was out of her thick hair, it was Jamie's turn, and moments later both heads were clean and conditioned.

Each woman lathered up a soft cloth and washed every square inch of her partner, spending extra time on some of the most prized real estate. Jamie was forced to snatch the cloth away when Ryan started to stray into forbidden territory, and gave her partner a playful slap on the hand.

They dried each other with fluffy beige bath sheets, and then Jamie used a smaller bath towel to remove the bulk of the water from Ryan's hair. Sitting the tall woman on a small stool, she carefully combed her hair to remove any tangles, pulled out a blow dryer and blew the dark hair dry, combing it straight back off her forehead. Ryan once again echoed her lover's actions, quickly blowing Jamie's hair dry.

They returned to their own room where they each playfully brushed the other's teeth. This task was not particularly easy, but it was fun to try, and when finished, they kissed a few times to test for cleanliness.

Walking back into the bedroom together, Ryan checked her watch. "It's just a little after nine, hon. We've got an hour to kill."

Jamie tilted her head and considered their options for a moment. "We could go downstairs and see if Conor's up," she suggested. "We didn't get a chance to spend much time with him yesterday."

"I've been spending time with Conor for twenty-four years," Ryan said with a frown. "I'm not really interested in that proposition."

To Ryan's amazement, Jamie seemed unable to think of any pastime that could occupy them for an hour or so. She blinked up at Ryan and asked, "Do you have anything you'd like to do?"

"Gosh, Jamie," she said slowly, trying to hide a grin. "It's the last day of our honeymoon … we've got over an hour to kill … we're sparkling clean … my legs are all smooth—just waiting to be touched … or licked." She shook her dark head slowly and muttered, "Nope. I can't think of a thing."

"Oops!" Jamie was truly embarrassed to be so oblivious, but when she considered the proposal, she realized why it hadn't occurred to her. "I don't really want to need another shower. I'd really like to be close, but could we maybe just lie together for a while?"

"Of course we could." Ryan smiled as she gathered her in a hug. "It's the closeness that I really need, too. Let's spend the last hour of our honeymoon in each other's arms."

Obviously not as well rested as they had thought, they both fell asleep within minutes of climbing back into bed.

A small noise woke Ryan and, staring at her watch in amazement, she nudged her partner and asked, "Jamie, do you know what time it is?"

"No," she mumbled. "Can't we talk about this later?"

"No," Ryan insisted. "It's ten-fifteen."

"*What!* How can that be?" Jamie shouted as she leapt from the bed and ran to her closet.

"That's more like it," Ryan decided, getting to her feet and trying to stay out of the way.

Only by rushing faster than she ever had, was Jamie ready by her self- imposed deadline. But even in her great haste she looked adorable to Ryan's appreciative eyes. She was wearing a sleeveless cotton batik dress in shades of yellow, gold, and orange. The dress was quite short and showed off her smooth, tanned legs, which were somewhat needlessly covered by sheer pantyhose. Simple gold earrings, a matching necklace, several gold bangles on one wrist and her slim gold watch on the other were the perfect accessories. She had on a touch of makeup that accentuated the golden highlights of her tanned skin, and a little splash of perfume that made Ryan's mouth water. Ryan was absolutely mesmerized, staring at Jamie the whole time she was getting dressed.

When Jamie was ready, she turned to make a comment to her partner and was struck by the lovesick expression on Ryan's lovely face. Her heart clenched in her chest, and she felt the first stirrings of desire flare. Echoing the longing she saw in the deep blue eyes, she murmured, "God, I don't want this to end."

Ryan closed the distance between them in the blink of an eye, wrapping her beloved in an emotion-filled embrace. "I don't either, sweetheart, I don't either." They hugged so fiercely that Jamie was afraid she'd have to change clothes to avoid being a wrinkled mess, but she didn't mind a bit. Being held in Ryan's arms was worth any sacrifice.

"You could go with me," a small voice floated up to Ryan's ears.

Pausing a second to make sure she gave the correct impression, Ryan demurred. "This is something you need to do alone. I really think I'd be in the way."

Jamie started to disagree, but Ryan silenced her with a gentle kiss. "If you're worried about going alone, or you need to talk about it some more, I'll drive you and hang out in Palo Alto while you go to the ceremony, but I really think you need to go to the graduation alone to be able to let go of some of this."

"I have let go of him, Ryan! Really, I have!" The look on her face was a combination of embarrassment and fear as she tried to convince both Ryan and herself of the truth of her statement.

Ryan's hands lifted and gently grasped Jamie's face. She tilted her head just enough to be able to gaze directly into her eyes. Her voice was soft, but firm as she said, "I know you have. But this chapter of your shared lives is still open. You wouldn't have wanted to go if it wasn't, baby. I think this is something that you need to do, and I support you completely. I really want you to go." Ryan's face reflected her sincere wishes, even though she surprised herself a little when she expressed them.

"You're right," Jamie muttered, nuzzling her face against Ryan's chest. "I don't want to go."

The mere fact that Jamie was so reticent to leave made Ryan feel immeasurably better. "I know, I know." They stood and held each other gently until Jamie absolutely had to leave. With a small kiss on the top of her head, Ryan said, "I love you more than words can say. You make me happier than I ever thought was possible."

"I'm gonna spend the rest of my life trying to make you happy, Ryan." She reached up, then slipped the other blue diamond into Ryan's right earlobe. "I need to wear a matched set today. So you keep mine safe for me until we're together again," she said as she stood on her tiptoes and kissed her ear.

They walked down the stairs hand in hand. As they entered the kitchen, Conor was sitting at the counter, fully dressed, with an anxious look on his face. "Thank God you finally came down! There was no way I was going to disturb the honeymooners!"

They both laughed at his predicament, with Jamie placing her arms around his neck and kissing his cheek. "Sorry we got such a late start, Conor. But you've got plenty of time to get to the course."

He smiled up at her, all of his anxiety now gone. "I hope you have fun today too, Jamie. I wish you could go with us."

"I do too. I don't know how I'm going to survive without this one for a whole afternoon." She gave Ryan a big hug.

Ryan leaned down to kiss her tenderly, grasping her hand and leading her outside. Conor followed along behind them and tried not to watch as his sister said her goodbyes. Jamie got into her car, and Ryan sat down on her haunches to be able to reach her through the low door. She kissed her several times, each kiss getting a little more fervent. She finally lifted her head and smiled at Jamie. "I think we'd better stop, or Conor's gonna get a show."

"Now you have fun today, Tiger, and don't forget to drive those other cars. Why don't you take one to the course?"

"Could I?" she asked with her eyes wide.

"Oh course, baby, Daddy wants you to drive them. It's okay if Conor wants to drive, too. Daddy really likes people to enjoy his little toys. Oh, I forgot to tell you that I already signed for your golf today. I also paid for Chip's time since it's going to be a playing lesson, and I left a nice tip for him so you don't have to worry about that. I opened a tab for you at the restaurant, too. Have lunch there and sign my name. I've just gotten some weight back on you, so you eat up."

"You're much too good to me, you know," Ryan insisted. "You're really going to spoil me."

"I can't think of anyone I'd rather spoil," Jamie said as she puckered up for another kiss. After several more tender kisses, she started to pull away, but stopped about twenty feet down the drive. Ryan trotted over as Jamie leaned her head out. "I need one more," she pleaded.

Ryan stuck her head in the window and gave her a doozy. Jamie had to fight to focus after the searing kiss. "Whew!" she breathed. "Hold that thought until I get home tonight, Tiger."

"If Conor wasn't here I'd like one more little taste of you."

"You read my mind, baby," Jamie agreed wistfully.

Ryan leaned in and gave her a final kiss, then reluctantly stood and waved good-bye.

Conor was standing on the landing by the back door, hands on his hips. Ryan lifted her shoulders in a shrug as she gave him a guilty smirk. "I've got it baaaad, Conor."

"It's the worst case I've ever seen," he agreed as his wrapped his arm around her shoulders.

They had less than ten minutes to get to the club, so rather than drive one of the muscle cars, Ryan decided to go in Conor's truck, since his clubs were already loaded. They flew into the parking lot and had to run to get to the clubhouse on time. Chip was waiting for them and after quick introductions they headed out to the first tee.

Conor was like a kid in a candy store, "oohing" and "aahing" at all of the sights. He and Ryan rode together, and she pointed out all of the interesting trivia that she had learned on her earlier round. Conor was really on his game and made quite a respectable showing. Ryan also played significantly better, and both Chip and Conor were generous in their praise of her improving game.

Conor had to brag about her a bit to Chip, informing him about what a natural athlete his little sister was. He had Chip in stitches by the time he finished regaling him with stories of a young Ryan beating her older brothers in nearly every game they played.

When they stopped at the snack bar after the ninth hole, Ryan grabbed twenty dollars worth of food and Gatorade, with even Conor expressing astonishment at her purchases. "Jamie made me promise to eat a lot today," she protested.

Conor laughed at her as she gulped down the large bottle of Gatorade. "You wouldn't be so hungry if you came downstairs and had breakfast like normal people."

"I'm sorry for worrying you this morning," she said sincerely. "It really would have been okay to come up and check on us."

"Well," he admitted, "I heard you playing in the bathroom at eight, so I assumed you were up. But when you didn't come down by ten I did tiptoe upstairs and I didn't hear a sound. So I made just enough noise to wake you up. I do respect your privacy, but I wasn't going to miss playing this course!"

As they drove to the tenth tee, Ryan leaned over and gave Conor a kiss on the cheek. "What was that for?" he asked.

"I missed you these past two weeks. I was really disappointed that I didn't get to see you before we left to come down here."

He gave her a big smile as he patted her on the leg. "I missed you too. Da and I were talking about it the other day. It just doesn't feel right at home when you're not there."

Chip was waiting for them when they pulled up, so Ryan was unable to pursue the conversation. But she decided that she needed to revisit the topic at lunch.

The rest of the round flew by, with the threesome getting along quite well. Ryan loved seeing her brother enjoy himself so much, and she thought that one of Conor's most endearing traits was that he was unafraid to show his true feelings. He wasn't the type of man who felt he had to play it cool. He let his boyish enthusiasm show through in nearly everything he did. Ryan studied him as he stood on the tee to hit his shot. When she really thought about it, she realized that he had changed very little since they were children. He was still full of energy and always ready to play a practical joke or engage in some form of competition. She was pleased to see that being an adult hadn't hardened him, like so many people his age.

He came back to the cart, grinning widely at his excellent tee shot on eighteen. "I fail to see what's so hard about this little course," he said smugly. "I see the pros out here every year just hacking away. I don't get it."

Ryan laughed as his bravado. "This is the very rare day when the wind isn't blowing, Conor. Add a twenty-five mile per hour wind, and this place can eat you alive."

"I don't know, Sis. I think I've just got what it takes," he said with a grin.

When they finished their round, Chip made Ryan promise to tell Jamie that he was always available to help her with her game. He gave Ryan his card and wrote his home number on the back. "If her relationship doesn't work out, I'd be happy to help her in other ways, too," he grinned.

Ryan promised to relay the message, ignoring the tension she felt building from her brother. They said goodbye to Chip and began to walk toward the clubhouse for lunch.

"The nerve of that guy!" Conor fumed. "Who the hell does he think he is, trying to horn in on you!"

"It's okay," Ryan said. "He doesn't know we're together."

"I don't care! You shouldn't go sniffing around a woman when you don't know what the situation is. For all he knows, she's going out with me!"

"I guess you do have a point there," Ryan agreed. "But if you were dating Jamie, you would have made a point to mention it at some time during the round. I'm not able to do that given our situation."

"That really makes me mad. I don't see what the big damn deal is. So you're both women. So what! You show each other more love than any ten straight couples I've seen. Why can't people get over themselves?"

"Well, you know I haven't spent much time in the closet in the last seven years," she said. "But Jamie's not in the same place that I am with this. She needs time to figure out how and when to tell her parents, and the other people in her life. I'm afraid it's going to take a while for her to be comfortable being fully out."

"I wish this were easier for you both, Ryan. It must be hard for you having to hide how you feel about each other. Actually," he laughed, "I don't know how you do it. It's so obvious how totally in love with each other you are. I don't know how you fool a soul."

"We haven't had to fool anyone besides Chip since we've uhm ... you know," she blushed. "I do think it's going to be a whole lot harder now than it was before."

"Yeah, you two have really turned up the volume," he grinned.

After they were seated they looked at the menu quickly. Ryan wanted two of everything, but she settled for a turkey club and a bowl of minestrone. Conor ordered a cheeseburger and fries. That sounded good to Ryan too, so she asked for fries also. After the server left Ryan asked, "Do you think it'll be awkward having us around the house?"

"No!" he said emphatically. "Why would you even ask that?"

"I don't know. I'm just afraid that it'll upset our normal dynamic. Jamie and I touch each other every minute of the day, and I don't want to make you guys uncomfortable with that."

"Ryan, we're all cool with you being a lesbian. Being happy with that implies that we're happy about you sleeping with women. We're good with it, honestly. Aside from the fact that we're all jealous that you snagged Jamie, we want you to be happy. It's obvious that Jamie is the best thing that ever happened to you, so why wouldn't we want her in our home?"

"You know, Conor," she said as a tear threatened to leak out, "I don't tell you nearly enough how much I love you and Rory and Brendan. I couldn't have chosen better brothers."

"We did pretty well for ourselves too, Ryan. Plus the added benefit of having a little jewel like Jamie added to the family is just icing on the cake." He smiled broadly as he added, "Although, if I got to play Pebble Beach once in a while, you could date a jerk and I'd still be happy!"

Their food was delivered promptly, and they tore into it quickly, all conversation at a standstill until a substantial dent was made in the repast. When her hunger was sated enough for her to be able to speak, Ryan brought up their living situation again. "Do you think Da is really okay with us living in Berkeley during the week?"

"I think he is. Now, I'm not denying that he's sad about it, but I know he understands your reasons."

"This really is going to be an adjustment for us, Conor. This is all so new for Jamie, I want her to be able to get comfortable with our relationship this summer. It's so ideal having her roommates gone, I really feel we need to take this opportunity to get to know each other better."

"I understand. But Da's still upset about Brendan moving out. His ideal would be to have all of us married, all living in the house, with a bunch of kids running around."

"Well, Jamie and I are going to do our best to fulfill some of his wishes," she said with a grin.

"Wow! I assume you mean Da's number one wish to have a bunch of grandchildren. Are you planning on doing that anytime soon?" he asked.

"Not soon, but eventually."

"Do you … uhm … need any help?" His tanned face grew a little pink as he blushed at the implications of his offer.

Ryan gripped his arm and gave it a squeeze, reassuring him that she was comfortable with the topic. "It does seem a lot more real now that Jamie's in the picture, doesn't it?"

The relief showed clearly as Conor blew out a breath and nodded his head. "When we talked about this before it was so hypothetical."

"It's still pretty hypothetical," Ryan assured him. "But we discussed it a little bit this week. Jamie was kind of ambivalent about whether she wanted to bear a child or adopt one, but when I told her you had offered your services, she changed her mind immediately. She would love to have you be the father, if you were still interested."

"Do I get to do it the old fashioned way?" His leering face indicated that this was just the beginning of the teasing she would face.

"Yeah, no problem. We could have a three-way!" she suggested, with a totally genuine looking smile on her face.

"Well, doesn't that just take all the fun out of it." He made a sour expression that caused Ryan to laugh out loud. "You really know how to spoil a party."

"We're a long way from taking that leap. We both want to go to graduate school, so it'll be a few years. And you never know what could happen during that time. You might be with someone who doesn't want you to have a child by another woman."

"Not a chance of that, Ryan. I would never be with a woman who didn't understand my commitment to my family. You and the boys will always come first with me."

"I hope that's always true for all of us, Conor. That is one of the things that I found most attractive about Jamie, you know. She was crazy about all of you from the first time she met you."

"Just another indication of her excellent taste," he said.

"Speaking of taste, where's our server? I need some dessert!"

On the way home Conor asked, "Are we going to take off now?"

"Not quite yet. I promised I'd do a little favor for Jamie's dad. You could help me if you wanted to."

"What's the favor?"

"He's got some old cars that he needs me to drive. Are you interested?"

"Since I'm guessing that he doesn't have a backyard full of junkers up on blocks, I'm definitely in!"

When they arrived back at the house, Ryan ran in to get all of the keys. Conor was walking around the yard looking over the property when she returned. He pointed to Jamie's tree house and asked, "Was that for Jamie when she was little?"

Ryan nodded her affirmation. "Pretty nice for a kid, huh?"

"I'll say. I wonder if it's big enough for an adult to fit in?"

Ryan blushed and replied, "Yeah, it's big enough."

"Ryan! You two didn't desecrate a child's playhouse, did you?"

A guilty shrug was his only answer.

"Boy, she is a little live wire, isn't she?"

"She's all that and a bag of chips," she smugly replied. As they approached the garage Ryan said, "I'm not sure what we're driving today. I was so overwhelmed by the first two cars that I drove that I didn't have the strength to look at the last two."

"How many cars does he have?" Conor's blue eyes were dancing with excitement, and Ryan was very pleased that she was able to share this with her big brother.

"I've been afraid to ask. He's got three muscle cars down here and a new NSX, plus a Suburban. I know he's got a seven series BMW and a Range Rover in the city. And you saw her mother's CLK. But I have a feeling there are more cars that I haven't heard about. Her dad is a real car nut."

"Why couldn't our dad be a car nut?"

"Conor, if Da was a car nut, all he could afford would be magazines with pictures of the cars he wanted. Jamie's dad can actually buy what he wants."

"Well then, why couldn't Jamie's dad be our dad?"

"I know you're kidding, but you have no idea what you're really asking for. Jamie really is the poor little rich girl. We've spent more time with Da this year than she's spent with her dad her whole life."

"What about her mom?"

"From what I hear she's much worse than that. She took her to the opera and the symphony when she was three years old! Not that it's a bad thing to have some culture, but she didn't get to do any kid stuff. They never even took her to the zoo! They had all the money in the world, and she's never been to Disneyland. They've traveled all over the world, but what kid wants to see the Louvre?"

"I'm twenty-eight years old and I don't want to see it. I can't imagine being dragged through museums when I was little. Gee, Mama hated to take us to church, and it was a mortal sin not to do that!"

She stopped and looked at him for a minute, "I don't remember that," she said with a somber look flitting across her features. "Tell me what it was like."

Conor truly hated that his sister had so few memories of their mother. The four-year difference in their ages gave him a much larger catalogue of impressions, and he did his best to share them whenever he got the opportunity. "I don't remember going when I was real little, but when I was six or seven I was in charge of you during Mass. Da would sit on one end and Mama on the other. You'd be next to Mama, and she and I had to tag team you. Rory would be by Da, and Da and Brendan would try to keep him quiet. By the time Mass was over, you'd be half undressed, and you'd usually be next to Da since Mama and I had given up on you."

"Come on, I wasn't that bad," she argued, unable to dispute Conor's memory, but thinking it unlikely that she had been the little terror that he portrayed.

"You were worse than that! You hated to wear dresses, but Mama always had a frilly little dress on you for church. You had those cute little ruffled panties on under it, and you loved to pull your dress up over your head and show everyone your underwear. You'd get your socks and shoes off in no time flat, and it was a constant struggle to stop you from throwing them at people. You had a gun when you were just a baby. I swear you could hit the back of someone's head from six pews back!"

"Hmm, Jamie's always threatening to adopt so she doesn't have to have a kid like me—maybe she's right."

"I wouldn't have traded you for anything," Conor said sincerely. "You were wild, but you were always a ton of fun."

"Speaking of fun ..." she said as she opened the garage door. Conor stood and stared in amazement at the condition of the Mustang, one of his all-time favorite cars.

"This car is a masterpiece," he said reverently as he walked all around it.

"Jamie said you can drive any of them you want," she informed him, unable to suppress a wide grin at the look of delight that sped across his features.

"I'm not worthy," he moaned, his eyes wide and unfocused.

Laughing at his reaction, Ryan moved to the next car. "Let's see what else we have here and then you can drive ... if you're able," she added. He helped her take off the cover of a 1967 electric blue Chevy Malibu Supersport. "Wow!" they said simultaneously.

"This is soo hot," Conor muttered. "I think I'm gonna try and hold out for those cousins of Jamie's. It's worth the risk."

"They're on her mom's side of the family, so I don't know if they have the car nut gene," she warned him. "On the other hand, that's where the dough is, so you could get them hooked on a new habit." She could nearly see the gears turning in his agile mind, and imagined that he was computing the minimum age at which he could make his move on the teenagers.

Next was a 1970 Pontiac GTO, in a brilliant da-glo orange. "This one is really rare," Conor said, walking around the pristine car. He looked like he wanted to run his hands over the paint, but there wasn't a smudge on the entire surface, and he didn't want to leave a mark. "There are tons of Mustangs around but not that many GTO's were sold. It's hard to find one in perfect condition like this one." He walked around each car again, stopping to look carefully at each one from every angle. "Can I really drive them?"

"Jamie assures me that her father wants them driven, and that he wants some carbon burned off the plugs. You up for it?"

"I'm not sure I can move," he admitted. "These are works of art, Ryan. Are you sure he doesn't mind?"

"He left a note asking me to drive them, so I'm sure he doesn't mind."

"Then what are we waiting for?"

Ryan let Conor drive each of the cars in the collection. He was truly in his element when he drove a hot car, paying rapt attention to every detail of the experience. Ryan could tell that he was listening to each of the individual elements of the car, gauging their performance as he put each one through its paces, turning them quickly to judge their turning radius, mashing down on the brakes to determine their stopping power. He got each car up well over the speed limit, but she felt perfectly safe because of his dexterity with the machines. He pushed each one, but never past its limit.

Tooling down Highway 1 in the GTO, Conor grew pensive. "Do you have a read on Jamie's parents yet?"

"Mmm, I'm not sure what you mean." The growl of the engine forced her to raise her voice a little higher than normal.

"I guess I wonder how they're going to be about you two." It was clear that Conor was a little worried about his sister, and Ryan smiled, even though he couldn't see her.

"It's really hard to tell, Conor. There have been some positive signs though. I met her Dad after the ride and he was very friendly. He knows that I'm gay, and he knows that one of the reasons for Jamie's breakup was because of her relationship with me."

"Yeah, but he's a lawyer, Sis, you know they can make you think they're your friend while they stab you in the back."

"Hey, Bren is a lawyer, too! He's not like that!"

"He's not the head honcho of a big firm either," Conor reminded her.

She nodded her head at the truth of that statement. "Well, even if he's being disingenuous, her mom tried to pry the truth out of Jamie, and she didn't seem upset at the time. Jamie says she knows lots of gay people, so I'm hoping that she'll be cool."

Conor gave her a small smile and patted her leg. "I wish this was easier for you, Ryan. It pisses me off that it has to be an issue at all. You'd be such a great addition to any family ..." His voice trailed off as he found it difficult to comprehend why anyone would try to subvert the obvious bond between his sister and her partner.

"Hey, don't worry about it, Con. No matter what happens, Jamie's a member of our family now. The worst thing the Evanses can do is stop speaking to Jamie or withhold her money. I don't want either of those things to happen, but if they do, it won't affect the way we feel for each other."

Conor shot his sister a fond smile. "Jamie's still a pretty good choice, even with no dough."

"She's a damn good choice if she were ten million in debt!" Ryan decreed with a touch of hyperbole.

When he finished with each of the vintage cars, Conor's lustful blue eyes lingered over the Acura. "Okay," Ryan said slowly, as she tossed the keys to him. "Here's the keys, but be very, very careful with this one. We'd have to become Mr. Evans's personal slaves if you wrecked it."

His eyes lit up as he snatched the keys out of the air and slid into the black leather seat, almost in the same motion. A deep sigh of pleasure came from his lungs, and Ryan smiled at the look of supreme satisfaction on his handsome face. As he turned over the engine he looked at her dreamily and said, "This is better than sex."

As the car backed out of the garage Ryan replied, "You, my boyo, have been having sex with the wrong people."

"Come on, Ryan," he argued. "You love cars nearly as much as I do. Are you telling me that driving this baby didn't make you hot?"

For the tenth time that day Ryan blushed deeply, causing Conor to laugh at her embarrassment. "You didn't do it *in* the car, did you?" He was having a very good time at her expense, but his teasing was gentle, and sprinkled with a good helping of envy, so Ryan didn't get angry.

She paused for a minute, debating whether or not to tell him the whole story. She had always been very open about her sex life, and even though she neither wanted nor needed to talk about her intimate life in detail, she had to admit that she liked having Conor as a confidant. She let a sly smile escape, as she replied, "No, not in the car, but I will admit that we couldn't wait to get home. We stopped at a motel." She couldn't stop the adolescent giggle that accompanied her revelation.

"You know, Ryan," he said as he narrowed his blue eyes at her, "you're not making me any less jealous by telling me these things. You've got a gorgeous, smart, funny, rich girlfriend, who can cook no less, and she's as hot as a pistol!"

"It's all true, Conor," she admitted. "I haven't been able to find a fault in her yet. I keep waiting for the police to show up and tell me she's a con woman perpetrating a massive fraud on this naïve rich couple, but so far she's legit."

"I've never been one to pry into your life, Ryan, but I'm telling you now, if you let her get away, I'm going to have you committed!"

"Not gonna happen, Bro." Her dark hair trailed over her shoulders as she tossed her head confidently. "If we ever split up, it'll be her doing. I'm in for life."

"You're really sure, aren't you?" he asked thoughtfully.

"Absolutely positive. Jamie's the last woman in my life." The conviction in her voice caused him to offer his little sister a fond smile.

"I'm happy for you, Ryan. I really am." As he turned to glance at her he noticed the sapphire blue diamond in her ear. "Hey, where'd you get that?"

Her hand lifted to touch the jewel. "Little honeymoon present," she informed him with a laugh. "Jamie's great grandmother willed a pair of diamonds to her. She had never had them set, but when we fell in love she had them put in this setting and she gave them to me on Monday. I didn't feel right taking them, since they're a part of her family, so I made her a deal: I'd wear one if she wore one. We went out yesterday and each got another piercing so we can wear normal earrings too."

As she turned her head he noticed that she wore both diamonds. "Why do you have both on?"

"Until the new piercing heals we have to leave a sterile stud in. Jamie wanted to wear a pair of gold ones today, so I'm holding hers for safekeeping."

"How did you hold up when you got it pierced?" he asked gently, knowing his sister's propensity for fainting at the sight of needles.

"I went out like a light," she admitted, laughing at her foible. "I can hear Da now, 'That's your punishment for desecrating your body, Siobhán. If the good Lord wanted you to have another hole in your head, he'd have given it to you'," she said in her perfect imitation of her father's brogue.

"I don't know, he might go easy on you since it's a gift from Jamie. I don't think she can do any wrong in his eyes."

"We've got to figure out a way to use her to our advantage," Ryan said carefully, blue eyes narrowing in thought. "She might be a good foil for some of our misadventures."

"Yeah, but where was she when we really needed her? We sure could have used her assistance when I helped you buy your first motorcycle."

"I can still remember the look on his face when he saw it," Ryan remembered. "I honestly thought I saw steam coming out of his ears."

"Yeah, well, you just got yelled at. I got the 'If you don't love your baby sister enough to stop her from spilling her brains on the pavement' speech."

"You've got to admit he's a master at the guilt trip," Ryan said fondly.

"A legend in his own time," Conor agreed with a smile.

When all of the cars were put to bed with their covers tucked around them securely, they went back into the house. Conor wanted a quick tour and Ryan obliged, but his professional eye told him volumes about the home and the taste of the owners. He walked around the house, noting the craftsmanship of the carpentry and the quality of the fixtures and appliances. "The last house I worked on that was this well appointed was one of the mansions up in Pacific Heights. One of the chairmen of a Silicon Valley software firm paid about three mil for the house and spent another five mil fixing it up. This place isn't as high tech as his was, but the detail in here is just as amazing."

Ryan nodded her agreement as they went from room to room. He was truly impressed with the master bath. "These people spend their money on quality stuff," he said. "I really like this Japanese toilet," he said as he indicated the strange commode that Ryan had seen, but not commented on.

"What's the deal with this?"

"It's a regular toilet and a bidet all in one. It saves you from having to have separate fixtures, which really comes in handy in older homes where space is at a premium."

"Oh, I've never used a bidet," Ryan said excitedly. "Meet me outside," she instructed. "I've gotta try this out."

Conor laughed at her excitement, but did as he was instructed. Moments later she emerged with a crooked grin on her face, "That was … different," she said slowly.

"I would imagine they'd take a little while to get used to," he admitted, as he returned her grin.

They finished their tour in the kitchen. Conor spent a few minutes looking at the butler's pantry, again marveling at the efficiency of the design. "They spent some bucks hiring a good designer," he said. "In an older home like this you really need to hire someone who knows their stuff."

"Jamie's mom is really into the house. I assume it was her pet project to have it done right. And when money is no object, I guess you can take as much time as you need to have it done the way you want it."

"How do you feel about her money?" he asked seriously. "Has it been hard to get used to?"

"We've just started to work on that," Ryan admitted. "We're both going to have to give a little bit on the issue."

"Does it bother Jamie that you don't have any money?" He was reticent to ask this question, but the thought had been worrying him.

"No, not at all. She has a great attitude about their money. She feels like it's an accident of birth, rather than anything she's entitled to. It's gonna be a big adjustment, since she wants to be able to spend more on me than I'm comfortable with. Like these earrings," she said as an example. "I can't even imagine how much these are worth. And she bought me some clothes the other day that must have cost a ton. She practically crawled on the counter to stop me from seeing the receipt," she said with a chuckle. "I don't feel comfortable having her spend lots of money on me, so we're going to have to work on it to reach an agreement."

"Well, I understand that it might be tricky to work out, but you've got to admit it's a hell of a problem to have. 'My rich girlfriend buys me too many nice things,' next on Jerry Springer."

Ryan laughed as she admitted that it wasn't a terrible problem to tackle. "But one neat thing is that we're going to work together to find a way to distribute a lot of her money to a cause that we both support. We haven't decided how to do it, but I'm excited about having the opportunity to help other people."

"I think you two are going to be a force to be reckoned with, Sis," he said admiringly as he wrapped his arm around her waist and gave her a squeeze.

# Chapter Seventeen

Jamie arrived in Palo Alto nearly an hour before the graduation was set to begin. She had decided that she would sit alone, not wanting to make the Townsend family uncomfortable. She didn't know what, if anything, Jack had told them about their breakup, but she wanted to avoid any unpleasant questions. Although they were very nice people, and she knew they wouldn't consciously offend her, she knew that if they knew about Ryan they might feel obligated to say something, and she wasn't in the mood to discuss her lover with them.

She strolled around the law school campus, reminiscing about all the good times she and Jack had shared at the school. Passing by the administration building, she recalled going with him for his first registration, when he was nervous about his new adventure. They'd only been dating a short while and they hadn't yet learned much about each other. They stood together in the various lines, her hand resting on his back. Her presence seemed to soothe him, and by the end of the day he was his normal, confident self. That day had done a lot to cause her to fall in love with him. The fact that he was not only willing to share his vulnerability with her, but was also willing to let her help him through it, was completely charming to her.

She let her mind wander through their three years together. It became clear to her, in retrospect, why she had fallen in love with him. He was so like her father, it was almost eerie. But he was a little bit more emotionally available than her father had been. Perhaps that was only because he was a student, and didn't have the demands of work that her father had. She suspected that in reality, her father was absent because he needed the space. She knew that he loved her and her mother, but she guessed that he could only handle small amounts of that love at a time. Jack seemed to have a larger capacity for closeness, but he still had a lot of her father's quiet reserve. She thought that was what made him feel so safe and comfortable, almost from the start.

Since she had never allowed herself to acknowledge her innate attraction to women, she had never known the power of fierce sexual attraction. Because of this, she had felt that the desire she had for Jack was what everyone felt. She had found a good man who would be a good father; it made sense to snatch him up while he was still available. She had to acknowledge that being with Jack had prevented her from exploring her deep, hidden feelings. She would never have cheated on Jack, no matter how strong the attraction, and the thought occurred to her that perhaps she was subconsciously trying to permanently remove the possibility of succumbing to her latent desires. Perhaps taking the lesbian sexuality class was a sign from her subconscious to burst out of the confines of her safe choice and take a risk. Whatever the reason, she knew it was the best decision that she had ever made.

Jamie walked past the area where the graduates were lining up, many of them posing for pictures with their families. She thought she spotted Jack's tall blond head, and as she came closer she saw that her guess was correct. He was standing with his parents and getting ready to pose for some pictures. He looked so handsome in his cap and gown that she felt a small stirring of emotion that took her by surprise. His gown was black, but he wore a cowl of a deep burgundy and white, along with a gold cord that she knew symbolized an honor. She assumed he would receive honors for being editor of the main law review, but he might have merited other commendations that she was unaware of. She felt a pang of loss at not even knowing how his last semester had gone, a sharp pain deep in the pit of her stomach.

Fighting to control her emotions, she was struck with the thought that she had given herself to this man. She knew now that she had not given herself totally, but she had not known that at the time. It was deeply painful to watch him move on through his life without her, even though she was so much happier now. There was a part of herself that she had permanently given to Jack; she could never hope to reclaim that part, and she wasn't sure that she wanted to. The things they shared were all in the past now, but they were important to her. She wanted to treasure the good times they had together and mourn the bad ones.

She wiped the tears from her eyes and decided to go say hello before the ceremony began. Just as she took one step towards him, she saw why they had been waiting to take the pictures. His law review partner, Natalie, approached the group. Jamie watched, transfixed, as Natalie walked up and slid her arms around him and gave him a very, very friendly kiss.

Jamie stood, unable to move, as Natalie greeted Mr. and Mrs. Townsend. Her legs felt so weak that she nearly collapsed before she could stumble to a bench and collect herself. Every rational thought in her head screamed at her to leave at that moment. But the urge to observe the pair tugged at her like the need to look at a car wreck.

Fighting back her tears of outrage, Jamie stared at the happy graduates. Natalie and Jack posed with their arms around each other as Mr. Townsend snapped a few pictures. Jamie was in the middle of a fierce debate with herself over her desire to go take a swing at her former fiancé when the graduates were called to line up for the procession. Jack gave Natalie a very tender kiss as she moved away to find her proper place in line. As she stared at the besotted man, she felt her stomach turn when she recalled him kissing her in exactly the same fashion. Jamie watched his face as he watched Natalie walk away. *Two months ago that look was reserved for me*, she thought as the flames of jealousy burned at her soul. *Or was it? Maybe he always felt that way for Natalie.* She remembered the long afternoons and even longer nights that they spent together working on their article. *He was very defensive when I compared my relationship with Ryan to his relationship with Natalie*, she thought suspiciously. *I swear that if I find out he was screwing around behind my back, I'll kill him!!*

She found Natalie in the crowd and spent a few minutes looking at her, feeling an overwhelming sense of hatred for the oblivious woman. She was tall, about five feet ten or so. Her long auburn hair curled around her shoulders, and her figure, although mostly hidden by the robes, looked to be as attractive as Jamie remembered.

As the graduates began to walk toward the stage she debated whether she should leave immediately, or stay to cause a massive scene. Her irrational jealousy was beginning to overpower her and she had to fight with herself to go sit down and think things through before she left. She walked to the very rear of the gathered families and found a bench behind the neatly arranged folding chairs, just barely able to hear the speakers as they began the ceremony.

She sat quietly and tried to still her raging thoughts, taking several deep breaths as she tried to focus her rational mind. *Okay, what you know is this*, she thought. *You know that you were largely unavailable to Jack because of your growing feelings for Ryan. You know that you pushed him away and began to give more of yourself to her. You know that he wanted to be closer to you. You know that he was more than willing to have you back, but you would have had to give up the dream of being with Ryan. And you know that being with Ryan is the best thing that ever happened to you.*

Here she dropped her head in shame as she recalled their last conversation. *He went out of his way to call you and wish you well. He genuinely wanted to know that you were happy. You are happy. You're happier than a person has any right to be. Why can't you be as loving to him as he was to you? Doesn't he deserve that after all that you put him through? You did break his heart.* A wry smirk crossed her face as she amended that detail. *Obviously, his heart wasn't terribly broken, or he's a really fast healer.*

Focusing her thoughts on being her most generous self, she thought, *You owe him your thanks and your appreciation for all that you meant to each other. Be the person that you would admire. Go up to him and wish him well, and mean it!*

She concentrated on this mantra for the rest of the ceremony. When Jack's name was called she found herself standing and applauding enthusiastically for him. No matter what had happened to them as a couple, she knew that there was not a person at Stanford that had worked harder to get where he was than Jack Townsend. Even though she didn't feel responsible for his efforts, she had to acknowledge that her two and a half years of support made a difference in the effort that he could expend, and she took some small measure of pride in having been there for him.

Jack's name was near the end of the alphabet, and since she knew that the ceremony would be over soon, she left her bench and went to the reception area, feeling the need to see him quickly so that she could leave before her good thoughts evaporated.

As the joyous graduates passed, she reached in and grabbed him from the queue. He was totally shocked, but as his initial surprise faded, he seemed genuinely pleased to see her. He wrapped his arms around her, and the comfort and familiarity that she felt in his embrace shocked her so much that she began to cry. "I'm so proud of you, Jack," she sobbed. He patted her back and murmured comforting words to her, just as he had during their time together. She clutched herself to him and let herself mourn for the sadness they had caused each other. She saw Natalie out of the corner of her eye and felt Jack tense up when he caught her glance, but when she looked up, Natalie was gone and Jack had relaxed again.

"Hey, are you all right?" he asked solicitously. "Is everything okay between you …?"

"Oh yes," she said as she shook her head. "Things are great with me, Jack. I don't know what came over me, but seeing you today made me really feel all that we had and all that we lost. I'm so sorry for how I hurt you," she said sincerely, tears freely rolling down her cheeks.

"I'm okay, Jamie," he said soothingly. "I'm going on with my life, too."

"I know," she said softly, her shoulders still shaking with the betrayal. "I saw you before the ceremony."

He looked decidedly uncomfortable with this revelation, but summoned his usual direct approach and looked right into her eyes, asking, "Does it bother you that it's Natalie?"

She mutely nodded as the tears continued.

"I swear there was nothing between us when you and I were together, Jamie. I was devoted to you. I never would have cheated on you. You meant the world to me," he said as his own tears fell down his cheeks.

"When?" She asked the one-word sentence that would either reassure her or prove that Jack was lying.

He took a deep breath, hoping that Jamie would believe him. He wasn't even sure why her opinion mattered so much, but it mattered a great deal. "When we … broke up in February … she was … she was there for me, Jamie." He fixed his light blue eyes on his former lover. "It took a while … a few weeks I guess, but eventually she stopped seeming like just a friend. We were just starting to explore getting together when you … gave me another chance." His face reflected both his complete honesty and the lingering hurt that obviously still pained him.

"Did you tell her …?" Jamie's voice trailed off, but it was important to know that Jack was honest with Natalie, too.

He laughed softly, shaking his head a little. "Yeah. I told her." He tilted his head and fixed Jamie with a gaze that she had seen hundreds of times on his handsome face. "She wasn't happy with me." He paused a beat and added with a twinkle in his eye, "But if I were you I'd stay out of dark alleys when she's around. She kinda thinks you're evil incarnate."

"*Me!*" Jamie was stunned that she had turned out to be the bad guy in this little soap opera. But after just a minute of reflection, she had to admit that she was entirely to blame for jerking Jack around during their futile reconciliation. "I'm glad that she's angry at me, rather than you," she admitted, smiling up into his eyes when he shot her a grateful grin. "She won't be angry with you about me being here, will she?"

"No, don't worry about that." He gave her his most charming boyish grin as he assured her, "She's very easy to get along with. You're the only person I've ever heard her say a bad word about."

"That's very reassuring, Jack," she said with a bit of her sparkle showing again.

"I'm glad that you understand. I need to move on, and I think Natalie is going to be good for me. I hope you know that I'd do anything not to hurt you." Without thought, he raised his hand and trailed his fingers down the side of her face, brushing his thumb against her lips in an achingly familiar gesture.

Her shaky composure shattered, she threw her arms around him and hugged him tightly. "I loved you, Jack, and part of me always will," she whispered fiercely into his flushed ear. "I gave you everything I had to give, even though I know that it wasn't all I was capable of. I'm so very sorry it couldn't work out. But I truly want you to be happy, and if Natalie can do that for you, then I'm glad."

Releasing him, she reached into her purse and pulled out the gift she had brought. "I hope you enjoy all of the happiness that you deserve, Jack. Take care of yourself." She stood on her tiptoes and kissed his cheek, relishing the feel of his smooth skin one last time. By the time he composed himself enough to reply, she was gone.

Jamie spent the next several hours driving around Palo Alto, passing all of the places that they went to as a couple. She got out of her car and walked around the campus for a while, finally finding the grove of trees where Jack had proposed to her. She sat on the bench where countless students had declared their love and cried until she had no more tears to shed. She felt absolutely empty—her emotions overwhelming and raw. It took a while, but she finally composed herself. Almost as if her car was on automatic pilot, she drove by Jack's apartment and sat out in front for a long while, remembering when she helped him move in.

*It had been a long day, and they were both hot and tired. When they had carried the last box in, they sat out on the steps to catch their breath before they went back inside to start unpacking. A stiff breeze blew the door shut as they simultaneously realized that the keys were inside. A few seconds of shock were followed by near hysterical laughter from both of them. That was when she realized that he might be "the one." Even hot, and tired, and cranky, he could still see the humor in the situation. He didn't blame her and he didn't get mad at himself—he just laughed until his stomach hurt. He had to stay at her parents' house overnight since they couldn't get the management company until morning, but he didn't let it bother him one bit. He stood outside her room that night and spent a long time kissing her. Her resolve almost melted that night, but she held firm and he took it well, merely giving her a final kiss and a crooked grin as he walked down the hall to his room.*

Her thoughts turned to the night that she decided to sleep with him, just a few days after she had accepted his marriage proposal. *She was at his apartment on a*

*Saturday night, just after finishing her sophomore year, and she was planning on staying at her house in Berkeley for another few days while she cleaned up some last minute details.*

*She normally stayed in Palo Alto all day on Saturday and left around midnight to return home. This night it was near midnight, and she was being driven absolutely crazy by his kisses. He looked at her with such longing and desire on his face that she could no longer refuse him, so she stood up, and he gazed up at her with his normal stoic face. This time she held out her hand and, as he took it, she pulled him to his feet, wrapped her arms around his neck and whispered, "Let's go to bed."*

*She would always remember the look of joyous anticipation on his face as he gazed at her to make sure she was certain. He didn't ask her for confirmation, but he put his hands on her shoulders and held her at arm's length, gazing deeply into her eyes. He saw that she had made her decision, and was ready to take their relationship to this next level, so he bent over and took her into his arms, carrying her to his bed. Their lovemaking was feverish and passionate, both of them being carried along by the stored up feelings they had harbored for so long. But what she most remembered was the tenderness of his touch after they had finished. He gently touched her face as he trailed his long fingers along her cheeks, then ran his hands down her body, soaking up the sensation of finally being able to love her completely. She recalled the tears in his eyes as he looked at her with such love that her heart ached in remembrance.*

Even though they would never share another intimate moment, Jamie realized that having fond memories of her time with Jack was a very positive thing. She felt all of the anger from earlier in the day begin to lift.

Squaring her shoulders, she started the car and slowly drove past some of their favorite restaurants and bookstores. When she had seen every place that had meant something to them, she drove back to the spot where he had proposed, getting out of the car to sit on the bench again. She let the memories wash over her once again, and as they passed by she felt the pressure in her chest start to lessen. For the first time all afternoon she allowed herself to think of her beloved Ryan, closing her eyes to picture her lover in her mind. Finally back on track, she stood up and took a deep breath. "I'm sorry I wasn't the woman you needed, Jack. But you weren't the woman I needed either," she said aloud as she got back into her car to be with the woman that she would always need.

Jamie had driven no more than ten minutes when her cell phone rang. She smiled to herself as she opened it and touched the button. "Hi, gorgeous," she purred into the phone.

"How'd you know it was me?"

"Well, I only date gorgeous women, so I knew it would be one of you."

"Conor misses you and wants to know when you're going to be home," Ryan joked right back.

"You tell Conor I miss him too, and I'll be home in about forty minutes," she said. "And tell his sister that I can't wait to get her alone in bed."

"I know his sister will be very glad to hear that," she purred. "I miss you, sweetheart. Drive carefully."

"I miss you too, Ryan. I'll be there soon."

When she pulled up in front of the house, Ryan and Duffy were sitting on the front steps. Ryan had changed into a favorite pair of navy blue sweats and a long sleeved white T-shirt. She had obviously been exercising, as her blades were still on her feet and her hair was wet, her face pink from exertion. Even Duffy was panting, further evidence of their shared activity. Her face broke into a luminous grin when Jamie stepped out of the car and both she and Duffy bounded off the porch, with Duffy arriving first due to his advantage in dexterity. He jumped all over Jamie until she squatted down and let him lick her all over her face and neck. She giggled from the assault as Ryan stood by, arms crossed over her chest, and let him have his way with her.

When Duffy had finished with her she stood and shot an accusing glance at Ryan. "I thought you were supposed to protect me."

"Hey, it was either him or me," she explained. "He just got there first."

Holding her arms out to her partner, Jamie smiled and offered, "Come on … start licking."

Ryan chuckled at the invitation and indicated her sweaty body. "I need a shower before I'm worthy of your attention."

Jamie wrapped her arms around her tightly, unaccustomed to her partner's increased height. Her head rested against Ryan's breast, rather than her chest, but she didn't mind the new view in the least. She held on so tightly that Ryan knew she was upset. "Hey, hey," she said softly. "What's wrong?" Her long fingers reached down and tilted Jamie's head up. On closer inspection she could see that her partner had been crying today, quite a bit, if her swollen eyes were a proper indication. "Tell me."

Jamie sucked in a deep breath and shook her head. "I had a lot of memories to purge today. It caught me by surprise," she admitted.

"Do you need to talk about it?" Ryan asked. "Or do you want some physical comfort?"

"I don't want to talk about it now. I might take you up on your offer later, though."

"Anytime, sweetheart. I'll always be here for you."

"You really will be, won't you." There was not a hint of question in her statement.

"As long as I live," Ryan whispered, nuzzling her chin against the top of Jamie's head.

They stood on the quiet street, cuddling for a few minutes. When they finally released each other, Jamie looked up at her partner and asked, "Any big plans this evening, Tiger?" She fixed Ryan with her best sultry gaze, leaving little doubt where she thought the evening would find them.

"That all depends," Ryan mused, leaning against the Boxster to better equalize their heights.

"On what?"

"Oh … mostly on how tired you are." Ryan had something on her mind, but Jamie knew she had to let the little guessing game play out.

"I'm not very tired physically," she said. "Emotionally, I'm toast, but as long as we don't get into any big emotional scenes, I'm good to go."

Ryan laced her hands behind Jamie's neck and gazed at her fondly. "You're quite the little trooper, aren't ya, sparky?"

"That's me." Jamie smiled and kissed Ryan on the tip of her nose.

"Well, I have good news." A sly grin was curling the corners of Ryan's mouth and Jamie knew she was being set up, but she didn't mind a bit. "I've spoken to the committee and you'll be glad to know that I have been given permission to extend full membership privileges in the lesbian community to you." Waggling eyebrows punctuated this announcement.

"Wow," Jamie said, playing along with the joke. "I think we'd better get right to bed so you can show me the benefits package." She started to pull away, but Ryan gripped her a little tighter.

The dark head shook as Ryan informed her, "That's not how the initiation is performed, babe. You're a member of a community now—even if you're only in the group by marriage," she added, trying to let Jamie know it was perfectly fine if she didn't feel like a member of the lesbian nation.

The blonde eyebrows knit in confusion. "I don't have a bloody clue what you're talking about, Ryan O'Flaherty."

"Jamie?" Ryan said, leaning her head to one side and appraising her partner carefully, "do you remember New Year's Eve?"

The dark blonde eyebrows edged closer together; the small woman scrunched her face in puzzlement. "New Year's Eve?" she repeated slowly. "Uhm … yeah, I think I remember most of it." She rolled her eyes, recalling the hideous hangover she had suffered on New Year's Day. Ryan obviously had a point, but she was certainly taking her time to get to it.

"Do you remember coming to the Mark Hopkins?"

"Yes, dear, I remember stumbling across the street just to see how you looked in leather pants. It was worth the effort, by the way."

Ryan smiled at the compliment and continued her questioning. "Do you remember what I asked you that night?"

"Asked me?" Now the puzzled face took on a blank look. "You asked me something?"

"Yes," Ryan drawled. "I asked if you were there for a special purpose. You weren't ready then, but you've displayed a marked aptitude, and I now think you're ready." She said this with such a serious look on her face that Jamie was even more confused.

"I … I don't," she stammered, embarrassed that she had been too drunk to remember an obviously important exchange.

"Jamie," Ryan said as she reached down to grasp her partner's hand, "tonight, you are finally going to learn the secret handshake."

"The secret …" Jamie's questioning voice trailed off, and the look of puzzlement on her face was replaced by a broad grin. "The secret handshake," she repeated with confidence, anticipation bringing a sparkle to her eyes and a very becoming blush to her cheeks. "I've enjoyed every single thing you've ever taught me, Ryan, and I doubt that this lesson will break that string."

The two young lovers tilted their heads together and ascended the stairs to the O'Flaherty home, laughing the whole way.

The End